THEY DARED TO HOPE

"Mrs. Hastings." Gill dug deep inside himself to try to find some of the impudent brass he had had before the war. He needed all the gall he could beg or borrow to ask her what he was about to ask.

"Yes?"

"If I agreed to this coddling, will you agree to something I want?"

"What's that?"

"That we be married right away."

Jennifer opened her mouth to speak and nearly choked on her own caught breath, and then her heart began to beat painfully hard. She wanted to say yes so much. Too much. She wanted the chance to be a wife again, to be Zachary's mother for real and for keeps. She wanted to have her own home, to make a cozy warm nest for her own family. She wanted someone to give her love to.

But she wasn't what Gil thought she was. Or at least, her past wasn't, and although she had firmly turned her back on it, could Gil, if he knew? Would he want anything at all to do with her when she fell off her pedestal?

By Lee Scofield

A Slender Thread
Taming Mariah
Sweet Amity's Fire

Available from HarperPaperbacks

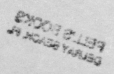

A Slender Thread

⊠ LEE SCOFIELD ⊠

HarperPaperbacks
A Division of HarperCollinsPublishers

This is a work of fiction. The characters, incidents, and dialogues are products of the author's imagination and are not to be construed as real. Any resemblance to actual events or persons, living or dead, is entirely coincidental.

HarperPaperbacks   *A Division of* HarperCollins*Publishers*
10 East 53rd Street, New York, N.Y. 10022

Cover illustration by Jean Monti

First printing: February 1995

Printed in the United States of America

HarperPaperbacks, HarperMonogram, and colophon are trademarks of HarperCollins*Publishers*

❖ 10 9 8 7 6 5 4 3 2 1

In memory of my mother,
Jonybelle Nash Scofield Patterson,
who encouraged each and all of her children
to develop their talents.

Prologue

Dusk had fallen. Jennifer thought she'd better make her trip to the privy and get it over with. Get back into the house and lock the doors. Saturday night wasn't a good night to be out wandering around, even if she was in her own backyard and at the outer edge of town. A woman alone had to take care of herself. Although, when she hadn't been alone, her circumstances had gained her little protection.

A loud popping sound followed by shouts and a barking dog came from two streets over, the town's main street, where five saloons and two bawdy houses were located. She shook her head in wonder. Trouble bloomed early tonight. Ever since the war broke out last April, the rowdiness in the town had grown generally worse.

In spite of that, she stood at her opened back door and listened. She liked watching and listening at dusk. And often, at dawn, as well. Her observations of life around her filled a lot of lonely hours.

Sometimes she thought this little Kansas town on the edge of the prairie was livelier, noisier than downtown Philadelphia, although she must admit she hadn't lived even close to the rougher elements there, as she did here. Her existence there had been among the well-to-do who lived in elegant homes in quiet, modulated neighborhoods. In many ways, she'd been cosseted and shielded from the kind of reality she now faced every day.

But in the end, her reality there had been far more horrible.

She didn't miss that lavish life much. Well, maybe she did miss one or two things, she wryly confessed to herself, like never having to use an outdoor privy. But living here gave her a different slant on life, and most of the time it kept her busy enough. It was easier to keep her unhappiness at bay when she was busy.

Mrs. Gallaghar, two doors up, called her little hellions, Tommy and Joey, to come in from their play. "Aw, Ma, not yet," the boys protested at the top of their lungs. "You git in here or I'll wallop you, ya hear me?" she heard Mrs. Gallaghar give her usual threat. It was too often an idle one, which the boys frequently ignored.

Lights flared in the house beyond the vacant lot. She switched her attention to it in time to see the outline of old Mrs. Davis as she yanked her curtains closed.

Jennifer sighed. Better go and attend to her own business. Then she could settle down to study the new readers that had arrived for Becky Dillon and the Gallaghar brothers. July was not too soon to prepare for September. And she had her treat—fresh blackberries to eat just before bedtime.

She made the trip briskly. Full dark had fallen. The last

few yards returning weren't so bad because she could see the light she'd left burning in the kitchen lamp. She hated entering a dark room. In fact, she hated the dark, but it was a part of her character that thoroughly shamed her. A grown woman, and a schoolteacher at that, should never fear something so elemental.

The wooden porch creaked a bit when she stepped up. One more step, and she'd be cozily inside.

She had her hand on the post when the deep voice came.

"Ma'am?"

Jennifer jumped. Her heart plunged, then raced.

Poised, she waited, blinking toward the voice's point of origin. It came again. "Mrs. Hastings?"

"Y-yes?"

The man stepped out of the deep shadows, yet the only thing she could see in the blackness was his tall outline.

"I didn't aim to scare you, ma'am. I'm sorry. No harm intended."

"I . . . it's all right." Until proven different, she had to accept his word. Nevertheless, she remained wary. Her arms hugged her waist. "Who are you? What is it you want?"

"Well, ma'am, I hoped we could talk. I'm Gil Prescott."

Gil Prescott. The name rang a faint bell.

"Does your family own a place north of town?"

There was a rustling movement; she heard the clink of a spur, then he stilled. "Yes, ma'am, my pa does. Ma's gone, four years ago."

"I see." She cleared her throat, then said in her best schoolteacher's voice, "How may I help you, Mr. Prescott?"

"It's a special matter, Mrs. Hastings. Might take some explaining."

Jennifer contemplated the request for a long moment. He didn't seem threatening, and there was an air of quiet urgency about him, but still . . .

She never received male callers. It wasn't acceptable in her position—a woman alone, who, as the town teacher, had to maintain a spotless reputation. Even now, the neighbors would surely gossip, if they were watching, generating all kinds of speculation about her male caller, and what he was doing at her house after normal hours.

Nevertheless, there was that sense of urgent need about him, and she couldn't remain standing on her back porch talking to a strange man in the dark.

"Very well, Mr. Prescott. Come in."

Leaving him to follow, she entered the kitchen, picked up the glowing lamp, and went through to the parlor. She pulled the curtains tightly closed, then turned and set the light on the small table beside the sofa. A minute later, the tall man stepped into its soft radiance.

She remembered his face, now. She had passed him a time or two in the mercantile.

Jennifer studied him. He was a husky, well-toned man with broad shoulders, about her own age, she thought. Early twenties. His clean features were even, but not outstanding. Except his eyes. A sober blue-gray, they were deep and long lashed, and just now held a world of sorrow, she mused, as her gaze lifted to meet his. He appeared to have returned the study, for his expression also held a hint of respectful admiration.

They stood thus for a long moment before she finally broke the silence. "Now, Mr. Prescott. What is your business?"

"It's this, Mrs. Hastings." He shrugged his left shoulder, and a bundle, secured by a leather strap, swung from his back to his chest. It looked like dirty laundry wrapped in a dark blue shirt, but he held it in a cradling fashion.

"Mrs. Hastings, I want you to take my son. He needs a mother."

"W-what?" She blinked rapidly, disbelieving what she'd heard. "What did you say?"

"I want you to raise my son, Mrs. Hastings. He's only a few weeks old and there ain't nobody else. I'm leaving to fight."

"You can't possibly be serious." Her heart began a double beat. This was impossible; she must be hallucinating. He couldn't have asked what she thought he had. "Why, I'm . . . I'm a stranger to you. Where is the child's own mother?"

"She died giving birth."

"Oh. I'm very sorry, Mr. Prescott. You do have a predicament. Well, had your wife no people who would care for him?"

He paused a moment. "I'd rather they not raise him, Mrs. Hastings."

"But if they are relatives, surely they would want the child."

"Ma'am, my wife was a Cherokee Indian. She was a fine woman, but I don't want him raised Indian. I want him raised white."

"I see. What of your father, Mr. Prescott? He—"

"No!"

A spark of fierceness flickered in the blue-gray eyes. His mouth went straight while a dull red crept up his cheeks.

"I didn't mean to shout, ma'am, it's just that Pa and I

don't see things in the same way. He didn't approve of me marrying Morning Rain."

"Perhaps if you explained the situation?"

He shook his head. "He didn't just disapprove, Mrs. Hastings. He never accepted the marriage a'tall. We did it in an Indian way. He's called the boy a bastard and I'll not stand for it. He'd treat him like one, too."

"Oh. But Mr. Prescott, I'm a stranger," she said again. "There must be people in the town, friends, or . . . or . . ."

He shook his head as his chin thrust forward in bitter defiance. "Most of the people in this town feel the same as Pa."

A tiny mewing punctuated his last statement. Jennifer's eyes flew to the shirt bundle. It started to move.

"Mr. Prescott." Her heart fluttered, her stomach fluttered, and her hands started to shake. A baby. A baby for her very own? She had put away her deepest yearnings years ago. Could she—dare she—keep this child?

She had to clear her throat before she spoke again. "Why have you brought him to me? I'm a woman alone; you know nothing about me. Why would you entrust him to me? How can you be sure I would be good to the child?"

"Ma'am, I know more about you than you think."

Startled, her heart picked up its beat again. What could he possibly know? She had told not one soul in this little Kansas town a single detail outside the background she had carefully invented. She had been scrupulously cautious. And after three years, she still kept her friendships here at acquaintance level; despite her loneliness, she didn't dare take the chance of anyone knowing her true past.

She gave him a wary, questioning stare.

He answered. "You're quality, Teacher. A real lady. You have a fine way of talking, but you never put nobody down. And even though you're a widow, you don't hold with flirting. None of the men around here who would court you are ever encouraged.

"You're a good teacher; the kids like you. And you have a good heart. Every day during school last year, you stopped at Lindermans' grocery store and picked up a big tin of fresh milk. Even apples, sometimes. Tattle around town says you fed it to those three Schiller kids. They often didn't have much more to eat than the milk and bread you brought 'em. Everyone knows those kids' pa is a good-for-nothin' and gambles and drinks away most of his money."

"A little kindness isn't much. A good teacher wants her pupils alert, Mr. Prescott. Children cannot be alert on empty stomachs."

"You've been teaching Bessie Terrell to read."

She made a slight grimace. "How do you know about Bessie?"

"There ain't many coloreds in Kansas, Mrs. Hastings. A pretty piece like Bessie stands out at a place like Jasmine's. Uh, sorry, ma'am. But you're bound to know about Jasmine's if you took Bessie on."

"Oh, my heavens above. That girl promised she wouldn't tell a soul. She begged me to teach her, saying she wanted to get out of her, um, position at . . . that place."

"Uh-huh." His blue-gray eyes glinted with a sparkle of humor.

"She comes at first light on Sundays and is gone by the time most people are up," she protested.

"Well, Bessie's so proud at learning to read, you didn't really expect her not to tell nobody, did you? It didn't take long for the story to get around. And Sunday morning still has its early risers, Teacher, so it wasn't likely to remain a secret, anyway."

Jennifer sank onto the edge of a chair. "If the secret is out, I suppose I'll hear from Mrs. Portland and Mrs. Gallaghar over the matter."

"I don't think so, ma'am. Good teachers are in short supply, especially now that the war's on. If you don't make a big thing of it, they'll just pretend they don't know about it."

Silence drifted down as she considered everything he'd said. Her protests hadn't dissuaded him.

It was impossible to assimilate all the possibilities and practicality of his request. How she would feed the child until he could eat regular food, what supplies she would need, what people would say—none of it made a dent in her usually logical mind. That side of her wouldn't cooperate. At the moment, all she could do was want, and her want was growing stronger by the moment.

"The baby," she murmured. Dare she?

His voice dropped to a low pitch. "I'm asking a lot, Mrs. Hastings, I know that. But I've thought and thought. I gave you reasons why I know you're of good character. But it's more than that. You won't hold it against the boy that he's a half-breed. You haven't even asked which side I'll be fighting for, so I know it ain't politics or where my boy comes from that counts with you. With you he'll get the best of mothering and raising, and I ain't sure I'll come back."

"Mr. Prescott, you mustn't think in a negative fashion."

He gave her an uncompromising stare. It gave her a world of insight. This young man didn't want to come back.

Jennifer sighed deeply. He seemed to know exactly when her arguments had run out.

His mouth folded with determination, then relaxed. His gaze dropped to the bundle in the blue shirt. Hers fixed there as well. Without another word, he gently placed the child in her arms. Reverently, she accepted him.

Hands trembling, she gently folded back the shirt, then the piece of blanket beneath it. The baby stirred. A tiny fist waved. Black, black hair covered his head above tiny scrunched-up features. He popped one dark eye open and looked at her, then closed it and returned to sleep.

Jennifer's heart was instantly lost. "Who has cared for him until now?" she whispered.

"An Indian woman. But her family was moving on and I couldn't let him go. Maybe I should have, but I have to know what will happen to him."

Her arms started a rocking motion. "Will your father object to me having the baby, Mr. Prescott?"

"No. Relieved, most likely."

"Does he know you plan to join the war forces?"

"He'll find out soon enough."

Her gaze left the baby and raised to the man's. "If I do this, if we agree, I insist you give me full entitlement to the child until you return. I don't want a fight with your father if he changes his mind about wanting his grandson. Do you agree?"

"Yes."

"Are you willing to write a letter to that effect?"

"Yes."

"All right, Mr. Prescott. I will take the boy. And I will pray for your safe return and a swift close to the war."

"Thank you, Mrs. Hastings. My most heartfelt thank-you."

"Now then, Mr. Prescott. Tell me the child's name."

"Umm, well, he doesn't exactly have one." His shifting feet made him seem on uncertain ground for the first time.

"You haven't named him?"

"No, ma'am. You see, the Indians usually wait awhile to give a name and I've had much on my mind and I didn't have a name already thought out."

"My heavens above! Mr. Prescott, this child cannot go another day without a name. Haven't you anything in mind at all? What about your father's name, or a grandfather's?"

Silent for only a moment, he looked at her hopefully as he said, "One of my grandfathers was called Zachary. That'll do as good as any, I guess."

"Zachary is a fine name," she affirmed. "I had a grandfather called Zachary, also."

"Okay. He's Zachary Prescott. Now, ma'am, if you have paper and pen?"

Twenty minutes later he was ready to leave. Overawed at Gil Prescott's trust in her, Jennifer stood in the back doorway and clutched the baby and the paper to her bosom as she held out her other hand to say good-bye. Now that it had come to this, she could scarcely believe it.

In her heart, a slender thread of hope was born. A baby, something her heart had never stopped hurting for, had been given to her out of the blue. It seemed to her God smiled on her once more in replacing the one she had lost.

Gil took her hand in both of his. Callused and work toughened, nevertheless, his large hands communicated unspoken thoughts. The starlight caught a shimmer in his eyes, and Jennifer realized his emotions were close to the surface.

"There's no words to say thanks with, Teacher." His murmur was deep and rough edged. "But I feel 'em."

"There's no need. I feel them, too, because—" Her voice cracked, and she paused. She hadn't confessed her loneliness to anyone and was uncertain how to express her own mixture of hope, need, and enormous thanksgiving at his gift. "Mr. Prescott, most women want a child of their own and I . . . well, I'm no different. Now you've given me one. At least until you return. I am the one to say thank you. I will treasure him, you may be certain of it."

He bent his head and, spreading open her hand, pressed his lips into her palm. Warm and tender, his mouth at that moment evoked nothing but sweet gratitude. But when he raised his eyes to hers for a long, last gaze, her heart stirred. Slowly, her hand closed around the place where she could yet feel his lips against her sensitive skin, and she placed it against her breast, next to the baby's head.

Gil then kissed the baby, his ashy-brown hair softly brushing the back of her hand in the process, which gave the contact intimacy, before he turned swiftly and strode away. At the edge of her yard he hesitated but did not turn around again. After a moment, he walked on.

Jennifer watched, the baby against her bosom, until the dark swallowed him. It took her a long time to step back into the house and close the door.

Later, she found a deerskin bag lying on the kitchen table where he had written his consent. It held only a few coins. It struck her that it must have been all he possessed. That thought seemed to join the lingering imprint of his kiss and the soft, sweet presence of the baby against her breast. He had given her, Jennifer, all he had.

1

The bucket, being much too full and heavy for four-year-old Zachary to carry with ease, sloshed water out too far as he tried to tip it onto the brown earth. Some of it arched onto Jennifer, wetting the hem of her gown and foot. She placed her hands on her hips and gave him a mock scowl.

"Zach, you little rascal, you got me all wet!"

His feet straddled the row of cabbage. He tipped his head at her, his dark eyes full of merriment while the corners of his mouth curled up in spite of all he could do to keep it in. "Didn't you need watering too?"

"Well, I guess I could do with a bath, all right. But not a muddy one, thank you!"

"But didn't you tell me once you knew some lady in Phil'delphia who liked mud on her face?"

"Yes, I did indeed. But that doesn't mean *I* like mud. And, young man"—she shot him a challenging look as she bent to scoop from the bucket—"I think you could do with a little watering yourself!"

"Un-unnh, no ma'am!" His denial was vehement but his eyes danced with expectation. As the sparkling drops hit his cheek and slid down his neck, he let out a shriek of laughter. It lit her own, and Jennifer could no longer hold back the giggles.

Eyeing her, his grin wide, Zach sank both hands in the bucket and came up with water flying. It hit her chest and she gasped, loudly. The day had been blistering hot, a true August day, and the spring water was cold; it felt pleasant to be cooled, but it was a shock just the same.

Jennifer looked at her little boy with pretended menace, and he almost doubled over with mirth. She grabbed him up and swung him around as they both laughed, then hugged him close while he clamped his legs around her waist. Teasingly she remarked, "Well! I can see I really have you under my thumb."

Zach slid his arm around her neck and kissed her cheek. "I'm too big to be under your thumb, Mama. I'd sit on it and squash it!"

She brushed at his gleaming black-brown hair. The downy-fine baby texture had long gone, leaving it springy under her touch. It was straight as a poker and grew faster than the weeds in her garden. Perhaps she'd trim it this evening before bedtime.

"Squash it, huh? Someday you will be too big, that's a fact. But until then . . . What are you looking at, Zach?"

"Mama, there's someone at the top of the road."

Jennifer spun around. They had few visitors out this way. The Prescott place was rather off the beaten path, which suited her most of the time, but she had to be alert to any possible danger, and that included strangers.

The setting sun caused her to squint and she placed her palm above her eyes to shade them. The man and horse were very still; how long he'd been observing them she couldn't guess.

"Who is it, Mama?"

"I don't know." Didn't she? Her heart unaccountably started to pound. Her arms tightened around the child.

As if he knew of her sudden apprehension, the rider heeled his mount into a slow, unthreatening walk. Jennifer and Zach watched his approach with growing curiosity.

As he drew nearer, the first thing Jennifer noticed was how thin he was. And battered. It wasn't that he carried visible bruises or scars beyond his threadbare clothing—yet, his nose didn't appear quite as straight as she remembered—but she recognized suffering, just the same. The blue-gray eyes she distinctly recalled were sunk deeply into his skull, throwing his cheekbones into almost harsh prominence, while his mouth was white beneath a scraggly, days-old beard. He looked much older than he was.

His mare halted a few paces in front of them, and she and Zach silently stared at him. He stared back. His gaze seemed to devour her and Zach, while giving out a deep but weary gladness that struck her as beyond his ability to speak.

"You're home at last, Mr. Prescott! Where have you been all these months?" It came out with more asperity than she intended. Was that all she could think to say? The man had come through years of war with its horrors and destruction, suffered wounds and privation far from home and his boy, and all she had thought to do was question his whereabouts?

But the war had been over for months. She had begun to think that, indeed, he would not return.

Gil felt a proper oaf for staring, but he could not tear his gaze away. He couldn't look at Jennifer enough.

And the boy, reflecting his own eyes. *His son!*

It was as though every cell in his body was starved for them; he wanted to drink them both into his soul.

Had he recalled her correctly? Yes. He had not misremembered. Beautiful in every graceful line of her, Jennifer stared at him with the same wide, delft-blue eyes he recalled from the night they'd parted. Only then, she'd been primly precise, with every golden hair smoothly in place and her white shirt buttoned to her lovely round chin. Her skin had been all top cream, that night.

Now shiny blond curls bounced around a tanned face and hung down her back, tied loosely with a ribbon. Her mouth, though pensive, held a sweet shape that appealed to him mightily.

He couldn't have described what she wore, he only knew it showed the shape of her womanly body, and the sleeves, rolled to her elbows, gave him a glimpse of well-shaped arms and wrists.

He suddenly wanted to touch her, hold her, to mold her body with his hands to see and feel that she was real and not a dream.

Then she'd spoken to him. It took him a minute to pull his thoughts together, to hear what she'd said. Jennifer was real enough, by thunder, the actualization of the woman who had haunted his dreams for years.

Gil answered slowly; a tinge of teasing overlay his serious words. "I'd have been home sooner, Teacher, except I was recovering from a wound that didn't want to heal."

Jennifer felt a tinge of embarrassed blush heat her cheeks and didn't know what to answer. "Of course. I should have thought of that. Are you better now?"

"Pretty much."

She wasn't too sure of that, by the look of him. "How did you find us?"

"Mr. Linderman at the grocery store in Osage Springs told me you and Zach were out here."

"Mama, who is he?" Zach had been unusually quiet, Jennifer suddenly realized. Now he pinched her chin, as he sometimes did when he wanted her full attention.

She looked down into his young face, his bright dark eyes earnestly questioning. She couldn't keep her tone less than solemn as she told him, "This is someone you've been waiting a very long time to meet, Zachary. He's your papa."

"My papa?"

"Yes."

"*My* papa?"

"Yes."

"My *real* papa?"

"Yes."

Zach returned his solemn gaze to Gil. They eyed each other, man and boy, each sizing up the stranger that was most important in their lives. Jennifer remained quiet while she continued her own study.

"You're a soldier," piped Zach.

"Yeah, son, I've been a soldier. But not anymore. Now I'm just plain me."

"Oh. Are you going to stay for supper?"

"I thought I would, if Teacher invited me."

"Who's Teacher?"

"Your mama."

"Oh. Well, my mama makes food real tasty." Zach turned to her, his young face eager with excitement. They had very little company. "He can stay for supper, can't he?"

"He most certainly may. And after the long ride he's had, I suspect he's ready for a good hot meal, don't you?"

"Uh-huh. Hey, Mister Papa, d'you want me to show you where you can put your horse?"

A softness settled in the corners of Gil's mouth. "That's very thoughtful of you, son. Would you like to help me ride Sally, here, to the barn?"

"Yes, sir. Can I, Mama?"

"I think that's an excellent idea. Then the two of you can wash up at the back door before you come in."

It was the perfect way for father and son to get acquainted, Jennifer thought. Zach didn't take to everyone so swiftly, and it would make the coming adjustments easier for him to have these first few moments alone with his father.

Gil nudged his mount to take a few steps and Jennifer walked toward him. She lifted Zach's small body, and Gil's long arms reached.

For the space of a heartbeat, she caught the utter reverence that flooded Gil's face as he held his son high before settling the boy on the saddle in front of him. When his gaze dropped to the top of Zach's head his mouth softened even more, while his eyes misted. One hand tentatively smoothed the dark hair, almost as hers had done only moments before.

"Okay, gitty-up, Sally," Zach sang out. "You can have some supper too, when we get to the barn."

Gil flicked her a glance full of unspoken feelings as he touched his heels to the mare's flanks. She watched them head for the barn, then walked toward the weathered, partly logged farmhouse.

Jennifer, herself, was a little overwhelmed. Zach's father was home!

Was she about to lose Zachary? After all this time, would she have to give him up? Give up this life?

The thought of giving up her self-contained existence with Zach caused her heart to plummet. Well, she silently scolded herself, she'd known this time would come, however much she had put off thinking about it. But whenever she'd thought of Gil's return these last months, she'd had so many emotional conflicts about it that she had pushed it right out of her mind again.

Now Gil was back and she had to face reality. Zachary was *Gil's* child. This was *Gil's* land, *his* home.

He had come home to reclaim them. It was only right.

Jennifer reminded herself that she'd always known she was but a temporary mother; she should be grateful for the years she'd had Zach. But inside, she cried out against surrendering Zach to anyone. Zach may be Gil Prescott's blood child, she thought fiercely, but he was the child of her heart. And this place . . . it had become her home, too.

Would she be asked to stay?

Maybe Gil wouldn't stay. He hadn't wanted to return, all those years before.

Yes, he would, her common sense declared. He was hardly the same young man who had gone, leaving behind a weeks-old baby.

If asked to leave, where would she go? How could she bear to leave Zach? The anticipation of such an event almost tore her heart out.

But she couldn't think any more about it just now, she resolved, as she glanced around the small kitchen.

She had supper to prepare and it must be special. Something Zach would remember for the rest of his life, a celebration of the night his father had returned from the war.

And it looked as though Gil needed a little celebrating, too—a bit of pampering. That haunted, ill pinch to his face told its own story. Yes, she'd make the evening a memorable one for both father and son. That way, she could fight her dismals.

She turned to the old cast-iron stove. What to serve? She had planned to feed Zach the leftover stew, but there wasn't much left to feed a grown man. Besides, that would never do for a welcome-home party.

There was the venison haunch Mr. Jackson, the nearest neighbor, had brought her. That would do it. She had planned to serve it for Sunday dinner, when Bessie often came, but now would be better.

Jennifer hurried the several yards from the back door of the house to the root cellar. Grabbing the rusty iron handle, she tugged. The heavy wooden door wouldn't budge.

She stood back and gave it a disgusted glare. Sometimes Jennifer wondered what good it was to have a fine cellar if she couldn't get into it. Often, it took her and Zach combined to raise the stubborn door.

Well, she couldn't allow it to get the better of her today. Gathering her breath, she pulled another heave, all the while muttering under her breath. "Come on, you blasted thing. This is no time to . . . give . . . me . . . trouble."

Finally, it swung upward. Relieved, she ran down the steps.

The venison hung from the rafter. She placed a wooden crate underneath it, stepped up, and unhooked it. Hopping down with the meat cradled under her arm, she then surveyed her vegetables and fruits.

She'd already put up a goodly stock—green beans, peas, pickled beets, blackberries. And thankfully, she had fresh potatoes and corn to serve. It was too bad she hadn't been able to get some of those peaches at the grocery before they were gone, but her table would not be disgraced. Mr. Linderman had promised to save her some the next time Mr. Bailey brought them.

Choosing sweet potatoes she'd wrapped only days ago, and fresh squash she had picked that morning, and jarred peas, and the blackberries she'd hidden from Zach in order to save for Christmas, she carefully filled her apron to carry them to the house. She would send Zach to pick fresh corn.

When she returned to the house, she set to work preparing the best dinner she could think of on such short notice. Biscuits. Venison steaks. Four vegetables. Blackberries. And fresh beaten cream.

Cream! She'd forgotten it. She'd have to go back to the cellar for the cream. Well, later.

Jennifer built up the fire in the stove then dipped her favorite cup for measuring into the flour. She dumped it into the mixing bowl, then looked at where it measured against the sides. Better make a double batch, she decided. She scooped another cupful of flour, added salt and baking powder, stirred, mixed in the lard, and lastly, buttermilk.

She heard a light tread, then a heavier one on the back step before Zach's head peeked around the door.

"Mama, we're gonna do the milking, all right?"

Jennifer looked up in surprise from shaping the biscuits. "Why, surely. That would be a great help. Make certain you wash your hands first."

"Okay. Papa," she heard Zach, now out of sight, say, "Mama says we have to wash our hands. Right there's the wash pan."

"Then we must see that they're extra clean, if Teacher says," the baritone replied.

A few minutes later, Gil stood on the back threshold, drying his hands on an old flour sack. "Ma'am, if you'll tell me which bucket you use for milking?"

"It's that one by the door. Here, let me give you a clean cloth to cover it when it comes back."

Jennifer bent to the shelf and pulled out another piece of cloth sacking. Zach popped into view around the door.

"Zach, be sure to show your papa just where to pat Flossy so she won't be nervous."

"Okay."

She handed him the cloth and a pan. "And will you kindly go to the corn patch before coming back to the house? We'll need five or six ears."

"Yummy. Corn."

Jennifer glanced at the small, animated face and smiled. The boy gave her such joy. His face, so openly honest, gave away his every feeling. Seldom irritated or unhappy, his disposition was usually sunny. He found delight in almost everything. As now, he didn't grumble about the need to pick the corn, he only thought of the pleasure of its goodness.

Her gaze sought Gil's face. Isn't he a wonderful child? she wanted to ask him.

Gil met her look and smiled. His eyes shone softer, alive with pride. He's a fine boy, they seemed to answer.

"Now don't be too long. Supper will be ready as soon as you come in."

"Okay, Mama."

"Yes, ma'am."

Jennifer set the table with the blue-flowered dishes. She had found them last winter, nearly a complete set, packed away in the storage area under the eaves. She'd carefully washed them and put them out, but she and Zach used them only for special occasions. For the first time, she wondered if they had belonged to Gil's mother. Would he mind her using them?

The back door, opened to catch the cool air of early evening, gave Jennifer a partial view of the back path to the barn, so she was aware when Gil and Zach returned. She also heard Zach. He was chatting and asking questions, his ongoing volubility punctuated with grunts or syllables of encouragement from his father.

Did he, Papa, live here when he was a little boy? Mama thought so, but wasn't sure. Did he have any brothers or sisters? Mama never had any. It used to make her sad, but she wasn't sad anymore, 'cause now she had him. That's why Mama liked him so much, he was a good playmate, she had told him so.

Mama said his grandpa used to live in this house, did he know that? Did Papa have a mama? Mama didn't have a mother or father, she had an aunt. She grew up back east where lots of houses were all bunched together like mushrooms. She liked it here best of any place she ever saw.

"Is it the best place you ever saw?" Zach said as he crowded through the door side by side with his father, his small hand curled around the pail handle alongside Gil's huge one.

"I reckon it is, son." Gil's gaze flickered her way and lingered. "The very best place."

"Set the milk in the dry sink and I'll strain it after

supper," Jennifer directed. "Come and sit down now. The food is hot."

"It looks mighty good, Teacher. A feast."

"I hope you'll enjoy it, Mr. Prescott. Please sit there." She indicated the chair at the head of the table.

Zach climbed into his usual place and waited for her. When she was seated, he announced, "It's my turn."

Jennifer contemplated a moment. Saying grace was one of Zach's favorite things to do, but traditionally it belonged to the household's head. Gently, she said, "Yes, I believe it is. But perhaps, now that your papa is home, he would like to be the one to offer thanks."

The boy turned questioning eyes toward Gil. Jennifer thought it was his first inkling that another male might usurp his place in the household.

"Ah . . . I would be most pleased to hear Zach's, tonight."

Zach eagerly folded his hands and bowed his head. "Thank you, God, for our food and nice house. And please make it rain. Amen." His head raised, a smile hovered. Then without warning, his head ducked back down. "God, I forgot. Thank you for bringing Papa home. Amen!"

Quiet reigned for a moment. Gil's gaze rested on his empty plate. His lashes, as long as Jennifer remembered, lifted slowly, and Jennifer probed the depths of his blue-gray pupils. They held an unaccountable sense of anguish and yearning.

Whatever was the cause, Jennifer couldn't guess, but she felt an immediate response—a tug so insistent, a need to soothe and comfort as she would Zach, that it was all she could do to remain in her chair. Instead, she picked up a serving dish.

"Would you care for sweet potatoes, Mr. Prescott?"

"Thank you, I would."

However, he didn't put much on his plate, she noticed.

"I want some meat, Mama."

"Wait until it passes your way, Zach," she admonished in her usual gentle way. "Be sure your papa has a biscuit."

Zach handed his father the biscuit basket. "Mama makes biscuits light as goose down, Papa. That's what Bessie says."

"Bessie?"

A slight blush crept up Jennifer's cheeks. "Bessie Terrell. You remember Bessie. She comes to visit once in a while."

"Yeah," Zach said. "Bessie showed Mama how to milk our cow when we first got her 'cause Mama never milked before."

Which reminded Zach of something he was eager to tell Mama. He swiveled his gaze from one adult to the other. "Mama, you know what? Papa squirted milk right into kitty's mouth! Did you ever see such a thing as that? Kitty was meowing an' meowing, and Papa called to her. She ran up and Papa squirted."

Zach raised his fist in the air and squeezed to demonstrate. "It went *shhhhish* and kitty got a mouthful. Boy, it sure was funny."

Jennifer chuckled, then looked at Gil when Zach asked, "How did you do that, Papa?"

"We had a barn cat when I was a boy. A real orange tiger cat. That cat knew exactly when it was milking time and came running. I always gave him a squirt."

"What happened to him?" Zach wanted to know.

Gil thought a moment. "I don't know, exactly. Pa sold our milk cow after Ma died, and the cat left by itself, I reckon."

"My mama got our cat from Mr. Linderman. She traded him needles for it."

"Needles?"

"They were scarce during the war years," Jennifer explained. "Luckily, I had a goodly supply from . . . my days in the East. Zach and I thought a cat would do us more good at the moment."

"I see." Gil's eyes narrowed in thought.

Wanting to change the subject, Jennifer said, "Would you care for another biscuit, Mr. Prescott?"

"Why do you call him Mr. Prescott, Mama?"

"Um, why, because that's his name, Zach. Like yours. Zachary Prescott, Gil Prescott." She hadn't expected this question quite so soon and tried for diversion. "More potatoes, son?"

"Uh-huh. But Mr. Linderman calls you Mrs. Hastings. And—and Mr. Jones and Mrs. Gallaghar do, too."

"Yes, they do. My name is Jennifer Hastings."

"Well, Tommy and Joey's mama is named Gallaghar, the same as theirs. And their papa's, too."

"That's right," Jennifer agreed.

"Mr. Linderman's mama—I mean his wife—her name is Mrs. Linderman, remember?"

Jennifer hid a sigh. Why had Zach picked now to raise such questions? But he had a tenacious streak, and obviously this was one he wasn't going to let go. She threw a glance at Gil; shouldn't he be the one to answer his son? He didn't appear to be preparing to do so. Perhaps, unused to small children, he didn't know how.

At least his emotions had come under control, Jennifer thought. He didn't look quite as unhappy as he had. In fact, behind his questioning gaze, she detected a glimmer of amusement. In spite of herself, it sparked her own. Apparently she was to teach them both.

She laid down her fork. "Zach, you remember last spring when we saw a wedding party going on at the church?"

"When that lady wore that long curtain on her head?"

"A veil, yes. Well, when a man and woman marry, the lady takes her husband's last name. It's called the family name. Any children born afterward have the same name."

"But yours is different," he insisted.

Jennifer reached out to take his hand. "Yes, mine is different than yours. Remember when I told you about the mother who gave you life before she went to heaven?" She waited for him to nod. "Her name was—"

"Morning Rain," Gil said in a gentle voice. Then his tone strengthened. "She was from a Cherokee family. When we married, her name became Morning Rain Prescott."

"Oh."

"But when she"—Gil flashed Jennifer a look of confirmation, then continued—"went to heaven, I needed to find you another mama quick, because I couldn't take you with me. So I looked around for the very best one I could find. I felt very fortunate Mrs. Hastings agreed to be your mama."

"But why—"

Jennifer jumped up from the table and carried her plate to the dry sink. "I think we've discussed this enough tonight, Zach. Besides, do you know what we have for dessert? Blackberry shortcake! Only I forgot to get the cream from the cellar." She dried her hands on her apron, grabbed a lantern, and started out the back door. "You men just finish your vegetables and I'll be back faster than you can say Jack Frost."

"Yum, blackberries." Zach turned to Gil. "Only I better go help Mama. She can't hardly lift the cellar door without me. 'Sides—" he leaned in and lowered his voice. "Mama doesn't like the dark. But don't tell her I said so, okay?"

"No, I won't, son. But I reckon you're right. We should go help."

2

"When did you move out here, Teacher?"

Gil descended the last stair into the living room, which was located almost immediately next to the kitchen door. The staircase led to the one room sandwiched into the eaves.

Jennifer had made the room into Zach's bedroom in June for his fourth birthday, making a big-boy rite out of the project. The child had welcomed it, telling her he was too old, now, to sleep in her room. As indeed, he was. Even while proud of him, a part of her sorrowed for Zachary's long-gone baby days.

Jennifer gave a last swipe to the dishpan and wrung out her rag before giving Gil a casual answer. "Oh, May of last year. Did Zach finally settle down?"

Gil chuckled, his eyes lighting up with sheer delight. "Mmm. Does he always ask so many questions?"

"Frequently." Jennifer flashed her own smile. "But I must admit he was in rare form tonight. I guess it was to be expected, though, with your homecoming. You've become real to him at last."

"I suppose it's been hard for him to think of having an honest-to-goodness pa. It might take some getting used to for both of us. But, I welcome it, Mrs. Hastings, I really do. These last years I've chewed on it a lot."

"Have you, Mr. Prescott? I often wondered . . . well, you never wrote and I thought perhaps you didn't plan to return at all."

He didn't answer immediately, but then he did, his voice strained. "I'm sorry, Teacher. I guess I should've written. I just . . ." He shook his head as though the thought eluded him.

The jumbled reasons seemed lamer than a one-legged goose to Gil now, but for a long time after he left Kansas, he had thought only of the mess he'd made of his life and speculated that it was better to cut any ties; that way, when he died, he would leave no grief behind him. His will to live had returned only slowly.

The memory of this woman had been a major part of it.

"I sent money when I could. You got it, didn't you?" It seemed the only thing he had to offer for his lapse.

"Oh, yes. It came through Mr. Linderman, and we appreciated it. But, Mr. Prescott, a child needs more than an occasional bit of money to answer his needs. He needs human contact, a human touch . . . a child needs love, and—"

Jennifer stopped scolding abruptly as Gil rubbed the back of his neck wearily. His face looked pinched and white, and she suddenly noticed he was leaning rather heavily on the back of a kitchen chair. Instantly ashamed of her runaway tongue, she laid a hand on his arm.

"Forgive me, Mr. Prescott. It isn't my place to scold and you have only come home. Please sit down, you look tired to the bone. Or perhaps you should go on up to bed."

"Not yet, Teacher, if you don't mind. I'm still too restless to sleep. But I'll sit a moment, if you will."

"All right." Jennifer lowered herself into a kitchen chair as he did, and was silent. The kitchen was cooler now, a breeze coming through once in a while from the opened back door. Idly, she lifted her hair off her neck to catch it. "I'm glad it isn't as hot as July. Zach has trouble sleeping upstairs when it's too hot."

Gil watched the feminine gesture, storing to his memory the way her long fingers patted and smoothed, wanting to be the recipient of those pats and strokes, soaking up her very presence as the wheat would the sun. Did she have any idea how completely lovely she was? And desirable?

"What do you do then?"

"We make a pallet on the parlor floor. He likes that."

"Mmm."

"Would you like a cold biscuit? You didn't eat much at supper."

"No, I . . . supper was the best I've tasted in years, Mrs. Hastings, thank you. But my appetite hasn't been much good lately."

"When were you wounded?"

"In February."

Just before the end, Jennifer mused. Was that where he'd sustained his broken nose? What had happened? There were another dozen questions vying for expression, but she asked the one uppermost in her mind. "How badly?"

"Bad enough," he said wearily. "Teacher, I'd rather hear about you. And Zach. How's it been for the two of you these last four years?"

Jennifer accepted Gil's reluctance to discuss his war experiences, instinctively feeling they were too painfully recent for him to talk about. Although she wanted to know, she recognized it might take him a long while to recount them, so she didn't urge him. Instead, she smiled into Gil's eyes. Behind his expected curiosity, Jennifer sensed a depth in his longing to know all about what he'd missed in his son's life.

"Zachary is a joy, Mr. Prescott. And you can see for yourself he is healthy. Growing so fast, I'll need to make him new pants soon. I found some old clothes under the eaves last winter which I can cut down. And some with very good buttons. I can use . . ."

But would she be here to make them? Would there be a place for her now in Zachary's life? The questions seemed to jump up to hit her in the face. What *would* happen now? To her, to Zach? Would she be expected to return to her previous life? To teaching other people's children but not her own?

How soon would she have to face the fears that plagued her?

Jennifer let her chatter drift into silence, then gave a slight shrug, as though to say it was nothing important. Noticing a haze of puzzlement in his gaze, she covered her agitation by asking, "What else do you want to know?"

"When did you quit teaching?"

"Two years ago."

"Why?"

"Well, Zach . . ." She dropped her lashes, her fingers playing idly with the sugar bowl lid. She didn't want to burden Gil with distasteful details on his first night home. "It was just time, that's all."

Gil gave her a disbelieving look that she caught as he said, "Ah-huh. Mr. Linderman told me my pa died winter before last and left you permission to use the ranch, but you'd already stopped teaching. Spoke of some ruckus over a couple of the older boys at school picking on Zach."

Jennifer stiffened at the remembered insults and petty cruelty some of the children had shown the child. As they grew steadily worse, she had felt them personally. Rather than create a full-blown fight over what the children had done, thus pulling the parents into it, she resigned her position. However, she didn't want Gil to feel guilty about her choice of removing Zach from the situation.

"I won't tolerate bullies in my classroom, Mr. Prescott," she answered, crossing her arms and fighting the angry blush that crept up her cheeks. "Of any kind, toward anyone. And the school board understood my position. But all in all, I thought it best to resign."

"I'm deeply sorry, Mrs. Hastings. I never imagined you would be put in that kind of a rocky place."

Her tone softened. "It's all right, really. We've gotten along just fine. Why, we have become regular farmers."

He nodded his understanding, his eyes picking up a twinkle as he asked on a lighter note, "Tell me how you got Flossy?"

"Oh, you mean Zach didn't fill your head with that story?" she said and flashed a smile. "Well, I had some earbobs that I never wear, and Bessie knew I wanted a milk cow. She worked out a sale of the earbobs for me to a . . . a woman working at Jasmine's, then Mr. Linderman helped me buy Flossy from Mrs. Dillon.

But I didn't know a thing about keeping a cow or milking, as Zach told you, so Bessie and I traded instructions. She taught me everything about Flossy, and I taught her how to add and subtract on paper." Jennifer laughed in delight. "I had the better bargain that time because Bessie knew arithmetic just fine when it came to counting money. She learned it in a snap."

Gil made no comment on the story but chose, rather, to respond over her delight in it.

Jennifer noticed how Gil's smile spread from his lips to his eyes. Those sparkling eyes said things his lips did not, Jennifer thought. She marveled at how it changed his rather ordinary looks to one of sweet appeal. It called forth a ready response of shared feeling, a touch to a heartstring.

And for the first time she realized how much Zach resembled his father. Except for his darker coloring, Zach was almost a replica—deeply set eyes being his most striking feature. Would she have a chance to learn how to read Gil's thoughts as easily as she did Zach's?

"Now we trade butter and milk along with eggs with Mr. Linderman for other things we need," she remarked.

His face sobered. His long discussion with his old friend, Mr. Linderman, had given him some worrisome news. Not only had he then learned of his father's death and of the run-down condition of the ranch, but of how hard life had become for Mrs. Hastings and his son. His indebtedness to this woman was mountain high.

He was an unworthy son of a coyote and hadn't deserved such devotion to his affairs. He swallowed hard and spoke humbly. "I'm right sorry you've had such a hard time, Teacher. Losing your teacher's post and then having to trade away your things to keep food on the table. I'll never be able to repay you."

Jennifer saw the strain in Gil's face and reached out to touch his fingers in reassurance. She wanted to ease his distress. Her touch registered the fact that his skin was too soft for a man—the kind of softness which reminded her he'd probably been immobilized during his recovery.

"Zach's worth everything, Mr. Prescott," she answered in a soft, compelling voice. "And as I've said, we've gotten along all right and we . . . I've been . . . more than content."

Yes, she had been more than content. She had even, in spite of all her difficulties, been quite happy in their rather isolated, simple existence. Yet she hesitated to express it; happiness was an elusive commodity, one easily lost. Once, ten years before, she would have been gushing to spill it, to share it and every one of her emotions. However, past experience had taught her well; a carelessly shared heart was to risk betrayal.

Gil's long lashes flickered downward and his gaze rested on her fingers where they covered his. His expression softened. Instantly, Jennifer pulled back, even while wondering what Gil was thinking, and folded her hands in front of her. She wasn't ready to take this particular risk just yet.

Gil changed the subject, his voice dropping to rough edges as he said, "Tell me what you know of my pa's death."

"I don't know all that much. I heard of his passing away from a man named Bill Wallace."

"I know the man. He worked for Pa."

"Yes, well, he knocked on my door in town early

one morning, sometime in late March of sixty-four I believe, and told me of your father's death. Then he handed me a letter that authorized me to take over this place for Zach. I have it in that first drawer of the desk if you want to see it?"

"Later. Go on."

"Mr. Wallace told me he was leaving the area and for me to see Mr. Linderman, who had also received a letter verifying my right to be here with Zach until your return. That was all."

"Did Bill tell you how Pa died?"

"Pneumonia, he said."

"Mmm." Gil turned to look into the dark beyond the door. The old chair creaked as he shifted to lean back. Even though he tried to hide it, pain laced his next question.

"Did my pa ever ask to see Zachary?"

She hesitated a long moment on her answer but finally decided he deserved the straight truth, however discomforting. "He never communicated with me directly, Mr. Prescott, for any reason. But he saw Zachary once that I know of, when Zach was about two."

At Gil's questioning look, she told of the incident. "We were walking toward Mr. Tige's mercantile when those little ruffians, the Gallaghar boys, barreled past us and, deliberately in my opinion, knocked Zach down. They were off and away before I could either prevent it or take them to task for it. But Zach didn't cry. He just picked himself up, dusted his little hands, and said, "C'mon, Mama," as though he couldn't be bothered with what had happened. When I looked up, your father was standing close by. I'm sure he saw the whole incident."

Thoughtful, Gil remained silent a long moment.

Then he changed the subject once again. "Was there no one on the place when you came?"

"Not a soul. Mr. Linderman told me there should have been two men and some cattle, but I found no one, and no animals at all."

She didn't see that it was necessary to tell him how dirty the house had been, or that half the household equipment had been rusty and damaged beyond use.

"Damn!" Gil rose and paced into the parlor and back.

It was worse than he'd thought. What little he'd seen of the conditions around the house and barn, of the other buildings and equipment—or the lack thereof—had been an eye-opener. It surpassed even what the storekeeper had told him. And by Jennifer's very subdued account, he knew she'd walked into a sorry mess. "Uh, pardon, Teacher."

"I understand your disappointment, Mr. Prescott. And I regret adding another disquieting factor, but, I must tell you . . . more than a week lapsed between the date Mr. Wallace said your father died and the delivery of the letters to me and Mr. Linderman. No accounting of the number of cattle, horses, or other animals or equipment was given. When Zach and I arrived, the place seemed unexpectedly quiet, out of kilter, not as I would have thought a man of your father's reputation for exactitude would have left it. Without the cattle or horses, and no sign of the men, I've concluded you were robbed by your father's hired men."

Gil dropped into his chair again and heaved a heavy sigh as he rubbed the heel of his hand against his cheekbone and fingered the broken ridge of his nose. "Peder Linderman indicated there were problems, but I'd no idea how big. How have you managed?"

Gil's sense of indebtedness and wonder toward Jennifer Hastings seemed to spill over into a second mountain heap. It was painful to contemplate. He could never make it up to her.

"I grew up learning to make a penny stretch, Mr. Prescott." She turned out her hand, palm up. "I guess my Aunt Agnes gave me skills beyond her intentions, but they've come into good use. Zach and I have bargained for our needs as often as possible, and I've a little money, a twice-yearly income, which goes for the things we need to buy."

Jennifer fell silent again, waiting for his response. His gaze flickered away, seeing something beyond the blackness outside, and for a long stretch he didn't speak, as though his thoughts were too painful to share.

But then Jennifer saw his mouth tighten with anger. "Teacher, I don't want you using any more of your money. It ain't right! I don't know how I stand here, if there's anything left besides these buildings and land, but by thunder, this is my place and I'll take care of the paying from now on. Tomorrow I'll ride out to look things over."

Jennifer dropped her gaze. She shouldn't have told him just yet about her annuity. Gil's embarrassment was obvious, and there were going to be more problems for him to work through. And when he found out she'd ordered and paid for winter wood yet to be delivered, and Flossy's hay and grain for the winter— it had cost her half her yearly income—his pride might further suffer.

Well, she'd deal with that problem when it came and not before. Enough had been said tonight. She stood.

"You are tired, Mr. Prescott, and you have come a long way home." She wanted to mention how drawn he looked and how, because he was apparently still recovering from his wounds, he should rest tomorrow, but she thought it might cause him additional discomfort. Instead, she picked up the lamp and reached for another.

"Morning has a way of making things look brighter," she told him as she lit the second lamp, then handed it to him. "The main thing is, you're home in one piece and Zachary has his papa back."

Gil's eyes silvered as he studied her. They captured her gaze and made a soft, yearning impact. For the first time in years, Jennifer suddenly felt a womanly fluster, because Gil's expression didn't hold the look of a tired and recovering man. No, sir. Those eyes held a definite glint of male interest.

She blinked rapidly while all her hard-won containment seemed to fly away. She was abruptly aware of her probable bedraggled appearance. Her hair, too curly to lie smooth, frequently sprang away from its pins to surround her face with unruly corkscrew curls. Usually she didn't care if it made her look like a porcupine; there was no one to see. Now she wondered if he found her looks amusing—she thought she must appear so.

Startled at her own reaction, she spun away with a "Wait here a moment," and hurried into the small bedroom off the parlor that she'd taken for her own. Picking up the best of the two feather pillows from the bed, she took a deep breath. Then more composed, she returned to the kitchen and handed it to Gil.

"I think the bed upstairs is big enough for the two of you. But Zach has only one pillow."

He smiled, the edges of his mouth creasing the corners beguilingly. Once again she was reminded of how much he and Zach looked alike.

"We'll manage. That was my bed when I was a boy."

"Oh, of course. I should have realized it."

"Good night, Teacher. Thank you for welcoming me home."

"Good night, Mr. Prescott."

As the gray light of dawn lifted, Jennifer rebuilt the fire in the kitchen stove, poured the last of her water into the kettle, and set it to heat, then listened for any possible stirring from above. All was quiet.

She sat to pull on her old boots before taking the two water buckets to the spring, a quarter of a mile from the house. Hopefully, she could make her first morning round before Gil and Zach wakened.

But it was not to be. She heard the stairs creak and recognized Gil's descending tread.

"Good morning," she greeted him brightly. "I trust you slept well in spite of a rolling four-year-old."

He grinned his response. "It was a new experience, right enough. But after years of sleeping wherever my body fell, I didn't mind it a bit."

He didn't add that, as the sun filtered into the attic room, he'd watched his son's small features in wonder this last half hour. The tenderness that took a tight hold of his heart was an emotion he'd felt only rarely.

"The kettle will boil in a few minutes, Mr. Prescott," Jennifer directed, "and you will have hot water for shaving. If Zach comes down, please tell him breakfast will have to wait a bit this morning." She pulled on a pair of old cotton gloves. "I'm off to fetch water."

Jennifer caught the slight puzzlement on Gil's face but didn't enlighten him. He would find out soon enough, she reasoned.

And he did. Twenty minutes later, Jennifer found the back door opened for her by an impatiently waiting man, wearing a scowl.

"Why in thunder didn't you tell me the well had gone dry?" Gil accused, as he took one of the heavy buckets from her.

Jennifer avoided answering as she assessed his anger. Apparently, he was the type of man who wanted all the facts set before him immediately. He didn't like it that she'd omitted telling him of the dry well.

"I told Papa about the well, Mama."

"Thank you, Zach." She spared a smile for the boy. He sat at the table, innocently swinging a bare foot. "That's very helpful."

"How often do you make the trip to the spring?"

She turned from setting her bucket on the worktable and faced Gil. "Most days, two or three times. But when we don't get rain, we need to water the garden."

His scowl deepened. "How many times?"

"I don't bother to count."

"Yes, you do, Mama," Zach reminded her, then turned to his father, counting on his fingers. "Once for the kitchen. Once for washin'. Once for the chickens. Sometimes for Flossy, but Mama said she usually has enough water from that little stream at the bottom of the pasture. An' four times for the garden."

Gil bit down hard on his teeth. "How long has the well been dry?"

"I don't know, exactly. It got us through that first summer, barely. But the water was muddy. Then when we discovered the spring, we started using that. . . ."

She had needed the well badly, and they could do with a windmill, too, but she hadn't enough money to pay for a new well, yet, much less the windmill. When her July check came in, she'd had to make a decision between the well and other needs. She had opted for buying hay and animal feed, and wood for the coming winter—last year, they'd frequently been very cold—and a paid-up bill at Lindermans'. It had made her feel good to owe nothing.

But as soon as her next check came in at the first of the year, she would have enough money to pay for a new well. In fact, she'd already discussed the problem with Mr. Jones, a farmer located on the other side of town. He and his two sons had agreed to do the work next spring.

But right now, she'd have to be very careful how she approached Gil about the matter. This was his place—he might have different plans for it. Besides that, even though having good water was of paramount importance, after last night's adamant command that she wasn't to use any more of her money, Gil wasn't likely to take her intentions with equanimity.

Her intentions. She brought herself up short. Why was she worrying about it? She didn't even know if she would still be here next winter.

He hasn't asked me to stay, yet.

Where had that reminder come from? she asked herself. But would he? And would she? Zach still needed a mother, but would Gil want her to stay? Perhaps he had someone else in mind to be his wife.

That thought caught her unaware. After all those years when she had sworn never to marry again, she hadn't even realized the idea lurked in the back of her mind—to become a wife once more. But it was the only way, as far as she could see, to keep Zachary.

However, if Gil should want to marry someone else . . . If that should happen, Jennifer didn't think she could bear the thought of giving up Zach.

But if Gil should ask her, could she accept?

Zach's piping voice intruded on her introspection. "Mama's saving money to get a new well dug, Papa."

Uh-oh! Now the cat was out of the bag.

Jennifer ducked her head as she swiftly turned toward the stove. She waited for Gil's next question or comment. Or explosion. She didn't know, yet, the temper of Zachary's father.

She dug into the coffee jar and measured out an extra scoop for the pot, then placed it where it would quickly boil. She sliced bacon and laid it in precise rows in the frying pan. Behind her, the quiet was filled with Zach's chatter, giving his father the details of how much water they fed each vegetable.

"Excuse me, Zach," she quietly interrupted. "Do you want two eggs or three, Mr. Prescott?"

"I want two eggs, Mama," the child announced.

She gave the boy a look. It was going to be difficult for him to give up his cock-of-the-walk status. Indeed, it was difficult enough for her, and she didn't know if she could do it. She'd have to be careful not to make it harder for Zachary. Using her gentlest voice, she said, "Yes, Zach, I know you do. But you haven't allowed your father to answer."

Zach's face lost its happy glow. His gaze flew from her to Gil. "I'm sorry, Papa."

"That's all right, son. But I'm glad to see you practicing your manners."

The little boy relaxed and smiled again while Gil turned a thoughtful, sober gaze to Jennifer. "I'll have one this morning and try for two tomorrow, Teacher."

She nodded her understanding and cracked five eggs into the bacon grease. After dishing up the eggs, bacon, and toasted biscuits left from the night before, she poured milk for Zach and coffee for Gil and herself. Silently, she sat down and listened to Zach's morning prayer before beginning to eat.

Gil said nothing more about the well, but his attention to breakfast and Zach was given halfheartedly. A few minutes later, he stood, sudden impatience lining his stance. "Zach, run up and get your boots on, pronto. We ride out in five minutes."

Zach, his eyes big, shoved a last bite of bacon and biscuit into his mouth as he hopped off his chair. "Where're we going?"

"I reckon we'll check out the south section today. It'll take us quite a ways past the spring," he explained. Then playful, he ordered, "Now git."

Zach thundered up the stairs. Jennifer, her gaze on her plate, listened to his progress as she sipped her second cup of coffee as calmly as she could. She wished she'd been invited to go, too. A day roaming with the two of them would have been fun. But Gil hadn't included her, and anyway, with Zach using old Ben, the nag she used to take her to and from town, there would be no mount for her even if she spoke her desire to go.

Ah, well, she consoled herself. She had plenty of work around the house to do, and she hadn't had a day completely to herself for years. Four, to be precise. And the plan was all to the good for Zach. He needed to start cutting the apron strings.

Gil needed to begin being a father.

The man turned to her. "Can you pack us a lunch, Mrs. Hastings?"

His formality hurt after his calling her Teacher in that gentle way. She schooled her features to blandness before raising her lashes. "Certainly. What time shall I expect your return?"

"Late in the afternoon." His jaw hardened as he ordered, "But you're not to water the garden before we get back to help. And let Flossy find her own water down at the trickle."

"Yesterday was an exception, Mr. Prescott. I usually water the garden in the morning. It is better for the plants."

"You're not to haul water," he insisted. A command, really. "I'll do it when we get home."

"Very well." She rose from the table and gathered together bread, bacon, and pickles, putting them into sandwiches, wrapping the food in a clean flour sack with the last of day-before-yesterday's cookies. They were molasses, Zach's favorites.

Zach was clumping down the stairs before Gil spoke again. Almost as an afterthought, he asked, "You'll be okay here alone, won't you, Mrs. Hastings?"

"You needn't worry, Mr. Prescott. I have plenty of work to occupy my time, and being alone is not a new situation for me."

"'Bye, Mama," Zachary called over his shoulder as he ran out of the door. Blithely. With his excited attention completely focused on Gil.

Jennifer's heart turned. The child and she had seldom been apart for more than an hour or so, before. It was a mark of his growing up that Zach did not look back.

The day stretched before her, looking long and lonely. Was it to foreshadow her future?

3

Jennifer spent the day canning corn, making corn relish and a triple batch of sweet cucumber pickles. She had found, last year, that they sold well in the Lindermans' store. She had used her profit for Zachary's Christmas presents.

She missed Zach's bright chatter. His small presence usually filled such a day with small adventures and laughter. Now the hours, while busy, seemed to trudge uphill. As the sun sank lower in the western sky, Jennifer eagerly watched the southern horizon for Zach and Gil's return.

Normally, after she had spent a long hot day in the kitchen, Jennifer was too tired to serve anything but a cold supper. Zach never complained, and she didn't care, for herself. But tonight she put in the effort to make a venison pie and a pudding for dessert.

The table had been set for an hour when she heard Zach's shout. "We're home, Mama." He appeared at the opened back door with a grin. "What's for supper?"

Gil's low rumble interrupted. "We need to see to the horses first, son."

"Okay. I'll be in pronto, Mama. Me'n Papa are starved."

Jennifer smiled at Zach's use of the new word *pronto,* which he'd learned only hours ago from Gil, while she hurriedly dished up generous portions of food on their plates. She felt rewarded when both Zach and Gil tucked into it as soon as the evening thanks were offered. They were indeed very hungry.

And very tired, Jennifer observed moments later when Zach's eyes began to droop halfway through their meal. He was in the middle of a sentence, struggling to tell her everything they'd done during the day even as his speech slowed.

"We rode all the way over the hill and a long—" he paused for a huge yawn, "loonnng way to where Papa says our land stops. We found three cows. We saw a rattler, even. But Papa killed it."

Gil rose and scooped the small boy into his arms. "C'mon, son. Time for bed."

"He really should have a quick wash, Mr. Prescott. He's filthy."

"I reckon he is, Teacher, but it won't hurt him for one night to go without. Don't think you could keep him awake for another minute anyway."

It was true. Zach's head lay heavily on his father's shoulder, his gentle breathing deepening as he succumbed to sleep while she watched. She saw the white lines and dark shadows of exhaustion in Gil's face as well. They had pushed themselves too hard.

"Very well. This once."

"I'll be back to finish my supper in a minute."

Jennifer resumed her own meal while the minutes ticked by. From above came the soft rustling of quiet movement. Zach's faint protesting murmur, answered by Gil's, reached her. A boot thumped on the floor and a bedspring squeaked. After what seemed a long time had passed without Gil's return, she listened from the bottom of the stairs. There was no sound except a single sighing breath.

She lifted her skirt and climbed the stairs on tiptoe. Just as she'd suspected, she thought, halfway between amusement and annoyance. Gil was as fast asleep as his son.

In the gloom of the attic room's one window, she stared at the two figures stretched out on the bed. While Gil had succeeded in removing Zach's boots and pants, he, himself, lay sprawled fully clothed, an arm curled around Zach's shoulders. One hand, looking too white and thin, spread across his chest, the wrist bones sharply prominent.

She moved quietly to tug at Gil's heavy, army-issued and now-patched footwear, all the while mentally scolding. He was obviously as worn down as those old boots. Why couldn't the man just admit he was not yet in robust health? Why did he insist on taking up a full-day's work before he had completely recovered? He would ruin what little health he had left.

Three cows. Was this unhealthy exhaustion worth those three measly cows? If they hadn't gone anywhere for years, they weren't likely to get lost now. And his land . . .

Compassion flowed through her even while she fussed and all her momentary irritation drained away. Those cows would more than keep them in meat all winter, and if any of the three were young enough, perhaps Gil could sell one. Or use it to help start a new herd.

She knew what it was like to lose everything, what it was like to be ill. And while Gil hadn't lost his land, he had come home to a run-down ranch. It would take several years of hard work as well as the blessings of God's own to make the place successful once more.

She wished she could talk him into resting for a few days before wearing himself out like this, but she suspected his pride wouldn't allow him to entertain the idea. Manlike, he would test himself to the hilt. And somehow, after their earlier discussion, she knew Gil wouldn't be satisfied to scrape along as she and Zach had, either. Gil had changed. That night when the young Gil had given over Zach's custody to her, she had received the impression he had led a somewhat careless existence until then. Now this Gil had become a man of responsibility and ambition.

Again, she wondered how she fit into his scheme of things. Would his plans include her? She still didn't know and couldn't guess. His only thoughts seemed to concern this place and Zach. *His* place and *his* son.

Jennifer pushed her anxieties aside once more and concentrated on what she was doing. Gil grunted softly as she finally succeeded in removing his boots. She set them on the floor, then unbuckled his belt and loosened his clothing. Leaning across him, she brushed Zach's hair back from his forehead, her usual goodnight gesture, then spent a long moment just looking at the two of them before tiptoeing back downstairs.

Soon after clearing up the kitchen, Jennifer went to bed, too, falling asleep on the thought of the garden's need for water and the changing pattern of her days. And the new element in them . . . Gil.

*   *   *

Jennifer swung over the last rise on the far side of the house and headed for the garden, the heavy buckets splashing only a little water as she kept her stride long and smooth. The first sun rays sparkled with the promise of another hot day. She hoped the heat wave broke soon. She still had about three days of canning to do, by her mental accounting of the garden produce, and spending those days in a sweltering kitchen would be hellish.

Without a word of warning, Gil walked up from behind her, his footfalls silenced by the soft earth, and lifted the buckets from her hands. Though her breath caught in surprise, she made no complaint as she followed him into the neat rows of the new plantings of green beans, peas, and spinach she was trying as fall crops. Without speaking, they poured water on them together in about half the time it usually took her. It was a relief to have someone around to share the work.

As the last drop disappeared into the ground, Gil said, "I'll hitch Ben up to that old pull sled and haul the rain barrel down to the spring and fill it. That ought to be enough water to finish the job and then some."

She started to voice her opinion that he needed to regain his strength before tackling such a heavy load as lifting a barrel full of water, but then thought better of it. Instead, she couched her thought in a way she hoped would give him pause. "That's a wonderful idea, Mr. Prescott. That heavy barrel—I would never have had the strength to lift it, even empty. Full of water, it would be impossible."

But the understanding that he might not be up to it, either, didn't seem to occur to him. He acknowledged her compliment with a pleased nod. "Good. I'll go right away."

She turned. Men's egos and misplaced pride had always been a mystery to her, but she recognized Gil's, just the same. "Very well. I'll have breakfast on the table by the time you return," she said.

A few moments later, Zach bounced down the stairs and looked eagerly about the kitchen. Finding no sign of his father, a sudden worried frown creased his forehead. "Where's Papa? Did he leave already?"

"He went after water."

"But I wanted to go with him." Zach never cried over a mere disappointment, but now his chin wobbled.

"He's coming right back, Zach," she reassured him, her heart tender. "Why don't you help me with breakfast so that we'll be ready by his return."

Somewhat mollified, Zach dutifully put flatware on the table. But when Gil came, he didn't hesitate to voice his fears as he watched his father gather the buckets to milk the cow. "I thought you'd gone away, Papa."

"Nope. Only as far as the spring."

"Are you going to ride the land again today?"

"Yep, sure am."

"Me too?"

"Uh-huh, you bet."

"I was 'fraid you might go without me."

Gil stopped in the middle of his stride out the door. His eyes were solemn as he returned Zach's troubled gaze. "I might have to go somewhere, Zach, now and then, when I can't take you with me. Like to town for a few hours or something. But I'd let you know, if that was the case."

"You won't go away and never come back? Like before?"

Gil flashed Jennifer a brief glance before answering, his deep voice ringing with promise. "No, son. I don't plan to leave you behind ever again. You can count on that."

Zach, his fears laid to rest, took one of the buckets from Gil's hand. "Okay. Mama, me'n Papa will eat a mountain of biscuits this morning when we get back."

Jennifer's heart felt likely to turn over. Gil had said exactly what Zach needed to hear for his son's world to feel secure. But not her own. Zach had so quickly taken to leaving *her* behind in favor of going with his father, and even though it was to be only a little while, it was lonely in the house without him.

She hadn't expected to feel such mixed emotions. She hadn't at all. Why couldn't she cope with them?

Being with his father was good for the child. A son shouldn't cling to his mother's apron strings, she reminded herself, and Zach was old enough to be taught manly ways. Was she jealous over having to share Zach's attention? Or Gil's?

Was she fearful that the two of them could get along without her altogether? Was she afraid of being left on her own again?

Ashamed of her selfish thoughts, Jennifer hurried to finish her preparations.

That morning, true to his word, Gil ate two eggs, several strips of bacon, and three biscuits. Gratified, Jennifer later packed a lunch without comment, and the two males left after promising to return for supper earlier than the day before.

"I'll need old Ben tomorrow," Jennifer announced that evening after Zach had been put to bed. She wiped the last big pot she'd used for the day's canning, and put it on the back of the stove. "I usually go to town on Wednesdays and Saturdays, and sometimes an additional day, as well, to take my eggs and such to Lindermans'."

"All right," Gil answered. He had no quarrel with her plans. After all, Jennifer owned Ben and her produce.

Jennifer glanced at him. He was being very accommodating.

He sat at the table, a brooding stare at nothing on his face while both hands circled his coffee cup. He appeared just as exhausted as the night before, she noted, but at least freshly scrubbed tonight. His brown hair curled long against his neck, glistening in the budding lamplight. True to his promise, he and Zach had bathed at the tiny spring before they brought the water up to the house. "I'll go along, then Zach can double up with me. No use making your ride more troublesome."

"Oh, it isn't troublesome," she answered, hoping to ease his conscience. "I've been using the old buggy I found in the barn. We've just enough room in it to transport a few things besides ourselves."

"That thing? I did see it, of course, but I didn't take time to look closely. If I remember right, that was in sorry condition even before I left."

"It serves," Jennifer answered absently. Gil had hauled more water for her just before supper, and she gratefully looked forward to her own sponge bath. She would have to take it in the privacy of her room, though, rather than here in the kitchen, as she'd done before.

"I had the blacksmith replace a wheel and repair the brakes," she added. She turned her back to him as she counted jars for the third time that day, lining them along the dry sink to be transferred to the cellar tomorrow. Eight quarts of pickled beets and the last of the green beans.

"And you settled your account with more of your jewelry and such, I suppose?"

The tinge of accusation in his voice caused her to look at him over her shoulder. That was it, of course. His pride still smarted over her way of paying for what they'd needed. "I don't see—"

He eased back in his chair, watching her. "How much?"

She didn't want to tell him, but knew she must. "A velvet cloak with a fur collar I no longer wore. His wife looks lovely in it."

"Ugh! What else?"

"Else?"

"What else don't I know? Bills and the like? How indebted am I?"

"Mr. Prescott, you can't expect to come home to find everything just as you left it," she defended with some asperity. "And we must live. Anything I've done has been toward investment for our future. That is, Zach's and mine . . . and . . . and to . . . to advance our progress."

She decided not to tell him how she got her first chickens; they had already paid for themselves, anyway. Instead, she added, "I couldn't know if you would return."

"But I have," he replied gently, refraining from pointing out the obvious, that Zach and this place were his responsibility.

She tried to redirect the conversation. "Why, my eggs are considered the freshest in town, Mr. Linderman tells me, and my butter, the sweetest. The hotel now pays a premium for my produce."

"I never said anything against your excellent management, Teacher," he said, showing his first sign of real irritation with her. "You would put a beaver to shame. But I must know all of what you've spent to get started here again, and what's owing now."

"Really, Mr. Prescott, we could save this discussion for a later day, when you've been home long enough to feel in full health."

"In full health? Putting it off ain't going to win any favors, is it? Or help me feel better. What are you afraid of? Is there much you haven't told me?"

"Well . . ."

"Come on, Mrs. Hastings," he said, letting the irritation cover his feelings of failure, then instantly ashamed of his tone, softened it. Despite everything, over the last two days he'd strengthened his resolve to win this woman for his own, and his first step seemed to be to settle his obligations. He was determined to know of every penny she'd spent. "It doesn't sound like all I know of you to put off something that has to be done. Or said. I always admire how you go right to it."

No one could ever call her lazy over physical work, it was true. But she had been a coward, sometimes, when faced with a difficult decision or an emotional turmoil. If Gil knew how often she'd been guilty of that very fault, would he still admire her?

Yes, indeed, she'd gotten herself into deep trouble by putting things off in the past. And once, it had cost her horribly dear not to face an issue square on; her problems hadn't gone away or solved themselves. No, they had escalated to an irreparable stage and she had paid the price by being left to pick up the shattered pieces of her life and start again. Alone and friendless.

Now Gil's blue-gray gaze pinned her to the wall.

He was only asking what he had a right to know—all of her business transactions that concerned the ranch and his son. She sighed, and without more ado told him of the wood and hay she'd ordered from Mr. Jones. "The hay will be delivered sometime in early September, he said, and the wood no later than October."

"How much is Jones charging you?"

Jennifer named the sum. Gil whistled through his teeth.

"He's making more than his share of profit from that price," Gil said in disgust. He rose and stretched, his annoyance with her apparently over. "Well, I can talk to Jones in a day or so. See if we can strike a better trade. We'll need to take the hay, of course, but Zach and I'll find wood on our own. No use—"

"Mr. Prescott, I fear you don't understand. I've already paid Mr. Jones."

"You've what?" His expression was almost blank in his shock. No one ever paid for a service or product before it was done. No one with any sense, that is. He realized there was a human streak in Teacher.

Jennifer refused to feel defensive, or tried to. She folded her hands at her waist, unconsciously taking a stance that her former students would mark as a no-nonsense one of preparing to lecture a recalcitrant student.

"Mr. Jones has already received payment. He wouldn't hold it for me at that price unless I paid in advance."

Gil gave an angry snort, his eyes snapping with outrage.

Jennifer hurried on with her explanation. "The quality of the wood is guaranteed to be the best, you see, hard burning wood to last us the winter in comfort. And he said he could get twice his hay price in town, or triple, if he hauled it to Topeka, Lawrence, or Kansas City, and I expect he is right. Too many people are in need, still, and prices are high."

Gil walked a circle around the table, watching his feet, filled with feelings of impotent rage and nowhere to put them. Jennifer had done only what she'd had to, he suspected. His admiration for her industriousness climbed, but he wondered just how gullible she'd been.

He'd met Jones a few times before the war, but never had dealings with the man. He tried to recall anything said against him in town, but nothing came to mind. Was Jones completely fair and honest in his business? Had he taken advantage of a woman alone?

Probably. As he had, he reminded himself.

He had taken great advantage of Jennifer Hastings, and he felt deep shame over it. He'd had no idea . . . Watching her neatly hang her drying cloth over the wall hook reminded him that she'd given up a much easier life in town to come out here. She'd made a vested interest in the place.

But, like the war, that was water under the bridge, and there was no use trying to call it back.

Now he wondered just how much Jennifer had, indeed, sacrificed for him and the boy. Were there yet secrets to discover? It bothered him more than he'd like her to know, his uncertainty of it all. She was so noble, so giving. He had seen how hard she worked; it would make her old before her time, like his mother.

Jennifer shouldn't have to; she was an educated lady and used to better.

His head ached slightly, and from habit, he rubbed the base of his skull. For the ten thousandth time he wondered why Jennifer hadn't married again. She could have had her pick of men around Osage Springs before the war, and she was damned beautiful, with those silky sunny-blond curls and delicate features and refined manners. She could easily grace even a governor's table. But four years ago, people said she was a bit starchy and reserved, a natural loner.

He knew better. She had generously taken Zach, hadn't she?

In her private moments she wasn't standoffish or starchy at all. She sometimes hummed, or laughed at little things, and she was very lively when she was alone with the boy. He'd discovered how really lovely she was during those first unguarded moments of his arrival. The two of them were happy together, that was as plain as the nose on his face. So happy that it made him feel almost an intruder.

How did Jennifer feel about him? He was nothing but an ignorant overgrown farmboy in her deep blue teacher's eyes, he suspected. Why would she ever look at him as anything else? Had he given her reason to think otherwise?

Yet, he remembered she was sometimes nervous with him. Like a skittish horse that had been mistreated and didn't want to let another rider near it. Maybe that was it. Or maybe she had never gotten over the death of her first husband. Or maybe—the thought filled him with horror—she was one of those women who simply had no use for men.

Resolutely, he shook that idea from his mind, but other doubts plagued him. Was she unhappy he had returned? Would she want to stay after he really settled in?

Why should she? he chided himself. He had nothing to offer her except himself and this land, and neither one of them were in any great shape. Although she heartily loved Zachary, she owed him, Gil, nothing; the owing was all on his side and he had already taken four years of her life and all her money and assets.

Which brought him full circle. Did she have anything left? Was she only biding her time until she could leave?

Jennifer's tone took on additional firmness and his thoughts were pulled back to the moment. "The war took its toll here, as well, Mr. Prescott. You may think I acted out of haste, but I feared we would be left with nothing to feed our animals during the winter. And Mr. Linderman has been a godsend to advise me. He assured me that Mr. Jones will deliver what is promised."

Gil cleared his throat. "Let's forget it. I mean, if Mr. Linderman says Jones is honest and straight dealing, I'll take his word on it. But the cost . . . I'll pay you back, some way, Teacher. I swear it."

But could he? Ever?

4

Jennifer, with Zach next to her, drove old Ben sedately into town while Gil rode along beside the buggy. She found a place to park close to Lindermans' grocery store and pulled the horse to a stop. Gil dismounted and was beside her in a flash to take her elbow.

She gathered her basket of eggs while Zach ran ahead to open the door. Their actions were those of a practiced routine, Gil noticed. A team. He almost felt like the odd man out. It wasn't the first time that thought had crossed his mind, but he refused to let it take root and grow.

Yes, the two of them needed him, he mused as he pushed the uncomfortable thought away. Zach needed his pa and already had taken to him like a duck to water. It pleased him mightily; now he could admit to being afraid that the boy wouldn't.

Teacher needed him, too. It just might take her longer to believe it. Her struggles to make a living for herself and the boy were nothing less than heroic, and he felt an odd pride in the mental strength she showed in moving out to the homeplace alone with the boy. But she still needed him to make it more than merely a get-along life. But how would she take to him? As a man?

Gil sucked in his breath. He sure as hell needed her. He knew his own mind these days, too; he felt none of the uncertainties of those weeks and months before he'd left. Now all he wanted was to get his place back in shape, live out his life there, and raise his son in peace. But it would be difficult to do it alone.

And he desperately wanted Jennifer Hastings for his own. He didn't know what he'd do if Teacher decided that she'd had enough of the hardships, had finished her good deeds, and wanted to leave him and Zach.

"Here, I'll take that," Gil said as he reached for her basket.

"No, I have it," Jennifer replied, while ignoring the dry-goods salesman staring from his shop doorway two doors down. The man had been insolent to her once, after looking Zachary over; he'd made a sly proposition for nighttime visits in trade for goods. She had frostily ignored his offer, whereupon he'd given Zach a pinch-faced glare and a sharp-tongued command not to touch anything with his dirty little hands.

Jennifer had refused to set foot in his store again.

"Perhaps you would be good enough to get the other basket," she told Gil.

Gil noticed the dry-goods clerk, someone he didn't know, and nodded before obliging Jennifer's request. The man coldly acknowledged his silent greeting, then turned away with a supercilious air.

Gil shrugged. The town was full of strangers these

days, he thought idly as he reached for the wide laundry basket, and many of them still held hostile feelings from the war. Well, he'd had enough fighting to last a lifetime and he was quite willing to let time settle things down.

Surprise caught him as he lifted the second basket. It was heavy. Glancing down, he noticed two small crocks of butter, and half a dozen jars of cucumber pickles and beets. More trade on all of Jennifer's hard work. He remembered his mother doing the same, trading produce for other needs from the store.

"Why, Gil. Gil Prescott, you old son of a gun." The familiar voice made Gil turn. It was a boyhood friend, Frank Able.

"Frank! Nice to see you, you old sodbuster." Gil smiled and shifted the basket so that he could offer a handshake before he realized his old friend had lost an arm. His smile faded as he shook Frank's left hand.

"Glad to see you made it home, Frank," he said more seriously, noting the new lines in Frank's long, thin face. "See you paid your dues."

"Yep. In the Shenandoah Valley. You too, Gil. When did you get back? Hadn't heard anything about you for so long I thought . . ."

Gil nodded. "Only a few days ago. Wasn't too sure, myself, if I'd be coming home."

"Are you back at your homeplace? Heard about your pa's passing. Shame about them scalawags stealin' your stock."

A faintly familiar dark-haired young woman wearing a cotton sunbonnet walked up to them with a blue-clad baby in her arms and stood listening as Gil replied.

"Yeah, Frank, I'm at the homeplace. And I've found a few head of cattle, though not much else."

"We hear that teacher took up the place with a boy. . . . Is the kid really your son?"

Gil chose not to take offense at what he knew Frank was probably thinking. It was no more than what the town thought and most likely gossiped over, that he'd fathered a half-breed bastard. He'd been something of a hell-raiser some years back, he was quick to admit. Now he had some tall fence mending to do in Osage Springs and around the territory for folks to accept him again, and eventually, his son.

"Yes, Mrs. Hastings has been very kind to keep the house from falling down around her ears for me. And she's done a fine job of raising my son, Zach," he said in a smooth voice, hoping to set boundaries Frank would recognize and honor.

The young woman's wide brown eyes showed her curiosity, but Gil thought they held a bit of disapproval as well. Frank seemed to take little notice of her attitude and made proud introductions. "You remember Mary Sue Tabor, don't you, Gil? Well, she's now Mrs. Able. And this is little Frankie."

"Congratulations, Frank. How do, ma'am," Gil responded, and touched his hat brim. Mary Sue returned the greeting in a shy murmur.

Lindermans' door flew open, and Zach rushed through. "Papa, are you coming? Mama says she needs the basket."

Zach slowed to a walk, then to an amble, when he saw the Ables. Gil held out a hand to the boy. Shyly, Zach sidled up to him as he stared solemnly at the couple.

Gil thought it a perfect opportunity to reinforce his

intentions of establishing Zach as his legitimate son. "This is my son, Zachary Prescott. Zach, say your how-dos to Mr. and Mrs. Able."

"How do you do, sir. Ma'am," Zach dutifully responded.

Frank, his thumb in his suspender, replied with "Hello, there, Zach. Your daddy and me used to go huntin' an' fishin' together as boys. We always had a grand ol' time."

Mary Sue nodded her pointed little chin stiffly at Zach but said nothing. Gil pretended he didn't see her nudge her husband.

Frank, after glancing at his wife, said, "Well, good to see you home, Gil. Mighty good. When fall comes round and we get a little huntin' time, we could go out in the hills, I reckon. I can't use a rifle no more, but I got a new dog that's a dandy. Well, I guess we gotta get on to the livery stable. Got a saddle there I'm aimin' to buy."

Gil bid them good-bye and turned to the store, pondering about how lucky he was to have come home with all his limbs. "Come along, son."

He carried the basket through the door and laid it on the counter near where a graying, rounded Mrs. Linderman counted eggs. Gil recalled that Maude Linderman was probably the only other soul alive who remembered his mother, and he was hit by a wave of unexpected sentimentality. Mrs. Linderman had been his mother's closest friend.

He smiled tentatively as he removed his hat. "Morning, Mrs. Linderman."

Much of that friendship spilled over onto him now as she greeted him enthusiastically. "It's about time you wandered home, Gil Prescott, you young rascal.

You took long enough. I'll swan, but you do look a little peaked as well as thin as a rail. Are you ailin'?"

"Not anymore, Mrs. Linderman," he replied with relief at her friendly greeting. "Now that I'm home."

Jennifer stood in the back, waiting while Mr. Linderman wrote in his ledger.

"That brings your credit up to three dollars and fifty-five cents, Mrs. Hastings," the skinny storekeeper told her. "Anything you need to spend it on today?"

"Yes, I need flour, cornmeal, and salt. And I'd like to take some of those peaches you promised to save for me, Mr. Linderman, if you have some."

"Ah, *ja,* I remember. And some good ones came in yesterday from over Missouri way. Maude, did you put back a peck of them peaches for Mrs. Hastings here?"

"Sure enough did, Peder." Mrs. Linderman picked up the egg basket. "They're in the storeroom, Mrs. Hastings. Do you want to come with me to get them? How's the rest of your produce coming along, anyway?"

"Pretty good. Better, now that Gil is hauling enough water for it up from the creek. But we need some rain. I have high hopes for the pumpkin patch."

"Pumpkins . . . now that's gonna be a good trade. I'll take all you got, when the time comes."

"Wonderful."

Gil tipped his head at Linderman as the two women disappeared into the storeroom. The old man nodded and moved away from the two male customers that were standing beside the cold stove quietly arguing over the latest newspaper stories. A third customer seemed content to browse among the barrels of kraut and pickles in the back corner.

Zach stood nearby and Gil said, "Here, son, why

don't you choose a candy stick and go outside to the porch awhile." Gil indicated the three jars lined up on the front edge of the counter.

Mr. Linderman nodded at Zach's questioning look. "Cinnamon, sassafras, or licorice?"

Zach chose licorice and skipped outside.

"See you made it on home the other night without any trouble, Gil," Mr. Linderman said by way of opening. "Ever'thing like I told you out at your place?"

"Yep, it's all just as you said, Mr. Linderman. It's in a pretty sorry state. The place ain't like Pa would of left it, if he'd had a choice—he must have been sick a long time before he died. Makes me wonder what those no-good hands were up to besides stealin' Pa blind. Lots of work to be done, and that's a fact. Mrs. Hastings has done her best, but . . ." He trailed off with a shake of his head, then offered, "Thanks to you, nothing came unexpected, except . . ."

"Except?"

"Well, I understand Mrs. Hastings had to sell many of her things as well as spend whatever real money she had just to feed herself and the boy and hold the house together. It's a wonder she made it through last year."

"*Ja, ja.* It's a shame, to be sure." The old man took out a white handkerchief and wiped the sweat from his balding head. "But times've been real hard, Gil, for most folks. Still are. You ain't the only one."

"Uh-huh. I can guess. I've been thinkin' on it." Gil shifted his stance and leaned against the counter. He'd grown up with an independent streak a mile wide, with a lot of pride thrown in—false pride, he now knew it to be. He'd gotten those things from a strong-minded father who had always been the boss and took no sass from anyone. And he'd been the boss's son. Except for his time in the army, Gil had never worked for anyone else.

It cut his pride up considerably, but he had to ask. "Mr. Linderman, is there anyone around who's hiring? I need to find work."

"Ain't heard of any, but . . ." Mr. Linderman thought a moment. "There's always the railroads, you know."

Gil shook his head. "I'd have to be away for months at a time, and I promised Zach I wouldn't leave him again."

He didn't mention his not wanting to leave Jennifer, either. Now that he had come home, he felt strongly about not leaving either one of them again. Or his place. He hadn't realized how much he loved it until he left it.

"Hmmmn. Lot of building going on over to Kansas City an' up to Topeka," Mr. Linderman said. "Might find work there, but it'd be the same thing. You'd have to stay through the month. Uh, pardon me, Gil, while I tend to this customer."

Jennifer came out of the storeroom with Mrs. Linderman, and Gil wandered over to the pots and pans rack while she completed her transactions. He'd noticed how worn the enamel was on the bottom of their coffeepot—it wouldn't last much longer. But hell, he hadn't even the money to buy a new coffeepot, he thought with disgust as he fingered one of the cheaper ones.

He turned when he heard Mr. Linderman answer a question. "No, mister, I don't know nobody in town who does gun repair," Mr. Linderman said. "I sent a pair o' Colts east to the maker, not long ago, but they'll take weeks to come back, I'm thinking."

Gil stepped up. "I know a little about guns, mister. Maybe I can help. What's wrong with it?"

The man explained his problem as Gil fingered the weapon. As well as needing the sight straightened, it could use a good cleaning. He could see rust in the barrel.

"You know about guns?" The customer glanced at Mr. Linderman for confirmation.

"Yeah, a bit. Worked in ordnance during the first year of the war. Learned even more on the line, when a weapon needed a simple repair."

"War service, eh?" The customer gave him a quick once-over, but to his credit in Gil's eyes, refrained from asking which side he'd fought on.

"I might be able to take care of it for you, if you want to leave it with me. I can have it back to Lindermans' here, next week."

Mr. Linderman gave a quick nod. The man agreed and was just asking Gil about his charge for the service when a sudden shout came from the street.

"Papa!" Zach ran through the door. "Papa, there's a fire up the road."

Everyone's attention jerked to the boy. Fire was a deeply dreaded foe.

"Where, son?" Gil spoke even as he pivoted and raced for the door. Already, he heard the commotion of loud voices outside, and the pounding of running feet. Beside him, Mr. Linderman muttered while the men in the store all rushed to leave.

"Don't know," Zach answered. "A man said . . ."

Gil didn't linger to hear any more. "Stay with your ma, Zach," he commanded as he left.

Jennifer grabbed the back of Zachary's shirt just as he would have chased after Gil. "What is it? What's going on?"

"It's a fire, Mama. Can't we go see?"

"Oh, heaven have mercy!" Mrs. Linderman said wildly. "Who's on fire?"

"Close the store, Maude!" Mr. Linderman said as he stripped the apron from his body, hurrying to join the fire fighters. "Ain't gonna be no customers for a while. I'll go see what we can do."

Standing in the street a moment later, Zach tugging her while she held his hand tight, Jennifer stretched to her tiptoes, hoping to see more than flames and smoke and swarming men and women. But she could see little else. Behind her, she heard Mrs. Linderman slam the door of the store, and then the older woman joined her.

"What's on fire, Mama? Is it going to burn everything down?" Zach asked on a worried note.

"I don't know, Zachary. Your papa and the others will try to prevent that from happening."

Jennifer heard someone say it was the livery near the schoolhouse that was on fire. Mrs. Linderman had mentioned that there would be children there today getting the place ready for the new school year. Automatically, her heart thumped fearfully.

How many children would be there? Surely they would have gotten out. There was another new teacher this year—Amelia Smithers, a former student of hers. But Amelia was so very young and inexperienced that Jennifer worried she would panic. What if the fire spread? It would be so easy for the flames to leap those few yards between the buildings.

She couldn't just stand there; she had to see for herself that the children were all right.

"Mrs. Linderman, hold on to Zachary for me, please," she instructed as she broke away and started up the road.

"Mama?"

"I'll be back when I can, Zachary," she called over her shoulder. "You be a good boy and stay with Mrs. Linderman."

Jennifer hiked her skirt to her knees and ran. Her feet felt as if they had wings of their own as her momentum picked up. She had to be where she was needed. She dodged a frenzied horse as it galloped past her, and leaped to the side of the road to avoid a runaway team and empty wagon, but she kept going. The closer she got to the fire, the blacker the smoke became. Her eyes smarted with it and her nostrils and throat felt scorched.

Jennifer pushed her way past a dozen people who were already passing pails of water from hand to hand. Almost upon the schoolhouse, she saw flames leaping out toward it, short by only inches. Any minute that building might be on fire, too.

She leaped up the school's steps and through the wide-open door, praying all the while that she would find the building empty. And empty it was.

Jennifer nearly sagged in relief. Thank God, Miss Smithers had had the presence of mind to get the children out. But where were they? Then, through all the shouting and roaring noise of the firefighters, she heard them out back on the rough grassy terrain that they'd marked off as their playground.

A mouthful of smoke made Jennifer cough. For a moment, all her senses reeled and she leaned against the doorjamb to steady herself. She had to get out!

As she hesitated in the doorway, Jennifer noticed there was a second bucket chain forming, drawing water from a nearby well. A man threw a pail of water toward the schoolhouse in an effort to prevent the fire from spreading. Beside her the sheet of water hit the front corner of the schoolhouse, spattering her as well.

She paid it scant attention as she looked around for Gil. Where was he? Was he safe?

She finally spotted him close to the fire itself, shouting instructions to others as he threw water onto flames that roared through the livery doors. She should help the bucket brigade, she thought, but something about the children's shouts drew her more insistently.

"Get outa there, ma'am," someone shouted to her. She leaped to the ground without answering. Briefly, she wondered if anyone had been caught inside the livery barn and if all the horses had been saved. But while she recognized the reek of burning wood and hay, she didn't think it told of burnt flesh and blood.

She had no time to think about it further as she circled the schoolhouse. Out back, on the prairie side of the building, Jennifer rushed into a crowd of jumping, milling, screaming children.

"Oh, Mrs. Hastings. I'm so glad to see you." The slight figure of Amelia Smithers ran up to her, tears streaming down her face as she wrung her hands. "What shall we do? I can't get the children to listen."

Jennifer immediately took charge. "Come, come, Miss Smithers, none of that. You have done splendidly in getting the children out. Are they all here?" She didn't wait for an answer. She saw that even some of the little ones had come to help the new teacher prepare for the coming year.

"We should move them away from the vicinity, I think. Lavinia Schiller," she addressed a small blond twelve-year-old she knew could be trusted, "take little Sara's hand, please. And you, Bonnie, follow with Hazel, Anna, and Molly. And George Schiller, you line up the boys. We will head toward Lindermans'. Remember all of our emergency practices. Now, march."

She took Amelia by the elbow and steered her to the head of the little band, then dropped back, giving encouragement as they walked. A moment later, Mrs. Linderman fell in beside her with Zachary.

"You don't mind if we shelter at your store for a while, do you, Mrs. Linderman? Then we can calm them down a bit and the little ones won't be so frightened. I'm sure the children's parents will gather them up as soon as the fire is put out."

"Of course I don't mind, my dear. I think we might even raid the cracker barrel and cut into a round of cheese. Feeding them is the quickest way I know to quieten young'uns."

The women sat the children down on the wooden sidewalk and porch in front of the store, and then fed and played games with them to keep them occupied. Progress of the fire trickled in. As the day went on, some of the older children left for home, taking their younger siblings with them until only Lavinia, George, and Molly Schiller, the Dillon girl, and Zach remained by the time the tired fire fighters started streaming by on their way home.

The Gallaghar brothers, Tommy, twelve, and Joey, ten, looking bedraggled and dirty from the smoke and ashes, came along and flopped down on the edge of the store's porch. Jennifer admitted only to herself that she didn't like the boys; they were overgrown bullies.

"You sissies had to stay with ol' Teacher while we gotta watch the fire," Tommy boasted. "It was a bang-up lulu."

Lavinia answered smartly, to which Tommy took exception, and a squabble started. Jennifer, tempted to step in, instead put it out of her mind—it was up to Amelia to settle it. Besides, she saw Mr. Linderman and Gil approaching, and any desire she had to revert to her teacher status fled as intense relief rushed to take its place. Until that moment, she hadn't realized Gil's safety had concerned her so deeply.

She rose slowly from her place on the porch bench.

Mrs. Linderman hurried to meet her husband and began to scold gently about how smelly and dirty he was, all the while softly patting his hand. Zach ran to his father and hugged him unabashedly around the legs.

Jennifer took a long breath, fighting the sudden impulse to do the same as she saw Gil caress his son's head. Instead, she contented herself by carefully looking him over from head to foot. Thank goodness, he didn't appear injured anywhere, but his eyes were bloodshot and white lines of exhaustion showed through all the grime he wore. Once again he had pushed his strength beyond what he should have, and she wondered how long he could continue to do so without breaking down his health completely.

"Is it all over?" Mrs. Linderman asked her husband.

"*Ja, ja.* It's over. But poor Samuel. He lost most ever'thing. His barn, two or three saddles he rents out and his hay . . . even that buckboard got one side burnt afore someone beat out the fire."

"That's a downright shame," Mrs. Linderman murmured.

"Are you all right, Mr. Prescott?" Jennifer asked. "Was anyone injured in the fire?"

"Mostly only some minor burns and scrapes except for Sam," Gil answered. "It's a wonder, though, as fast as it went up, that someone didn't get caught in it.

Sam had to jump from his hayloft . . . has a broken leg, I think. Cracked some ribs, too, maybe. That youngster of his took him over to Doc's place."

Up the street, first one then another of the saloons seemed suddenly to come alive after long hours of quiet. Men who had taken part in the fire fight were recounting every incident about it, celebrating their victory, and most likely, Jennifer mused, bragging about their bravery. Several women straggled by, looking as tired as the men; they had fought as valiantly, she thought, on the water chains. Mrs. Dillon broke away to gather her child from the porch, said thank-you to Jennifer and Mrs. Linderman for looking after her, then left again.

Two men joined their circle, Mr. Tige from the mercantile, the town's unofficial mayor, and John Perry, who owned the meat market next door to Lindermans' grocery.

"What about the animals?" Jennifer asked.

"Had only five horses in the barn. Leastways, that's all I could find," Gil answered.

"You? You got the horses out?"

Mr. Tige answered for him. "Yeah, Gil here got ever' one of 'em out while we was gettin' the pails gathered up for the water chain. And it was him who got that burnin' buckboard out, too."

"Gil." Jennifer started to protest his foolish actions, but thought better of it. It could do no good now, it was all over and he wasn't harmed. But no wonder he looked as he did! How could he have done all that when he was still recovering from his war wounds? Undoubtedly, he'd stressed them. And he had just returned to his home and child—what was he thinking to put himself in jeopardy that way?

Gil, taking one look at Jennifer's face, explained. "I went into the barn to make sure there wasn't anyone in it. Frank Able and his family were heading that way when I came into the store this morning, and I worried. . . . But they weren't there. I never even saw them."

"I did. . . . Leastways, I saw Frank," said Mr. Linderman. "He was on one of the waterlines toward the back."

"That's good," Gil murmured in relief. "Has only one arm, now, you know."

"Don't you worry none, now Gil. Frank is gettin' along okay, one arm or no," Mr. Linderman put in. "And they live with Mary Sue's family an' she's got three brothers to do the work that needs two hands."

"Couldn't save much of the livery barn." Mr. Tige broke into the conversation as he shook his head in sorrow. "But leastways, the schoolhouse was saved."

"Thank goodness," Amelia muttered. "But everything is going to smell something awful now. I don't know how I'll ever manage—" She broke off to settle another tiff between Tommy and Lavinia.

"Yes, I was worried some about the schoolhouse," Gil said as he leaned tiredly against the storefront.

"You'll manage very well, Miss Smithers," Jennifer assured the girl kindly before turning to the others. "Well, if there is nothing more we can do, I think we should start for home. Gil, you get into the buggy, and we'll tie Sally to the back. Zach, you may sit on my lap, beside your papa. But don't chatter too much. Papa's tired."

A flicker of amusement tugged at Gil's mouth as he straightened to stand tall. He wanted to deny his exhaustion, but he didn't think he had a leg to stand on with Teacher. She wouldn't believe a word of it. And if they weren't with a group of townspeople, he would swear she might scold him the way she occasionally scolded Zach—gently, but brooking no nonsense.

Besides, she was right. "Yes, we need to get on home. Chores to do."

They bid good-bye to everyone and climbed into the buggy, where Jennifer picked up the reins. In spite of his slender frame, Gil filled the seat next to her, his arm almost touching hers. Zach wiggled onto her knees while Gil held the peck of peaches. Her other purchases were safely tucked into the tiny space between her feet.

"Where's your hat, Papa?" asked Zach as they trotted out of town.

"Don't know. Reckon I lost it somewhere in the fire."

"Do you have another one?"

"No, don't reckon I have." Gil shifted and placed his arm along the back of the buggy to give Jennifer more room.

The odor of burned fabric seemed to stay with them, Jennifer noticed. Glancing sideways, Jennifer saw tiny burn holes in Gil's sleeve. Had he suffered any burns that he wasn't telling her of?

"You can have my other one; it's too big for me," Zach said. "It's the one I found in the attic."

Gil smiled at his son's generosity. "That's right nice of you, son. Thank you, kindly."

Zach leaned his head back against Jennifer. The brush of his hair against her chin felt sweet and familiar. He would be asleep soon, she was sure. Next to her, Gil's arm occasionally rubbed along her shoulders. In contrast, his touch felt both alien and yet companionable.

Gil allowed his head to loll, unable to fight his exhaustion any longer, and a moment later Jennifer felt the weight of him slide against her, his cheek coming to rest against her shoulder.

Jennifer allowed him to stay. He desperately needed the sleep. Besides, it seemed silly to push him away when she'd been making claims to his need to rest more. And she liked the feeling . . . very much, she realized. Except for Zachary, she had experienced no personal touch from another human being for eight long years.

True, that choice had been hers. But somehow, Gil . . . Gil was different from other people. He gave her a feeling of security; she trusted him. A tiny bit of her relaxed past the mountain-size barrier she usually put up toward men.

A full five minutes drifted by in contented silence. Jennifer let old Ben slow to a sedate walk. Then drowsily, out of the blue, Zach asked, "What's a by-blow, Papa?"

5

Gil's head lifted sharply, all his own drowsiness gone while his eyes flashed a spark of anger. "By-blow? Who—?"

Quickly, Jennifer transferred the reins to her left hand and then wrapped her right around Gil's wrist to give him caution. She couldn't see Zachary's face to assess his expression, but she saw the angry jut of Gil's chin, and she knew Zach was too intuitive not to pick up on his father's mood.

She wanted to avoid any additional agitation today— they were all too worn out to think about anything clearly. Certainly, Gil was in no shape to tangle with more. Besides, this question was bound to rear its ugly head again and yet again; there would be more than one chance to deal with it, and later would be better.

Zach tilted his head to look up at his father. Only the tips of his long dark lashes and the curve of his nose were visible to Jennifer. Relaxed in confident trust, he pressed his warm little back against her. It was a trust she treasured.

Jennifer resisted the impulse to hold the child tighter; he was beginning to grow up and she had to let him.

Now she wanted to know why, and how, Zachary was asking the question, in order to diffuse its power to harm. She suspected he asked with quiet but real curiosity. Zachary had been openly called a bastard before, but he'd been too young, then, to know what it meant or to question it. Even at four, in her opinion, Zachary was too young to have to deal with it.

He had, though, known the malice that was intended. She'd tried hard to protect Zachary from people's ill will, but she'd also known she couldn't do it forever. A child never misunderstood blatant emotions, whether good or bad, she'd discovered.

By-blow. An expression used for ugly intent. Who had said it? A number of people might've. But to call too much attention to it would be to add more importance to it than she wanted Zach to take in, for now.

Gil's face softened only a little as Jennifer's fingers patted the bare skin of his wrist gently, but he seemed to accept it as an action intended to soothe him. He held his speech, for the moment.

"Why do you ask, Zach?" Jennifer spoke calmly. "Where did you hear that expression?"

"Tommy said it. He said I was a by-blow. Joey said it too."

"Oh, Tommy." She said, making a little moue. "Well, you know those Gallaghar boys. They like to make trouble with everybody. They'll say any old thing to pick a fight."

"But what does it mean?"

"Oh, nothing much."

"Pull over, Mrs. Hastings." Gil spoke with quiet determination.

"Mr. Prescott, I really think it might be better to wait," she protested.

"Nope. Right now!"

She wanted to argue the point further, but to do so would only make it worse. Besides, she couldn't undermine Zachary's father, she thought with a sigh. She had to adjust to the fact that Zach now had two parents.

"Very well," she said and did as he ordered. She brought old Ben to a stop under the shade of a lone sycamore tree, where the late-day sunshine reached them only in small spots.

Gil gently lifted Zach from her lap and set him on his own, turning the boy so he could see his face.

"Now, Zach. You know I'm your pa, don't you?"

Zach nodded, his dark eyes wide and pensive.

"And your ma . . . I mean the mother that did your birthing, she was Morning Rain, remember?"

At Zach's second nod, Gil continued. "Well, some people don't like Indians. And some people think their ways are just too different. So, when I married Morning Rain, they thought it was wrong. Now, a baby that is born when the ma and pa ain't married is called . . ."

Gil glanced at Teacher, silently beseeching her help. He wanted to use the correct word, by thunder. He wouldn't have his son battling with the stigma of bastardy, and the quicker Zach understood the matter, the stronger he could withstand the insults that would come his way. And there would be plenty of them, that was for damn sure.

He guessed his homecoming was timely, right

enough. As much as he stood in awe and appreciated all that Jennifer had done, he thought Zachary needed some fathering as well as mothering. Coddling him about his parentage wouldn't prepare the boy to handle the matter with know-it-all, prejudiced neighbors.

"Illegitimate," Jennifer supplied.

"Yep, that's the word. And that's what by-blow means. And the word *bastard*, too," he said, allowing his anger at the terms to show. "You'll likely hear those words again. But Zach, you're legitimate, so there ain't a need for you to feel ashamed, like those pups of a coyote want you to."

"But Tommy said—"

"Well, you can just tell Tommy he don't know what he's yappin' about. You ain't a bastard or a by-blow. You were born after Morning Rain and I got married. We were married in an Indian wedding just as real as that one you saw where the lady wore 'that curtain thing' on her head. Just because someone told Tommy that it was wrong to marry an Indian don't make it less than a real marriage. So you see, you're my lawful son."

"Tommy is very stupid, sometimes." Jennifer let her innermost thought pop out. She surprised herself and blinked rapidly at Zach and Gil. She usually kept her private thoughts under tighter control, working hard to keep her emotions evenly tempered under a smooth facade.

Years before, she'd been all too openly emotional over everything and it had given her nothing but grief, so she'd grown a tough shell over her feelings. Loving and caring for Zachary had been the only feelings that she'd allowed free reign these last four years.

Zach and Gil both looked at her in surprise, too. It

was unlike Teacher to voice her dislike for anyone, Gil thought, let alone a child, and especially a child she'd had as a student. Her good manners never allowed it.

Zach suddenly giggled. "Mama, you said a bad word."

She smiled in return. At least the seriousness of the conversation had diminished. "I'm sorry, Zach," she said smoothly. "Stupid isn't a bad word, really, but it was unkind for me to say that about Tommy, wasn't it?"

Gil felt both admiration for Jennifer's ability to handle the matter so calmly and delight in her sudden outburst. Teacher was a pure, perfect lady, she was. But for an instant, she had looked very young and fierce, her blue eyes snapping, and he knew she was as incensed about the insults flung at Zach as he was.

"Never mind. Let's get on home. We got chores to do."

"The only chore you have to do, Mr. Prescott, is to take a long hot bath before bedtime. I won't have you getting the clean sheets I just put on your bed all gritty with ashes and soot. It might be impossible to get out."

"Speak for yourself, Mrs. Hastings. You look a little sooty yourself."

"I?"

"Doesn't she, Zach?"

"Uh-huh. You have dirt on your face, Mama," Zach responded with delight, "a big black streak across your cheek and nose."

"Everyone who fought the fire ended up filthy," Gil said with a chuckle. "We'll all have to have a bath, I reckon."

"Oh, my goodness. Why didn't you tell me before?"

"Didn't see a need to. But that reminds me—you

were at the schoolhouse," Gil said half-accusingly while his smile faded. "I saw you run into it when all the sensible folks were fighting the fire from the outside. What were you doing in there?"

"The same as you, Mr. Prescott," she returned with a bit of asperity, "when you risked your own safety to help an old friend. I went into the schoolhouse to make sure all the children were out."

"Yep, just as I thought. But you scared the livin' daylights out of me, you did, running right into a building that could go up in flames any minute that way. I couldn't leave the line I was on to go after you . . . didn't breathe easy till I saw you leave."

"I suppose we are tit for tat, then, Mr. Prescott. You shouldn't—"

Jennifer broke off when she saw Zach's wide, curious eyes. She saw no need to distress the child just because she and his father were on the edge of a quarrel.

But were they? Suddenly she couldn't be sure, for behind Gil's words, she captured a hint of a dismissing grin. Well, she could see that Gil hadn't taken her reply seriously, and anyway, he was far less easily appeased during a discussion than his son. She thought he might challenge her regularly.

"We will have ample time to finish our, um, debate later, Mr. Prescott," she explained rather formally, barely avoiding the sniff she wanted to give as she picked up old Ben's reins and smartly turned him back into the road. "For the moment, I think we should continue home."

"Yes, ma'am," Gil replied with a bit too much compliance. From the corner of her eye, Jennifer saw his grin stretch, then she caught his wink at Zach.

That rascal! Gil was teasing her!

She found herself fighting to keep a responsive grin at bay while pondering at the wonders of heredity. Zach teased her with a bit of the same art of ridiculousness, sometimes. But she had the feeling the talent was much more potent in the grown male sitting beside her, and certainly more developed, than it was in the still emerging child. And though they both tickled her fancy, her response to Gil felt decidedly different.

Had Gil been a charming heartbreaker when younger? Before war and devastation had robbed him of it? By all that she knew, he had undoubtedly been more carefree.

But he could be stubborn. Well, stubborn or no, and charming though she was finding him to be, she and Gil would have to finish their discussion later, for there were a few things she intended to say.

Gil was almost asleep when Jennifer pulled into the yard, but he roused himself promptly. It was not without effort; he ached all over and felt weak as a kitten. His recovering wounds demanded a little more respect than the hell he'd put on them today, he mused as he stumbled to the ground.

He glanced at Teacher; yes, by gum, he thought she had noticed. He hated like poison to have her see him in such a condition. It was a good thing he'd filled the water barrels before going to town this morning; he didn't think he had an ounce of energy left to do it now.

"Go on into the house, Mr. Prescott, while I put Ben away," Jennifer ordered gently. "I'll be in presently."

Gil wanted to protest. He should tend to the horse himself. But his side smarted and his head pounded. He wanted to fall asleep where he stood.

Now wouldn't that be an impressive sight for the

teacher, he silently mocked himself. And more trouble for her, to boot.

"All right," he conceded reluctantly. "Zach, you go and help your mama. I'll get the fire going."

He walked into the house. Finding only two sticks of wood in the firewood box, he went out to the backyard to get more. He filled his arms with a load and carried it inside. All his movements felt as slow as molasses poured from a jug that had been sitting in the snow.

Carefully, he rebuilt the fire in the stove and then filled two of the biggest kettles with water, placing them on the stove to heat. He sat down at the table to rest a moment. Only a moment. Jennifer seemed a long time at putting Ben away.

Jennifer and Zach found Gil sound asleep a few moments later, his head resting on his folded arms. Jennifer put her finger to her lips for quiet. Zach nodded, and thinking it a wonderful game, tiptoed around the kitchen as they prepared a cold supper while the bathwater heated.

A long time later, Gil thought he heard the beguiling voice of an angel. "Mr. Prescott. Gil? Come along, now."

The soothing tone near his ear slowly penetrated his sleep. For a moment, he confused it with the one he still heard in his dream—a winsome, seductive dream. In it, a lovely woman whose long golden-streaked hair rippled over her shoulders in satiny curls, spoke to him.

It was an illusion he'd experienced before, only this time it was different. It coaxed him to wakefulness and reality even as he ran after the dream.

"Let's get you into the bath while you still can."

"Hmmm?"

"The bath, Mr. Prescott. Would you like my help?"

A feminine hand at his shoulder urged him to respond while the sweetness of the voice enticed him to open his eyes. He watched her for a long moment with a hazy gaze. *Yes, you've been with me before,* he wanted to say. *You're my dream, my angel. Yes, I would like your help in the bath. In the bath and more.*

The beautiful face was only inches from his. If he lifted a finger, he could trace the line of her straight little nose and feel the curve of her cheek against his palm. Would her lashes feel as soft as they appeared?

Her pink mouth parted slightly in an unknowing invitation to a kiss, while delft-blue eyes looked at him with concern. Vaguely, he noticed that her face was free of soot and she smelled clean. The fragrance of rose water tickled his nose.

This was no dream Jennifer. He felt himself slide into all-out arousal and wanted with all his heart to press his lips to hers.

As he stared, her eyes grew more puzzled.

Had he voiced that sentiment? Had he told her how much, how desperately he wanted her?

"No." He finally answered her question as he sat up and rubbed his eyes to remove the last of his drowsiness. Needing diversion, he glanced around.

Shadows filled the little kitchen—where had the rest of daylight gone? He noticed the remains of bread and milk on the table where Zach had eaten his supper. Evidently, he'd slept through it, undisturbed.

He stood up. "Where's Zach?"

"Gone to bed."

"Ummm. Well, I'd better get the milking done."

"Zach and I did it."

"The chickens?"

"Fed, watered, and in the coop for the night."

He stood motionless a moment before he said quietly, "Sorry, Teacher."

"You mustn't be sorry for something you can't help, Mr. Prescott. You simply have to recognize your limits and stop pushing yourself so hard before you're well enough to do the work you've set for yourself. You need to relax and rest for a few days, and nourish yourself with decent food. Now, about the bath. Do you need help undressing?"

He paused a moment before answering. "I can manage."

"The tub is ready," Jennifer said unnecessarily, for the old bathtub stood in plain sight near the stove. It was one she'd found in the house when she had come there, so he must have used it as a child, she thought. He looked at it anyway, as though he had never seen it before. Obviously he knew she'd only just poured the hot water in, because steam vapors wafted from the tub.

Jennifer pursed her lips, trying to gauge Gil's state of health. He still appeared half-asleep, his blue-gray eyes filled with a misty seductive quality; she wasn't sure he really could manage on his own. She'd been quite concerned with his extreme exhaustion.

"And here is a new bar of soap," she continued. "You may use these towels, one for your hair and the other . . ." She glanced up and caught the mischievous beginnings of a grin. Had she been prattling on again? Or taken on too much mothering?

"Thanks, Teacher. I'll manage."

She backed away a step as his grin spread. Something

about it didn't have the ring of exhaustion at all. Or any indication he thought of her as a teacher in spite of his pet name for her. "All right. I'll—I'll be just—just in the bedroom there, if you should need me."

"I'll keep that in mind," he murmured low.

Jennifer felt the heat climb her cheeks and practically scurried around the corner and into her bedroom. What had gotten into her? Gil wasn't Zach, or anything close to a child at all. He might well have taken her remarks as an invitation of the wrong kind.

She sat down on the edge of the bed, folded her hands, and listened for the sounds in the other room. Satisfied when she heard a small splash, she lit her lamp and turned its wick high. There was always mending to be done.

Gil had one extra shirt but no extra trousers, she'd noticed, so her present task was to add more length to the old brown twill ones she'd found in the attic. The darker fabric she was adding didn't match, but the results would still be the same—he'd have clean pants to put on.

She stitched for thirty minutes, whipping the raw edges under to give the seams added strength. Occasionally she heard the water swish and the slap of the washcloth. But after she'd heard no sound for a while, she wondered if he had fallen asleep once more.

She had completed her task. She clipped the threads and laid down her needle, then rose and listened at the door. Nothing.

She hurried into the room only to come to a dead stop. Gil wasn't in the bath any longer; he stood in the altogether, facing the warmth of the stove, his head bent to look at his side. She had a clear view of the long lines of his back, hips, and legs.

Without warning, she let out a little "ohhh."

He turned to look at her over his shoulder, his eyes dark and unreadable.

Jennifer couldn't have said he was beautiful; he was too thin by half, and his face, now with his broken nose, too roughly fashioned. But given some flesh on his bones . . . Instantly, she recalled he'd been on the husky side before the war. Now his shoulder bones, still broadly structured, looked even sharper beneath the skin than she'd guessed. As her eyes traveled downward, she saw the ugly red evidence of his wounds, long scars that curved along his rib cage.

Pity for what he must have suffered flooded her soul, and real compassion assailed her heart. Her eyes smarted with tears, and she swallowed hard to keep them under control. Slowly, her gaze traveled back to his face.

"Oh, Gil. I knew you hadn't let yourself get completely well." She gestured feebly toward his side. "But this . . . this . . . oh, my dear! You must allow yourself to rest and heal properly."

"I haven't time, Teacher. There is far too much to do."

His tone was matter-of-fact. He kept his back to her and reached for his trousers.

Jennifer's compassion touched him deeply, but he wanted more from her than her pity. All that she'd already done for him and his son almost laid him flat. He didn't deserve all her kindness.

Those feelings didn't keep him from wanting her, though, and he felt compelled to get back on his feet as swiftly as possible. He couldn't let her go on as she had been, with so little for herself. If he had even a prayer with her . . .

Without thinking about the propriety of the situation, and ignoring his nudity, Jennifer strode forward and thrust out the clean pants on which she'd just worked.

Gil barely glanced at them as he took them. Instead, he raised a brow, amusement at her boldness written on his face.

Compassion still held sway in Jennifer's heart, but his expression gave her pause. What had she done this time, she wondered, to make him laugh? Why wouldn't he take her kindness seriously?

"But you can't go on as you have been," she burst out. "You've greatly overextended your resources as it is. What were you thinking today, throwing yourself into that fire fight when you . . ." She shook her head, only keeping herself from shaking her finger at him by a mere thread of control. "You will make yourself ill again!"

He shrugged as though it didn't matter, and thrust one leg then the other into his pants. The action only served to heat her irritation into real anger.

"Gil, you have to think of your son. Now that you're back, Zach has grown enormously attached to you and if anything should happen, if your health should break down completely, where would that leave him?"

He turned quickly, still buttoning his last two buttons. Jennifer caught a glimpse of dark, straight hair arrowing downward to where it disappeared beneath the pants before she resolutely raised her gaze. But her senses seemed to linger on the way his hair broadened over his chest muscles before she once again studied the scars on his side.

"Maybe better off and no different than before," he said.

"How can you say so!"

"He'd still have you."

Something in his tone made Jennifer raise her gaze to his. His eyelids drooped but his expression was filled with admiration and a wistful longing.

It made her uncomfortable even while it quickened her heartbeat. Gil shouldn't put her on a pedestal that way; she didn't deserve such a position and it frightened her a tiny bit. If he only knew.

But he didn't, thank goodness, and she reminded herself how hard she'd struggled to truly put the past behind her. She enjoyed a fine, respectable reputation in this community, and those incidents that had caused her such deep pain eight years before, in another time and place, no longer had any power to hurt her unless she let them. Now her life consisted of new and different problems and she felt grateful for it.

"Does it pain you?" she asked gently, gesturing to the red and white marks on his side.

He hesitated before he answered. "Sometimes."

"Then that settles it." Jennifer resumed her teacher's mode. "You may rest for the next few days. Your healing will quicken if given a chance."

"I can't."

"You must!"

He looked at her a long moment, his eyes narrowed, while his mouth once more spread into a smile. "Did anyone ever tell you you're a bossy woman, Teacher?"

"No, not exactly." No one ever had; long years ago she'd been rather meek and far more biddable, but only when very young. All at once as she thought about it, she discovered she liked being bossy. She grinned back at him. "No, but I don't mind being called that if it gets the right job done. Now, Mr. Prescott, I

think it best if you use the downstairs bedroom for a
few days and—"

"Mrs. Hastings." Gil dug deep inside himself to try
to find some of the impudent brass he'd had before
the war. He needed all the gall he could beg or borrow
to ask her what he was about to ask. He'd do anything
to have her.

"Yes?"

"If I agree to this coddling, will you agree to something I want?"

"What's that?"

"That we be married right away."

Jennifer opened her mouth to speak and nearly choked
on her own caught breath, and then her heart began to
beat painfully hard. She wanted to say yes so very much.

Too much. She wanted the chance to be a wife again,
to be Zachary's mother for real and for keeps. She
wanted to have her own home, to make a cozy, warm
nest for her own family. She wanted someone to give
her love to.

But she wasn't what Gil thought her. Or at least, her
past wasn't, and regardless of the fact that she had
firmly turned her back on it, could Gil, if he knew? And
she couldn't bear him children. Would it be fair not
to tell him?

Gil waited for an answer, his face quiet, his eyes
growing guarded as the minutes slipped by.

Jennifer found it difficult to know how to answer.
She wanted to say yes. Oh, God, she wanted to. To
leap at her chance for total happiness. To see the ful-
fillment of that slender thread of hope that Gil had
given her the night he'd given her Zachary.

But after all the speculation she'd done on the matter, and all the agonizing during these last months

since the war ended and she knew Gil would be coming home, now that he *was* home, now that he *had* asked her, it had, after all, come so suddenly. She'd had no time to lay any groundwork, to prepare Gil for the truth of her past. The scandal.

What should she tell him? It had all been so sordid and wrought with so much grief . . . and guilt. How could she ever explain that she was a divorced woman, convicted in the eyes of Philadelphia society of deceit and adultery, of deliberately losing a baby, and of driving her former husband to suicide.

She'd nearly lost her own mind over the vile accusations hurled at her and over the very public display of her pain. The printed word and sly whispers had had the ring of truth even when she'd protested her innocence. How could she expect Gil to believe anything good of her after hearing the story? No one else had.

Perhaps Gil wouldn't even want to hear it, but doubts clung to her mind like cockleburs. Would he still want her to be his wife, or mother his child, if she told him all of the ugliness?

Would he want anything at all to do with her, then, when she fell off her pedestal?

6

The silence between them stretched long. Then Gil burst out with, "Sorry, Mrs. Hastings. I guess I took too much for granted. I know I ain't much, and I've not a lot to offer, but I hoped—"

Shamefaced, Gil reached for his shirt, shoving his fist through the sleeve as though he would strike out at something. "Shoulda known better," he muttered under his breath, "presuming . . ."

A quick shiver shot through his long body and his mouth tightened with pain.

Jennifer saw it and, turning abruptly, snatched up the damp towels and folded them, her fingers smoothing the cloth to cover her own agitation, then put them on the table. The cold supper she'd left for Gil sat nearby; he hadn't touched it.

She felt miserable. Gil did, too, she could see.

Her unrest increased. She didn't know what she would do if forced to leave Zachary and this place, but the bigger question was, What would Gil do? How would he manage without her? He needed her as much as she needed him. Surely they could make a marriage on that.

"Mr. Prescott . . . Gil."

"Never mind, Teacher. Pretend I didn't say it."

"No, it isn't that."

"You don't haveta explain nothin'."

"Gil, please. You didn't presume, really. I am honored that you asked me."

She felt rather than saw him turn to her, waiting. She kept her gaze on one wrinkle in the towel before her, fingering it over and over. "It's only that I—I don't feel I can."

Why couldn't she just marry him? She'd thought about it and thought about it into the wee hours of the morning ever since he'd returned home. Why couldn't she have what she wanted with all her being, what she'd never had, which was to be part of a complete family?

But she had to decide how much to tell him.

Jennifer took a huge breath and looked at him. "Won't you please sit down? I have something I need to tell you."

He glanced her way warily before he eased onto a kitchen chair. He leaned forward, his elbows on his knees, looking upward through his long lashes with an edge of challenge. Jennifer slowly sank into the opposite chair. Only inches separated their knees.

"All right, Mrs. Hastings. What is it?"

"Please don't look so," she cried. "I . . . it isn't that I don't want to marry you. But—but *you* may not want *me,* when you hear . . ."

Gil sat straighter. "Just tell me."

In her nervousness, Jennifer had to force her hands to be still; she folded them in her lap, her fingers gripping tightly. She sucked in another breath, then began.

"Long ago, I made some terrible mistakes. I—I . . . um . . . married my husband when I was barely eighteen. He was older, and very wealthy, you see, and among the social elite. My aunt Agnes pushed the match, but I—I must confess, I wanted it too. I was so impressed, you see, with his gifts and attention, and his houses, his standing in the community, and the parties and the like that he took me to."

She lowered her gaze. "Anyway, it didn't turn out very well. He was rather a cold person, and didn't . . . well, never mind. Let's just say we didn't suit each other. I was happier when I found I was to be a mother. I think he was too, and for a while I had high hopes that everything would be better. But then . . . then one night we fought and I . . . I lost the baby."

Jennifer finished on a flat, whispered note, then swallowed hard; her insides hurt. She hadn't talked to anyone about the old pain for many years and, until now, there had been only one person to whom she'd ever wanted to explain it all—Aunt Agnes.

She hadn't realized talking about it now would bring it back so vividly. If only Aunt Agnes had lived long enough to understand, if only Jennifer had gained her forgiveness, then perhaps those events wouldn't still have the power to hurt. But her aunt had died believing her an adulteress and worse.

Jennifer pushed the memories of her aunt aside. That too, was in the past, she reminded herself, and she could do nothing to change it.

There was still more to tell Gil. "A few months later,"

she said, her voice low, "my husband . . . died. That's when I came out here."

Understanding softened Gil's heart. All this time he'd thought Jennifer remembered her husband with fondness, so much so that he'd feared she never wanted anyone to take his place. But if he'd heard her right, she was trying to tell him that she'd never loved the man, that she had made the mistake of marrying for money.

Well, that wasn't such an awful sin, people did it all the time, and she'd been young. He couldn't hold it against her; he had his own shame to put behind him and he'd made his own share of wrong turns.

He felt downright expansive, and the tightness in his chest eased. Now that he knew Teacher wasn't remembering anyone else, he couldn't see any reason why they shouldn't be wed. They'd bury the past together and make a new start. Their own union would work, by thunder. He'd love her so hard she would eventually love him back. He'd give her every reason to.

And they'd turn this place into a fine home with none of the bickering and petty spites his father had harbored and perpetuated. They both wanted a family, he was sure of that. Jennifer loved children—it was as plain as the nose on his face. And he did, too, he suddenly realized—a dozen or so would be nice, if the good Lord blessed them—and he sure as heaven looked forward to the making of 'em. Lord, did he ever. He could start right now, if she'd let him, even if he was tuckered to the bone and still smarting from the heavy demands he'd made on his body today.

Ashamed at where his thoughts were heading when he could see Jennifer was on the verge of tears, he said by way of sympathy, "I'm real sorry, Teacher. Must've been a helluva time."

Unconsciously, Jennifer hugged herself. She hesitated a long moment before she quietly answered.
"Yes, indeed, it was a type of hell."

Hell? How could hell itself have been worse? Even
now it made her shake with erupting emotions: grief
and guilt and despair. She wasn't sure she could survive the deeper telling. Neither would Gil's admiration, she was certain.

She sincerely hoped Gil never asked her for the
horrible details of that time or about the events that
had led up to that dreadful day of losing the baby,
and the repercussions and scandal, and how Willard
had died. Again, she asked herself, could Gil respect
her if he believed her an unfaithful woman? Or knew
she'd driven her husband to suicide?

All her determination to give him the whole truth
fled. She couldn't risk telling him. He now knew the
bare bones of her past. It was enough.

Yet she had to give him the most important detail.

"But that's not all of what I need to tell you, Gil.
The fact is, you see, that the doctor said I couldn't . . .
can't . . ."

Tears clogged her throat and her lips trembled as
she whispered, "Gil, I can't give you children."

Gil's rosy wandering thoughts came back into sharp
focus as he slowly took in what she said. No children.
She couldn't conceive again. The words seemed dis-
jointed while his dream of their future shifted and
reshaped. There would be no children of their own.

But they had one—Zach was as much her child as
his.

"Do you understand?" Jennifer said into the silence.

"Yes, Teacher, I heard what you said." Real empathy
and disappointment touched him, and he let her see it

by a soft touch to her hand. But he couldn't let his own emotions get in the way; he wanted her to be his wife no matter what. He shifted in his chair and leaned closer. "It's a disappointment, to be sure. And for you, it's somethin' that's hurt you a lot, ain't it?"

Surprised at his insight, Jennifer merely nodded.

"And you thought I'd be put off?" He spoke gently, and didn't allow her time to answer. "Well, you're still too good for the likes of me by a long shot, but I'm bold as brass to ask you anyway. Say yes, Teacher. Say yes and we'll make it a good life. And we have Zach. He's enough son for any man to be proud of."

She looked at him helplessly, afraid to hope, but hoping anyway, feeling teary with it. Didn't he truly care about her disability?

"And, if you've a mind to accept me, we can make a real go of this place. I know you ain't afraid of hard work and you'll soon find that I ain't. But it's gonna take some time, and first things first. Like that well, now, that's bothering me not a little. We need that well before winter, today's fire proved how badly, and by thunder, we gotta get it. Besides, I ain't havin' you livin' more primitive than I can help—"

Hoofbeats of several horses sounded from up the road and then a call.

Jennifer welcomed the unexpected interruption even though, embarrassingly, she'd been caught with her emotions showing. It seemed she'd been battling tears all evening, and now she quickly wiped her moistened eyes while Gil turned to the door.

"Hellooo, Mr. Prescott? You to home?"

Jennifer didn't recognize the voice; he sounded young, though. Gil rose and motioned her to stay where she was, then cautiously stepped out of the back door. A moment later she heard him answer from the dark side of the house.

"Who is it?"

"It's Homer Burns, Mr. Prescott. Sam Burns's son."

"Ah, Homer." The tension in Gil's voice eased. "Thought you might've been less welcome company, when I heard all those horses coming."

Gil referred to the bands of men who sometimes still roamed the countryside looking for mischief in the name of the recent political conflict, Jennifer knew. She'd had one near brush with night riders last winter and been very frightened at the time.

"Sorry to give ya a scare, Mr. Prescott," Homer replied. "Got some business to talk over with ya. I come at my pa's bid." Then seeing Jennifer in the front doorway, he tipped his hat. "Evenin', Teacher."

She remembered him now; a skinny child with homely features, notably his big ears. Homer had been a student of hers for about two years, but his learning had been rather slow and indifferent. He'd hated school and his father made no objection when he quit, saying the boy was needed to work at his livery business anyway. Jennifer hadn't argued the point, although she felt saddened for Homer.

"Well, get down and come in, Homer, and welcome," she said, smiling to put him at his ease.

"Thank ya, ma'am." Homer swung to the ground, gripping the reins of the six riderless horses he'd brought with him. As soon as he had carefully wrapped the reins around the front post, he turned to Gil. "It's these here horses I come about, Mr. Prescott. Pa wants to know if you'd keep 'em fer a spell."

"Well, I reckon we can manage that," Gil said in a dry, humorous tone. He had land in abundance, much of it good pasture going to waste without animals to graze it. "Come on in and tell me what your pa has in mind."

The youth glanced shyly at Jennifer once, nodded, and then clumped through the doorway. Thereafter, he wouldn't look at her.

"How is your father doing after that nasty fall?" Jennifer asked as she lit another lamp and then pushed the coffeepot onto the back stove plate where it would heat.

Homer stood stiffly, his troubled eyes on his hat, which he continuously turned in his hand. "Um, not too good. He's done broke some ribs, Doc says, an' cracked a laig."

"I'm very sorry to hear that. He must be very distressed over losing the stable, and to be injured as well. Did you lose all of your holdings?" She busied herself with cups and saucers, giving the youth time to take in his surroundings and relax a bit. "It's just you and your father, isn't it?"

"Yes, ma'am, just me an' Pa."

Zachary thumped down the stairs, then came to a sudden stop beside Jennifer. Although he was very close, he didn't cling to her skirt as he might have last year, or even hang back as he would have a month ago, Jennifer noticed.

"Who's here, Mama? I heard a lot of noise."

"This is a friend from town, Zach. You may stay up for a little while, but you must be quiet while your papa conducts his business," she instructed the child.

"Sit down, Homer, and have some coffee while you tell me what your pa needs," Gil lightly commanded.

"Yes sir." The youth awkwardly scraped a chair out from the table and plopped into it, his knees seeming to stick out sharply.

Seeing Homer's quick glance at Gil's plate of cold supper, Jennifer said, "Did you have supper, Homer?"

"Yes'm, Mrs. Linderman, she fed me."

"Well, I was about to serve Mr. Prescott some pie with his supper, Homer. Won't you have a piece too?"

"Don't want to trouble you, ma'am."

"It's no bother," she murmured, already reaching for the berry pie left from yesterday. She gave Gil a meaningful nod toward his own plate, trying to send the silent message that the boy would relax more if Gil ate too. With his eyes twinkling, Gil returned the nod.

Zach sidled up to his father, eyes and attention fixed on their guest. Automatically, Gil lifted the child to his knee, then reached for his plate of meat, cheese, pickled beets, and buttered bread, then made a sandwich and broke off a piece for Zach.

Jennifer poured coffee for the men and milk for Zach, then sat down to join them. Homer ate in great, consuming gulps, Zach drank his milk silently, and she sipped her coffee. Gil took a huge bite of his sandwich, cutting his eyes her way to make sure she noticed, and then chewed thoughtfully while Homer shyly explained, around a mouthful of pie, his purpose in coming.

"Pa's athinkin' that it's gonna be awhile afore he's back on his feet. Doc says mebbe a couple of months, mebbe longer. Dunno when the livery'll be back in business. Lost everything in the barn 'cept the horses you got out an' that wagon that partly burnt, an' the three mounts that was out on rent, o' course. Couple of 'em came back in after the fire was put out. Anyways, Pa said to tell you he's right grateful to ya for savin' 'em an' all you did."

"Glad I could, Homer, but the whole town pitched in to put out that fire," Gil remarked.

"Uh-huh, that's right, they did, and me'n Pa are plumb grateful, but nobody went in after them horses like you did, Mr. Prescott. It makes a heap o' difference to Pa an' he says to ask ya if you'll graze them horses fer him while he's laid up an' till he knows what he's gonna do about startin' up the livery again, and then ya can use 'em in trade fer their keep, if ya think that's fair."

"It's more than fair," Gil responded eagerly. "I'm obliged to your pa for offering me their use. I can think of a dozen ways. A couple of months, you say?"

"Yep, looks like it." Homer gloomily trailed off.

Jennifer frowned. "Homer, it seems to me that I heard you and your pa lived in a back room in that barn. Is that right?"

"Yes, ma'am."

"Then where is your pa now? Who's looking after him?" she asked.

"Uh, Widow Portland, ma'am," Homer answered. "She's been acourtin' Pa, ya see, an' offered to do the nursin', so some o' the men carried him on over there after Doc was through with 'im. She's right happy, I'm thinkin', to have him stay with her," he ended on a note of disgust.

After a lightning glance at Jennifer, Gil asked, "What about yourself, then, Homer? You need bed an' board, too, don't you?"

"Well, Widow Portland said I could sleep on her back porch," Homer mumbled.

"I think we can offer better than that. I can't pay you wages, Homer, but we can sure give you a bed in the old bunkhouse, and keep you until your pa needs you again."

Homer sat up straight. "Would ya, Mr. Prescott, honest?" He looked beseechingly at Jennifer. "I'll work fer it, Mrs. Hastings, I really will. It ain't like schoolin', ya know, I know how to do lots of things in a reg'lar way an' I cain't abide that Widow Portland."

"I'm sure you'll be most industrious, Homer. We would be happy for the bargain."

"Really, sure 'nuff? Can I bring my dawg?"

"Yes, of course," she assured him.

"Then I reckon it's a trade," Homer said. "I'll fetch 'im in the mornin'."

"Done," Gil agreed, and offered his hand. The youth broke out in a grin and shook it.

After that, Jennifer tucked Zach back into bed while Gil and Homer left to take care of the horses. Then she gathered up a blanket and the only remaining sheet she had, and headed for the bunkhouse, a few yards from the barn. She had cleaned it early in the summer, but then had closed it up tight again, since there was no one to use it.

Gil caught up with her, Homer at his heels, and held the lantern high as they entered. The air smelled musty and the room looked stark and bare except for four narrow bunks along the walls, and an old stove in the center. There wasn't room for anything else.

"I'm afraid it isn't much," Jennifer began.

"Oh, this is Jim Dandy, Mrs. Hastings," Homer exclaimed. "I'll have a real bed an' I won't haveta listen to Widow Portland natter on an' on."

While she made up one of the cots, Gil opened the only window the structure boasted to allow fresh air to flow in. "You can come to the house for meals," Gil said. "As to water for the animals, you'll have to water 'em down at the trickle, for now. It ain't much, and it sure the hell ain't convenient, but that well is the first problem I'm aimin' to fix. Now with your help and the use of your horses, I think I can. Meantime, your first task in the morning is to fetch water from the spring down yonder up to the house."

They left the youngster to himself. Gil took her arm as they strolled back to the house, the lantern he carried flooding a small area around their feet with light.

"It's a shame to benefit by others' misfortunes, but it seems to me that you've just come into a piece of luck, Mr. Prescott," Jennifer remarked.

"Yep, it sure does. Imagine that. Here I was cogitating how to get this place goin' again, just to get a handle on it, and get another well dug—"

"Don't you think you should wait for more help to dig that well?"

"Got help now."

"But you promised to rest."

"No rest for the wicked, my ma used to say," he returned with a chuckle.

"Gil Prescott, you don't take me seriously!"

"Oh, yes I do, Teacher. I take you very seriously. In fact, I think you were right earlier when you said I should sleep in the downstairs bed."

"But that was when I thought you too exhausted to climb the stairs!"

"Oh, I am, Teacher. Too exhausted. In fact, I think I can barely stumble to bed by myself. Here, can I lean on you?" He stepped closer and one arm came around her shoulders, his hand dangling just above her breast. "I might need you to undress me and tuck me in like you did the other night."

Jennifer jerked sharply away. "Why, you impertinent—"

"Sorry, Teacher, but you did offer." Laughter laced his voice.

"Well, my offer was for the bed only, it didn't include any *extra*, um, er, services, you can be sure. And if you have enough strength to tease me so, I think you can climb those stairs well enough, and just stay there."

"Hmmm. Does that mean you're not ready to marry me?"

"Pardon?"

"Earlier you commanded me to rest up and finish healing before taking on any kind of hard labor. I agreed, providing that we don't wait to wed. That doesn't take hard work," he said, still on a teasing note.

They reached the house and Gil pulled the door wide for her to enter. Gil blew the outdoor lantern out and set it on the floor by the door. Jennifer picked up the table lamp and held it shoulder high so she could see his face. In spite of his joking, Gil was running on sheer willpower, she was certain.

And he was ignoring all she had told him of her past.

"Well, we never quite finished our discussion. Do you think we should rush into it? There is still much you don't know of me."

Gil, finally sedate, leaned against the door to her bedroom.

"It ain't wise to put it off, I'm thinking. If town gossip ain't caught up with the fact that I'm back home before now, they'll know it after today, and the fact that we're living under the same roof. It'll cause talk if we don't marry and you don't move out, neither. You don't want Tommy or the like to fill Zach's ears with more sh—"

He stopped abruptly and rubbed the back of his neck. "Excuse me, Teacher, I've been around soldiers and rough men too long and my tongue gets the better of me, sometimes. But you know what I mean."

"Yes, I suppose I do."

"Then I think we ought to visit the preacher in town tomorrow. Get it done. I don't have to have . . . I can wait . . ." His gaze grew somber, and he said in a more diffident tone, "Hell, Mrs. Hastings, I'll keep my distance, if that's what you want, until you feel ready to . . . All you got to do is say the word. But when we officially visit town again, I reckon you oughta be Mrs. Prescott."

Jennifer thought about it a long moment. "All right. I suppose that would be best. I can see that waiting would serve no good purpose, under the circumstances."

"You do? You will? Aw, Teacher." He took one exuberant step forward and swept her into his arms.

"Gil, the lamp!"

"Hold on to it," he murmured, drawing her body into alignment with his.

And there was nothing she could do except hold the lamp high with one hand and grasp his shoulder for support with the other while he kissed her.

His lips were warm and tender, needy and seeking. They took all of her mouth in a way she hadn't expected. She allowed him a long moment of contact, wanting to give him the pleasure and emotional healing he sought while she made a silent pledge to honor this agreement in every way.

Then she forgot all about her high-minded intentions as slowly she found her body responding to the sensual pressure of his. His kiss heightened all of her own senses—she took in the way he smelled of the soap with which he'd bathed, the hot feel of him against her mouth, his hands against her, one inching closer to the underside of her breast, waking her to her own yearning need to be touched there, all the while glorying in the way his other hand circled her waist even tighter.

Jennifer never thought she'd ever feel that hot desire she'd only glimpsed before, but her limbs felt weak, her blood heated. She heard and responded to the appeal of the low, agonized groan in his throat by a faint whimper of her own.

When Gil finally pulled away, she was dazed with pleasure and regretted the separation.

"Sor—" His voice cracked and he started again. "Sorry, Mrs. Hastings. I said I'd wait and not push myself on you, but I couldn't help myself just now. I've been wantin' to do that since . . . But I won't do it again till you say. I promise."

Jennifer stared at him and pulled a long, shuddering breath. A moment ago, her intentions were to wait until they knew each other better to allow Gil to consummate their agreement. She had thought the pleasure would be all his, that she'd be doing all the giving on that level. Now she couldn't think, she didn't know—

Yes, I do!

Her mind went spinning into a stark revelation. She wanted him—her need was as great as his. She was stunned with the knowledge.

I do know, and I want to take him to my bed!

Oh, my! Oh, my yes, she certainly did! Gil was right. They had better visit the preacher tomorrow.

Nevertheless, a whisper of fear about the speed of it all drifted past her haze of delight. It was too much to love Gil as well as Zach, to have it all. She shouldn't allow herself to want it; she would be tempting fate.

As once before, she silently begged God to tell her she was doing the right thing, to give her some sign, any sign. She'd made so many mistakes, she didn't want to make another. But she heard no thundering voice or whispering of the Almighty around her, saying either yea or nay. Only the sounds of their own excited breathing filled her ears.

She had to make up her own mind.

Then she remembered; she wasn't alone in this. She and Gil were taking this step together, with Zachary. Her hopes lifted. The slender thread strengthened.

7

They were married very quietly the next day just before sunset at the newly built church on the edge of town, standing with Zachary between them and the Lindermans as their only witnesses. Gil had gone into town early that morning to make the arrangements.

It was the first day of September. Because it was her birthday month and a new school year usually began then, Jennifer had always thought of September as the month of new beginnings. That was how she would view this day, she decided firmly.

At breakfast, Jennifer and Gil explained to Zachary what was to take place that day. Zach immediately became concerned with what Jennifer would wear on her head, asking—while Gil ducked his head to hide a chuckle—where she was going to find "that curtain thing" in time to wear it to be married.

"I have a straw hat with blue ribbons that's packed

away which will do very nicely," she assured him. It was old and out of date, but it had once been a fashionable delight during her days as a social butterfly. She'd worn it only once since coming west.

"What hat, Mama? Does it have a—a . . . that thing on the front?"

"A veil. No . . . well, a wisp of one, but it doesn't cover my face. Is that what you wanted to know?"

Zach nodded but continued to wear a puzzled expression. "But don't you have one?"

"It isn't necessary, honey," she told him. "Besides, those are worn by very young brides who are getting married the first time. Do you see?"

"Okay," he answered doubtfully.

The day flew toward the late afternoon, the time Gil had set with the preacher, and when it was time to leave for town, Zachary rushed upstairs and down again, something white fluttering from his small hand.

"Wait! Mama, wait!" he cried.

"We aren't going to leave without you, Zach," Gil said, amused at Zach's urgency. "You're part of this, too."

"Uh-huh, but, here, Mama," Zach said as he thrust out his hand. A limp piece of gauzy cloth lay there.

At first, Jennifer didn't know what it was or where it had come from, but she instantly knew what Zach intended it for. His dark eyes shone with excited triumph.

She slowly reached for the cloth. A white square of unhemmed cheesecloth, ragged on one corner, floated to a drape as she shook it out.

"It's a veil, Mama."

"Son, I don't think—" Gil began, then quieted at Jennifer's cautioning look.

She dropped to her knees so that she could talk

face-to-face with the child. "Zachary, you are so thoughtful to go to all that trouble to find a veil for me. But do you think my hat needs one?" She turned her head from side to side to show him her hat, where the bows she'd refreshed that morning stood up in peaks and covered the brim.

"Guess not."

"But do you know what? I do need a handkerchief. Is it all right with you if I have this cloth for my very own wedding handkerchief? Then I'll keep it for always and always and never use it for anything else so that when I am old, I'll still have this as my special gift from you. Is that all right?"

Zachary smiled his response. "Uh-huh."

She tucked it into the front of her dress, an ice-blue silk taffeta afternoon gown with flounces and tiny pleats; it, too, was a leftover from her former life, and she'd even pulled her hooped underskirt from storage to make the skirt stand out as it was designed to do.

She rose and turned toward the door where Gil waited. The admiration and pride in his expression were mixed with a wary diffidence.

Perhaps it had been a mistake to wear the expensive garment, for it clearly shouted wealth and pointedly reminded her, and now Gil, of how she'd once lived; but then again it was the best she had and, womanlike, she felt pride in how well she looked in it.

But all doubts fled when Gil whispered, "You look prettier than a prairie sunrise on a frosty winter morning, Teacher."

His imagery called up a picture in her mind of how the frost sparkled like diamonds on the hills and how the prairie grass that stretched for miles around them was rimmed with gold on a sunny winter morning. It was the sweetest compliment she'd ever received, Jennifer thought, as she recalled the multitudes of mostly empty ones she'd once enjoyed.

Now, with the sun's rays streaming through the church's west windows to edge everything around her with light, she felt the warmth of Gil's sincerity wrapping her with promises to love, honor, and cherish, reminding her of her own promises that she was making this day.

"You are now husband and wife," the minister said.

Gil turned to face her, his eyes filled with a momentary awe. "I'll do my best to make you happy, Mrs. Prescott," he murmured humbly as he gave her the lightest of kisses. But before she could respond, the Lindermans were congratulating them.

"I wish you a long and happy life, my dear Jennifer," Maude Linderman said, and hugged her. Then she turned to Gil. "And you, you young scalawag, I hope you know what a lucky man you are. It'd be a proud day for your ma, if she was alive to be here."

"Yes, ma'am, I do know." He nodded solemnly.

Zach beamed at everyone and allowed Mrs. Linderman to kiss his cheek.

"I wish you great joy, Mrs. Prescott," Mr. Linderman said, and shyly touched Jennifer's hand.

But he wrung Gil's hand exuberantly. "Congratulations, there, Gil, ya done the right thing. Ya sure are a lucky son of a gun, I can tell you. An' you, young fella," he added as he ruffled Zachary's hair.

"Might I add my hearty blessings, also, Mr. and Mrs. Prescott," the preacher politely intoned. "I do hope we may see you in service from time to time?"

Zachary eagerly pulled Jennifer down to whisper in her ear. "Mama, did you hear? He called you

Mrs. Prescott. Your name matches mine and Papa's now."

"Yes, Zachary, he did, and it does," she acknowledged with a huge smile as she hugged him. "Now my name is Jennifer Prescott." Her heart rejoiced that she no longer had to worry about leaving Zachary. She was his mother legally; he was her child. No one could ever take him from her.

Jennifer kept him close against her side for the few remaining moments of their stay in the church.

As Jennifer settled herself in the buggy to leave, Mrs. Linderman laid a box in her lap. "For your wedding supper, my dear," she said, then leaned closer to say confidentially, "I'm so glad you decided to marry Gil and stay on. Gil needs a good woman to steady him, you know, and the two of you, and little Zach, will make a fine home together, I'm sure of it. His ma would've liked you."

"Thank you, Mrs. Linderman, I do hope you're right. You have been so kind, I thank you." Jennifer hadn't felt such comfort from another woman in a long while, and it warmed her heart.

They didn't linger in town. Homer joined them on the outskirts, having spent the time visiting his father.

While the men attended to the evening chores, Jennifer changed her clothes and set about preparing supper. When she opened the box Mrs. Linderman had given her, she found a cake, intended to mark the day as one to celebrate. Another kindness, she mused, fighting the sudden sentimental tears. After all this time it seemed almost too much, that too many good things were happening.

She set the cake in the center of the table, a place of honor.

Well, she'd take all the good wishes that came her way, she decided, and then had no more time to think about her change in status because the men came trooping through the front door, wiping their feet without her telling them, laughing at some joke they shared while Gil set the milk onto the dry sink, filling the kitchen with all the sounds of a happy family.

Supper was a merry party. The two boys tucked into the food as though they hadn't eaten all day, and even Gil, trying to please her, ate better than he had before. But even so, he still showed lines of fatigue by the time she served the spicy fruit cake. He nibbled valiantly on a tiny slice.

Homer soon excused himself and left for the bunkhouse.

"It's time for bed, Zachary," Jennifer said quietly as she collected dishes to be washed.

"Right now?" was the protest.

"It's been a long day, honey. Everyone is tired."

"But—"

"Mind your ma, Zach. Bedtime."

Zachary started away, then turned back. "Aren't you coming?"

"Mmmm, in a little while. I want to talk to your mother for a bit. But I'll come along and tuck you in."

"All right," Zachary conceded.

Jennifer took her time with the cleaning up. When all grew quiet from above, she wondered if Gil had fallen asleep again. Which was disappointing, she thought; she'd grown used to having adult conversation in the evenings.

Oh, phoo. In the mere few days he'd been home, Jennifer admitted, she'd grown used to having *Gil* around, to his easy company, to his teasing nature in the face of their hardships, to the sharing of their routines and things that concerned Zach, and plans and ambitions for this place. The fact that from now on she had a right to share everything gave her a sense of joy and a peace she hadn't known in a long time.

His tread was soft as he came down the stairs. "Is the milk ready for the cellar?"

"Yes, it's ready. I'll have to churn butter again in the morning. Flossy seems to give more milk for you than she does for me."

Gil chuckled as he picked up the two buckets, one full and one half full. "Well, you have to sweet-talk Flossy a bit, Teacher. She's a proud lady. Besides, you have twice as many mouths to feed now than you did a week ago, so we need the extra milk."

"Yes, indeed. I've been thinking to double my hens next season. Now I'm sure to do it."

Gil melted into the dark of the backyard with the milk, and a moment later Jennifer heard the creak of the rusty cellar hinges. Another two moments brought the sound again, as he closed the cellar. Then he was back.

In silence, he reached for a dish towel and picked up a dish she had laid on the table to dry.

"Gil, you don't have to do that," she gently admonished.

"I used to help Ma with the supper dishes," he replied.

"You promised."

"What?"

"You promised that if we married right away you would take more care of your health. You're tired. You have had days, probably weeks, of hard work and worry. Your wounds . . ."

She finished her last pot, then wrung her cloth out and hung it over the stove handle.

"I ain't as—"

"I am not, not I ain't," she said automatically.

"Pardon?"

"Um, sorry." She flashed him an embarrassed smile. "I guess once a teacher always a teacher."

He grinned, acknowledging her correction with a nod. "Oh, well, *I'm not* as delicate as you think, Mrs. Prescott. But I don't mind givin' in to some of your coddlin' if . . ."

"If?"

"If you let me do some courtin' while I'm whilin' away the time."

"You want to court me?"

"Yep, think I ought to. Or rather, I think we should. This whole business has been backwards anyway an' fast enough to spin heads. I think we already got rushed enough."

"Oh, I see."

He threw his dishcloth over a chair and turned to face her. "Don't know if you do or not," he said a bit roughly.

Gil held Jennifer's puzzled gaze, thinking she was the loveliest woman he'd ever seen, a Miss Prim and Proper most of the time, even a touch-me-not in the eyes of the town, but underneath that exterior, he was certain Jennifer was as warm and loving a woman as God ever made. And he barely resisted grabbing her into his arms and tearing her clothes off. He'd dreamed of her often enough these last years; now they were married and the barriers between them were gone.

"The plain raw truth is, Teacher, that I want you awful bad. I been with rough soldiers, mostly, for years, an' I ain't had a woman in so long—"

He stopped and gritted his teeth. He couldn't tell her

he felt so lusty he might end up too rough with her. He'd never raped a woman in his life and he didn't plan to start with his wife, but he knew it could happen that way if he let his need get out of hand. He had to be patient with this thing they'd started between them, he cautioned himself. He had to build for the years they'd have together.

"I want us to be man an' wife, Teacher, an' I want to make love to you somethin' fierce, but I want you to like me when I do."

"I like you, Gil. Enormously."

He felt some of the tension go out of him, and grinned. Then scared of the mere three feet separating them, he moved away from her toward the parlor. "That's a start. Well, what about it?"

She followed. "I think courting is a fine idea, but I have a condition or two to make."

"What conditions?" He took a stance by the stone fireplace, leaning against the mantel. "I thought you only wanted me to rest up?"

"Yes, that is foremost in our bargain, to be sure." She sat on the old horsehair sofa. "But for the courting, you must call me Jennifer. At least in our private moments."

"All right. Jennifer. What else?"

His voice sounded almost reverent as he said her name, low and husky. Only familiarity would ease his attitude toward her, she knew, but the sooner he looked on her as an ordinary woman, the better for them both.

"You shall sit with me in the parlor each evening," she said and patted the seat beside her, giving him the broad hint that she wouldn't mind if he sat there now, "and sleep a while each afternoon." She nodded toward the bedroom.

His eyes flashed with fire before he dropped his gaze.

"Okay, sittin' with you in the parlor won't be hard to take and sleeping in the afternoon is part of the coddlin', I guess." He shoved his hands in his pockets and remained where he was.

She bit her lip in thought before she said, "And another thing. I think it should go both ways."

"What should?" He looked at her again.

She held his gaze. "The courting," she said slowly. "Courting is intended to give a couple a chance to know each other, and, if they suit each other, to allow a certain, um, intimacy to develop, wouldn't you agree?"

"Yep, that's what I had in mind."

"Well, I want to do some of the courting. Since we have done everything backwards anyway, as you say, I see no reason I should not be allowed to offer you a gentle caress occasionally."

Although Zachary had filled a great need in her, Jennifer realized she'd been starved for the kind of loving she had in mind to give this man. She had a longing to kiss Gil on the ridge of his nose where it had been broken, and the back of his neck. . . .

Gil's eyes went silvery. "Jennifer, honey, you can offer all the caresses you've a mind to give me, and I won't fuss a'tall, not a bit"—the mere thought of her touching him in an intimate way had him in a white-hot heat—"but I'm not sure it will work."

"Why not?" she asked innocently.

"Because if you touch me I just might explode. I don't know how long I can last as it is."

"But you kissed me last night and nothing further happened."

Gil thought she had no idea how difficult it was for him to leave her at the bedroom door. It had taken all of his reserves, for he knew if she'd said no to his proposal last night he'd have had to sleep in the bunkhouse, putting at least that amount of distance between them for her protection.

"Only because you're Teacher."

"But I'm not. Now I'm your wife."

He groaned. "Don't say it like that, in that soft voice. You'll undo all my good aims."

Jennifer pulled a long breath. "Very well. Perhaps we should go to bed, then. What did you have in mind? I mean, how long do you see this courting period lasting?"

"Don't rightly know. Just want it to come naturally."

"Hmmm." She rose and strolled toward him. "In that case, I'll use some of my courting privileges to kiss you good night."

Gil watched her come, his heart beating in double time. When she reached him, she stood on tiptoe to slowly slide her fingers around his neck, stroking the skin there, ruffling his long hair a moment before laying her mouth against his.

He let her kiss him for thirty long seconds without moving a muscle. He felt her lips tentatively explore his, while his delight climbed apace with his need to mate her. She was the warmest, sweetest woman he'd ever known, he thought before every common sense intention left him altogether.

Hold steady now!

He tried to hang on to that thought. He really tried.

Jennifer felt very bold as she deliberately deepened the kiss, pressing against him, wanting to give him the same feelings that he'd given her the night before. She hadn't the nerve to tell him that she desired him, too—it had happened with all the speed of a tornado and she couldn't explain it—but she could show him.

And then she knew she had, for his arms came crushingly around her as he invaded her mouth, pulling her so close to his hot body she thought they might be fused together in one quick flash.

Slowly, as though through pain, he pushed her away and held her at arm's length. "Teacher," he croaked.

"Wife!" she whispered.

"Jennifer, then. This isn't—"

"I know," she agreed, whereupon, she leaned into him again and lifted her lips.

"Jennifer, you don't know what you're asking for."

"Yes, I do. I'm a grown woman, Gil, not a tender, unknowing child."

"But the courtship—"

"I hereby declare it suspended. You may court me tomorrow and for a month thereafter, but tonight I want to be your wife."

He opened his mouth to speak, then had nothing more to say. He simply lifted her straight up, strode into the bedroom, set her down again, then immediately began to kiss her ardently. On her cheeks, her chin, beneath her earlobe, all the while holding her head firmly, his fingers in her hair and his palms against her cheeks, as a starving man might hold the vessel of his nourishment.

Their lips joined again, and Jennifer met his demands with equal fervency. Her fingers unbuttoned his shirt and pushed it aside, then she laid a palm over the scarred ridges on his side. He reacted as though touched with fire, drawing in a sharp, hissing breath between his teeth. Under her sensitive hands, his chest felt as tight as strung wire.

Gil sought the front closure of the print dress she wore, tugging impatiently, then finally getting it opened enough to slip a hand around one firm, heavenly soft breast.

Her body shuddered with the contact.

He frantically thrust her down on the bed, shoving her skirt and petticoat up as they fell on the coverlet. He stroked her inner thigh above her cotton stocking, then kneaded the firmness of her flesh as he jerked her underdrawers down, driving her hunger higher, and his own. His patience ended, and with a wildly impassioned murmur, he joined himself to her with great force, climaxing immediately.

He slumped against her and stilled, his breathing so ragged it sounded painful. Jennifer felt the slowing of it, and putting aside her momentary frustration—after all, he had warned her how close he was to a sexual explosion, and part of her mind felt an amused affirmation of his true assessment—she gently caressed his head where he lay, his mouth and cheek against her one bared breast.

Gil soaked up her touch through a mountain of regret, sorry to have disappointed them both with his precipitous need, and with "awkward oaf" and "stupid fool" only the milder terms he mentally called himself. Had he hurt her?

They lay in the middle of the bed with clothing bunched between them along with bare flesh still entwined with bare flesh. "Teacher, I tried not to let it happen that way," he finally said. "Too fast."

"It's all right, Gil." She let her thumb stroke the tender skin under his eye and remembered how exhausted he must be. "You may begin your courting tomorrow night and we'll try again. You know the old lesson rule. If at first you don't get it right, practice, practice until you do. Sleep now, my dear husband."

Gil could muster only a faint chuckle at her sober teasing. He felt himself drifting and tried to stay awake; he despised feeling so weak at the end of the day and fervently wanted all his strength back. He wanted to love her properly. He was a selfish bastard to take her without giving her pleasure in return. He should be the one holding her in the aftermath, but at the moment, the life-giving sustenance he drew from her arms felt too vital for him to move.

He was so tired, he let his innermost thought slip out in whispered wonder. "Is it really true? You're my wife?"

But sleep claimed him and he didn't hear her answer.

8

Gil slept like the dead until well past dawn. Forcing an eye open at last, he found he was naked under the sheet and alone in the tiny bedroom. He didn't remember undressing completely. Jennifer must've finished the task.

He felt better rested than he had in months. And oddly peaceful. He should get up pronto, he told himself. There was all kinds of work to be done, and Teacher would already be at it. But for one long moment he couldn't help himself. He luxuriated in the soft feather mattress that his ma had made as he glanced around the room that he'd occupied only once before when he'd been sick and Ma had wanted to keep an eye on him.

The room didn't look much like it had when his parents had used it. Jennifer had made the room her own. Blue print curtains, tied with a bit of lace, hung at the window. His practical mother never had lace of any kind, for anything. But then, she'd never had a chance to own anything that nice, either, he remembered.

From the back of the closed door hung a dark heavy shawl and winter bonnet, seeming to his unpracticed eye to be of fine quality. Books, tumbled or stacked or neatly resting together, filled the night table, the chest, and the floor's corners. His mother hadn't known how to read well and hadn't practiced the skill. Of course, teachers did enjoy reading, didn't they? Ma would've approved.

Over the foot of the bed was a woven blue counterpane, half trailing in disarray on the floor. He stretched lazily and recalled what had happened yesterday and the night before, and in remembering, his body came alive. The mere thought of Jennifer caused hot stirrings of desire to hit him in full force and he groaned aloud, wishing she was still in bed with him.

He had to get up. The rumble of Homer's buckboard going past to the garden drifted to him and, from the kitchen, the gentle voices of his son and his wife.

His wife. Teacher was his wife. He couldn't quite take it in or believe his great good fortune. But he recalled last night well enough!

Then the doubts set in. How had he lost control of his carefully planned courtship? He'd wanted to be so gentle with Jennifer that she wouldn't mind giving in to his male needs, and instead he'd ended up as a crude, mindless jackass, doing exactly what he'd sworn not to do.

Berating himself soundly for starting his marriage off so poorly, Gil discovered that bone-deep embarrassment was not the lightest or easiest of emotions for a grown man to ponder. What was Teacher to think of the husband she'd so generously taken on when the first thing he'd done was selfishly to take his pleasure, then instantly fall asleep? She must think she'd married a dolt for sure. And worse, she might never want to let him near her again.

Somehow, he had to correct his mistakes.

He heard Homer slam through the front door, reminding him that he was lazing away the morning. Yes, there was work to be done, not the least of which was mending his fences with Jennifer, so shoving the sheet down, he swung his feet over the side of the bed. His clothes lay neatly over the chair in the corner. He dressed hurriedly.

"Papa," squealed Zach when Gil entered the kitchen. The two boys sat at the table.

"Mornin', Zach." He leaned against the doorway, pretending to be half-asleep. He thought it his best defense until he knew how the land lay.

"Mama's making apple flapjacks for breakfast. They're special, 'cause this is the first day we're altogether a family."

Still festive with the yellow and orange sunflowers that Jennifer had put there yesterday, the table was neatly set for four, and he knew they'd been waiting on him.

"That so?" He watched Jennifer from the corner of his eye. Her back to him, she stirred something at the stove.

"Uh-huh. And sausage, too."

"That sure 'nuff does sound good. I'm very hungry."

"Already got the garden done, Gil," Homer said.

"Good, good." Shifting his feet, Gil stood straight. Wouldn't she even look at him? Had it been that awful for her last night? Had he hurt her?

He looked her over worriedly, letting his gaze travel

from her head to her feet. She seemed all right. Her shining blond hair was in its usual bun, and she wore a yellow dress he hadn't seen before that fit her slender curves very nicely.

Lord Almighty, yes! She was all womanly as she stretched to reach for her flour on the shelf above the dry sink. He recalled how she felt, too, how she'd filled his hands. If they'd been alone, he'd have reached for her now, touched her, kissed her, buried his lips against her skin. He suddenly shoved his hands into his back pockets and shifted his feet again. He wanted to, by golly. Instead he greeted her with polite formality as if there'd been no intimacy at all between them. "Good mornin', Mrs. Prescott."

"Morning, Mr. Prescott," she returned crisply over her shoulder as though just realizing he had entered the room.

"Homer's been watering the garden this morning and Mama and me already milked Flossy," Zachary informed him.

"All done, huh? I've been a lazy son of a—" Gil cut himself off sharply. Pretending to be half-asleep didn't give him an excuse to let his language foul up the morning.

He grabbed another peek at Jennifer, now busy at the stove. She hadn't turned around once to look at him since he'd come into the kitchen. Was she that flat-out disgusted with him?

"I guess that leaves me free to go after the stone this morning for the new well," he said, halfway dejected.

He had in mind to quarry a rocky area that was still on open land, well beyond his place. One trip a day, though, was all he could expect to make with his limited resources. But with Homer and his wagon and team, he thought they'd only have to go two or three times.

Jennifer whirled to look at him. "Oh, no, Gil, it's much too soon for you to do all that heavy labor, you'll wear yourself out."

A warm flush that had nothing to do with her close proximity to the stove crept up her cheeks, and he caught an embarrassed flash of her eyes. Why? Why would she feel so? Then he wondered if the same notion that had crossed his mind had dawned on hers—that their lovemaking last night had plumb worn him out. Or maybe that she didn't *want* him worn out before they got to the lovemaking tonight.

He grinned. Yep, it had indeed taken his all, although he looked forward to the time when his stamina returned and he could not only make love to his wife more than once a night, but give her the kind of blissful completion he'd attained. He felt a bit sheepish over feeling so good about it, but he hoped to let her know he'd take that kind of wearing out any time he could get it. "I feel right sprightly this morning, Teacher."

"That is all well and good, but—" She stopped as she saw his grin and suddenly flushed again.

Gil's spirits picked up. "Yes, Mrs. Prescott?"

"You must rebuild your strength slowly, Mr. Prescott. Remember our agreement."

"Ahh. Sure 'nuff I do remember it. Let's see, I have to sleep later in the mornings, rest in the afternoons, eat well, and what else? Oh, yes. I must practice, practice, practice, too."

Jennifer thought his grin was just too much, and the light in his eyes told her he had indeed remembered what she'd said last night in the intimacy of the moment. She couldn't imagine now why she'd been so bold as to say such a seductive thing, but in the cold light of day she was appalled at herself, and so trying to restore a semblance of control, she gave him a curt nod. "Good. I have a nice bit of calf's liver for your dinner. Mrs. Linderman assures me it will build up your blood."

In spite of his best effort to match her sober tone, Gil couldn't contain his humor. His eyes sparkled with it, and Jennifer instantly realized the bawdy connotation he'd put on her comment. "By thunder, that's just what I need, Teacher, a blood builder to regain my strength."

Jennifer nearly gasped at his implication.

Homer, who'd gone outside for something, swung through the door in time to hear the last exchange. "Liver? Teacher, ya ain't gonna make me eat no liver, now, are ya? That gol-dern stuff is worse'n what Mrs. Portland makes me eat."

"No, Homer, you may have soup and cornbread."

"Well, now, you know, I don't really cotton to liver any more than Homer does, Mrs. Prescott."

Jennifer firmed her mouth. "You will eat it anyway, Mr. Prescott."

"Mama will read you a story, if you do, Papa," Zach offered. "She always reads me one when I'm good."

"She does, huh? How 'bout it, Teacher? Will you read me a story before bedtime if I eat my supper?"

"I might, Mr. Prescott." Jennifer couldn't keep the soft emotions from swirling around her as three pairs of male eyes hung on her answer. Especially those shimmering blue-gray ones. "If you all finish your work before sundown, then I will read a story before bedtime."

That night, Gil stoically chewed his way through a

good-sized piece of thin liver, cooked to a degree of bare doneness. Coupled with onions and potatoes, he decided, it wasn't too bad, but he didn't want to let on that he found it acceptable. He liked Jennifer's gentle badgering.

Finally, he laid his knife and fork down.

"Very good," she remarked teasingly as though speaking to Zachary.

Gil raised a brow and gave her an answering glance. "Thank you, Teacher. Okay, boys. Let's finish stacking that stone."

They had brought back a good-sized load this morning, then true to his word to Jennifer, he had rested for part of the afternoon.

"Umm . . . no, I think the stone can wait until tomorrow," Jennifer admonished.

"I'm fine." But then, seeing the look on her face, Gil changed his mind. "I reckon we can stack the stone tomorrow, though."

Satisfied, Jennifer rose and began to gather up the dishes, and because the boys were excited about the prospective treat, they helped her clean the kitchen without being asked.

"Here, Mama, sit here," Zachary said when it was time for the story. He pushed the light armchair closer to the settee where his father had settled, then climbed into Gil's lap. Homer sat on the floor by Jennifer's feet.

Jennifer had frequently read to Zachary from one of Jacob Abbott's Rollo books or a tale from Hans Christian Andersen, but after serious consideration to her present audience, she now opened to the first page of *The Last of the Mohicans* by James Fenimore Cooper.

As she read, she watched Homer's eyes glaze over

with fascination, and Zach, usually restless after a few minutes, grow still. Gil listened, his body relaxing, with his head thrown back against the settee, his eyes drooping, but more often than not fixed on her face. By the end of two chapters when the light had failed, Jennifer saw that she had started something that would be hard to end, so she said, "We'll take up the tale tomorrow evening after all the chores are done."

Homer left for the bunkhouse and Jennifer put Zach to bed. Gil remained in the parlor.

Jennifer returned and noticed that only one lamp remained lit, its wick turned rather low.

"Are you tired, Jennifer?" Gil spoke in a soft, rumbling tone, and when she glanced at him, she realized he'd set his boyish teasing aside.

"A little," she admitted.

"Can we talk awhile?"

"Why, of course. What is on your mind?"

"I thought maybe we might start some of that courtship now."

"All right." The lines around his eyes and mouth didn't appear as harsh tonight, which gave Jennifer a great deal of satisfaction. The rest had been good for him.

She sat again in the chair she'd occupied earlier, wondering what kind of courtship he had in mind. Last night she'd been as sexually aggressive as she'd ever been in her life, far more so than when she'd been accused of being a slut and a whore, and now it embarrassed her. Yet, she wasn't sorry. She and Gil needed each other, and they needed to be acquainted quickly to cement this marriage.

But she wanted to know more of him than that he was attracted to her. She'd already discovered that

Gil had a lighter side to his character than the serious young man she'd first met. However, questions now tumbled through her mind without rhyme or reason.

What little things made him happy? What did he want to do with the ranch, beyond the obvious need to make it yield them a living? Did his son remind him of the Indian wife he'd had? Had he loved Morning Rain deeply? Did he love her still? He'd refused to talk about his war experiences; had he come away with scalding hatreds as other returning soldiers had? Or emotional wounds that she hadn't yet noticed? How long did he think it might take to get the new well in?

She wondered what he was thinking now, for the silence stretched while he watched her.

Finally she asked the first thing that came to her. "Were you able to repair that gun to your satisfaction?"

"Mmm . . . yes." He'd worked on it all afternoon. "Should run it into Lindermans' tomorrow," he answered with ease. "And I need to stop by to see Sam, to see how he's mending, and let him know his horses are doing fine. Homer, too."

"Very well. Perhaps you'd drop my produce off at Lindermans' for me, then I wouldn't have to go into town myself. Now that I have a little time, I'd like to explore that section of woods toward the east for nut trees."

"As a matter of fact, Ma used to gather black walnuts in there. But I don't want you going alone, Teacher." Then at her cautionary look, he corrected himself. "Ah, Jennifer. Wait a few days and I'll take you."

"Why? Is it dangerous?"

"Well, now, times haven't exactly been certain, you know. Strangers everywhere, some of 'em pretty rough. Could be anything or anybody in those woods."

Jennifer refrained from mentioning that she and Zach had been alone on the place for well over a year before he returned home, and she'd learned to be wary a long time ago. "Very well. We'll plan on going at the end of the week, then, shall we?"

"Sure, that'll be okay."

Another silent wait. Spying her mending basket on the small lamp table at her elbow, Jennifer reached for it.

"Jennifer."

"Yes?"

"You said last night you would sit with me sometimes."

She looked up. "I am sitting with you."

"Here," he said, patting the sofa seat beside him, much as she'd done last night.

Without comment, she exchanged her seat. Gil took the mending basket out of her hand and replaced it on the table, then took her hand. Slowly, he ran a finger along hers, traced the lines in her palm, and examined a scar along the base of her thumb. "How did you get this?"

"Oh, when I was learning to cook. About ten, I think." The feel of his fingers wrapped around hers felt secure and inviting. She wondered how such a simple touch could make something inside of her melt. "Aunt Agnes let me begin by peeling potatoes. When did you start learning chores?"

He continued to explore her hand, inspecting the way her short nails shaped the fingertips, and was inordinately pleased at their cleanliness. He thought of her penchant for the daily bathing routine. He liked the practice himself, especially now, after years of frequently going without, of enforced conditions where such a simple pleasure as regular bathing had been a privilege.

His jaw tightened in determination as he gave thought to their water problem. They needed that well and he intended to see they got it without any more delay. They *had* to have convenient water—it wasn't fair for Jennifer to have to stint on it.

"So young I don't remember," he answered, putting aside his worries. Besides, Jennifer was right there beside him with her soft skin clean and inviting, and he wanted to hold more of her than her hand. She smelled so damn sweet it made him crazy to put his nose right against her face and neck and between her breasts and just sniff. And taste. And kiss.

He drew a breath to try to control his urges. "Pa believed in earning your keep and despised laziness, or softness, as he called it. But I could seldom please him. I'd polish a harness 'til it shone or plow a field 'til I couldn't see, but it was never enough."

"Is that why you didn't get along?"

"Yeah, reckon that was part of it. I got rebellious. Sometimes I just ran off and went hunting or to town. Got into my share of trouble there, too."

"What kind of trouble?"

"The usual kind a boy gets into. Stole tobacco from Mr. Linderman, then got sick as a dog when me and Frank smoked it behind the barn. Then Pa found out."

"What happened?"

"Pa whupped me good with his belt and Ma made me work off the debt. Never stole anything again." He spoke with a quiet, old bitterness, as though it was worn out but yet had a sting.

"Did your father . . . did he whip you often?"

"Not so terribly often, now that I think on it, but

when he did it was a powerful hurt. He was a mean old bird, even so, and Ma . . . I could take my lickings, but he shouldn't of been so hard on Ma. She worked harder than a dozen women trying to make him happy, and he never had a kind word or a smile for her. It killed her, eventually, and I ended up hating him for it."

Jennifer felt a greater connection to him then, at that moment, remembering his hidden desperation the night he'd brought her the tiny bundle that had become the joy of her life. "Is that why you brought Zachary to me that night?"

"Mostly. Yeah, I reckon that was it. I couldn't stand for Zachary to grow up with him, just as I said. Pa would've made the boy pay for my sins."

"Tell me of your mother."

"She was gentle, like you. And small."

Gil obligingly talked of his mother, tiny Alice, who'd been a domestic servant in the East before she'd married his farmer father, a hulking man in his prime, and how she'd come west with her husband and son and a pioneer spirit, with high hopes to make a home of her own. From his description, Jennifer felt a kindred spirit with Alice. Gil had gained his gentle spirit from her, she suspected.

They talked until the lamp sputtered. "Time for bed," she murmured.

"Yep, reckon so." At his reluctant agreement, she gazed at him questioningly. His expression was intent with longing. "It ain't that I want to sleep upstairs, Jennifer. But after last night, I think I better."

"Why?"

"Well, I promised you a courtship. And sleeping in the same bed . . . I don't think—*I know* I couldn't keep from—I want you now just as much as before," he finished saying with some force. "But it might not be any better than last night for you."

She nodded. "I know. I understand."

"You do?"

"I think so. But Gil, I think you should sleep in our room anyway. I didn't dislike it, and it will improve if we give it a chance . . . give each other a chance."

"You wouldn't mind?"

"No."

"I didn't disgust you?"

"I told you, Gil. I want to be your wife."

"Oh, God, Jennifer." He pulled her across his lap and kissed her with all the fury of a gale wind, his lips begging and taking, while his hands eagerly did the same as they sought her breasts. "I *need* you," he said, his voice hoarse with emotion, "with . . . every . . . breath . . . I draw."

"Mmmm," she answered as his mouth wandered across her face. "I know."

"You know? How? How do you know?"

Because I feel that same need!

The loneliness of years seemed to peak for her then, and she answered with her own lips on his, pressing into him with her own fervency. It was as though the night before had never been, for there was no slack of want between them.

The touch of him sent her into a blaze, further igniting her passion. She thought she'd die of pleasure as he succeeded in baring her shoulders and breasts. When his mouth pressed against them she felt she'd been waiting eons for his touch while it had only been one day, and slid her hands against his neck and cheek, wanting, needing, *desperate* to touch him back, to let him know . . . to tell him . . .

They lingered on the small sofa kissing and fondling until Gil tried to lay Jennifer beneath him, only to find they couldn't fit themselves onto the small settee. With lightning speed, he switched her to the braided floor rug, shoving a small, hard pillow under her head only a moment before thrusting himself into her warm responsive body. It lasted barely seconds longer than the night before, except this time he lifted her with him and felt her shudder wildly while the blood roared through his own head.

But he knew he hadn't satisfied her.

They lay entangled together, motionless, saying nothing, until the floor beneath them began to feel very hard and their clothes lumpy.

"You must think you married a rutting pig, Teacher." His tone was full of embarrassed apology.

"I think I married a man, Gil. A fine man, and with a man's needs. And I'll remind you that I'm the *woman* who has become your wife," she gently emphasized. "And that's how you make me feel. Like a real woman."

He chuckled shakily, his breath flowing softly against her neck. His wife seemed to have the power to lighten his mood, and his embarrassment lifted. "I hope to heaven that the next time you feel womanly, I have enough damned male patience to get *all* your clothes off first. It's downright mortifying to be so hasty."

A light breeze reached them through the open door; the days were cooler now, and the nights, too. Jennifer watched shadows dance on the ceiling for a moment while she contemplated the thought of being totally naked with the man she'd married. "Um, how is your masculine patience right now, Gil?"

"Midlin', I'd say, fair to midlin'. How's your womanly feelings?"

"Oh, I think I could last until we reach the bedroom."

"Awh, Jennifer, I'm not sure I could . . . you know. . . . I haven't regained all my strength yet."

"Cuddling was all I had in mind for the rest of tonight, Gil. The other will eventually happen. But I do have a wife's longing to lie in husbandly arms."

Shocked at the sudden realization that his self-contained-perfect-lady wife was asking to lie next to him completely nude, he responded with a slow gentle kiss of promise. For even in his exhaustion, Gil had heard the loneliness in her voice.

In the bedroom, with infinite patience, Gil finished undressing his wife. He lowered her to the bed, then stepped out of his own clothes, and lastly, lay down beside her and pulled her close. Under the sheet, he stroked her arms and back with loving hands even while they both descended into sleep.

Jennifer sighed in blissful content.

A long while later, something dragged Gil out of the depths of sleep into semiconsciousness. Jennifer was dreaming, and not pleasantly.

Her whimpering turned into a soft pitiful crying. It tore at his heart, and he closed a hand over her fist and brought her knuckles to his lips. "Hush, sweetheart, don't cry," he murmured as he drew her closer. "Everything's all right now. It's only a dream. You're here with me and I won't let anything hurt you, I promise."

The crying slowly ceased. Her breathing evened out, and thinking she had never truly wakened, he drifted back to sleep. He would ask her about it tomorrow.

Beside him, Jennifer lay very still and willed her clenched stomach muscles to relax. She had had the old, frightening dream again, the one where the monster had taken her baby while she fought him alone.

Quietly, she wiped the tears from her cheeks. It had been a long time since she'd dreamed that one—years, in fact. It made her distinctively uneasy. Why now?

In the dark, her eyes wide, her teeth came together in a tight clamp. Would those horrible long-ago events continue to haunt her all her life?

But she wasn't alone anymore, she reassured herself, acutely aware of Gil's body next to hers. She'd awakened to his soothing words, and the power of the ugly dream had lessened. Gil had gone back to sleep now, but he still held her hand against his chest; it gave her comfort.

Nevertheless, she unfolded her fingers to lay her palm wide against his skin to draw upon his warmth.

She wouldn't be haunted by it any longer, she decided, that was all there was to it. Her past was over. She was plain Jennifer Prescott, now, not Patricia Jennifer Mitchell, cold-hearted adulterous socialite. She was going to build her future with a new husband and son—with this tender man who needed her, and Zachary. She'd never let anything from her previous life steal a jot of this precious existence.

But why, after these years, had she dreamt about losing her baby?

9

The swiftness with which Jennifer fell in love with Gil shocked her. During those rare times that she had allowed herself to contemplate the future before Gil's return, she hoped and prayed for consideration and respect from Zachary's father, when he finally did come home. And even though she looked upon Zachary as a blessed gift, one she couldn't conceive of giving up, she'd also hoped for acknowledgment and recognition from Gil of who she was in his child's life and what she could continue to give him.

But deep down she'd yearned to love a man again, and her very daring to hope and dream of finding that had frightened her. Deeply. So much so, that she'd ruthlessly pushed those dreams down into a tight little ball and decided she could, and would probably have to, accept simple contentment.

Now Gil had given her all she could ever want—all of

his world and beyond. Himself and Zachary. Passion, laughter, sweetness in life, dreams for themselves. Love.

A few days after her nightmare, and after nights of simply going to sleep in each other's arms, which was enough at times, they made love again.

That morning Jennifer walked up to the barn where Gil was replacing old rotted-out boards on one side of it.

"Where are the boys?" she asked as she glanced around the dim interior.

"Homer went after a couple of nags he left in the far pasture and took Zach with him," Gil replied. He rose from his haunches, gauging the effects of his efforts where he'd just finished nailing a new board at the bottom of the wall.

"Oh, he took Zach?"

"Don't worry, Jennifer," he said, rightly guessing what the tone in her voice meant. "Homer can look after the boy."

"I guess so, it's just . . ."

He glanced at her over his shoulder, saying gently, "You're thinking like a mama. But you have to let Zach grow up a bit now."

"I suppose I do," she agreed with a tentative smile. "But he's still so little."

"Um-hmm. And he's our only chick." He laid his tools down and came to her, lifting her chin. "It's hard, I know. It was hard on my ma, 'cause she had only me. But you wouldn't want Zach to grow up not knowing what a boy should know, would you? Or without a boy's need for some freedom?"

"No, of course not."

He kissed her, a soft gentle kiss. "Teacher, you've

been a wonderful ma to Zachary. I can't ever thank you
enough, not in a million years, for the job you've done."

Her eyes misted at his praise. "Oh, Gil, if only you
knew."

"Knew what?" His thumb brushed her cheek, loving the way her skin felt as soft as freshly spun cotton,
loving the contours of her delicate jaw, and delighted
with the springy curls along her nape. She was altogether so beautiful, he never tired of merely looking
at her.

Even yet, sometimes he could hardly believe she
was actually his for the wanting. The stirrings of
desire hung low in his groin now. They'd had three
nights of tenderness between them, but suddenly, he
couldn't wait a moment longer.

"Nothing. I was only being sentimental."

"I know one thing. It ain't only gratitude I feel for
you." Merely gratitude? That didn't begin to describe
his feelings for this remarkable woman who had
become his wife. He couldn't put them into words or
even describe them to himself, he only knew he never
could get enough of her. Hungry for her, his mouth
sought far more than a gentle kiss. His hands roamed
over her, shaking with need. "Jennifer."

His arousal pressed against her, hard and rigid, and
she felt his urgent heat through her clothing. Helpless
against the appeal in his voice and hands, she couldn't
deny her own deep response. Yet she made an effort
to point out, "It's the middle of the day."

"That don't matter. C'mon, sweetheart, let's go into
that corner where the new hay is stacked."

"The boys."

"They won't be back for a good while."

"Well, I have work to do." She broke away and

backed up a step, a teasing smile on her lips while her heart began to hammer.

"Not for the next hour." He followed with mock menace, purpose in every line of his body.

He teased and chased her; she didn't try very hard to escape him, daring him with her glances. He caught her easily as she leaped over a pile of boards. Thereafter, he held her fast. And she let him.

They laughingly spooned in the scattered hay in the corner where a beam of bright sunshine filtered through the boards to light their faces. Jennifer kept her gaze on Gil's features, observing her husband's deeply intent expression as he loomed above her, discovering anew the worshipful way he loosened her hair and returned her soul-deep stare before overpowering passion took him completely.

Jennifer found it utterly wonderful. She put aside her effort to correct his view of her as a woman on a pedestal. She simply enjoyed his hands, his mouth, his body.

They almost did get caught, though, just as Gil pulled his trousers back over his hips, because the boys returned. Homer's clear musical whistling, with Zachary's higher key barely audible, floated to them in warning.

Jennifer scrambled to right her clothing while Gil leaned up on one elbow and groaned. "Damnation. I'll have to think of a chore for the boys that'll take longer next time," he said.

"Gil, you can't possibly plan—"

"Yes, I can," he replied impishly.

The boys were closer. She could hear Zach's voice. Hurriedly, she jumped up and shook out her skirt and hair, while Gil mischievously ran a hand up under her hem.

"Gil, stop that!" she whispered. It tickled, besides other things.

"Hmmm, Teacher, you have nice legs, did you know?"

"Gil!"

The boys stood in the barn doorway. "Papa?"

"Okay, okay." He laughingly whispered with glowing eyes. "We'll try again tonight, Teacher. Tonight we'll take it slow. Real slow. Tonight is the night I'll get you properly all-the-way undressed *before.*"

Jennifer tossed him her sauciest stare over one shoulder, her mouth trembling with joyous response as she whispered in turn, "You need the practice, hmm?"

"You bet! Again and again, 'til I get it right!" Then louder, "I'm coming, son."

Jennifer laughed delightedly as she left the barn. She found it *all* completely wonderful!

True to his promise, Gil made slow delicious love to her that night, and again every night that week.

And to Gil's total wonder and awe, Jennifer responded with what seemed like a mountain of stored-up passion. Half the time he couldn't help but feel as though he were living a fantasy, or that it was all a dream left over from the hell of war, when those long months of illness and recovery from his wounds caused him to drift into another world. Sometimes he worried that his nights of unparalleled passion and days of equally satisfying companionship would suddenly cease and he would wake and find that Jennifer, as his wife, didn't exist, and that his boy wasn't the fine youngster that was Zachary.

Slowly he regained his strength. He felt reassured and comfortable. More and more often as the days ran together he put his doubts aside and simply enjoyed every experience, whether it was Zachary's endless questions, Jennifer's gentle teaching through their nightly readings, or observing the way she handled Zachary and Homer. He gloried in the increasing amount of physical work he took on and the satisfaction he found in the doing, and the real, though small, progress they were making as a unit. Every day felt freshly new.

Another thing he was decidedly happy about was that he'd gained more control over his starving body. That's the way he had viewed himself when he first met Jennifer again—a man literally starving for his woman. Thank God she had agreed to marry him right away. He shuddered to think how he'd have survived without her, without her comfort and caring. Thank God she'd been kind and patient. Most women would not have been, he suspected, but Jennifer . . .

His wife was an unusual woman.

It frightened Jennifer to look too closely at her happiness, so she no longer did. She only knew, as the weeks flew by, that whether they talked around the breakfast table, including the boys as they easily discussed the needs of the day, or read together in the evenings, or whether, after closing their bedroom door at night, she and Gil made love or merely went to sleep holding each other, she was happy.

She was still blithely happy some weeks later as she stepped up to the wooden sidewalk in front of Lindermans' store, struggling to lift her basket filled with small pumpkins, the last of her fall garden produce. They were heavy. Five large ones waited in the Burnses' buckboard for Gil and Homer to carry for her.

Gil hopped out of their buggy, lifted Zachary down,

and then looped old Ben's reins around the hitching post.

They were returning the buckboard to Sam Burns today, so they had come to town in both vehicles. Sam had started up his livery business again and needed his equipment and horses back. She and Gil understood his need. It had been almost seven weeks since the fire, and Sam's mode of income had ceased with it.

Homer was returning to his father today as well, although regretfully. The youth, they'd discovered, liked working for them and they liked him. She, Gil, and Zach would miss Homer—and the use of his buckboard, of course. Homer had worked hard and had earned far more than his keep. As Gil's strength slowly returned, he and Homer had finished quarrying the stone they needed to build the new well. Also, the two of them had hauled additional stone to sell in town, which enabled Gil to put a down payment on a buckboard of his own and hire the labor to get the new well dug.

They had proudly celebrated its completion ten days ago.

Gil now insisted on paying Homer a man's wages for the days they'd worked so hard at the quarry and hauling.

Homer, impressed with the first money he'd ever earned, jingled his coins in his pocket and grinned. "Pa'll be bug-eyed when he sees what my wages got me. I aim ta buy me some new duds."

"Shouldn't you talk it over with your father first, Homer?" Jennifer asked.

"Nope. Pa'd likely take my money away from me and spend it on somethin' else of his own choosin'."

"Oh, surely not . . ." She drifted off, remembering that Sam Burns could be somewhat chary with his son. He'd made it clear when the boy had quit school that he didn't plan on wasting the resources of the boy's labor. She didn't think all that highly of Sam for that.

But Gil and Sam had come to an agreement about pasturing the horses during off seasons, and Homer planned to continue at the quarry with Gil two days a week until snowfall. Gil felt confident that his business arrangements with the Burns men would profit them all. He was even thinking of raising a few horses for the livery trade himself and had used Sam's best stud horse to mate Sally.

Homer promised to visit them often if he could listen to the nightly readings. Jennifer had to be satisfied with the knowledge that she'd made progress with the boy's education, for he'd begun to take an interest in reading for himself and had borrowed some of her Rollo books.

Gil and Homer hefted the big pumpkins out of the wagon and carried them into the store. Zachary wanted to help, so Jennifer gave him one from her basket to take in, then Gil was back for more. Setting her basket on the sidewalk, she leaned against the store post and rested while supervising the rest of the unloading. She didn't know why she felt so tired this morning.

"'Bye, Mama. I'll come back with Papa."

"I should hope so. I wouldn't want you to get lost coming all that way," she teased, referring to the two and a half blocks they would traverse back to Lindermans' on foot.

"We'll be back in about thirty minutes, Jennifer," Gil told her as he swung Zach onto the buckboard seat. "Tell Mr. Linderman I'll have that Henry rifle back to him by next week. Couldn't repair it until I had a good vise to hold it."

Jennifer smiled as she returned Zach's wave, then gave her husband an understanding nod. Gil had repaired half a dozen firearms since that first pistol, and the Lindermans now had a small sign that advertised Gil's gun repair service. The trickle of income it brought gave Gil pride, and she in turn felt pride in Gil. He was doing everything he could to bring in money.

And he looked well, robust, and able. That seemed to give her the most pride, these days. However, although Gil had put on weight and his body had taken on the muscled tone of an active man, she suspected he would never return to being the husky young man she saw before the war.

She loved him with every fiber of her being, Jennifer realized, as she watched the men, with Zach between them, drive out of sight toward the livery barn. Why, exactly, she couldn't say. His features had always been rather ordinary, except for his deeply set blue-gray eyes and long lashes, but now, with his broken nose and etched lines around his eyes and mouth, his face had taken on maturity and character, and even could look somewhat fierce, at times. She didn't mind. His masculine appeal strongly attracted her.

She seemed to be in a dreamy state today, she admitted, for she was wont to linger against the porch post with her thoughts and sigh with her musings.

Gil's masculine appeal wasn't all there was to the loving. Was it because he was Zachary's father? Or merely because of their deep need of each other?

Or because he taught her to make love so exquisitely and made her feel so prized?

Jennifer sighed again and gave up trying to figure it

out as she started for Lindermans' door. Perhaps she should just settle for the fact that they had both been ready for love, like the vegetables in her garden coming to fruit when it was their time.

It was all of those things, she knew, and thinking about it brought a secret smile to her lips. Because whatever it was, something between them had gloriously exploded into life like a cataclysmic clashing. But it had happened so very fast, she felt as though they'd been caught up and carried to the top of a whirlwind, and she was afraid of what would happen when they came to earth again.

Her thoughts were diverted when she saw Bessie Terrell leave the bootery two doors up.

"Bessie," she called.

"Miz Jennifer," the pretty young woman answered with a smile, moving toward her. Bessie wore a demure rose-colored dress today, but the fit left nothing to the imagination as to her ample shape. Her dark eyes darting about to see who might notice them, she lowered her voice to a half whisper. "Ya shouldn't speak to me on the street, Mrs. Prescott. Respectable folks'll have a cow if they see us conversin'."

"Nonsense, Bessie. My reputation is quite safe. Why haven't you been out to see us lately?"

"You're a married woman, now, Miz Jennifer." Her eyes snapped with wry humor. Their friendship had been important to them both, but Jennifer's marriage had changed the status of it. "I ain't sure your man would welcome someone like me at his house."

"Gil will always welcome you, Bessie," Jennifer insisted. "He knows how much help you've been to me and Zachary these last years while he was away. Besides, you're my friend and I miss your company."

"That's right nice of you to say so, Miz Jennifer," she replied, her light brown face aglow even as her voice took on sadness. "I miss our visitin' times, too, but I reckon I'll have to be movin' on sometime soon anyway, so might's well get used to it."

"Moving on? To where?"

The young woman hesitated for a moment before saying, "I ain't as young as I was, Miz Jennifer. Ain't as fresh. Lots of my old regulars ain't comin' around no more an' Miz Jasmine ain't pleased. Reckon my customers won't be as perticular farther west."

"Oh, Bessie, I'm very sorry to hear of your troubles. Why didn't you marry that bartender that asked you last month?"

"Didn't like him much. 'Sides, he just wanted me to keep on workin', if you get my meanin'."

Jennifer did, and she felt resentment flame against the unknown man on Bessie's behalf. "Can't you find other, less . . . um, less . . . er, more desirable work?"

"Now Miz Jennifer, you know there ain't much for a woman out here less'n she's a whore or a wife. 'Sides, a wife ain't much more'n a slave most times, I'm thinkin'. Of course there's always backbreakin' work, like laundress or waitressin' or somethin', but most folks around here wouldn't hire me for wages I could live on."

"*I* would, if I could." She hated to see Bessie start the downward spiral that seemed to plague the women in her profession. She bent to lift the basket. "But right now I'm no better than anyone else. I couldn't offer you anything but room and board in exchange for hard farm work. However, if you should ever need . . ."

Jennifer blinked rapidly. Bessie looked very fuzzy, suddenly.

"No call for you to feel bad for me, Miz Jennifer. You

been real kind to me and the only white woman friend— Here, what's the matter? You feelin' under the weather?"

"No, not at all. I'm just fine. I merely felt a bit dizzy. It's passed now."

Bessie gave her a strange stare. "You best watch those dizzy spells, Miz Jennifer. You gotta take care of yourself, you know."

"I'm quite all right, Bessie," Jennifer lied blithely. In truth, she was feeling a bit woozy. "But I must go. Please come to see me before you leave town."

Jennifer said her good-byes and continued on into the store while Mrs. Linderman held the door wide.

"Jennifer, you do make the strangest friends, at times. Why would you stop to talk to that common person on the open sidewalk in the middle of the day?"

"Bessie has been a good friend to me, Mrs. Linderman," she answered in mild reproof. "I couldn't bear to be unkind to her. Anyway, I happen to know the girl had little choice in the profession she's in."

Bessie had long ago confided that she'd been sold into prostitution at the age of eleven, going from bordellos to whorehouses in Mississippi. She'd landed in Kansas, where she at least had the appearance of being free, about a year after Jennifer.

Jennifer felt an affinity with the girl. They'd both been forced into poor circumstances while very young, and then had had to take leaps of faith in coming to Kansas, and to make drastic changes to improve their lives. Jennifer still admired Bessie's determination and courage in coming to her to learn to read and write. She'd wanted to improve herself and she had.

Jennifer knew there was a fine line between Bessie and herself. She'd never turn a cold shoulder to such a woman.

But she would've, once.

Slowly, she put those thoughts aside and began her business with the Lindermans.

Two doors away, a dapper, expensively dressed middle-aged man stood very still in the shadowed doorway of the bootery. His small mouth pursed upon his thoughts and raging emotions, yet he knew that anyone looking at him could not guess at them. He had long ago perfected the art of concealing his every thought.

What he felt at the moment was stunned gleeful elation. He could scarcely believe it! Lady Fortune had favored him at last, for it had been only chance that his travels had brought him to this small prairie town. To find *her* there. *Patricia!*

At last, at last! But deadly annoyance filled him, too, unknowingly darkening his eyes to almost blackness, as he realized how many years and how much money she had cost him. After he'd given her his all, after he'd even sacrificed his best friend, his cousin, for her, she had run from him. The unfaithful slut.

He had searched everywhere for her after he ascertained she had left Philadelphia. In New York. Boston. Europe. He had found traces of where she'd been in Europe, but never could catch up to her. She had eluded him again. Determinedly, he had even sent men south to look for her during the war. She had believed she could hide from him forever and had succeeded.

Amusement curled inside him, then uncoiled like a slithering snake. Almost succeeded.

He felt a growing victory. He had found her. She would be his again. And she would repay him . . . oh, yes, she would repay all those years of fruitless wanderings.

"May I be of further assistance to you, sir?" the store clerk asked as he hovered just behind him.

"No."

He answered curtly, as though brushing off a fly. Then thought better of his attitude.

"Can you tell me, my good man, who was that woman wearing the blue dress? She just entered the grocery establishment."

"Didn't see her."

"Surely, you noticed her. She is dressed like a common farm woman, but she's very beautiful."

The bootery clerk raised a brow and gave closer attention to the stranger's question. He was a rich dude if his clothes were anything to go by, and since the clerk, himself, aspired to be a well-dressed, leading town merchant, he noticed these things. "Why're you asking, stranger?"

"Oh, nothing very significant." He gave a deceiving, negligent shrug. "I merely thought she resembled someone I once knew. But, no. That woman she conversed with was a whore, and I doubt the lady I knew would sully herself with such a public acknowledgment."

Suddenly, the clerk looked knowing. "Did the woman in question have yellow hair? And did she have a dirty little Indian boy hanging on to her skirts?"

"I didn't see a child," he said, feeling his certainty slide. He had been told that Patricia couldn't have more children. And an *Indian* child? "But she is a blonde."

"Bet it's her anyway."

"Who?"

"Mrs. Hastings. Or was. She was the teacher round here for about five years."

"And who is she now?" He asked in let-down idleness now, feeling that perhaps his eyes had deceived

him. Patricia, a schoolteacher? He rather thought not.
Yet the name Hastings had a familiar ring.

"Mrs. Prescott. Strange woman."

"Why do you say so?"

"She lived by herself for years. Seemed poor, but had
some expensive stuff that she traded round town. You
know, clothes and jewelry stuff. Saw some blue diamond
earbobs oncet, that she'd traded."

The stranger almost allowed a smile to escape him as
elation flooded back. It *was* her! He'd given her those
earbobs. He must keep the fellow talking.

"Most interesting, I must say. What else about her
did you find as strange?"

The store clerk gave the stranger closer attention. He
was all-fired raring to hear about Jennifer Prescott, though
he pretended his nosiness was of no account.

"Well, sir, she didn't make no close friends while school-
teachering. Snubbed most of the courting men in town,"
he said, disparagingly, "like she was too good for 'em,
and some of 'em good men, too. Then she up and took on
that half-breed bastard kid of Prescott's to raise. Married
that fella Prescott soon's he got home from the war."

The store clerk continued to chatter, but Robert
Quiller didn't hear another word. A red haze drifted over
his eyes while disbelief stabbed him like long sharp
darts.

It couldn't be! She had *married* again and it had
not been to *him!*

After Willard, Patricia swore she'd never marry again.
He hadn't cared, for himself—he'd have no less control of her, as his mistress, than as his wife; he'd have
seen to that. And he would have taken excellent care
of her even as his mistress—exquisite care.

But she had run away from him, damn her. After

all he'd done to rid her of that cold bastard Willard, now she'd given herself to another man. How could she have done it? He, Robert, should have had her. She *belonged* to him.

His fingers crept to his watch pocket, where a lock of her golden hair lay curled inside his watch. He wanted to take it out and look at it, yet he couldn't bear to share it with the store clerk. Patricia.

He could taste the saliva in his mouth, sweet and salty as he thought of her. The young beauty had led him on for months, like the easy trollop that she was, both before and after she married Willard. He had honored her with his own courtship and proposal early in their acquaintance, but she'd taken his cousin Willard instead.

Then despite her marriage vows she had continued to accept his importunities, teasing him, teasing him, teasing him endlessly with her beauty and flirtations, letting him glimpse the ecstasy she would bring him, promising heaven with her smiles, as though she had every intention of succumbing to him soon, disregarding the scandal their flirtation fostered.

But in the end, she had refused him once again. He'd set into motion a nasty, public disgrace.

Patricia hadn't liked it. She had abhorred it, but he'd found it necessary to gain her. She would come to him for solace when society snubbed her, he reasoned. The scandal had been easy to create, and after all, it was her own fault.

She had let another man claim his paradise?

He felt sick with rage, remembering.

She had left Philadelphia, leaving him a note to say good-bye. A mere note! She'd chosen not to return, it said.

At first he'd waited, certain she would in spite of the note. Then after some weeks went by and she did not, he began to look for her. He'd looked for her ever since.

Now Patricia had gone to another man!

His anger was so immediate that it was as though no time had passed at all. His blood raced with growing venom at his recollections. Why hadn't she returned to Philadelphia?

Pleading illness after she had lost Willard's brat, Patricia had shut herself away from everyone, from him—even put him aside. He, who loved her! Why hadn't she come to him? He had cared nothing about the scandal they'd created or what they'd called her in the newspapers. As far as he was concerned, those ugly stories would ensure his possession of her. And after Willard died, he'd waited for her to turn to him for comfort.

But she had given herself to another man!

The slut! Ignoring him all these years, after all he'd done for her. After he had . . .

Pure rage, jealousy, and hatred shot poison along his veins all the way to his heart as the present reality finally settled into his mind.

She'd chosen another man, had she? Well, not for long. He'd have her yet. She was his. His.

A sudden sharp pain pierced his head. For a moment, he couldn't see for the black curtain that seemed to descend over his sight. He held himself stiffly while it passed. That's what he always did when such an occurrence happened.

He'd have to keep a closer watch on his temper, he told himself sternly. He had almost lost control, right there on the street, and that wouldn't do. Not do one bit. He couldn't allow anyone else to see into his mind.

Slowly Robert forced a return of his rigid self-control. With great care, he returned his attention to the clerk. The way the man described Patricia's—now Jennifer Prescott's—behavior with a curl of the lip, gave the decided impression that the clerk had been one of those snubbed.

"Thank you, my good man, for your delightful conversation. I must be on my way now, but I am stopping for a while at the hotel," he said, handing the man a card.

His head was pounding. It was all her fault. The bitch!

"Perhaps we could talk again over a drink?" Robert continued. He could use one of Patricia's rejected suitors to his own advantage, if he was careful. As to how, he had to think out, but after this headache eased, and in private. He couldn't allow anyone, no one at all, to see into his mind when it burst open this way. Afterward, he would plan his strategy.

10

"*Frank and Mary Sue's* brothers want to go hunting next week," Gil thoughtfully informed Jennifer on their way home. "Mind if I go along?"

"Why should I mind?"

"Well, they want to go west a ways. They plan to be gone five, six days, even a week, maybe. Heard buffalo's been sighted out there. I wouldn't mind getting a couple of buffalo. Meat's good. I can sell what we don't want for ourselves, and the hides will be useful."

Jennifer hid a smile at all the reasons Gil'd lined up for going along on the hunting party, like a boy afraid he wouldn't gain permission. "Why do you hesitate?"

"For one thing, I promised Zachary I'd never leave him behind again, but he's too young to go. And sleeping out ain't—isn't—what it's cracked up to be." He shook his head in disgust. "Guess I've gone soft since the war. And besides, I don't cotton to the idea of—" Sudden color heightened his cheeks.

"Hmm?"

"Leaving you," he said under his breath.

"I think Zachary and I can get along without you for a few nights, Gil." She spoke in her crisp, teacher's voice, but her smile got away from her and she turned her head.

He gave her a quizzical side glance and then pursed his lips against his own smile. Had she let him see hers? she wondered.

"Well, don't go getting used to it, Teacher," Gil said in a mock threat. Then changing his tone, "Good, then I'll go. By the way, Frank's wife, Mary Sue, wants to call on you while we're gone."

"I would be pleased if she did."

"Well, her brothers . . . Ah, hell, you might as well know, Jennifer. One of 'em rode with the Jayhawkers that roamed this territory a while back."

Jennifer sobered and she remained quiet for a long moment. The worst scare she'd had on the place before Gil came home was one night soon after they'd gone to the country when night riders had stopped by to water their horses from the old well. All the horrible news accounts of what had happened to people and their homes had flooded her mind, filling her with dreadful fear. It had been very late; she'd gathered the sleeping child into her arms and prayed that Zachary would remain asleep, ensuring his silence. She had held him tight against her breast while they hid in a corner of the bedroom behind the old trunk.

But the night riders had ridden on without investigating the dark house, and she'd breathed deeply of relief. The next week, she'd heard of the damage done that night by the raiders to farmers and townsmen east of her who, some had said, had been Southern sympathizers. Ever afterward, she'd kept a keen watch at night with the handgun that Mr. Linderman had given her. But the night riders had never disturbed her again.

She'd told Gil about the incident during one of their long talks after supper. He knew she heartily disapproved of the tactics and purposes of the roving bands.

Even now, there were rumors some of the bands still met, although she hadn't heard where they'd hurt anyone or damaged any property lately. Hopefully, most of the raiders would melt back into their normal lives, now that the war was truly over.

"We have to put the war behind us, sweetheart," Gil murmured.

"Yes, of course. As long as Mary Sue is willing to be friendly, I'd be happy to reciprocate," she said. "But I hope you don't expect me to say nothing if she begins to reflect her brother's sympathies. Those bands were no less than murderers and thieves during the war, and I hear some of them are continuing their outlaw ways. I'm afraid my tongue might get the better of me were that topic to come up. I do hope you don't get mixed up with them, Gil."

He lightened his tone. "Don't you worry, Teacher honey. I only want to go hunting. I got no—have no, I mean"—he corrected himself with a teasing glance her way—"plans whatsoever to go along with that kind of tomfoolery. I've had a craw full of fighting. Besides, I have enough to do on this place without looking for trouble. But Mary Sue looks up to you, you know. Like me and Frank, she didn't get much schooling, but if given a chance, you're the kind of lady she'd aspire to be."

Jennifer threw her husband an exasperated look. He knew she couldn't resist an appeal to teach, whether formally or by example. But she also knew he could frequently sweet-talk her into seeing a matter his way. She decided to give in graciously. "All right, Gil. I'd be pleased to entertain Mary Sue Able, and I promise I won't say a word against her brothers."

The rest of the way home, Gil talked of the possibility of planting wheat next year. Without money to pay for extra hands, he didn't plan on trying to rebuild his cattle herd just yet, so he'd been looking at other options, and it seemed some of the farmers coming into the area were very enthusiastic about wheat. He had his land, and more of it than most farmers used, he enthused. If he teamed up with one of them for the first year or two until he learned what he was doing, he said, he figured he could work a wheat field by himself by the time Zach was old enough to help. His other endeavors would bring in cash money until then.

"Meanwhile, why don't we go to that town social on Thanksgiving weekend? The men are going to have a turkey shoot and there's a dance afterwards. Should be some fun, and the Ables and Lindermans are going."

"I suppose it would be pleasurable," she answered and smiled. The town had decided to organize a fire-fighting company, and the dance was a means to raise money as well as provide social activity. The current talk was of building cisterns in strategic places for the bucket brigades. "Yes, all right. I think a party would be lovely."

It seemed that Gil wanted to enlarge their circle of friends. Her husband was a sociable person and he had a knack with people, so it was natural he'd want to begin friendly exchanges with his neighbors. And she was willing, now. After all this time, she felt secure once more; she had a husband, a child, a place in the community. Yes, she mused, she could find a place in her heart for more friends.

It would also be good for Zachary. For too long they'd been almost isolated. They'd had no social life except for Bessie and the Lindermans. She discounted those business trips into town, which could be counted as social interaction, but not living friendships.

A boy needed children his own age with which to play. It was something she'd thought about before; as a former schoolteacher she'd recognized the importance of other children in Zach's life. But she didn't want him to get involved with anyone like those Gallaghar hooligans, who delighted in causing trouble, which also discounted the Jones boy who matched Zach's age, because he copied the Gallaghar brothers too closely for her peace of mind.

Perhaps as she and Gil made friends among the new families moving into the state, bringing lots more children with them, Zachary would find a friend for himself among them.

It tasted satisfyingly sweet to make such plans for the future after so many years of bleak prospects, she mused. Yes indeed, deeply satisfying.

Rain pelted the countryside the next couple of days, putting to rest the general fears of fire in the dry prairie. For this year, anyway. Gil tried to put the buggy's broken hood up, but failing that, insisted Jennifer stay home from their usual trip into town on Saturday. She hadn't been feeling quite well, a lingering malady of occasional nausea and tiredness, and was happy to let him go without her.

"I'll take Zach with me. You go back to bed, now, Jennifer, if you don't feel perkier in a while," he insisted.

"Oh, I'm sure it will pass," she told him, making a

face. The fact that she couldn't seem to recover was beginning to alarm her a bit. "I'll just indulge myself with a cup of tea, though, before I start my ironing."

Gil and Zach came home with news that Mary Sue Able would call on her next week, the morning the men left for the hunting trip.

"Mama, guess what? When I'm ten, I can go hunting with Papa and Mr. Able. And guess what? Mr. Able promised me a pup," Zach said, his dark eyes aglow with his news. "Next month, when one of his mama dogs has 'em."

"That's very kind of him, honey. Did you remember to say thank-you?"

"Uh-huh. It's probably gonna have spots like its ma, Mr. Able said. And Papa says he'll help me to train it. I'm gonna name it General, like Homer's dog."

"Won't you get them mixed up, then, when Homer comes to visit with his General and you call to him?"

"Nope."

"Why not?"

"'Cause mine'll know who I am."

Jennifer laughed delightedly at Zachary's logic and ruffled his hair.

"Sounds reasonable," Gil said, sharing her laughter.

Gil was gone for five days on his hunting trip. Jennifer and Zachary both felt lonely for him almost immediately, and it made Jennifer wonder how she'd managed those years of isolation with only Zach and her. But she consoled herself with the knowledge that he would be home soon.

On Wednesday, she took the opportunity to consult with Maude Linderman. Jennifer had never traded confidences with Mrs. Linderman before and felt a little unsettled about it now. But she'd already discovered the doctor wasn't in and expected to be gone for a few days on his country rounds. Jennifer thought she might burst with nervousness if she didn't have someone's advice on her discomfort. And the Lindermans had proved to be staunch friends.

"Mrs. Linderman . . . Maude, may I have a few moments with you in private?" she asked quietly at the conclusion of her morning's trade.

Speculation crossed Maude's face before softness replaced it. "Why, sure 'nuff, Jennifer," Maude said, her extra chins bobbing with affirmation. "Let's go upstairs and have a nice cup of tea. Got some cookies I baked just last night, too."

Maude glanced to see what her husband was doing. "Peder, you keep an eye on young Zachary there for a bit. Jennifer and I will be upstairs."

The older woman led the way up the back stairs to the living quarters above the store, which consisted of a kitchen-parlor and a bedroom. It smelled of bacon and beans and stale tobacco, which caused a sudden roll in Jennifer's stomach. Gingerly, she perched on the edge of a kitchen chair, wondering if Maude had noticed anything amiss.

Calmly, Maude put the kettle on the stove and set out her pink rose china set. After she'd poured boiling water into the teapot, she sat down purposefully across from Jennifer, her fading blue eyes kindly. "Now, my dear, tell me what's troubling you."

"Oh, Maude, I'm so puzzled about something. I really need to hear your common sense wisdom, I . . ." Now that she meant to confide her growing suspicion to Maude, Jennifer was trembling. It frightened her down to her bones to put her vague hopes into words. It was all too impossible. Too impossible. "I think I might be in a family way."

Maude stared at her in surprise and puzzlement. "My dear, how wonderful! But what is worrying you so and why is it baffling? It seems the natural progression of life, to me." Then noting Jennifer's distressed look, she said, "Tell me about your symptoms, my dear. We'll figure this thing out. How has Gil taken the news? Oh, he's as happy as a coon dog, I'm sure."

Jennifer's emotions climbed to the ceiling and slid back to the floor again as Maude asked her rapid-fire questions. She answered the one that concerned her most. "I haven't mentioned the matter to him yet."

"Oh? Why not?"

"It's so unlikely, I'm afraid."

"Childbirth isn't easy, Jennifer, but why unlikely?"

"You don't understand, Maude. Long ago I lost a baby. It was born too soon. The doctor said afterwards that I'd never be able to have any more. But, you see, I'm having all the discomfort and other symptoms of early gestation. I'm not an ignorant young girl, but how can I be pregnant?"

"Could be, Jennifer. Doctors don't know everything, you know," Maude said, pursing her lips in thought.

"Maude, I'm scared to death that I'm only imagining things and I'm so afraid to hope, and I couldn't bear to build Gil's hopes up either if it isn't true. Yet I know what's happening to my body." She swallowed down threatening tears. "What if I can't carry it? I was devastated when I lost the one before."

Maude spoke gently, patting Jennifer's hand. "Yes, yes, I do see. Tell me about it. The time before, I mean."

Jennifer did, leaving out all the horrible details of her

first, failed marriage, and gave only the bare facts of the pregnancy itself and the resulting stillbirth, then finished her recounting. "I was widowed soon after that."

"Oh, you poor dear, you had a tragic time of it, certainly. My, my, my! I can see why you're scared now. And a double loss for you, a baby and a husband. Yes, losing a baby is a dreadful hardship. I lost three before they were three months in my womb. After that . . ." Maude shrugged against her tears.

Jennifer, in turn, laid her hand on Maude's, her heart feeling the same pain. "I'm so sorry. I didn't know."

They were quiet as they silently shared the moment. Then Maude picked up the conversation.

"You were grieving, still, when you arrived in Kansas, weren't you? Peder and I suspected as much. But now, my dear, tell me why you think you are breeding again."

Jennifer explained her symptoms. "I know these things are real, but they're somehow different this time, and after what the doctor said, I've wondered if I've . . ."

"What? Wished it into being?"

Jennifer nodded.

"Well, if wishing could do it, I'd have had a dozen. No, my dear, I would dare to say that you are indeed probably expecting. When are you going to tell Gil?"

Maude appeared calm and matter-of-fact about her accounting of her previous pregnancy and the current symptoms. The impossibility of it slowly dissolved like a pat of melting butter from around Jennifer's heart. Could she really believe it was true? Could she hope for a healthy delivery, a full-term child?

"Not for a while. I just have to be sure, don't you see! I couldn't bear to disappoint him." Or herself. She'd take her hope forward slowly, she decided, and not leap into it until she could be absolutely sure. It frightened her to want it too much; too many good things had happened to her in recent months, her happiness with Gil was too precious. All that might be spoiled. She couldn't risk hoping, then finding it to be untrue.

And she'd been remembering the old nightmare.

"I'll find a way to see the doctor soon, after another monthly pass, you understand."

Maude nodded sagely. "Yes. A third miss would seem to clinch your facts."

Jennifer left the Lindermans' store in a lighter frame of mind. Confiding in Maude had been the right thing to do, she decided. And the truth would be obvious in a few weeks.

"Mama, can we go see Homer?" Zach asked. "I gotta tell him about my pup."

Despite her decision not to allow her hopes to surface, Jennifer couldn't hold them down. Instinctively, she *knew* it was true! Oh, she felt so *blessed!* She smiled and lifted her face to the November sunlight. The air was crisp and fresh, like the new life hiding deep in her womb. Surely nothing would go wrong this time. She wouldn't *let* it!

"All right, honey. A walk uptown will be nice. And I might just take a peek in at Tige's Mercantile. I think I may purchase some flannelette to sew on this winter." She was ready to indulge any whim her son asked at the moment as well as herself. Soon, he might be a big brother and lose his status as the only child.

The two of them strolled up the street, crossing the dirt road, then stepping up again to the wooden sidewalk that passed two saloons, the land office, and a bank on their way to Burns's Livery.

* * *

Watching them through the front window glass of Red's Barber Shop, Robert Quiller congratulated himself for his long-suffering patience. Putting up with this inferior little town's dusty streets and lack of true social graces had caused him a great deal of privation. A great deal, to his thinking. His waiting had been dull and tiresome, but it had been rewarded. This time he got a better glimpse of the woman than he'd had two weeks before.

Yes, it was Patricia. Nearly nine years older but no less enticing. His eyes narrowed. He stepped closer to the window, caring not if she should chance to turn her head his way. He itched to get his hands on her, to face her, to let her know she hadn't eluded him forever.

There was the child he'd heard about, dark eyed and brown skinned, clinging to her hand. A bastard child. He watched them share something amusing, for the child laughed and a glow came over Patricia's face. Her hair reflected the morning light, pale and gleaming against dove-white skin, and she walked as she always had, as though she floated.

Good God, she was more beautiful now than ever she'd been at eighteen!

The bitch!

Robert stepped out of the shop and followed at a discreet distance.

He was flamingly outraged at her audacity—and yet amused. How dare she be more lovely! How dare she flaunt herself with that bastard child!

He'd bet anything she'd slept with some dirty Indian and begot the half-breed herself, never mind what she'd told him about not conceiving again. This gullible town might believe that story she and Prescott put about, but he'd bet there was more to it than that.

But how she'd fooled everyone, he'd like to know! It would be just like her to go and have a bastard, after spurning him and Willard both.

If only he could tell Willard what Patricia had been up to now, when the absolute proof of her character was there for the world to see. He'd told Willard, hadn't he? Both before and after he'd married her. She was a slut!

However, she was *his* slut by all rights, and he would have her yet.

All those years ago, he'd secretly spread the rumors of Patricia's betrayal and even openly confronted Willard about his own affair with the girl. His own affair with her.

He'd lied about how far it had gone, of course.

Beneath the bland face he presented to those to whom he nodded as he passed, his body stirred. He'd possessed Patricia many times in his dreams and thoughts. Of course he'd lied about the actuality, but only because he could see no other way to get her free of his cold cousin.

And eventually, it wouldn't be a fabrication. He reached for his watch. Opening it, he glanced down at the pale curl lying against the face. Soon, it wouldn't be.

He laughed gleefully. Willard had refused to give her up. And wouldn't he be incensed if he could see her today? As a country matron, dressed in cheap calico and those dreadfully heavy boots on her delicate feet.

Alas, Willard was dead and would never know. Too bad. But Willard hadn't loved her, didn't deserve to have her, not the way he did.

Robert slowly licked his lips, his tongue slipping into one corner of his mouth. He tasted the alcohol in the cheap cologne the barber had used on his face. It was awful, but it sharpened his thoughts. He slowly returned the watch to his pocket.

Patricia was his now. Now that he'd found her again, he would claim her. It was only a matter of time until she belonged to him completely. She'd give him what he wanted of her then, and in exchange he would pamper her and dress her once again in finery that would enhance her beauty.

God, how she wasted it. He and she would be so handsome together. They would create beautiful things between them.

Yes. Beautiful things. He'd once wanted her to bear *his* children, he thought in maudlin self-pity. They would've been exquisite creatures. He had certainly offered his all. He remembered she'd almost died trying to give Willard a brat. He was glad it had died. And later, he'd made sure he no longer had to contend with Willard.

That woman had no idea what he had sacrificed for her. She'd rebuffed him most unkindly without ever knowing.

He'd make her pay for all the wasted years and for taking up with that bastard child. And another man.

Ah, yes. Yes, he would make her pay.

Mary Sue Able called. Jennifer guessed her to be about ten years younger than herself and vaguely remembered meeting her once in Osage Springs.

"Please sit down, Mrs. Able," Jennifer invited.

"Yes, ma'am." She was very stiff and formal, and sat gingerly on the edge of the sofa, holding little Frank, Jr., tightly and refusing to allow him to crawl on the floor.

Zachary, having very little experience with babies, was fascinated with the child and hovered close. "I can play with him, Mrs. Able," he beseeched. "I can show him my wooden horse."

Mary Sue's glance at Zachary was one of mixed horror and uncertainty. "I think Frankie should stay with me. He . . . uh . . . gets into things if I let him down."

Jennifer felt her own countenance freeze and wondered how Gil had handled Mary Sue's obvious dislike for their son when he'd taken him to call on Frank. He could have at least warned her, she thought in annoyance.

"Come sit beside me, Zachary," she ordered quietly. "Would you care for a slice of cake, Mrs. Able?"

"Oh, uh, yes, that would be nice."

"Perhaps it would be easier if we sat at the table."

"Yes, ma'am."

Mary Sue shifted the baby to one arm as she sat down at the table. Jennifer sliced a generous portion of cake and placed it in front of the young woman. The baby instantly grabbed a handful of it, his fat little fingers squishing it into goo. Two seconds later, he threw it all over the table.

Zachary giggled. Mary Sue's cheeks flushed.

"Oh, I'm so sorry," Mary Sue nearly wailed. "He's made a mess of it."

"It's all right, really. Babies can move quicker than the eye sometimes."

"Yes, ma'am, they can."

"Look, Mama, he's got it all over his face," Zachary reported gleefully.

"Zach! It isn't polite to laugh at, um . . ."

"But he's so funny. Look, he's laughing!" Zach was clearly delighted with the little urchin.

It *was* funny. Jennifer had trouble keeping a straight face, herself. Little Frankie had smeared cake and icing across one cheek, into one eyebrow, and in his hair. An impish gurgle ended on a shriek.

"Oh, you little dickens." Mary Sue grabbed one little hand as it snatched at more cake. In a twinkling, those baby fingers eluded her grasp and went right into his mouth. "I'm so sorry, ma'am."

"Don't worry, Mary Sue. We can clean him up in no time. And he certainly likes my cake. That's the best of compliments." She reached for a clean cloth from the dry sink and dipped it into the bucket of water.

"You're so kind to say so, Mrs. Prescott. I really am so sorry." Tears of humiliation stood in the young woman's eyes.

Zachary scooped a forefinger against the baby's cheek and placed it into the toddler's mouth. Frankie gave a gap-toothed smile. "Look, Mama, isn't he cute?"

Mary Sue sat very still and let Zachary feed the baby more cake.

Jennifer's heart was touched. The young woman was trying her best to be friends. If Mary Sue hadn't liked Zachary before coming, then it was up to her to change the woman's mind now. Gently, she said, "Oh, Mary Sue. Babies are only babies. It's when they're old enough to know better that poor behavior becomes unacceptable. Now let me tell you about how Zachary once wore his carrots in his ears to the Lindermans' store before I realized it."

"Oh, really?"

"Yes. I was so embarrassed. . . ."

*   *   *

When Gil returned home a few days later and asked how the visit with Mrs. Able had progressed, Jennifer smiled.

"I think Mary Sue and I are going to be friends after all," she told him. "And Zachary has learned a very handy new skill."

"What's that?"

"He's learned to entertain a baby."

And oh, how that skill was going to be needed, she thought happily. Every day she was more sure. She longed to tell Gil, but . . .

Only a few more days to wait.

11

The day after Thanksgiving, the town was all abuzz with festivities, filled with new sodbusting families who'd come from all over to farm the prairies; European immigrants who, while on their way to other parts, had stopped in or near Osage Springs to pass the winter, some to stay permanently; a far-flung rancher or two with lonely wives and children; a few friendly Indians; and a horde of single men looking for company and amusement—hunters, land speculators, businessmen, railroaders, traders, gamblers, and soldiers.

"Reminds me of camp when I first went," Gil spoke unthinkingly as he, Jennifer, and Zach drove into town. He rarely allowed himself to think about anything that had to do with the war. But he put the unpleasant comparison behind him; this was a celebration, and soon the weather would not permit this kind of gathering.

"I don't ever remember the town being so full," Jennifer remarked.

"Somebody's cooking something," Zach said.

"Reckon it's John Perry's Meat Market over there, son. Looks like John has a goodly flame going in his fire pit by the smoke he's making." They drove by, reading the sign in his front window that declared ROASTED SAUSAGE, HAM, PRAIRIE CHICKEN, AND BUFFALOE, READY COOKED TO EAT.

Even though a few businesses were closed for serious trade, Lindermans' and similar establishments were accommodating their normal customers and the swelling crowd by offering extra treats for sale. Maude, Jennifer knew, featured freshly baked pies and cakes today, made especially for the store's trade by Mrs. Dillon.

They passed Jasmine's. Raucous piano music spilled into the street, and with it feminine laughter. Bessie would be busy today, Jennifer mused.

She noticed that one of the saloons had opened at an earlier than usual hour with offers of a free sandwich with the price of a beer. Another promoted a half-price drink on every third purchase. Business, she suspected, would soar.

Miss Alberta's Breadbasket, a brand new German restaurant, found business brisk, by the look of the men standing around its doorway. Its success seemed assured. Though it might have more to do with the two pretty sisters that ran it than the food, Maude had told her last week.

"Saved yard room for old Ben and your rig, Gil, just like I promised," Homer said as Gil parked the buggy in the Burns's Livery lot. "Ain't got no more room left, after this."

Sam Burns had cleared his new barn of animals for the night, and he and Gil had built a low square stone fireplace in the center of the dirt floor for a campfire.

Bales of hay circled it for seating; it would serve as a gathering place for the overflow from the dance and for the children's activities. Sam had also put fresh hay in the loft for temporary sleeping accommodations for out-of-town families who wished to stay until morning.

"Much obliged, Homer," Gil said. "I reckon the outfit will rest easier here in your keeping, what with all the crowding in town. Business must be pretty good, huh?"

"That's so," Sam Burns said, pleased. "Every business in town'll make a profit today and everybody's promised to pay into the Firemen's Fund. Some of us men're rarin' to get organized. Too bad you don't live in town, Gil. Some of us woulda liked to see you be fire chief."

Startled at this information, and with a flash of pride, Gil glanced at Jennifer before answering. "I'm right flattered you and the others would want me, Sam. But it wouldn't do you any good to pick me to lead you when I don't live close enough."

"Know all that. Howsomever, we'd like it if you'd come to the meetings some. You was the one that got everybody goin' in the right direction the day the livery caught fire. You knew what should be done right off. We figure you might have some notions that would help in that kind of action in the future."

"I'd be honored to come." Gil turned to Jennifer, his eyes glowing. He pondered the possibility a moment. He'd do anything to make Jennifer proud of being his wife.

The townsmen thought he could be one of their leaders, did they? It was a far cry from the helter-skelter reputation he'd had as a youngster. Most of it had been deserved, he reflected, but those carefree days were long gone, and now his friends were taking note of his abilities.

Although he couldn't possibly accept a town position, the fact that he'd been considered gave him pleasure—those men thought him responsible and capable. It couldn't hurt his stature in Jennifer's eyes.

"Let me know when, now," he said in parting. Tucking Jennifer's hand through his arm, he started out of the livery yard.

"Are you going to sign up for the turkey shoot?" Homer asked as he hurried to fall into step beside Zach.

"Yep. Heading that way now," Gil replied. First prize was twenty-five dollars and Gil hoped to win it. He had every intention of using the whole of it for their first Christmas together. He wanted the best for Jennifer and Zach.

"Homer, you know what? Papa shot two buffalo. He can shoot anything!" Zach bragged.

"Not anything, son. Only game." Although he knew and respected firearms and was quite satisfied with his shooting skills, Gil had no intentions of ever using them again except when absolutely necessary. He'd hated that godawful war, despised shooting at other men, even his enemies. Hunting for meat had proved to be a chore, too, he'd discovered; his distaste for killing would last him a lifetime, he concluded.

Yet he had a talent with guns and was an excellent shot.

He'd become a practical man as well, and the buffalo he'd brought down last week had added to their winter stores. He'd taken the hides to the tanner, selling him one. The proceeds went to pay for the other one to be made into a warm buggy lap cover for Jennifer.

Yes, today he'd use his good marksmanship to his best advantage if he could. He wasn't fool enough not to go after that top prize.

Amelia Smithers stepped out of the schoolhouse,

her heavy brown shawl hugged tightly around her young thin body. A harassed expression gave way to relief as she spotted Jennifer. "Oh, Mrs. Prescott, I'm so glad you've come early. Would you be so kind as to give me a hand?"

"Surely, Amelia," Jennifer answered. "Gil, you don't mind, do you? I really would prefer to wait where it's warmer. I'll come along to the contest grounds in a little while."

"You don't have to come a'tall if you don't want to, Jennifer. Nothing much for you to do but stand around and wait. Besides, there's a cold breeze coming up. If it starts to gale, it might even cut short the turkey shoot."

He tugged the collar of her navy winter cloak up around her ears. Even though it was old, the garment had the feel of expensive wool. More evidence of Jennifer's former wealth, he noted.

The thought that he couldn't give his wife and son the best of things twisted his insides even as Jennifer's smiling blue eyes reassured him.

"No, I'll be there," she insisted. "And remember, you promised to dance with me this evening."

"I remember," he murmured. He'd been looking forward to it for days. The chance to show off his wife, to hold her in his arms, to dance with her in public—it made him so prideful he thought he might make a right good fool of himself.

Gil left her, taking the boys with him. Jennifer climbed the three steps into the schoolhouse.

"Oh, Teacher, thank goodness you've come. I mean Mrs. Prescott. I must confess, I was on the watch for you. I—I—" The girl burst into tears.

"There, there, Amelia," Jennifer said as she patted the girl's shoulder. "What's amiss?"

"Everything."

"Are those Gallaghar boys giving you problems?"

"Uh-huh. They have no respect for me at all and make fun behind my back. It causes all kinds of disruption among the children. And there's twice as many students as before, and I try to keep order, but it never seems to run as smoothly as when you were teacher, and those little devils never let up. They play havoc with the new children especially, and two of them can't speak English, and—"

"Slow down, Amelia, slow down. Now, what else?"

The young woman took a deep breath. "I don't know what to do about the Schiller children, either. Since their ma died, young George is starting to get mean and sullen, like his pa. Lavinia gets quieter every day and little Molly cries for no reason. George even picked a fight with the Gallaghars last week and then Mrs. Gallaghar complained, and Mrs. Dillon, too."

"It's a pity George didn't take Tommy down a peg or two," Jennifer murmured.

"I—I beg your pardon?" Amelia stared at Jennifer in shock.

"Never mind, my dear. Perhaps it is time for an open meeting with the school board. It seems the time has come to hire a second teacher, or a helper, maybe. And disciplinary action should be taken against anyone who fights."

"But they might fire me," Amelia wailed.

"No, no. Not if I talk to them."

"Would you? Oh, please, yes. I would feel ever so much better if you took my side in all this. They respect you, Mrs. Prescott, far more than me."

"Oh, I don't know about that," Jennifer said, thinking about her own previous run-ins with the Gallaghar family.

"Oh, yes, they do, Mrs. Prescott. You're the finest, best teacher we've ever had. Everyone knows you are."

Jennifer laughed, then looked around her. The schoolhouse had been cleared except for a few chairs at the back of the room. The teacher's desk sat in a corner. Red, white, and blue bunting streamed over it, waiting to be used for decorating the room for the evening's dance. "Do you need help with all this?"

"Yes, I surely do. Red Smithy, the young man whose pa started the newspaper, said he'd come to help if he could, but his pa's been laid up and he's had to do extra chores for the newspaper, you know. Mr. Brown promised, too, but I haven't seen him, either."

"Well, come along. I'll help." Jennifer began to sort out the bunting while Amelia looked for a hammer and tacks. Pretty soon Red showed up, then Andrew Brown. They both were courting Amelia, Jennifer knew, so it wasn't long before she left them to their friendly rivalry and excused herself to go along to the turkey shoot.

She found Zach and Homer on the outskirts of the area that had been laid out for the contest, then encountered Mary Sue and Frank Able among the watching crowd.

"Must be near a hunert men competing," Frank remarked.

"My brothers Merritt and Miles are shooting, too," Mary Sue said.

As the afternoon progressed, the breeze became heavier and gusty, a deciding factor in the marksmanship. Jennifer, Zach, and Homer unabashedly cheered for Gil to win at each round. In the final round, he took second place, which carried the ten-dollar prize.

"Great shooting, Gil," Frank commented, slapping Gil's back as the crowd broke up. "In spite of the wind."

"Done better," Gil replied, shaking his head in disappointment. But the ten dollars would still make a good Christmas, he supposed. He should be practical, he knew, but he had it in mind to buy one of those fancy combs for Jennifer's hair. "Wind had to be reckoned with, that's a fact."

Little Frankie became fretful and Mary Sue said she needed to nurse him, so the Ables and Prescotts parted company with the promise to join up again for the evening schoolhouse dance.

Supper with the Lindermans was pleasant, but quickly over. The women insisted they needed time to primp before the dance. Maude seemed very happy about something, Gil noticed. Jennifer, too. Must be something about the social that brought out their excitement.

Gil rubbed a hand over his jaw. He'd had the foresight to bring his razor. It wouldn't hurt any to shave again for the evening. "C'mon, young'un," he said to Zachary. "Let's you and me get spruced up too."

"We can use the back storeroom," Mr. Linderman offered, nodding. "Here, grab that kettle of hot water. I'll get towels."

A little later Jennifer emerged from the Lindermans' bedroom wearing her blue silk dress. All but one of her smooth curls were piled high at the crown of her head; the loose one enticingly framed an ear before falling to the ivory curve of her neck.

Gil recalled nibbling at that delicate ear only this morning. It had led to a passionate coupling; the memory of it sent shock waves of wanting through him now. He could never get enough of her, it seemed. She could send him into a tizzy by a look or a smile—it sure didn't take much.

As he allowed his gaze to roam over her, he saw an answering communication in his wife's eyes. They sparkled like a mountain lake in winter sunlight, Gil thought, cool and sharp and with unexplored depths. Yet he knew those depths belied the cool exterior.

It made his heart turn over yet again. How in the world had he won her? How had he found the audacity, the pure guts, even to ask her to be his?

"Mama, you look awful pretty," Zach spoke with total admiration. "Are you gonna get married again?"

"No, that one time is for always, honey. I just wanted to wear my best dress to the dance."

Gil bowed with gallantry, then offered his arm. "I see you're ready, Mrs. Prescott."

"Indeed, Mr. Prescott. I note that you are, too."

Dozens of lanterns lit the street and buildings as they strolled toward their destination. Strains of a piano and fiddle reached them as they approached the overflowing schoolhouse and livery barn.

They left Zachary with Homer at the livery. A dozen children already sat around the center campfire listening to old Mrs. Davis telling ghost tales.

"Zach'll be all right with me, I'll keep an eye on 'im," Homer assured. "I'll make sure he gets some eats, too."

Gil shouldered past the couples and scores of single men that clogged the school's one room and doorway so that Jennifer could squeeze through; they spoke to friends and acquaintances as they went.

A piano and player loaned by one of the saloons had been placed in the near corner and gave out a rousing waltz, accompanied by a fiddler.

"Come along, Maude, I'll give you a dance first before I find someplace to sit down," Peder said as the four of them moved along the outer wall. "My feet hurt."

"And that's the last dance I'll get from him, too, you wait and see," Maude complained to Jennifer.

"But it won't be your only one by the looks of all these men hereabouts. You ain't gonna sit out much, I betcha."

Maude giggled like a young girl.

To Jennifer's surprise, Gil was an accomplished dancer. Without hesitation, he led her into the waltz with a flourish, all the while smiling into her eyes. They finished their first set and then another before he took her outside to get some air.

A bonfire blazed in the school's backyard, silhouetting the men who sat on logs or stood around it. A bottle passed from one to another, catching the gleam of firelight as it was tilted to greedy mouths. Beyond was the dark prairie.

"Hey, there, Gil," one of them called.

"Howdy, Merritt."

"Come have a drink, fella."

"Not tonight," Gil answered. "Much obliged anyway."

"It's Gil Prescott, is it?" said a voice Jennifer didn't recognize. "C'mon over here an' have a drink, you son of a gun. Haven't seen you since before the war when we went huntin' fer some fun an' you was visitin' that little Injun gal reg'lar."

"That was a long time ago, Jim."

"Yeah, but not so long as to fergit how hot you was fer some—"

Someone gave a "shush" and a loud guffaw, effectively covering the remainder of the man's words. Beside her, Jennifer felt Gil's hand on her elbow stiffen as he turned her away from the men. "We'd better go, Jennifer."

"Wal, whut's the matter? Prescott was—"

"Hush up, Reilly," someone said on a nervous laugh. "Mind your tongue. Gil's got 'is wife with 'im."

"His wife? So whut? Can't a man get a drink without a henpeckin' woman botherin' him?" Reilly belligerently called again. "C'mon, Gil. Have a drink."

Jennifer glanced over her shoulder. Several men were on their feet.

"Shut your mouth, you dog-eared coyote," said Merritt on a roar, while firelight chased dark shadows across his bearded cheeks. "Don't you know who he married? That there teacher woman. She's a lady."

"You're joshin' me." Awe filled Reilly's accusation as he sank back down to his log.

"Nope, not joshin'. Damned if he didn't," Merritt answered, a mixture of puzzlement and respect in his voice.

Gil guided Jennifer toward the street. "I'm real sorry, Jennifer. Some of my old friends shame me, now. Hell, some of the things I did shame me. But you've already heard I was kind of a wild dog in the old days."

Even in the dim light, his discomfort at what had been said was evident.

"It's all right, Gil. What's past is past," Jennifer replied with finality, knowing her own wouldn't bear scrutinizing.

She didn't have time to answer anything more because Maude and Mary Sue called to them from the door.

"There you two are," said Mary Sue, waving at them. "Hurry up, Jennifer. The dance bidding is about to start."

"Dance bidding? What are you talking about?" Jennifer asked.

Mary Sue excitedly explained.

Since there were many more men in attendance than women, Mrs. Dillon and Mrs. Portland had devised a plan to add to the town coffers by selling dances with the women to the highest male bidders. The idea had caught fire and the room was clearing to permit Mr. Tige to start the bidding. Most of the women had agreed to it, even the married ones.

"Oh, I don't know. . . . " Jennifer began.

"It's only dancing, and no worse than auctioning off supper baskets at a church social," Mrs. Portland defended her suggestion. "And it's for a good cause. Think of the all that can be done for the fire department. Why, we might even be able to buy a fire wagon."

"Gil?" Jennifer turned to her husband.

"I—" He wanted to object and defensively shifted his feet. By thunder, he didn't like the idea a'tall. Jennifer would be bound to dance with whomever bid for her and he didn't cotton to the idea of watching just any other man putting his hands on his wife, even in a dance. But as he glanced into the faces observing him he felt like a skunk to protest. "I reckon . . . "

"What do you think, Maude?" Jennifer turned to the older woman. "Do you think it is appropriate?"

"I suppose it's all right this once. But mind you, Dora," Maude spoke strongly to Mrs. Portland, "this kind of thing should not become a habit."

"Oh, c'mon, Jennifer, it'll be fun," Mary Sue said eagerly, grabbing Jennifer's hand. "Let's line up with the other women."

"Where's Frank?" Gil asked Mary Sue.

"Oh, he's outside with that drinking bunch of rats," Mary Sue tossed over her shoulder with a sniff. "He won't dance with me because he has only one arm, he says. It'll serve him right if I have a good time without him."

Word about the auction had gotten around, for many of the single men standing outside began to jam into the schoolhouse. There was scarcely ten feet left clear for the dance floor.

Squeezed between Mary Sue and old Mrs. Davis, Jennifer stood with the other ladies who had consented to give three dances each to the auction. Around her, the room rippled with excited voices. The piano player gave an introductory chord.

Jennifer's nerves tightened. How had she allowed herself to do this?

Across the room, Gil leaned against the wall with the men. His hands were shoved into his pockets and his mouth looked stiff. He didn't appear any happier than she felt, Jennifer decided.

Mr. Tige stepped up on a chair. The room grew quieter.

"Now remember your manners, men. This ain't no dance hall or saloon. These ladies are respectable and they're giving out these dances to help out the town. Now." Mr. Tige began the bidding with the youngest girl to participate, a dark-eyed fifteen-year-old from one of the immigrant families. "Who'll bid two bits to dance with this lovely flower? How about a half-dollar?"

Several young men zealously responded, and the winner proudly escorted the shy young thing to the bottom of the room to await the first dance. Mr. Tige asked another young woman to step forward.

The bidding gained momentum among friendly, avid, or sometimes fierce rivalry as mostly the single men but even the married ones vied for the chance to dance with a woman. Every woman seemed popular. The zestful crowd began to call out challenges and nudged each other into higher bids.

"Now here's Mother Davis," said Mr. Tige. "She may be, uh, long in winters, fellas, but she can still dance right spry and give you a sweet smile that'll remind you of your own grandma."

Old Mrs. Davis gave a gap-toothed smile to prove Mr. Tige right, then batted her eyelashes at the handsome young escort that had won her bid.

"And next is Mrs. Mary Sue Able. She's a real dancin' sprite. What'll you galoots bid for a dance with Mrs. Able?"

No immediate answer came forth. Beside her, Jennifer saw Mary Sue blush and drop her gaze. Up until now the bidding had been brisk.

Surprised, Mr. Tige called, "C'mon, fellas. You all know her husband Frank."

"That's right, we do. That's why I ain't biddin'," called a young man in gray trousers.

"Aw, Leroy, that ain't no way to be," Mr. Tige replied. "We're havin' a party, here, and we ain't gonna allow no trouble about what's past."

"Naw, that ain't it, Mr. Tige. It's just that Mary Sue shore is pretty and Frank shore is powerful jealous. One-armed or not, I wouldn't come up against 'im."

The laughter that followed brightened Mary Sue's face. Jennifer chuckled as well.

"That's right good thinkin', Leroy," Frank said as he stepped forward from the crowd. "'Cause I'm claimin' all Mary Sue's dances myself."

The crowed roared and applauded while Frank swept his beaming wife to the other side of the room.

Jennifer was next. Listening to Mr. Tige introduce her as the former Mrs. Hastings, the town's leading matron of education, she suddenly wanted to smooth her hair or tug at her sleeves. Yet she remained composed and smiled across the room at Gil as Mr. Tige ended with "Now she's Mrs. Gil Prescott, our hero that day of the livery barn fire. All right, men, what're we bid?"

Gil stepped forward, his back straight and his chin

high. A proud smile hovered at the corner of his mouth as he raised his hand to give his bid.

From the opposite corner of the room, another bid superseded Gil's. A dapper, gray-haired stranger stepped forward. "I'll bid fifty dollars in gold currency for one dance with Mrs. Prescott."

Jennifer scarcely noticed the "ooh's" and "did you hear that's" as unadulterated shock hit her.

That voice! Gravelly, seductive, yet urbane.

It couldn't be. She must be mistaken.

She turned her head and she saw him.

Her heart jerked painfully hard against her chest; her eyes wouldn't focus. It felt as though the roof had caved in on her. She blinked rapidly against the reality.

Then the handsome, destructive face from another life came into sharp relief, a satisfied, victorious smile tipping his over-red mouth.

Oh, dear God, no.

But it was. *It was Robert!*

"Fifty dollars? You hear that folks? This gentleman is a real town booster."

Mr. Tige's pleased, booming voice seemed to come from a distance. Nearby, Amelia asked in alarm, "What's the matter, Teacher? Are you ill?"

There was no air!

"Fifty . . . anyone bid more than fifty?"

She couldn't breathe.

From across the room, Gil called. At least she saw his mouth move. Something . . . something seemed urgent, but . . .

Slowly, so very slowly, she crumpled.

12

Gil sprinted across the room toward Jennifer even as she fell.

"Get away! Give her some air," he commanded, shoving people aside ruthlessly as he made his way to his wife's side.

Amelia, thank God, had cushioned her fall. Looking stunned, the girl held fast to Jennifer's waist while Jennifer's head hung backward over her arm.

His wife looked as white as milk without cream, Gil was quick to note, making her dark blond lashes stand out like spikes against her soft skin. He knelt swiftly, scooping her out of Amelia's arms and into his own.

"Move back!" he ordered. Gil's glance skipped from face to face among the people who circled them. "Move back, I said. Give her some air."

What had happened? He'd caught a glimpse of desperation in her face before she fainted. Had someone hurt her? Carefully, he smoothed his hand along Jennifer's neck and shoulders. It seemed she had only fainted.

Where was Maude Linderman? She'd know what to do. "Can someone bring a cup of water?" he asked.

"Oh, Mr. Prescott." Amelia began to cry, patting one of Jennifer's hands. "I don't know what happened. She just didn't look right, and the next minute she just—just . . ."

"Hush, girl," said Mr. Tige. "I reckon she's only fainted."

Maude hurriedly pushed her way through the crowd. "Someone told me Jennifer—? Oh, dear, oh, my." Maude knelt by Jennifer's head and none too gently rubbed her cheek.

Jennifer moaned softly, then opened her eyes. She stared at Gil, disoriented. Then she remembered.

How foolish of her. She'd fainted only once before in her entire life: the night she'd found Willard's poor body. Her anxious gaze collided with Gil's. Had something dreadful happened?

"Jennifer, sweetheart?"

Gil's uncertain tone sharpened her attention. "Gil."

"You fainted, honey."

Yes, but why? Then she knew. The memory of the face she'd seen only seconds before she lost consciousness flooded back into her mind. Her enemy had found her. Robert Quiller.

While her blood raced with alarm Jennifer suddenly shoved herself to a sitting position, darting glances about her as furtively as she dared. Where was he? Where?

She was dizzy again and put her hand to her head.

"Now, now, Jennifer, take it easy," Maude said close to her ear. "Don't make any sudden moves."

Eyes stared at her. Old, young, men's, women's, all shapes, all colors. Curiously staring.

None were Robert's. Had she imagined seeing him? Hearing that insidious voice?

But Gil was there, only inches from her. His blue-gray gaze was compassionate, worried. She couldn't let him worry.

"Teacher," he whispered uncertainly, holding her closer. Did he sense that she'd had a blinding, earth-shaking shock?

"I'm all right, Gil. It was only . . . only that I became much too warm. I—I forgot to tell you. I don't do well in overcrowded rooms."

"It is a bit hot in here with all these people," Maude said, certain she knew what had caused Jennifer's faint but wanting to divert anyone's suspicions until her friend was ready to make her own announcement. "Don't you think so, too, Mary Sue?" Maude caught Mary Sue's gaze.

"Oh, yes. Yes, I was saying that very thing to Frank just a moment ago."

Someone shoved a tin cup of water under Gil's nose and he took it, then placed it to Jennifer's lips. "Sip some water, Jennifer honey. It'll help."

"Yes, Jennifer," Maude insisted.

She did so without protest. The cool water slid down her throat with difficulty, but it did help. "Thank you," she murmured. "I'm better now. I'll get up."

"No. I'll carry you." Gil lifted her easily, whispering in her ear to hold on tight and he'd have her out of there in three shakes of a lamb's tail, as he strode through the crowd toward the door. Maude accompanied them.

"Everything's all right now, folks. Mrs. Prescott only fainted from too much heat," Mr. Tige said to the assembly. "We'll go on with the dance now and finish the bidding later."

They were almost to their destination when someone said, "Too bad about losing that fifty dollars, though."

"Yes, it would be a shame for the town to lose out," said the cultured voice Jennifer remembered so well. "Perhaps we can come to another . . . agreement."

On pretense that she still felt faint, Jennifer pressed against Gil's shoulder, her eyes closed. Oh, please, please, God, let this be a nightmare, she silently begged. Let me awake and find this to be only my imagination.

Gil stopped as the well-dressed stranger who had bid for a dance with Jennifer stepped into his path. He'd never seen the easterner before, although he thought the man had taken an undue fancy to his wife. He clamped his teeth together hard as jealousy raged though his veins. He didn't understand it, but he didn't cotton to the fella a'tall.

"Pardon me, mister. You're in our way."

"Forgive me, Mr. Prescott. It is only that I want to make this evening's effort a true success. For the town, you might say." Robert's voice was smoothly considerate. "I shall gladly pay the fifty dollars as a personal contribution toward the Firemen's Fund if"—his tone was familiarly circumspect—"I may be permitted to reintroduce myself to the lovely lady who has become Mrs. Prescott."

Jennifer listened to it with growing panic.

It was no use. She couldn't hide. Slowly, she raised her lashes and stared into the face that had caused her downfall so many years previously. Her stomach roiled.

"Robert. How—how nice to see you again." She hoped she wouldn't be sick until they got outside.

"Who are you, sir?" Gil asked, none too patiently.

The man gave an exaggerated bow. "Robert Quiller, at your service. I do hope, my dear Mrs. Prescott, you will not bear a grudge against an old friend for having startled you?"

His smile appeared innocent. Only she would guess it was not. Underneath it, he was her enemy; Robert was the one true horrible mistake of her youth.

He had charmed and delighted her once. She'd been so young and naive, so gullible, that now she thought herself insane for not understanding what his intentions were before it was too late.

How had she let him do it? She blamed herself bitterly. Her youth had been no excuse!

Robert had smilingly led her down a garden path of missteps and wrong turns, deceiving her with inviting temptations into which she blithely stepped. She had barely avoided the liaison with him that he'd planned with care. Only at the last second did she recognize the trap and valiantly fight his rape, after which Robert, in his rage at being rebuffed, brought her to shame and ruin before she recognized the depth of his cupidity. And her own stupidity.

She had paid dearly for that stupidity, paid the price with her first marriage. She hadn't loved Willard, she was honest enough to admit, but she had grieved deeply over their ruined lives. Because Willard had believed more than the truth, which was shameful enough; she had allowed Robert liberties no married woman should. He'd also bought Robert's lies that they were lovers. So had Aunt Agnes and all the rest of Philadelphia.

Her society reputation was left in shreds. While it had shamed her, she hadn't felt it mattered as long as she could start again with Willard. She'd begged Willard to believe in her remorse over what she *had* done and her innocence in what Robert had claimed she had done.

Willard had believed his cousin Robert.

All of it, the heartache, lies, and endless quarrels and turmoil had made her lose the child. Willard had publicly divorced her, giving her only a small settlement.

Aunt Agnes had died of a broken heart by way of a heart attack.

Willard had died by his own hand.

The authorities had been called in, of course, questioning her part in his death; all of the previous scandal had been rehashed and renewed. Her name had eventually been cleared of Willard's death, but the resulting whispers and innuendos were monstrous. To Philadelphia she would always be an adulterous, immoral woman. She had been left alone and friendless.

There had been nothing left for Jennifer then in the huge mansion she once thought she'd wanted. She gladly turned her back on it and the fortune that went with it. Anyway, all of it had gone to Robert, Willard's cousin. Her enemy. Many times she had wondered if the fortune had been what he had been after all along.

Arranging for her small settlement to be sent through a lawyer, she'd fled the East, fled Robert, with his repulsive, demanding hands and lips, and his insistence that she was his.

She had wandered through Europe for six months before returning to America, eventually drifting to the middle states before deciding to settle in this small town. Teaching school had been useful; Osage Springs needed her, the children needed her, it was respectable. Using a different name to start fresh seemed natural, so she did. She had left her first name, Patricia, behind and used her middle name along with her mother's maiden name—hence Jennifer Hastings.

And here in this little town as Jennifer Hastings she'd found hope and life again, and for the first time, love.

Until now.

She stared at her relentless pursuer. Robert.

Would he ruin her life again? Would he tell Gil, who worshiped her, the ugly, sordid way she'd almost giddily given away everything? Everything that was precious?

Would he tell Gil, who had married her believing her pure of heart and soul, and these kind people, the Lindermans and Ables, the Dillons and Tiges, who respected her wholeheartedly, and Amelia and Homer, whom she'd fondly taught and who looked up to her? Would he ruin all that?

Would she lose little Zachary, the child born to her spirit and soul if not to her body?

Would Gil, the man to whom she'd given her heart, turn on her the way Willard had? Would Gil want her still after he heard Robert's accounting of their entanglement?

Jennifer felt immeasurably tired. But Robert stood squarely in front of them. He expected her to answer him. His stare relentless, it was the remembered slight flare of his nostrils that gave her the complete understanding of his demands. She had better play his game, his way.

With every fiber of her being, Jennifer drew her scattered wits together to answer civilly. Coolly. With deadly calm.

"No, of course not, Robert. How are you after all these years? Actually, you didn't startle me at all. I foolishly ate something at supper that I shouldn't have, and then this crowding, you see."

"Yes. I seem to remember that you did not like to be crowded. So sorry, my dear." Robert turned his gaze at last to Gil, lightening his tone. "Let me introduce myself, Mr. Prescott. I am Robert Quiller, an old friend of"—he hesitated only a second—"Jennifer's late husband. We were much of the same company."

"Uh-huh," Gil said, then gave a curt nod of his outthrust chin. "We'll be going now, mister. You can pick another lady to spend your money on."

Gil shouldered past Robert rudely, ignoring the affronted expression that the other man quickly covered.

The man's familiarity bothered Gil more than a mite. He reckoned he couldn't hold a grudge over Jennifer's past acquaintances, but he didn't have to tolerate them now if he didn't want to. And he damned well didn't like this one.

"Put me down, now, Gil," Jennifer said once they'd reached the road. "I am well enough to walk."

Behind them, the music started again and those that were hanging about returned to their own interests. Gil set her feet down on the dirt road but kept an arm tightly around her shoulders. She was grateful for his support in spite of what she'd said.

"Come along to our place," Maude said to Gil, "and we'll put her to bed."

"Reckon that'd be a good notion," Gil answered. "'Til we find out if it was only the heat and mob in there that made her faint."

"No!" Jennifer swallowed, then softened her response. "Um, no, thank you, Maude, you are most kind to offer it but I think we should go home." At the moment she wanted nothing more than to be in her own snug little house, to be safely tucked in their bed with Gil's arms wrapped around her and knowing Zachary was fast asleep in the attic room above them. "It's only half an hour's drive and actually, I feel much better."

"Are you sure, Jennifer? At least come back and let me make you some tea. In your condition, that might be—"

"Condition?" Gil's puzzlement was obvious.

"Oh, dear, there goes my tongue," Maude said, clapping a hand over her mouth.

"Gil, please. Let's get Zachary and go home."

He narrowed his eyes. "What condition?"

Even though she'd been too heated a few minutes before, now Jennifer shivered with cold. And mixed emotions.

She still hadn't consulted the doctor—she'd been too afraid he'd tell her it was all false expectations. She wasn't prepared to tell Gil yet of her hope, her suspicions. Now she must.

"Gil, I do have something to tell you, but can we discuss this later?"

Feeling her shiver in the frigid air, Gil remembered their coats were back in the schoolhouse. "Damn, Teacher, you're freezing. Maude, you stay with her and I'll get our gear."

But Peder came out with the outer wear over his arm as Gil reached the steps. Hurriedly, he helped Jennifer into her coat, then shrugged into his own. "Let's go, honey. To Maude and Peder's. When I'm sure you're okay, then we'll go on home."

"I'll get your team hitched and bring Zach on up," Peder offered. "Then if you decide to spend the night in town you can put the horses in our barn out back of the store."

"Much obliged, Peder," Gil said.

Jennifer gave in graciously. She walked the two blocks within the comforting circle of Gil's arm, and with Maude on the other side, she felt safe. Or at least less threatened.

But for how long? Robert had once delighted in emotionally torturing her and had even wallowed in his power to blackmail her. After observing the flash of triumph he'd given her tonight, she doubted if he had changed much.

Then again, why would Robert wish to do her harm, now? She had nothing he might want, nothing to give him. What would he gain by pestering her? And she didn't have to be friends with him any longer—she no longer traveled in his and Willard's elite circle of friends. She could ignore Robert completely, she mused. Surely after a while, he would be bored with what he considered "plebian company" and move on to wherever he was going.

Jennifer's spirits began to lift. If she just kept her wits about her and played it out. . . .

Maude went ahead of them to light a lamp, then hurried to stir up the stove and put water in her kettle. Gil eased Jennifer into the overstuffed chair by the front window, then lit another lamp on the table beside her. He pulled a quilt from the corner sofa and tucked it around her knees.

Jennifer didn't look quite as pale as she had, he noticed with satisfaction. He sank onto the edge of the sofa, his knees apart, letting his hands dangle. He'd been scared by her faint, he didn't mind admitting. He pulled in a deep lungful of air as relief washed over him.

Now he wanted to know what had really stumped her.

Maybe she really had fainted only from too much bustle and heat. Maybe she hadn't liked that auction bid; he remembered she'd mildly objected. Mayhap she'd even been frightened by it. But he thought it unlike her, if that was it. A woman who took charge of most situations as naturally as a battlefield general, however gently, was unlikely to let herself be overwhelmed by anything.

Hadn't she taken on an unknown half-breed newborn, a situation that flew in the face of custom? And with no hope of compensation, either. Hadn't she then moved with the boy out to an isolated farm where, for almost fifteen months, she'd existed with little help and few friends? Out where there were no town lights at night, when the one thing *he knew* she was afraid of—the dark—would be at least an overwhelming half of her existence?

Jennifer had done all that, tackled it all. His admiration for his wife swelled to boundless edges as he contemplated it. But however quiet he'd been until now, he still wanted answers for her upset.

Jennifer sensed Gil's unrest. He had been very tender with her, very solicitous, but very curious as well.

Maude brought a cup of tea and placed it in Jennifer's hands, insisting she sip it while it was hot. After she did, Maude asked, "Feeling better, my dear?"

"Yes. Yes, I am. Though I'm sorry to put you to so much trouble, Maude."

"Oh, poo, what trouble? Whatever I can do, I am glad for it." She gave Jennifer a meaningful glance, nodded toward Gil, then marched herself back to her kitchen.

Jennifer knew Maude could hear everything from the kitchen side of the room, but she still appreciated her attempt at giving Gil and her some privacy.

Jennifer set her cup and saucer on the nearby table then shrugged out of her coat. "Gil, darling." She leaned forward and took his hand. "There is something to tell you, but I don't want you to hope too hard."

His heart began to pound. Jennifer had never called him darling. Something was wrong. But had she said *hope?*

"Just tell me what it is, Teacher. I can handle anything if you're all right."

"Oh, I'm all right in the, ah, natural order of things. It's only that I'm . . . that we're . . . I know what I told you before, and Gil, that eastern doctor was so sure that I couldn't, wouldn't conceive again, but now—"

He stared at her dumbfounded for all of thirty seconds. Then he jumped straight up while his words shot from his mouth like a cannonball. "Oh, Lord A'mighty, are you sure? Is that why you fainted? Course it is, and I'm a fool. A lop-eared brainless jackrabbit is what I am. All the signs were there for me to read and I plumb missed 'em, like a wet-behind-the-ears shavetail."

As suddenly as he'd jumped to his feet, he dropped to his knees in front of her. He took her hands and laid her palms against his cheeks, needing to feel her skin, her warmth, to be a part of her while he made a desperate plea. "Oh, God, Jennifer, I was afraid somethin' bad was happening."

She refused to believe anything bad *would* happen, Jennifer thought fiercely. She wouldn't let it. Too many years of unhappiness and pain had been washed away these last few months. For both of them. And she was going to hold on to their happiness, for all three of them—no, now it would be four of them.

"I don't think so, my darling Gil. Unless your statement of wanting more children was untrue?"

"How can you say that? You know I want 'em. When? When will it be born?"

"Well, I haven't consulted Dr. Rosenberg yet, but . . ." Her eyes twinkled while her mouth pressed together, trying to repress a giggle. It escaped anyway. "In late spring."

All at once Jennifer looked about eighteen, Gil thought. He began to relax and grinned back. Sometimes, like now, he saw a very young Jennifer sparkling through her normally sedate demeanor, and it sent a shaft of pure joy through him. He knew why she giggled. Late spring, hmm? One of their first couplings had done it.

Was it that once in the barn? Or one of those first times on the parlor rug? Or the night he'd worshipfully kissed her all over, making her cry with passion? Or one of their tender early morning lovings when she felt sleep-soft and smelled like sweet woman and rose water?

He'd been as randy and ready each time as a young colt stud in a brand new harem, but she'd never turned him down and welcomed him with equal desires. By thunder, he hadn't stopped wanting her for a second either.

He'd need to take more care with her for the next few months though.

Zach came thundering up the stairs followed by Peder and Homer. Still on his haunches, Gil swiveled to greet his son, but he retained his hold on Jennifer's hand.

"Mama! Mama, you know what? I got a prize. It's a puppet."

"That's wonderful, honey. Where is it?"

"See?" Zach brought his hand from behind his back to reveal a brown sock puppet. He shook it, making its ears flop, and barked. "I'm gonna show it to General."

"What a nice prize," Jennifer responded, then glanced at Maude. The toy looked like her handiwork.

"But it needs spots on it so it can be like General. Can you sew some on, Mama?"

"I suppose we can," she said, smiling. "I'm glad you had a good time at the children's barn party."

"We had a right fine time, Teacher," Homer added. "Specially when that eastern dandy showed up with sarsaparilla and candy fer all."

"Who was it?" Gil asked warily. He didn't know anyone around here with easy money enough to buy treats for fifty kids at one time.

"That was that there Quiller fella," Peder said. "He come into our place and bought and paid for it days ago. Said he wanted to do his part in makin' the town grow."

Gil felt Jennifer stiffen. "Why? What is he doing in town?" she asked.

"Dunno," Peder answered. "Same as all the new people settlin' round here, I reckon. Makin' a livin'. Rumor has it he's with the railroad somehow."

Jennifer seriously doubted that Robert Quiller was connected with the railroad. He had no need nor had he shown much inclination in the past to involve himself in business. In fact, she remembered he considered business rather sordid.

But he wasn't above using anything or anybody to gain his own ends. What were they now?

What had brought him to this town at this time?

What did he want of her?

13

Jennifer left a note with Maude for Dr. Rosenberg, telling him she would be in the following week for a consultation. Yet she put her visit off once again when it lightly snowed; it was a convenient excuse to stay home. She wanted to allow some time to pass before the possibility of facing Robert again.

She'd heard nothing more about him from the gossip that Gil brought home from Osage Springs and she prayed he had left. But she didn't know where he was or what he was doing, and her imagination dreamed up all sorts of doubts and fears in connection with Robert.

Scolding herself didn't always help. Sometimes the old devastation weighed like a stone on her heart.

But as the days passed, her nerves settled down; whatever Robert was doing, his actions were beyond her control, she decided, and her daily routine was too full for worrying.

Mr. Jones and his sons delivered two more loads of the wood that Jennifer had paid for the summer before.

Gil spent a couple of days stacking it, and finally admitted to Jennifer that it was good hard wood. "It'll give us a nice warm winter, Teacher."

Gil and Zachary went to collect the new pup from the Able farm. Zach was in total delight with the small brown ball of fuzz, even though it didn't have spots as he'd hoped, taking it everywhere with him. But then, Jennifer tripped over the dog as General raced around the kitchen on the first morning.

"Now, Zach," said Gil, drawing the boy to him, "this is your dog and your responsibility, you understand?"

"Uh-huh."

"That means you're the one who sees to his feeding and you're the one to take it out when it needs to go."

Behind him, Jennifer pursed her lips. Did Gil really think Zachary would always remember to take care of the dog?

"Okay," said Zach.

"And you have to teach General his manners. He can't run under your mama's feet like that. It'll make her trip."

"Okay, Papa," Zach nodded vigorously. A minute later, he scrambled under the table in chase while the puppy wagged his tail and dashed away. "Here, General, here, boy. You be good, you hear? Or I won't tell you a story."

Gil gave Jennifer a triumphant laugh.

In the second week of December, old Ben died. When Gil went out to do morning chores, he found the horse's body in the corral, already stiff and cold.

"Reckon it was bound to happen sometime soon, the horse was so old," Gil remarked at breakfast. "I'll have to bury the carcass under some stones until spring."

"What's a carcass?" Zach asked as he climbed into his chair for breakfast.

Jennifer turned from where she stirred eggs at the stove and glanced at Gil. Zachary was so very young to understand death. "Gil," she said, shaking her head.

"Can't coddle the boy all his life, Teacher," Gil insisted. "Zach will know old Ben's gone and he's better off knowing the facts of life."

"Where did old Ben go?" Zach asked.

"He died, son."

Zach had seen a dead rabbit, he'd seen kitty with a dead mouse, and he'd seen Bessie kill a chicken. He'd listened to Papa and Mr. Able talk about killing buffalo. They had made it sound exciting, but . . . "What exactly is died?" he asked, earnestly staring into his father's face.

"Well, I reckon . . . you see, son . . . um . . . Ben's body was just too tired to do any more work. So he died."

"But what is it?"

"Well, you know . . . your first mama is in heaven."

"Uh-huh."

"She died, son."

"Oh." Zach turned to Jennifer. "If Ben is going to heaven, why does he have to have rocks piled up on him?"

Jennifer flashed a quick I-told-you-so look at Gil, then sat down in her chair with an exasperated fluff. Why couldn't men learn not everything was as easily explained as black being black and white being white to a four-year-old. "Zach, honey, do you remember seeing all those caterpillars last spring?"

"Uh-huh."

"I told you about how the caterpillars would make a cocoon and hide there for a while, and then come out again as a butterfly."

Zachary nodded.

"Do you remember when we saw bunches and bunches of butterflies in the summer? Well, those beautiful butterflies were the very same caterpillars that had made cocoons. They just left off being worms and decided to be butterflies, you see. Now old Ben is leaving his body behind and he . . . um . . . he . . . "

Jennifer caught Gil's mirthful stare. How could he make light of her serious explanation? She tried to kick him under the table but he was too far away; her toe made a glancing contact with General instead, which sent the pup scurrying from beneath their feet.

Gil laughed outright.

Jennifer glared at her husband.

"Here, General," Zachary called, and ran after him.

"I'm sorry, Zach," Jennifer said, raising a brow along with her chin at Gil. She felt foolish for having let her irritation at Gil's teasing get the better of her, but she wasn't about to cause an upset with Zach. "I bumped the dog."

Zach grabbed General and brought him back to the table, still insisting, "But what about Ben?"

Jennifer gave a long sigh.

"Okay, okay, Teacher," Gil said, mock apology in his voice. Giving Jennifer a nod, he took up the explanation. "Well, Zach, old Ben's gone on to a different place and we need to pile stones on his old body so he won't have to worry with it anymore."

"But he's too big to be a butterfly," Zach observed. "And we still need him to be a horse."

Gil nearly choked on his swallowed laughter, while Jennifer bit on her mouth to control her own.

"That's true, but—" Gil stood up, signaling it was

time to get on with the day's work. "It's time old Ben rested, son. And I need to go and build his cocoon."

He bent to ruffle the boy's hair, changing the subject. "'Sides, we're getting some new horses out here later this week from Sam and Homer, and we get to keep a couple of 'em permanent. I reckon you can pick one for your very own to ride."

"Really? What kind of horse? A big one or a little one? A papa horse or a mama horse, like Sally? Mama horses are different than papa horses, ain't they, Papa."

Gil looked at Jennifer with a "help me" expression before his mirth took over. This child asked more questions than a schoolbook, and went in more directions than a horsefly. It beat him all to pieces with the way Jennifer answered them all.

Hiding his laughter again became too much and he let it show as he stared at her from under his lashes. "Don't say ain't, Zach, you know your mama don't like it."

"That's right, Zachary," Jennifer said firmly, trying hard not to let Gil's charm affect her annoyance with him. But as usual, his blue-gray gaze held her captive and set her knees to tingling. She turned her back so he couldn't see her mellow reaction. She saw no reason to let him think he could get away with everything—even though he did.

"I think it best if you help me gather eggs this morning," she told the boy. "The hens aren't laying as many now, and I want to make sure I find every single one. You know some hiding places the hens use that I don't."

"Okay. But can General and I see old Ben's cocoon later?"

"Sure, son," Gil answered as he went out the door, his grin still hovering. "Later."

Toward the end of the week, Gil insisted Jennifer see the doctor.

"But I feel fine, Gil, except for being a bit tired now and then. And I don't need to see the doctor just yet. I'm sure now."

"I don't want to take any chances on anything being wrong, Jennifer. Besides, Maude's been asking about you. She'll be thinking I'm keeping you prisoner out here."

Gil was right, Jennifer mused. She had suspended her usual routine. If she didn't make an appearance in town again soon, Maude would grow suspicious of why she was staying away. So would Gil.

"C'mon, Mama. You won't be crowded in the buggy anymore 'cause Homer said I could ride my new horse home. I'm gonna name him Sergeant."

"What if your new horse already has a name?" she asked to stall her answer about town.

"He'll still be Sergeant."

"Jennifer." Gil gave her a no-nonsense stare.

"Well, I suppose I should see the doctor, and I do have business with Maude."

"I'll hitch up the buggy."

The weather was cold, with dark, heavy clouds on the horizon. "Looks like snow," Jennifer observed as soon as they were on their way.

"It does, at that," Gil replied. "But we'll be home long before it hits."

In town, Jennifer listened to all of Maude's usual gossip as she delivered her goods, hoping to hear about Robert's whereabouts or anything at all that might tell her about him. But his name didn't come up and she refrained from asking.

There were no weapons waiting for Gil's attention

this trip, Peder told him, which was a disappointment. He'd hoped to earn something more before Christmas so that he had cash money for gifts. His Thanksgiving prize money was now earmarked to pay the doctor when Jennifer needed him.

"Haven't heard about anyone else wanting stone, have you?" Gil asked quietly.

Peder shook his head. "Too cold for building right now, Gil. I 'spect it'll pick up again in the spring."

"Well, I'll just have to think of something else," Gil murmured.

If need be, he could still go after more buffalo, even if it meant traveling farther into the plains to find them. Frank would agree to go, he thought, or Merritt. The meat and hides would bring a fair price here in town and more than that if he took it all the way to Kansas City. He could do that, too, now that he had his own buckboard and the team he was getting from Sam. He just didn't want to be gone from his family all that long at any time, and especially not now with Jennifer expecting.

But he had to have more money coming in.

He left Peder at the back of the store and approached his wife, putting on a smile for her benefit. "Come on, Mrs. Prescott, it's time to go."

"Oh, but what about Zach?"

"Maude will keep an eye on him, won't you, Maude? It'll only be for a little while, and we'll be back to report our good news pronto."

Gil took her arm firmly while Jennifer made an unprecedented, childish face at him as they left the store.

"Didn't your aunt ever tell you your face might freeze that way, Teacher?" he whispered in her ear. "Or your teacher?"

"Did anyone ever tell you that you're a bossy man?" she shot back under her breath, reminding him of what he usually told her.

Gil chuckled. "I'm learning from a bossy woman, Mrs. Prescott."

Gil wasn't as easy with it all as he would like her to believe, Jennifer discovered. Although kindly, Dr. Rosenberg had to be firm about Gil not staying with Jennifer during the examination, to her everlasting gratitude. She knew she could answer the doctor's intimate questions better without her husband's presence and she also thought if she had to face unwelcome news it would be better to bear the disappointment alone at first.

In the examination room, Jennifer explained all her fears and doubts haltingly, but the doctor merely nodded. "I'll know more in a few moments, Mrs. Prescott. Now please just relax."

Gil paced the outer room. He hadn't let Jennifer see how concerned he felt about her, or let on how closely he'd been watching her these last few weeks. Most women didn't go to a doctor for just being in a family way until it was time for the birth, he knew. Or not at all. Many women had babies with only another woman or two present.

But Jennifer was different, she was delicate and fine boned and this pregnancy was unusual. He couldn't stand the fear of something going wrong, like she'd told him had happened before. Like it had for Morning Rain. Jennifer would have everything she needed, by thunder.

Nothing would happen to Jennifer! He wouldn't let it!

When Jennifer reappeared, she was smiling through tears. He stopped pacing and looked at the doctor.

"Congratulations, Mr. Prescott. You'll be a father by late spring."

Elation hit him. It was official. But . . . His gaze pinned the doctor while his heart felt as though it lodged in his throat. "Jennifer?"

"Now don't go borrowing trouble, young man. Your wife seems in good enough health, but she isn't as strong as some of the farm girls I see. However, I see nothing that should prevent a healthy birth. I would advise that she not overwork, though. No heavy lifting and such."

Gil nodded emphatically. "Gotcha, Doc."

"I do wish you two wouldn't talk as though I weren't here or that I couldn't take responsibility for myself," Jennifer complained. "I know all the right things to do."

"Very well, Mrs. Prescott. I'll trust you to come and see me, then, if you need to," the doctor said dismissively.

Gil held her arm tightly as they descended the steep outside staircase over the hardware store where Dr. Rosenberg had his office, and then during their return down the long block to Lindermans' grocery store.

"Really, Gil, I won't break if you loosen your grip a little," Jennifer said, laughing.

"Sorry, honey." Gil let out a gusty sigh. "Guess I just don't want anybody to bump you or nothin."

"At this rate I'll have a broken arm by the time the baby arrives," she joked.

"Well, there ain't nothin' wrong in a man protecting his wife, is there?"

But Gil did relax his clasp, and they both smiled as they entered the store. Since she was serving a customer, Maude merely nodded her acknowledgment with twinkling eyes. Gil left Jennifer to chat while he and Zachary went to complete their business with Sam Burns.

"Everything is just fine," Jennifer reported as soon as Maude's customer left. "But I don't know how well the expectant father might survive."

Maude laughed, but before she could reply to Jennifer's joke, Mrs. Dillon stepped up to the counter, Mrs. Portland at her side. She laid her freshly baked goods on the counter.

"Good morning, Mrs. Prescott," Mrs. Dillon greeted. "How fortunate it is to see you in town today. We need your advice."

"How so?"

"I think Miss Amelia Smithers has had all she wants of the teaching profession," Mrs. Dillon confided. "If I don't miss my guess, she'll accept a proposal from either that Andrew Brown or Red Smithy by Christmas."

"You mean she wants to leave in the middle of the year?" said Mrs. Portland, who, although she had no children in the school, nevertheless thought it her duty to be involved in the workings of it. After all, her boardinghouse gave her status in the town, the bony woman insisted. "Oh, dear me, that means we'll have to find a new teacher right away."

"It ain't a tragedy, Dora," Maude remarked as she stacked the baked goods on a low shelf behind her counter.

"What do you say, Mrs. Prescott? What should we do?" asked Mrs. Dillon.

"Why don't you see if there is a man who wants the job," Jennifer suggested, thinking that the Gallaghar brothers would be better disciplined with a man in charge. "And it wouldn't hurt to hire an assistant, as well."

"But there's only a few men that I know of who are qualified," Mrs. Dillon said.

"An assistant? Why, that would cost too much," said Mrs. Portland.

"There are a lot of new people coming west. You could advertise for one," Jennifer reminded.

"Yes, yes, I do understand that, Mrs. Prescott, but we'd have to pay a man more," Mrs. Portland objected again. "I don't think the town would stand for that."

Jennifer hadn't given much attention to the customer flow. Maude left to attend to someone in the back of the store while Peder climbed a ladder to put stock on his shelves.

"You might even consider hiring two teachers," Jennifer said. "I understand the school has almost twice the pupils it did last year."

"Two?" Mrs. Portland appeared shocked.

"Yes, I had thought the same," Mrs. Dillon said, nodding, as Maude returned to the group. "Certainly, we should take some quick action or we won't have a schoolteacher at all. Would you come and present your ideas to the town board, Mrs. Prescott?"

"Well! The town shall have to discuss it, I'm sure," Mrs. Portland insisted, her thin nose quivering. "Who's to pay for it all?"

Jennifer, glancing out of the store's window to see if Gil and Zachary were yet in sight, hid her amusement at Mrs. Portland. The woman had been the same when Jennifer taught school, objecting to every penny spent.

Peder called to her. "Gil and Zach are comin' down the back way, Jennifer. Looks like they got half a dozen horses in tow. You want I should load your beans an' flour now?"

"Yes, thank you, Mr. Linderman." She turned to the

ladies. "I would be honored to speak on behalf of the school's needs, Mrs. Dillon. If you will let Mrs. Linderman know when the meeting is to be, I'll be there."

On the verge of leaving the store, Jennifer suddenly felt a cold chill that had little to do with the opening and closing of the store's door. It raised goosebumps along her arms and the back of her neck. Turning abruptly, she stared squarely into Robert's face.

How long had he been standing there watching her?

A painful moment ticked by as Jennifer studied Robert's face, trying to read his intent. Did he plan to remind her openly of their past connections? Or challenge her in any way? His brown eyes glowed softly, covering his inner thoughts. Nothing of the evil he was capable of showed in his features, Jennifer noted. But they never had done, she reminded herself. On the surface he seemed to be only a handsome, polite man who was somewhat of a dandy and enjoyed the company of ladies.

Had time and events softened him at all? Surely he couldn't still be interested in her in a womanly way.

"Good day, ladies," he said, smoothing his thick graying mustache with one finger before bowing. "I must say, the three of you are this town's handsomest matrons. This crisp air has brought out the roses in your cheeks, hmm?"

"Oh, how kind of you to say so, Mr. Quiller." Mrs. Portland smiled and stood straighter to give her thin bosom a better display.

Mrs. Dillon nodded politely but said nothing.

"And my dear Mrs. Prescott," he said, turning a beguiling smile toward Jennifer while his voice deepened, implying an intimate acquaintance. "You are indeed as lovely as ever. How are you this fine winter's morning?"

Jennifer ignored the other women's curiosity and answered as though Robert was nothing more to her than anyone she might meet on the street. "Good morning, Mr. Quiller. I am very well, thank you. And now you must all excuse me, please," she said as she tugged her gloves over trembling fingers. "My husband is waiting."

Jennifer left the store without a backward glance. But she felt as though her back were burning with Robert's stare.

14

Snow mixed with sleet began to pelt down as they were halfway home, and Jennifer signaled Sally to pick up her pace. Poor Sally. She was an expectant mother, too.

At the rate the weather was deteriorating, it wouldn't take long for the road to turn to muck, and she'd rather not be caught in it. She and Zachary had had a miserable time of it last winter during one trip home in bad weather. Old Ben had worked hard to get them home at all. After that, she'd chosen her timing for trips to town with greater care.

She shivered as freezing drops hit her face and neck. Gil and Zachary were a few yards behind her with the extra horses. Turning, she looked to see how the boy was faring on the small roan that Gil had let him ride bareback. Although he looked cold—he'd pulled his head down inside his collar—he was so proud of riding all by himself she doubted that she could convince him to ride their last two miles in the buggy with her.

Gil waved at her from his position at the rear of the small band, and she reassured herself that he was keeping a close watch on Zach.

By the time they reached home, Jennifer knew they were in for the first bad storm of the season; it seemed a portent of the winter to come. She was smugly pleased that they were well prepared for it: the new well was very satisfactory, their wood supply was certainly sufficient, and they had enough food stores for half a dozen people, thank goodness.

Her only real worry was that the amount of hay she'd bought last summer wouldn't stretch to keep all of their new animals through the winter. "The horses will have to be content to winter on pasture grass for the most part," Gil told her when she had voiced her concern a few days before. "We'll hand-feed them only during the worst of it."

"I can't stand the thought of a living creature going hungry," she'd remarked.

"Your heart is bigger than the moon, Teacher, that's for sure. But me and nature will do what providing is necessary. Besides," he scolded, "you have enough to do with keeping up with the chickens and Flossy and the household. And now with a new child coming you have to take more care of yourself, Jennifer. You can't go round worrying over what you can't do nothin' about. What good would you do any of us if you neglected your own needs?"

Wide-eyed, Jennifer felt properly chastised but amused at the same time. Gil was proving to be a force with which to reckon when he got a bone between his teeth.

And now that the doctor had told Gil she needed

more rest than most pregnant women, Jennifer could imagine his anxiety over her eventual confinement. Ah, well, she had planned to do a lot of sewing and knitting this winter anyway. Gil needed warmer clothes and Zach was growing out of his. In fact, she'd begun her Christmas knitting early. Gil and Zachary both needed scarves and mittens. And Homer, too.

Their turnoff came into sight and Jennifer felt Sally take it without a signal. The poor animal was ready to feed, Jennifer knew, and as eager as she to get out of the storm.

At Gil's waving instructions, Jennifer pulled Sally to a stop at the house. He leaped down and was there to help her in a flash, trying to shield her from the worst of the driving sleet as he lifted her tenderly to the ground.

"Zach, you help your mama unload her packages while I get the horses put away. And take care of your dog right away, you hear? I'll be back for the buggy pronto."

"Okay, Papa." As much as he wanted to help with the horses himself, Zach recognized his papa's no-nonsense order as one he couldn't argue with and did as he was told.

Inside, Jennifer hurriedly stirred up the stove to heat the soup she'd prepared that morning, and by the time Gil stepped through the door, it was hot and a pan of corn bread was in the oven.

Gil sat down at the table and pulled off his wet boots as Jennifer dished up. "Whewee! Glad I'm inside tonight," he remarked casually. "Ain't a night fit for nothin."

"Yes, the storm is fierce." But Jennifer didn't feel threatened by it now that they were home. No, the storm didn't threaten her; they simply would ride it out.

And it would give her another excuse to stay home

during the next scheduled visit to town. She wouldn't have to face the possibility of meeting Robert again. The longer she went between visits the more she hoped that he wouldn't be there when she returned.

But he had been this time.

All the way home she'd been wondering what he was doing in Osage Springs in the first place and what might be keeping him there. A little town like theirs had nothing to interest him . . . except herself.

But Robert hadn't threatened her or said anything untoward today. In fact, he had said nothing to distress her at all, she reminded herself. In words.

No, not in words, but his very presence upset her. He wasn't the nice man he appeared.

"Did you hear any talk in town today about maybe a railroad coming our way?" Gil asked Jennifer as he reached for more corn bread.

"Oh, there's always railroad talk. What did you hear today?"

"Sam was full of it. Mr. Tige, too. He seems to think that fella you knew back east is here to scout out the possibility. What do you think?"

"Robert Quiller?" Jennifer couldn't prevent her surprise from showing. It didn't sound anything like the Robert she knew; he had been too indolent and preferred to leave real business dealings to others. Besides, she didn't think Robert knew anything about scouting out land for a railroad.

"Robert might well have placed some investments in railroads, but it seems unlikely to me that he would be involved in the actual building of any."

"Why do you think that?" Gil's curiosity was open.

"Oh, well, Robert isn't very industrious, you see, and his wealth doesn't demand it of him."

Gil nodded, then leaned back in his chair as he studied his wife. "Lazy, huh. Where you know him from?"

"Philadelphia, as I told you. He . . . he was a part of the social set to which Wil—my first husband belonged."

"What does Quiller do with himself then?"

Jennifer shrugged. The idle, pointless activities in which Robert Quiller and his ilk had indulged seemed outlandishly obscene to her now. She doubted if Gil had any inkling of that kind of life. "When I knew him, he gambled, spent time at his club, attended balls and soirees, and the like."

"Umm . . . Well, tattle about town is that he's right taken with Kansas. He's let drop that he's interested in the lay of the land hereabouts and he's wantin' to know what's open, what's government land, what's bought up. He's spent freely, too. Buys lots of drinks for folks."

"Yes, Robert would be sociable." Regardless of his low opinion of the down-to-earth company he found, Robert Quiller would put a good face forward. He wouldn't show his contempt for the people he met until he was through using them.

"But you don't like him." Gil made the statement with certainty.

"No, I don't care for him," Jennifer admitted.

"Why?"

What could she tell Gil without giving too much away?

"He . . . his ambitions in life didn't coincide with mine. I found him rather"—too much of a snake lying in wait to strike, with a poison so potent it would threaten the most stalwart of resisters—"rather too shallow."

"Mmm . . . Well, I don't know what business the man has here, but he's found himself a woman at Jasmine's."

That casual piece of information was like warm honey to Jennifer's tight nerves. Surely she wouldn't matter to Robert any longer if he had a woman at Jasmine's.

Gil bent to listen as Zachary started to tell him something about his new horse. Jennifer barely heard half of it as she finished her soup and reasoned with herself. Could she hope that Robert *was* here merely to attend to business? The war might have changed his priorities. He might well be following his investments.

Perhaps—oh, Lord, please let it be true—perhaps Robert wasn't the enemy anymore. What had happened between them was long ago. Wasn't she being a bit overanxious and conceited to think Robert cared any longer about what she did or how she lived?

"Time for bed, Zach," she said, feeling more relaxed than she had for weeks. Gil was right. She shouldn't take on worries she could do nothing about.

Gil crawled under the covers and pulled her close. Jennifer felt warm and cozy, loved and sleepy, before Gil broached the subject of going after more buffalo.

"You can't be serious!" she cried.

"It isn't the first thing I'd choose to do, Jennifer. But it is a way of bringing in money."

"Isn't hunting in the winter more difficult?"

"Yep, sure 'nuff is, honey. But I can make more, too. Not many men're willing to work against the winter weather. The meat'll hold with careful handling, and John Perry told me today he'd pay top dollar for any buff I brought back."

"But Gil, you'd have to be out in the worst of it and your health—"

"I'm fit as a fiddle, Jennifer. I feel fine. And I ain't stupid enough not to prepare for it."

"You can't go alone."

"I don't think I'll have to. Merritt'll go. And others. There's enough men looking for work."

"But Gil, the buffalo herds move south in winter. You might not find any close by."

"Not necessarily. Lots of herds hang around in the north. I reckon I will have to travel some, though. That's the bad part about it. I'll be gone a month or more."

"A month," she said on a gasp. "Into Indian territory?"

"Now, Teach. Don't borrow trouble."

"But why? Why do you want to go now?"

"Jennifer, love, I have to. I have to get enough money to carry us through the winter and to give me some seed money in the spring. If I can buy just three dozen cows—"

"I thought you wanted to plant wheat?"

"That too."

"But Gil, we have enough supplies to carry us through the winter. In fact, we're much better off this winter than last, and we—"

Beside her, she felt Gil stiffen. She could have bitten off her tongue. Why had she let that slip past her guard? There was no light in the room; Jennifer heartily wished she could see her husband's expression.

His next words were spoken calmly enough, but they carried an edge.

"Remindin' me of how much you and Zach did without before I came home only adds to my reasoning, Jennifer. It ain't gonna happen again as long as I have breath left. But it's more than that. I've got to get this place going again to hold on to what I have. What *we* have."

Tentatively, she laid her palm against his shoulder.

"Gil, please listen. You don't have to go. I have money

coming at the first of the year. We can use that to buy cows and seed."

"No!" He pulled from her touch and raised to lean on his elbows. "Now you know how I feel about that, Jennifer. I ain't gonna use your money!"

"But—"

"No!"

She was silent for a long moment. Her husband was as stubborn as a Missouri mule where it concerned money. His male pride was affected. Somehow he viewed the fact that she'd had to spend her income on this land before they married as shameful, and however their marriage had altered their situation, Jennifer didn't think this was one area where he would change his mind.

"Well, then, will you promise not to go until after Christmas?"

"Yeah." He relaxed back against his pillow. "I hadn't planned on going 'til then anyway. And I wouldn't leave you and Zach alone, Jennifer. Either you and Zach can move into town and stay with the Lindermans or I'll ask Homer to come out and stay with you while I'm gone."

She sighed deeply. "Your mind was already set before you brought it up then?"

Her rebuke was made gently.

"Reckon so."

His answer was obstinate.

Jennifer lay awake long after Gil fell asleep. She didn't understand why, but the idea of being left for a whole month without Gil's presence frightened her. It frightened her down to her toes.

Last winter had been long and lonely much of the time, even with Zachary's presence. Her only adult society had been from an occasional visit from Bessie and her trips to Osage Springs. She had felt capable enough to handle it. She'd made it through. Why didn't she feel she could do so now?

She hadn't known Gil, then. She hadn't known the comfort of his company and his strength. Or the feel of his arms around her.

Robert Quiller hadn't been in the vicinity last year either. Now his very proximity threatened her, so much so that she dreaded going to town these days. No, if given a choice she would remain on the farm out of sight.

Jennifer couldn't confide those fears to anyone, but she did broach her concerns for Gil's proposed absence with Maude when next she went to town.

"It must be your condition, dear," Maude suggested. "Being in the family way sometimes does cause a woman to get a bit nervy and full of fanciful imaginations, you know. And you can't fault Gil for wantin' to provide for his family."

"Perhaps you're right, Maude. I'll put no more stock in it. Now, are you and Peder coming to share Christmas dinner with us?"

It had been Gil's idea to invite the Lindermans and Jennifer gladly agreed. Christmas should be a real celebration, their first as a family.

"*Ja,* we're coming," Peder answered for Maude as he came around the counter. "But we bring the goose. John Perry got some fat ones in last week from over in Missouri and he's been feedin' 'em the best as geese ever ate. We ain't had goose for years an' my mouth is waterin' for it."

Jennifer laughed. "All right, goose it is. I don't think Zach has ever tasted it. It'll go well with the ham I've been saving from when the Ables slaughtered last fall."

Gil swung through the front door, looking pleased about something while Homer trudged behind him looking as though he carried a mountain on his shoulders.

"Howdy, folks," Homer mumbled, his hands shoved in his pockets.

"How do, there, Homer," Peder responded, then looked expectantly at Gil. "Ya look like ya done won a poker pot, Gil. What's on your mind?"

"Nope, never play poker." Gil let his grin spread. "But I got some news. Sam Burns says the army is looking to lease his barn for the winter. He'll do it if we can take over his stock."

"But how can he run his business that way?" Jennifer asked. "And how can we care for another dozen animals?"

"Got that figured. And Sam ain't too worried about a lot of winter business, Jennifer. There's less traffic and fewer calls for rental horses. But there might be a way to solve what need there is, if Peder, here, is willing to rent us part of his barn."

"You mean Sam wants to use my barn in back there?" Peder scratched his balding head in thought. "I dunno. Ain't much room in it."

"Room enough for a couple of nags, ain't they?" Homer asked.

"Sure, sure, but who's gonna take care of 'em?"

"Don't worry, Peder," said Gil. "Sam'll do it."

"Yeah, Pa'll do it. He might need the excuse of it real bad, real soon, anyways."

All eyes turned toward Homer. "He's gonna marry that Portland woman," he explained with disgust. "She wants 'im to help 'er run 'er boardin' house. When Pa gits tired of 'er, then he can say he hasta take care of the horses."

"Well, I swan," Maude remarked, putting her hand to her mouth. "Dora was in here this morning and didn't say a word about it. Are you moving into the boarding-house then?"

"Reckon so," Homer said in pure misery, his gaze on his boots.

Compassion turned Jennifer's heart and she lifted her gaze to Gil. It didn't take a second to realize he had already thought along the same lines as she. "Homer, why don't you move back into our bunkhouse?"

The boy lifted shining eyes. "Sure 'nuff, Teacher?"

"Reckon it'll be the same as before, Homer," Gil said. "We can't offer you any pay beyond room an' board."

"Don't care."

"Ain't digging stone 'til spring, which was our cash crop for making money and the way I paid you last fall," Gil said, wanting to be straight with the boy.

The boy, his underlip thrust out in stubborn resistance, merely shook his head. He didn't care for all that.

"And your pa'll want you to ride back and forth to town every day or two. You'll be fighting all kinds of weather."

"It'll be worth it," Homer insisted. "Can I still have my dawg?"

"Certainly," Gil replied.

"Hooray," shouted Zach. "Me'n you will have fun, Homer. Like before."

"And we'll have two dogs called General," Jennifer remarked with a laugh.

Hopefully, this new activity would cause Gil to give up his hunting trip, Jennifer thought. The additional horses would take more work. But now wasn't the time to broach the possibility.

On the drive home, Jennifer chattered gaily about

the full house they were to have for Christmas dinner. She felt exuberant. She hadn't encountered her enemy or heard anything of him. Perhaps her worries were for naught. "It will be a real family Christmas, Gil. We'll have to find some kind of a tree to decorate. We haven't had one before now."

"Reckon that'd be real nice. A tree, huh?"

"Yes, and we'll read and . . ."

"And?"

"Oh, other things. You'll see."

Gil felt more than a little happy, himself. His share of the budding partnership with Sam Burns would add to his savings for the spring purchases he planned. And he thought Jennifer was over her flare-up at him for making the decision about the hunting trip before talking with her about it.

"You're a real schemer, aren't you, Teacher?" Gil slanted her a teasing glance full of sexual promise. If they didn't have Zach in the buckboard with them he'd pull Jennifer aside for a kiss.

"Sometimes." She arched a brow and gave him an answering stare. "So are you, Mr. Prescott."

Gil grinned. He could hardly wait to have the evening over and have Zach tucked away for the night.

Jennifer came face-to-face with Robert in the mercantile store the very next time she was in town. She'd gone in to buy more yarn and to look at material for shirts for Gil, Zach, and Homer for Christmas. After nodding abruptly, she made her way to the yard goods counter where she inspected the wares.

She tried to ignore the fact that Robert had followed her and kept her gaze on the fabric she fingered.

"Ah, the chambray would be the better choice, my dear, among the poor goods that are offered," he said, his voice very near. "But I imagine your taste has turned to flannel these days, has it not? Your husband has no need for the, er, finer apparel."

She did not look up.

"You are quite right, Robert. My husband is a rancher. He prefers practical things." She couldn't bear to use the term *farmer,* although she felt no shame in it. She would be quite happy if that was what Gil wanted to achieve. But a rancher was what Gil aspired to be and the term would seem more prestigious in Robert eyes. It only mattered to her not to give him anything more in his arsenal with which to goad her.

"Are you happy, my dear?"

"Yes." She kept her answer short, hoping to discourage him.

"Really? I hardly think you could be, out in that god-forsaken place."

"You must not equate my desires from life with your own, Robert. They differ widely."

"Ah. A rebuke. So cold-heartedly given." He answered with gentle hurt and languid persuasion. "Perhaps you would care to enlighten me, my dear. Come to tea and explain what you mean."

"I cannot."

"Patricia—"

"Leave me be, Robert," she answered through her teeth. "My life doesn't touch you in any way now."

"Oh, but it does, my dear. It will."

"Never. Never again."

Jennifer turned and fled the store. Behind her, a sibilant whisper followed. "Patricia . . ."

15

Jennifer's heart pounded as she hurried down the street where she was to meet Gil and Zach. Robert might well be in Osage Springs for legitimate reasons, but he had no intentions of ignoring her or letting her lead her own life. As suspected, he planned to hound her—he loved making intrigues. She could only pray that he would grow bored with his game if she paid him no mind.

But at what cost? What damage would he do if she did ignore him? Or if she didn't?

It took her all the way home to calm herself, and she remained quiet and let Gil and Zach fill the void as they talked of the approaching hunting trip. Everything, it seemed, was set. Merritt Tabor and Gil would head up a party of two wagons and five men. They planned to leave the first of January.

Gil searched Jennifer's face a couple of times, thinking she was still put out with the idea. By thunder, he didn't want to go! Yet the money he expected to make was important to their future. Why couldn't she see that?

It seemed to him she'd been a mite touchy of late over everything. He'd heard her cry in her sleep again last night, a soft whimper like a hurt child; it ragged at his heart. It made him feel helpless to banish whatever plagued her dreams.

Dreams were right powerful, he knew well enough. He'd had his share of them, both good and bad. He'd drawn her into his arms hoping to comfort her, but he didn't know if he had or not. Surfacing a bit, Jennifer'd clung to him until she slept again. But come morning, she didn't mention the incident and he didn't either.

Maybe he shouldn't go at that, even though Maude had assured him that it was only Jennifer's condition that caused her to voice so many fears. If only he didn't need the income so badly.

In the next few days Jennifer refused to allow thoughts of Robert to interfere as she threw herself into their Christmas preparations, pushing him to the back of her mind ruthlessly. She had so much to do in making gifts and she wanted to take pleasure in the doing.

She took to staying up later at night, insisting to Gil that sewing and knitting were restful activities and required her only to sit. Her reasons were only partly due to the need to work on her gifts. She wanted to be too tired to think. Or dream.

For several nights in a row Jennifer smiled and excused the boys from kitchen work when they asked, with barely concealed excitement and mysterious glances at the supper table. It was the first time Zachary was aware of gift giving, she knew, although she was sure he remembered getting something last year.

Gil, too, went to bed later at night after long evening hours in the barn. He worked diligently to repair and restore the old buggy's torn seats and fold-up top and thought how much warmer Jennifer would be during her trips to town with her head buffered from the wind and the buffalo robe over her lap.

He and Jennifer had decided together to buy a small saddle for Zachary. The boy was old enough to begin a man's training since he was a rancher's son, Gil reasoned. Or would be after he got started again.

They had gifts for Homer, too. The youngster had earned them, Gil said. Jennifer had wholeheartedly agreed.

Gil yanked the heavy thread through the thick seam on the buggy seat. It snapped, and he glared at the thread in disgust. He needed something stronger, but this was the best he had, so he patiently tied the loose end and rethreaded the bone needle, and then went over the same seams to reinforce them. He fervently wished he had the money to buy Jennifer a brand-new vehicle.

He glanced over to the opposite corner where the boys worked on their own project. He thought it right nice of Homer to include Zach in his efforts. The two boys whispered and nudged each other at almost every evening meal, dashing away as soon as it was over to "attend to Flossy" or "brush down a horse."

He'd been a little hard put to find the privacy to repair the old halter he'd traded from Sam to go with Zach's saddle. But it had tickled his fancy, too. He liked having the boys around. They were good company. And the thought of a new child on the way gave him so much joy it went clear to his toes.

The only splinter in the smooth was his concern over Jennifer, and his heart often caught on that. What if she couldn't carry the child to the end? He wondered if that was the worry that plagued her. He'd wanted to ask more about what had happened, exactly, the last time, but somehow he knew she couldn't take the probing. What would she do, how would she feel if she lost the baby? He feared it might tear her up beyond repair. She seemed so delicate, sometimes.

But then again, her strengths staggered him.

Actual physical pain hit him as another fear broke through a hidden compartment of his mind. Women sometimes died in childbirth; it had happened to Morning Rain. What would he do if he lost Jennifer?

The possibility didn't bear thinking about. *He wouldn't!*

He thought instead of last Christmas. He'd been miserable, cold, and hungry—a marrow-deep lonely man among other equally lonely men who, facing frequent death and destruction, all longed for the same things. Families, sweethearts, wives. Home.

And the three Christmases before that seemed little more than blurred nightmares now, but he remembered the misery. He'd wanted to die.

Now the sky-high happiness he owned scared him breathless. He still couldn't believe it was his. And he'd do anything to keep it. Anything. Everything. That was why he was willing to leave his wife and son for a month. A month against forever didn't seem a high price to pay.

Patiently, he finished his stitching. He didn't have the money this year to buy his wife a new buggy, or other things she deserved, but by thunder, he would in the future.

*   *   *

On Christmas Eve, they attended the packed service at the little town church and heard the story of why they honored this day. They lingered only long enough to wish a few town friends well, then hurried home to their own celebration.

The Lindermans came with them. Zach had gladly given up his bed to them; he thought it a great adventure to sleep in the bunkhouse with Homer and the two Generals.

Jennifer served cookies and cider while they decorated the scraggly tree Gil had spent hours finding from that section of woods where she'd searched for nuts. Having a special pine tree of their very own to decorate was new to everyone except her.

She had saved bits of red yarn for bows and instructed Gil in making a star from a piece of tin. From her trunk, she brought out a box of exquisite hand-blown glass balls of green, red, blue, silver, and gold—a dozen in all; she'd bought them during her lonely sojourn in Europe so many years previously.

Everyone oohed and aahed at the sight of them.

"Do you remember these, Zachary?"

"Uh-huh, they're the Christmas balls. We put them in a bowl on the table."

"We did, indeed. Last year. But since we have a tree this year, let's put them on it, shall we?"

"Okay. Look, Papa. Homer, look. They'll be pretty, won't they?"

"Yes, they will, son. Right comely."

"I've never seen any as lovely as these, Jennifer," Maude remarked. "Peder and I have something for the tree, too. Get them, Peder."

Peder brought out six tiny candles set inside little tin cups made especially for them. "These are wonderful, Peder. Where did you—oh, you made them, didn't you?"

"*Ja, ja.* I did, sure."

Jennifer thanked the couple and with a glance reminded her husband and son to do the same. They sat on the floor by the fireplace where a warm fire snapped at its wood. Homer was there, too, watching all the proceedings with wide, observant eyes.

"Yes, these are perfect, Peder. We're much obliged for 'em. We'll use 'em every year, won't we, Jennifer? And we'll remember who made 'em." Gil spoke enthusiastically, then rose to his feet. "And I've got something I found in the barn to go under the tree, something that belonged to my ma. Just a minute."

He left for a moment, then came back into the parlor holding a wooden cradle, simple in design but full size.

It had been oiled and rubbed until the old wood shone. Gil stood with it in his arms, a tender smile hovering as he set it before Jennifer. "My ma said my grandpa Zachary made it for her. It's made of hickory and will last a long time, I expect. I thought it fitting maybe to put it under the tree this year?"

He'd hesitated to bring the cradle into the house so early. He didn't know how Jennifer would take it. Yet he thought it the perfect thing to encourage his wife.

He searched her face for a reaction. Had he made a mistake?

"Oh, Gil. Yes, it's very appropriate indeed." Jennifer smiled tremulously, then suddenly hugged her arms around her waist. She was so touched by his thoughtfulness that tears sprang to her eyes, but at the same time, she couldn't prevent a shiver of apprehension from traveling down her spine.

"Why, it's lovely, Gil," Maude quickly exclaimed. "I don't think I ever saw it before. You'd become quite a big young'un before we met you and your folks."

"What's it for?" Zachary asked.

"Well, it's for a baby, son." Gil forced his gaze away from Jennifer to focus on Zachary. "If I'd had it for you, it woulda made me proud for you to use it. But . . ."

"What's it do?" Zach put a tentative hand on it, setting it to rocking.

"You put a baby in it. See? It's a bed that rocks."

"What are we going to do with it? I'm not a baby anymore."

This would never do, Jennifer scolded herself after she had glimpsed a flicker of Gil's disappointment at her mixed reaction. Deliberately, she made an effort to shake off her foreboding. It was Christmas Eve and a joyous occasion.

"No, you certainly are not," she answered Zach very positively, then glanced at Gil. He'd brought the cradle in to show his love and happiness over the baby's coming and to represent what the holiday meant. It was a lovely gesture. She reached out to stroke the satiny wood.

Catching her husband's gaze, Jennifer smiled. Perhaps she could show him how she felt. It might be the right time to tell Zachary. They had to tell him sometime; she would begin to show soon and then the questions would fly.

"Zach." She lifted a questioning brow, then proceeded when Gil's mouth softened. He understood her gesture. "Your papa and I have something really special to tell you. You see, we're going to need this cradle by summertime. You're going to be a big brother."

Zachary stared at her. Then he looked at the cradle

suspiciously. Finally, he narrowed his eyes at his father. "We're going to get a baby in this cradle?"

"That's right, son," Gil answered as he went on his haunches to be face-to-face with the boy. "What do you think of that? Does it make you happy?"

"I don't know. I like little Frankie." His underlip poked out. "But little Frankie gets into stuff."

"Yes, babies do, sometimes," Jennifer said.

"Will he want to ride my horse Sergeant?"

"Maybe. But not 'til he's old enough," Gil assured. "By that time, you'll be older, too."

"Weelll, okay. But he'll have to do chores, just like me'n Homer."

"Right 'nuff," Gil said, nodding. "Every member of this family pulls his own weight."

"And I'm going to call him—"

Gil was positive Zach was going to say Major, for he'd asked a lot of questions about other army rankings besides sergeant and general only days ago when they saw a bunch of soldiers in town. He'd been intrigued with major.

"Son, you can't name him."

"A title isn't—" began Jennifer at the same time.

"He could always switch to admiral," Peder said as an aside, for which Maude gave him a poke in the ribs.

"Gabriel."

"Gabriel?" asked Jennifer, astonished.

"Uh-huh."

"Why Gabriel?" Gil wanted to know.

"Because that's an angel name. I like angel names."

"What if it's a girl?" Jennifer nearly gurgled on her suppressed laughter.

"Huh-ungh. My brother is a boy."

Zach's sense of logic broke out everyone's laughter.

After that Jennifer passed around the warm cider and cookies again and settled down to enjoy their Christmas tree. Even though they'd already heard it at church, Gil reread the Christmas story from his mother's Bible, for which he'd secretly practiced until he could read it without stumbling. He wanted to make Teacher proud of him; he wanted her to be proud he'd fathered her children.

His reward was the glow in her eyes at bedtime as they bid everyone good night. Jennifer, for the first time in weeks, slept soundly, and although Gil had hoped for more, he was satisfied she'd gone to sleep curled against him.

The morning dawned bright and clear. Jennifer scarcely felt Gil leave the bed, then sometime later she smelled coffee boiling. Hastily, she rose and dressed. She barely reached the kitchen before Zach and Homer were stomping through the front door.

"We left the dogs outside, Mama, like you told us," Zach eagerly reported. "When, Mama? When can we open presents?"

He tore out of his coat and mittens while his hair stood on end from the static. Behind him, Homer's shy eyes were wide with expectation as well.

"Hush, boys," Jennifer said, automatically smoothing down Zachary's poker-straight hair. "Our guests—"

"Are wide awake an' rarin' to go, too," Peder said, coming through the back door with Gil and a bucket of milk.

A blast of cold air did its best to help her wake. "Oh, my. I thought you'd still be asleep, Peder."

"Not at all, my dear Jennifer. I love being out early,"

Maude said, arriving through the door just behind her husband. "Especially on such a perfect winter morning."

"Oh, you too? Oh, my stars. It looks as though I've been the slugabed." Jennifer's hand went to her cheek in dismay. "And you've done all the chores. Oh, how rude of me."

"Oh, tush, Jennifer. I haven't fed chickens in years and I enjoyed it a heap," Maude told her.

"Now, Mama?" Zachary jumped up and down. "Please?"

"Oh, all right. I suppose breakfast . . ."

The boys raced to the parlor. Gil slanted a grin her way then followed the boys.

". . . can wait." Jennifer laughed.

"Whoopeee! A saddle for my own. Look, Homer. Now I can ride and ride."

"I guess he likes his big present," she said to Maude and Peder. They chuckled as they all hurried into the parlor. Jennifer shot out a hand just in time to rescue the lamp from the sofa table as Zach swung his new saddle around. Suddenly, it was too heavy for him and he sat down with a thump, the saddle atop him. He giggled uproariously.

Homer grinned and remained standing awkwardly.

"Here, Homer," Gil said. "A package with your name on it."

"Ya sure?"

"Yep. H-O-M-E-R."

The youth pulled the string from the brown wrapping paper, then held up a pair of boots. Underneath was a set of new underwear. His eyes went wide with pleasure while he blushed all the way to his ears. "Ain't never had no new boots just fer me," he mumbled.

Nor underwear, either, Jennifer guessed, by the way

Homer stared at the long drawers. She and Gil had chosen his clothing together. Seeing the boy shiver with the cold had been just more than she could stand. Obviously, Sam didn't always seem to notice what his son needed. Or that the boy had left childhood behind.

"Reckon you'll need 'em when you start riding back and forth for the rest of the winter, Homer," Gil said. "And a man needs proper boots when he becomes a cowhand."

Homer's grin stretched all the way to his red ears.

Gil's mouth softened as he ran his hand across the shirt Jennifer had made him. This was what she'd put in such late hours on, he was certain. Its softness and fine stitching proclaimed it a Sunday shirt and he knew he'd wear it with pride.

Jennifer passed around her packages of knitted scarves with mittens to match. Everyone seemed pleased with her efforts. She'd made the boys' in bright red, Gil's in blue, and the Lindermans' in green. Maude and Peder gave out bags of candy and bright red apples to the boys, and salted fish to Jennifer and Gil.

Homer and Zachary whispered for a moment, then went to fetch something. They each lugged an end of their object, Zachary teetering under the load, and all the adults watched in wonder. An old rag partially covered a thick slab of wood; Homer jerked it off as they got closer to Jennifer with it.

The bark had been peeled from its outside edges, but the roughly round shape and ringed circles on the flat top revealed that it had come from a very large tree. It had been smoothed to perfection.

"It's for when you make bread, Mama. We sanded it for a million hours."

"I hoped it would sit high 'nuff on the dry sink fer

you not to haveta bend yer back much, Mrs. Prescott."

"Why, Homer. This is wonderful. It is positively ingenious. My back shall certainly appreciate your thoughtfulness every time I make bread or roll biscuits for the next six months, at the very least. Please accept my most earnest thanks."

Homer's ears glowed.

"Me too, Mama."

"Yes, my darling Zachary, and certainly you too. Thank you."

"Mama, I'm hungry."

"All right, honey. I suppose we can have breakfast now."

"Whoa, not yet, Teacher. I haven't given you my gift yet. But you'll have to come into the barn to see it."

"Oh? What is it?"

Gil tenderly wrapped Jennifer's shawl around her shoulders. "Come and see, Teacher."

Horses snuffled while Flossy stomped and gave out a moo as they all trooped by to the rear of the barn. The old buggy stood in its renewed splendor with a dignified air.

"Why, Gil. Oh, how marvelous."

Gil's eyes shone at her reaction.

"And you won't be cold, neither, by gum," said Peder as he ran a hand over the buffalo robe. "Lookee here, Maude. Reckon we oughta get one of these."

"Is it from one you shot, Papa? Is it?"

"Yes, son, it is."

"This will be the best protection against every kind of bad weather," Jennifer said in praise. "Thank you, Gil. You and the boys have thought of everything for my comfort." It made her feel warmed and cherished and her eyes grew misty with it. "Oh, we're so blessed this Christmas."

"It's what I've been thinking, too, Teacher." Gil's voice was husky with his own emotions.

Between them, the love flowed in almost tangible force. Gil almost forgot there were other people around them as his blood rose in want and need. He'd been so careful with her. They hadn't made love in a week.

But then he was hit with the first inkling that maybe, just possibly, what he was feeling was more than only his needs and hers coming together. Somehow—and he stood in awe, for he didn't know how he had managed it—but he thought he'd won his wife's deepest devotion.

Homer left soon after breakfast. "Wish I could stay, Teacher. Rather be here. But my pa wants I should have eats with him an' his new wife at the boardin'house. An' I gotta take care of the horses that're in town, I reckon."

"I understand, Homer. It is quite natural for your father to want his son with him."

"I'll be back, though. Soon's I can tomorra."

It was after dinner when the men lounged in the parlor and Zachary had fallen asleep on his new saddle in the middle of the parlor floor that Maude suddenly burst out with "Oh, my goodness gracious me! Peder," she called as she put the dish she was drying and her cloth down on the table. "Peder, we forgot to give Jennifer and Gil that package."

"Sure 'nuff, we did. I'll get it," Peder said as he headed for the stairs.

"What package?" Jennifer asked, trying to recall if she'd ordered anything she might've forgotten about.

"It's from that man you know, Jennifer. Mr. Quiller."

Jennifer had succeeded in banishing Robert from

her thoughts all day, and now, rather than fear of what his intentions were about, she felt a burning anger that he had intruded on her perfect day. What could the dad-blasted man possibly want of her?

"What's this about?" Gil asked as he came into the kitchen.

"I don't know," said Jennifer uneasily.

"It's a Christmas package for you and your family is what Mr. Quiller said when he brought it to us," Maude said. "He asked us to see that you got it."

Peder handed the parcel to Gil, who, after a quick glance at Jennifer, laid it on the table and opened it. Inside was a box of very expensive chocolates imported from Europe, and a bottle of white wine, the label declaring it one of France's best champagnes.

Gil stared at Jennifer. Once again, her face had lost all its color. Her mouth looked pinched.

He let his gaze drop back to the table. Chocolates and champagne. Impersonal, even frivolous gifts, not improper in any way. Normally. But why were they even sent? Not only were these particular brand items costly, but they were hard to come by in this out-of-the-way little town. The man must have paid a fortune for them.

Why would a mere acquaintance send such expensive things? They were earmarks of courtship, to his way of figuring.

For the first time, he wondered if Jennifer had told him everything when she'd explained her past association with Quiller. Could this eastern man have meant something to her once?

16

Jennifer had another encounter with Robert the day before Gil left. He strolled out of a saloon and toward them on the street as she, Gil, and Zachary left the boardinghouse where they'd visited with Sam and Dora. Jennifer glanced back over her shoulder hoping for a quick retreat, but the newly married couple waved to them from their front porch, and somehow, since Jennifer had felt the visit to have been rather stiff and formal, she couldn't bring herself to intrude upon them again.

She darted a glance to the opposite side of the road. She wanted to cross, but to do so would have been quite obvious, and besides, Gil's grip on her elbow tightened.

"Ah, Mr. and Mrs. Prescott, good day to you." Robert greeted them pleasantly and tipped his hat. "I trust your recent holiday was a happy one."

"How do, Mr. Quiller." Gil politely touched the

edge of his own hat, but Jennifer knew that behind his calm exterior, he was on edge. Instinctively, her husband didn't like the eastern man, and rightly so; Jennifer fervently wished she'd had some of that instinct nine years before. "Yes, thank you, sir. Most happy."

"And you, Mrs. Prescott?"

She spoke with acceptable civility. "Our holiday was a joyous one, thank you, Mr. Quiller. And thank you most kindly for your remembrances."

"I like to remember . . . old times," Robert said, silkily smooth. An instant of implicated intimacy flashed from beneath his half-lowered lids and transmitted itself to his drawl. "And I wanted to salute better days ahead. For us . . . all of us, that is."

Gil's fingers dug into her arm and Jennifer firmed her mouth. "Yes, Mr. Quiller. I, too, salute better days ahead. Now if you'll excuse us, we must be going. We are expected elsewhere."

Without sparing him another glance, she sidestepped, her elbow jammed in Gil's side to signal him to move, and the two of them walked quickly away.

"This Quiller feller," Gil began after they were some yards down the street. "You knew him kinda well, before, didn't you, Teacher."

It was a statement rather than a question.

"I told you, Gil. He was a friend of my husband's."

"Close friend?"

"Yes."

"Seems to me he's right fond of you."

Jennifer was silent for a moment. "Well, that has nothing to do with us."

It was Gil's turn to be quiet a moment. "The man has a heap of money, I expect. Don't look like he was hurt none in the recent war. Leastwise, he spends a lot of money in this town. Wears fine clothes, smokes fine cigars. Stays in the best room at the hotel, I hear."

"Yes, that is how Robert Quiller would live."

"Runs with the highfalutin crowd in those eastern cities, I reckon. Bet he has a big house, too. Servants and things."

"Yes, I'm sure he does."

Another long silence.

"Don't you miss all that, Jennifer?" His voice was quiet.

She tried to hide a deep sigh; Gil hadn't asked those questions until Robert Quiller came to town.

"That sort of life is a part of my past, I do admit, but it is in the past." Then, trying to turn the conversation, she lightened her tone. "And I'm married to a hard-working rancher now, and what I will miss is my husband while he's gone."

She would miss him most dreadfully.

They reached the schoolhouse where Jennifer planned to spend an hour with Miss Smithers, who wanted her advice on the curriculum, while Gil met with the other men in the hunting party at John Perry's for an hour or so to finalize their plans.

All of a sudden, Jennifer felt the growing familiarity of a shiver crawl up her spine, and she wanted to turn to look back the way they'd come. Had Robert followed them? She wondered if he would actually do that. Really spy on her?

She grabbed Gil's hand and held on tightly. Gil stood very still, gazing down at her; his eyes reflected an oblique gray, she thought. She couldn't tell what he was thinking.

"Gil." Wanting to plead with him not to go, she yet refrained. He had to go without worrying about her and

Zach. She couldn't fault him for doing what he could to earn their living, but . . . "Please, Gil. Please come home safe and sound."

"Jennifer, honey, don't frazzle yourself so. I'll watch out for myself and Merritt. And the other men are all seasoned hunters. We can count on 'em to be careful. It's you I'm thinking about. It might be better for you to move into town with Maude and Peder after all."

She couldn't do that and risk seeing Robert every day. "No, I'm sorry to upset you, Gil. Zach and I will be just fine in our own home. And we'll have Homer, remember? And the two Generals. What can bother us with two generals to keep an eye on the place?"

Late one morning in the middle of January, Bessie came to visit. As always, she guided her horse to the rear of the house; no matter how hard Jennifer tried to explain to Bessie that she was welcome at her front door, Bessie preferred the back.

Jennifer guessed who her visitor was and threw her shawl around her shoulders to step out the back door to greet her.

"Bessie! My stars, am I glad to see you. What brings you out on this cold morning?"

"Heard tell that Mr. Prescott is away," Bessie answered. "And business is kinda slow. Thought I'd like it to come on out and have me a coze."

"Yes, my husband is away, but that shouldn't matter. You're welcome anytime, Bessie, as I've said before. Come on in, now, and I'll make some tea."

"That's why I come, Miz Prescott. For tea." Bessie never got tea anywhere but at Miz Jennifer's house. She liked the brew. Especially when she had ponderin' to do. She eased herself down to sit in a kitchen chair, then looked around. "Where's little Zachary?"

"Zachary isn't so little anymore, Bessie. He's out in the barn helping Homer Burns tend the animals. I'm surprised, though, that he hasn't noticed that we have a visitor and come running to the house to see what's going on."

"Ain't like the old days, is it? Just you an' him alone when you weren't never apart, I mean?" Bessie's smile was fleeting.

Jennifer chuckled. "No, thank goodness. My little boy is no longer a mama's boy at all. He seems to be taking giant steps to be like his papa."

"That's good, I s'pose."

Jennifer poured tea and wondered what was bothering Bessie. The young woman had barely looked at her directly, and shyness was not one of her traits. "Have you been practicing your reading, Bessie? And arithmetic?"

"Yes, ma'am, some. And countin' ain't hard. I like countin'." Bessie stirred hard at the liquid in her cup. Her stylish red velvet bonnet hid her face.

"Well, take off your bonnet, Bessie, and tell me what's going on in town. I haven't been in for a couple of weeks."

"Nothin' much." She untied the red ribbons from under her chin. "A pack o' miners came through afore Christmas an' I made me some nice money then, but . . ." she said on a sigh as she laid the bonnet on the chair next to her. "Not many folks passin' through in wintertime, you know. Lotta talk about folks goin' west, though, and about the railroad."

"More railroad talk, hmm? Gil has heard some of it, too. What have you heard?"

"Some sayin' it's comin' straight through this town. Some sayin' it's goin' north of here. Them's also sayin' there might be a spur to here. No tellin' yet 'til it happens, I'm sayin'."

"Well, a railroad would sure put Osage Springs on the map." For the first time, Jennifer gave the rumors serious consideration. Having her emotions in turmoil lately had certainly caused her to grow dull about what was going on around her, she thought.

"It would bring in all sorts of new business to town. I've been wondering why it seemed so crowded these past months. I've put it down to natural change, like folks wanting to move after the war and such. But a railroad . . ."

A railroad would cause land prices to rise. A wise investment now might prove to be a boon in the future. In land or in town.

"Fact is, I been savin' up what extra money I can like you told me I should, Miz Jennifer," Bessie turned Jennifer's thoughts back to the present. "Been thinkin' I'd like to open up a dressmakin' establishment. You think I should?"

"Why, yes, I think—Bessie! Where did you get that bruise?"

Bessie's hand flew to her jaw. "It ain't nothin' much, Miz Jennifer."

But Jennifer knew better. She'd seen Bessie with bruises once before, when one of her customers had gotten out of hand. This one showed purple against her light brown skin. "Someone hit you."

"Yes, ma'am, but it ain't nothin' new."

"One of your customers?" Jennifer felt incensed. "Did he hit you more than once?"

"Don't pay it no never mind, ma'am, I'm healin' now."

But Bessie shifted uncomfortably in her chair and Jennifer concluded that her friend had received more hurt than she wanted to tell. She leaned forward to touch her hand, urging, "Bessie, you must get out of that business while you can."

"Been thinkin' on it. I think I will, Miz Jennifer, soon's I save up enough money." Bessie pulled in a long breath. "My gentleman friend is at least generous. An' he's gone away now."

"Bessie—"

"'Sides, Miz Jennifer, he weren't mad at me when he done this. He was mad at some woman back east name of Patricia."

Jennifer felt icy cold. Robert! Robert had done this.

"You say this man has left town?"

"Yeah."

"For good?"

"Can't be certain for sure, but he said sompthin' about comin' back. He had one of his headaches when he was talkin' an' hittin', so I ain't sure he knows even what he was doin' or sayin'."

"How long do you think he'll be gone?"

"Now Miz Jennifer, you know a man like that ain't likely to confide his business to a woman like me."

Jennifer could only sigh. At least she had the relief of knowing Robert was out of her vicinity for a while.

"You'll stay for dinner, won't you, Bessie? I want to hear more about your dressmaking plans."

The not so distant howl of a wolf invaded Gil's sleep. Wakening instantly, he listened. A moment later, he heard another. More than one.

Where there were wolves, there might be game.

Gil rose from his bedroll and shivered, and then tightened the scarf Jennifer had made him around his neck. The younger men in their party, Willy Jones and Josh Babcock, had teased him about it but he'd only laughed back, knowing they were secretly envious.

He hunched down by the banked fire and stirred the coals. Damn, he did hate sleeping out. Even with a heavy tarpaulin beneath him and a warm blanket over him, he'd felt the damp cold.

Glancing at the sky, he noted the diamond-sharp stars against the blackness of the morning sky. Yep, it would be a clear, cold day ahead. An hour yet to sunup. He shivered again and wondered if he dared use more of the dry wood they'd brought; they had to ration it. They'd found neither wood nor buffalo chips for a couple of days.

Merritt crawled from beneath his wagon. He was a tall, lanky man who wore deerskin clothing. He frequently spoke only a word or two to communicate.

"Heard 'em?" Merritt asked as he hunkered down and held his hands to the fire.

"Yeah. How far do you think they are?"

"Mile. Mebbe less."

"What d'you suppose they're after?"

"Same as us."

"Think they've found buffalo?" They'd been gone two weeks with no luck finding big game.

"Mebbe."

"Well, let's go see. I'd like to go home with a couple of wolf pelts, at least."

Gil reached for the coffeepot and then headed for the water barrel. He filled it and threw in a handful of coffee grounds. His stomach sure was empty and growled to let him know it. Damn, he'd grown spoiled these last few months with regular, hot meals, clean clothes, and bathing. And loving his wife.

Lord, did he ever miss Jennifer and Zachary.

He set the pot in the center of the coals while Merritt wakened the other men.

"Fer Pete's sake, Merritt," Willy Jones said, adding a string of curses. "It ain't light yit an' there ain't no one puttin' us'ns under the gun. Why'd you wake us fer?"

Merritt didn't answer. Instead, he shook his brother Miles and then Josh.

Miles rolled out as silently as Merritt had; he spoke only a little more eloquently than his brother.

But Josh didn't mind talking.

"Willy, roll out, will ya? You got cooking duty this morn and I ain't about to wait half a day for you to fix some vittles. 'Course they mayn't be fit to eat with you doing the cooking, but no never mind, it's your turn and you ain't getting away 'thout doing your share like you done yesterday and day before. If you ain't up by the count of three, I swear I'll plumb dump a load of frosty grass and snow on you. Else, I'll do the cooking an'—"

"All right, *all right!* Else I'll lose an ear to your everlastin' jawin'. Hell an' damnation, yer as bad as my ol' gran'ma."

"Now don't go cussing 'cause you don't cotton to women's work. It ain't—"

Another howl, closer this time, tore the silence around them. Gil turned his head and held his breath, and then let it out, vaguely observing the vapor it made. "Willy, Josh. Get your gear into the wagons. Pronto!"

"What 'bout breakfast?" asked Josh.

"No time," said Merritt as he swooped on the coffeepot before kicking snow and dirt onto the fire. The sudden hiss made an urgent sound of its own.

Gil ran to his own bedding, rolled it all swiftly, and slung it into the wagon. Without a word said, he and Merritt harnessed the team of mules.

Behind him, a sound like muffled thunder rolled in the near distance. Concentrating on what he was doing, it took Gil a second to register what it meant. But only a second.

His head jerked up. By damn, it wasn't thunder. "Buffalo!" he shouted.

Around him, Willy and Josh scrambled to complete their tasks while he sprinted toward Miles, who led the riding horses into the circle. Within moments, he'd saddled Beau, the big bay stallion he'd traded Sam for, and mounted.

Beneath him Beau danced and stomped eagerly to be off. The sky had perceptibly lightened, but it was still too dark to run the horses in safety. It took Gil a full moment to gain control of Beau before he swung back to see how the wagoners fared.

A swift glance told him that Willy and Josh were ready. Gil didn't bother to look for Merritt or Miles. They were well able to take care of themselves.

The wolves gave their cry again. He leaned forward, holding Beau steady as they headed toward the growing sound of the moving animals. He wanted to let Beau go, to fly there, but despite what he'd told Jennifer, Willy and Josh were inexperienced youngsters and he felt compelled to stay close to the wagons.

As the sun rays spread over the hills, the noise quieted. Gil no longer heard the wolves. The predators must have brought down their prey and dropped the chase, he guessed.

Did that mean they had lost the herd?

He signaled a stop, then listened.

After a moment, he spotted Merritt, waving them forward.

They caught up to the herd by midmorning in a wallow by a half-frozen stream. Gil and Miles, moving downwind, cautiously approached on foot as close as they dared. The herd was smallish in size, less than a hundred. But it would give their party a goodly haul if they were lucky.

When the weather permitted Jennifer and Zach went to town for a few supplies.

"There's a message for you from Mrs. Dillon, Jennifer," Maude told her as she added up Jennifer's bill. "The school committee is meeting on Friday morning and they hoped you would come in for it."

"Has Miss Smithers given her notice, then?"

"Oh, she agreed to stay on until summer, but Mrs. Dillon took your suggestion to heart. The town has considerably more children than it did, and the school needs either a more experienced teacher who can handle all of the students or two of Miss Smithers's caliber."

"All right." Jennifer traveled to town these days in perfect peace of mind, knowing Robert was no longer there. She counted her coins into Maude's palm. "Please tell Mrs. Dillon I'll be happy to meet with the committee if the weather remains reasonable. But I'll have Zach with me."

"I think little Lavinia Schiller might like to earn a nickel," Maude suggested. "Poor little thing. Only twelve and doing a woman's job in trying to keep her brother and sister from starving."

"Mmm, yes. My heart goes out to those children,"

Jennifer agreed as she picked up her bag of flour. "I do wish there was more we could do for them."

"I wish they were mine," Maude whispered fiercely. Then realizing suddenly what she'd said, she glanced quickly around the store. Her face was pink with embarrassment. "Sorry, Jennifer. Sometimes . . ."

"Yes, I know," Jennifer answered in sympathy. She felt as Maude did. It was a crime the way some people produced children only to mistreat them. She knew her friend was particularly sensitive to the problem when she had wanted a child of her own so badly and couldn't have one. "I'm sorry it took us so long to be friends, Maude. I do understand your feelings."

Maude sighed. "Thanks, dear. It does ease the pain with the sharing. Well, that's neither here nor there. Peder and I are too old now to have children."

"You know, it's a downright shame." An idea filtered through her mind. She'd talked to Mr. Schiller once or twice when she taught at the school. He was hopeless, she'd discovered, and cared little for Lavinia, George, and little Molly. And the one time she'd met Mrs. Schiller before she died, the woman had let it be known in passing conversation that her husband would be off to the mining fields in the blink of an eye if she hadn't demanded he stay for her and the children.

Jennifer shifted her bag of flour. "Maude."

"Yes?"

"Would you and Peder really want those children?"

Maude's eyes went round. "Well, yes, but we're getting on in years, you know."

"Does that really matter?"

Maude thought about it. "Why, no. No, not at all. We could offer the children a trade, you know, teach 'em how to run the store. I daresay Peder would agree, but their father . . ."

"Why don't you ask him?"

"Do you think George Schiller would give his children up, willy-nilly?"

"I think he might. Especially if you sweeten the offer with a personal consideration."

A glimmer of excitement shone from Maude's eyes. Her mouth dropped open. "Well, I'll swan, Jennifer, I'd never have thought of it, but I'll go talk to Peder about it right away. He can talk to Mr. Schiller."

Maude hurriedly turned away, aiming for the back room where Peder was working. "Jennifer Prescott, you're an angel," she called over her shoulder. "A pure soul, my dear."

Jennifer nearly cringed at those words, however kindly meant. It reminded her too much of how easily her reputation could be destroyed if people didn't see her as an ordinary woman. She thought at last that Gil saw her that way, but Maude's remark bothered her all the same.

"No, I'm not, Maude. Nor have I ever been an angel."

17

Gil and Merritt chased and hunted the herd until late in the afternoon, leaving the kill behind to be skinned and butchered by Miles and the younger men. The low cloud cover that moved in toward mid-afternoon brought an early close to the day, and as the light began to fade, Gil slowed his exhausted horse to a halt beside a young bull that had fallen under his last bullet.

He dismounted and cautiously approached the dead animal. Magnificent, he silently enthused, a perfect specimen. As before, he felt sad for the killing. However, its hide, tongue, and haunches would bring good prices from the tanner and John Perry or the army up at Ft. Leavenworth.

Gil looked around him. He hadn't seen the wagons since a pale sun hung straight up, nor had he heard Merritt's heavy gun for the last hour. Its boom had kept him informed of Merritt's location. But then, the herd had split and he'd followed the smaller splinter.

Now he wondered how far back were those wagons? The party had necessarily spread out over the countryside, which wasn't too wise.

Deciding he'd better get to it, he ground-reined Beau, pulled out his knife, and began skinning.

He was about done when he heard it. The low thrumming gallop of a single horse. He looked up in time to see the rump of Merritt's horse, riderless, disappearing over a low rise.

Without a second thought, Gil swiped his knife clean through the snow and leaped into his saddle. He headed toward the top of the land rise cautiously. Anything could be on the other side.

But the vast prairie showed him little except the small band of buffalo he'd hunted. He started backtracking, looking for the larger herd, looking for movement, looking for signs. Somewhere, Merritt was in trouble.

On the last Saturday of January, Sam stopped Jennifer on her way to the schoolhouse where the committee meeting was to start choosing a new teacher.

"You ain't had word of Gil, have ya, Mrs. Prescott?" He glanced at her fleetingly, then away, as though something back at the livery stable interested him immensely.

Jennifer turned her head. The livery barn buzzed with uniformed soldiers in quick, sure motion. One private yanked at a strap as he buckled a canvas-covered canteen onto his saddled gelding while another private checked his horse's hooves. Their lieutenant pulled hard on the cinch in saddling his mount. All of the soldiers emanated a sense of urgency.

"How do, Homer," Zachary piped up. "Can you come and play with me'n Lavinia in the schoolyard?"

"Uh, not now, Zach. Got work to do."

Jennifer noticed a tightening of Homer's face. The tips of his ears whitened. Hurried deduction gave her a growing feeling that something was wrong.

She looked around for Lavinia, and then waved the girl forward. "Why don't you take Zach now, Lavinia, and start a game with the other children. Tell Mrs. Dillon I'll be there shortly."

"Have ya?" Sam Burns asked again once the children were out of sight.

"No, not yet. But I don't expect him for another week or so," she answered. "Why do you ask? Is there a problem with the horses?"

"Naw, nothin' like 'at, Mrs. Prescott. Homer, here, says ever'thing's okay with 'em. It's just—" Sam's glance slid away again, giving the impression of furtiveness.

Her nerves wouldn't stand for any shilly-shallying this morning, Jennifer decided. None at all. She drew herself up. "Come, come, Sam," she commanded in her best schoolteacher's voice, "you may tell me what concerns you."

"Miz Jennifer, them soldiers're sayin' there's a Arapaho huntin' party out on the plains the way Gil an' the Tabor men was headin'," Homer blurted out. "Word come that a wood wagon was attacked."

"Where, Homer? Where was the wood wagon?"

"Up round Ft. Leavenworth."

"But that's over a hundred miles north of here," she said, appealing for assurance and protesting her rising alarm at the same time. "And surely the Indians were only looking for fuel to keep warm."

"Yes, ma'am, but they left one dead an' two wounded," Homer said, staring at her worriedly.

Jennifer's stomach clenched. Her gaze flew toward

the soldiers. Silently, she watched as a few people gathered to witness the blue-coated soldiers mount and ride out, lined up in precision.

Jennifer hid her inner qualms and spoke calmly. "Oh, that is indeed dreadful. But that doesn't mean there is a war party out or that our men are in danger, Homer." What she said was true, but beyond that, she didn't want to add to anyone's panic. Especially her own.

Sam Burns jumped in with "Can't never tell what them savages'll do, ma'am. Never know where they'll be."

"Our men are careful, Sam, and most of them are seasoned veterans. They'll watch."

"We c'n only hope so, ma'am. They're a small huntin' party an' them redskins are sneaky devils, I'll tell ya."

He shook his head and walked away, leaving her to stare after him and the retreating soldiers in dismay. What if Sam's dire thoughts were on target and there were warring Indians out looking for blood? Could the hunting party withstand an attack?

But the chances for them even to cross paths were slim. She wouldn't worry. No, she would put it out of her mind.

Jennifer hurried into the schoolhouse. Mrs. Dillon, Mrs. Tige, Mrs. Gallaghar, and Dora Burns waited; at least they sat in the circled student desks chattering over town affairs. Someone shushed them as she entered the room, and several pairs of eyelashes suddenly dropped or flickered away.

Had they been discussing her?

"Oh, you must be so anxious, Mrs. Prescott," Dora Burns said, rushing to speak. "I told Sam, I said, that report about that wood wagon suffering an attack from those Indians, I said, it would frazzle my nerves something dreadful if my husband was out on the plains."

"Well, I've only just heard about it, Mrs. Burns. However, I have faith that Gil and the others will be on guard."

"Yes, I guess Gil Prescott does know about Indians, you might say," Mrs. Gallaghar put in with a sly glance from beneath her lowered lids. "He lived with a tribe of them before the recent civil disagreement, you know. But how silly of me. Of course *you* would know. There is the child, isn't there?"

Mrs. Dillon hastily cut in. "Ladies, ladies. We must get on with our meeting." She flashed Jennifer a sympathetic glance and nodded in greeting. "Good of you to attend, Mrs. Prescott. Thank you for coming to our aid in this matter of choosing a new teacher. Now, ladies, we may begin."

An hour later, Jennifer gathered her cape and mittens together, preparing to leave.

Dora Burns stepped forward. "Mrs. Prescott, may I have a word with you?"

"Why, certainly, Mrs. Burns. What is it?"

The two women stepped to one side.

"It's about Homer. Is the lad . . . is his work satisfactory? He isn't lazy or anything?"

"No, Mrs. Burns. Homer works very hard. We find his work very satisfactory."

Dora Burns sniffed, then asked, "He doesn't get cheeky with you, does he? If Mr. Burns ever thought . . . well, you say he's satisfactory?"

"Yes. Mrs. Burns, what is it you'd like to say?"

"Well, I was hoping you might keep the boy on permanently. He . . . um . . . well, you see, there really isn't enough room in my boardinghouse for him and

I'm hoping Sam . . . that is, Sam is considering selling the livery, and heaven knows I need his help around the boardinghouse, but there's Homer, you see. However I just can't give up a single room in my house to a nonpaying overgrown oaf of a lad like Homer. He's so clumsy, and I won't have that mangy dog of his. I told Sam, I said, the boy is old enough to earn his own living. It's time he went."

Jennifer drew a long breath and counted to ten before answering. After all, what was Dora Burns's loss was their gain. She and Gil both found Homer worthy of their care, and he certainly worked hard enough to find employment anywhere.

"Rest assured, Mrs. Burns. Homer can remain with us until he wishes to go. We have plenty of room for him."

"Thank you, Mrs. Prescott. I knew you'd come through. Why, I told Sam, I said, if that teacher took on that Indian bas—er, child of Gil Prescott's, she'd likely be happy to have Homer. Homer, at least, can earn his bread and butter, if he's a mind to."

Jennifer pulled her cloak close up under her chin. "I will talk to my husband when he returns, Mrs. Burns, but I'm certain he will be glad to have Homer with us."

"That is kind of you, most kind. And Mrs. Prescott, could we keep this little understanding to ourselves? I don't want to, um, upset Sam or count our chickens before they're hatched, as it were. And any change might jeopardize the possible sale of the livery, you see."

"I will certainly keep our conversation private, Mrs. Burns, if that is your wish. But why do you think a change in Homer's abode would cause you a problem?"

"Mr. Quiller hasn't actually made us an offer yet. He's only hinted strongly at wishing to buy the livery as it stands."

"Mr. Quiller?" Jennifer's mouth went dry. Was Robert back in town? And why would he even hint at buying the livery? "What has he to do with it? Where"—Jennifer tried to quiet her jumpy stomach and lessen her sharp tone—"where is he these days?"

"Well, he's away for the moment, but he promised to take the matter under serious consideration when he returns. He is interested in our little town and quite wealthy, you see. Oh, he has been so helpful. And very social, too. He's been to tea, you know." Dora Burns positively preened in the telling. "Twice. Only heaven knows why, but he likes talking to Homer, even though Homer doesn't have much to say, the big lump."

Jennifer nodded knowingly. She knew that Robert would appear very friendly and sociably charming while he courted whomever could give him what he was after. However, his attention could turn to cold disdain or to deadly verbal assault in the blink of the eye if he no longer found a person useful to him.

Why Homer? In this case, Jennifer truly wondered what Robert was after. How could Homer, Sam, and Dora Burns benefit the man?

Dora Burns's voice skipped on. "He has made friends with half the merchants, too. He has ideas. If he were to invest in some of our businesses and bring a railroad in, why we could expand Osage Springs to rival Topeka. I told him, I said, a man of his caliber could become quite a power in the state of Kansas if he chose to settle here. Even become a senator. He's so well bred, don't you think?"

Jennifer nodded again, giving the impression she agreed with her companion's opinion, while she tried to find a reason why Robert would want to invest in the livery or any other of the town's businesses.

Dora's praises suddenly turned sly when she said, "Of course, you know the charming Mr. Quiller rather well, yourself, don't you, my dear?"

Dora allowed her words to slither to a stop as her light brown eyes sharpened to points of inquisitiveness. Jennifer raised her gaze, her thoughts refocusing on Dora's question.

From her side vision, Jennifer noticed Mrs. Gallaghar turn toward them, as if listening to what she might answer. Mrs. Tige lowered her voice and let her conversation with Mrs. Dillon drift as her gaze flickered Jennifer's way.

There was no use denying it; Osage Springs had been aware since the Thanksgiving dance that she and Robert had once been acquainted, and he'd not missed a single chance to address her in casual meetings since. But now something more had been added, Jennifer guessed, a new element in the town gossip, and she wondered what Robert had said about her.

"Yes, Mr. Quiller was a friend of my first husband," she said calmly enough, giving full attention to pulling on her gloves. "We frequently attended the same social functions."

"That was in Philadelphia, wasn't it?" asked Mrs. Burns. "Mr. Quiller said you were quite the belle there."

"That was a long time ago, Mrs. Burns." Jennifer gave a quick smile, hoping to give the impression that the question and the bid for more information about her past was of little importance to her. "Excuse me, please. I really must go, now."

Behind her, she heard a whispered "Philadelphia? I thought she came from some little community near Boston."

"I don't know, but mark my words, Bridgit Gallaghar, that Mr. Quiller and our high-and-mighty, nose-in-the-air Mrs. Prescott were very close once."

Jennifer let it go and hurried out to collect Zachary. As bothersome as the local gossip about her was, at the moment she was more concerned that Gil could have possibly run into hostilities out on the plains. She hoped a talk with the Lindermans might help to alleviate some of her feelings.

And it did, a little. Peder insisted that Gil would be careful and said all the other things she wanted to hear.

But oh! She did wish for Gil to be home, safe and sound.

Gil found the place where he had lost sight of Merritt along with the main herd. The track was as broad in the crusty snow as though a whole army had tracked through. A much bigger herd had stampeded through than the one he and Merritt had chased. He'd heard it earlier.

He began to circle.

It didn't take him long to discover a wagon. His. It had turned over and meat and hides lay in a heap as well as scattered around it. Something had damn well spooked the horses, Gil surmised, but they were nowhere in sight. Neither was the other wagon. Nor any of the men.

Snow skids led over a western hill. It looked as if his team had dragged something, probably one of the men, along behind. Grimly, he followed the track. He could barely see in the darkening light. Thank the Lord the snow reflected what light there was because as soon as he crested the hill, he saw a dark shape lying in the snow.

Gil dismounted and rushed forward as fast as his snow-crashing steps could take him. Josh. Bending, Gil put his hand against Josh's face. His skin was cold and beginning to glaze. Instantly, he sharply patted Josh's cheeks and chin, then put his ear close to Josh's nose. A flutter of breath chilled his bare cheek. "Josh. Thank God."

Gil made a rough examination but could find no wound. Only unconscious, he decided. "C'mon, Josh, wake up."

Gil scanned the landscape, spotting more tracks. There was no help for it; they couldn't stay here. Gil lifted Josh carefully and placed him belly down over Beau's saddle. Leading Beau, they started forward again.

A few minutes later, he heard a wild sobbing. It came from an outcropping of rock. It had to be Willy.

"Willy?"

A low, rough catch interrupted the desperate sound of Willy's distress. Gil called again. "Willy, where are you?"

"Gil!" Willy stumbled forward from behind a boulder, knuckling his eyes. He didn't appear hurt. "Oh, thank God."

"What happened, Willy? Where's Miles?"

"Don't know . . . got turned over by a buff stampede an' drug. It was plumb awful, Gil. Terrible. Josh got left behind somewhere. Miles, he took his horse an' wagon an' said he was gonna foller Merritt sometime afore the big herd came arunnin' onto us. Ain't seen 'im since midafternoon."

Gil fervently hoped Miles had caught up with Merritt by now. The thought of three of them being left afoot was right troublesome. Josh moaned and Gil lifted the man down. "Well, I found Josh, anyway. Hand me the canteen, Willy."

"Josh? He okay? How'd ya find us'ns?"

"Wasn't hard," Gil answered. "Tracks wide enough for a child to figure out." He tipped a little water into Josh's mouth and was gratified when Josh swallowed. "D'you know what's happened to the team?" he said over his shoulder.

"Naw. Could be anywhere."

"Have you looked?" Gil demanded to know.

"On foot?" Willy said, horrified.

"On foot, your hands and knees, or even your belly! We need those horses."

"But Gil, I been drug an' spraddled an' I got bruised all over."

"You're on your feet, ain't you? Now git to the tops of those rocks you were hiding behind and look for 'em."

Willy stomped away, grumbling under his breath.

Josh began to move. "Josh, you all right?" Gil queried. "I couldn't find nothin' broken."

"My head."

"Yep, reckon you took a big lump there, right enough. Size of an egg. Can you stand up?"

"Reckon so." Although wobbly, Josh managed to find his feet, but he leaned heavily on Gil.

"Can you ride?"

"Reckon."

Gil wasn't too sure, but he heaved Josh into the saddle and held him there.

"See anything?" Gil asked Willy when they reached him.

"Nope. But I heard a whinny. From that buncha trees."

"Then go get 'em."

"But Gil, anythin' could be in them trees at night."

"Hellfire, Willy. Where'd all your wits go? We have to have those horses to get back to protect our haul. Those wolves'll make a feast on our buff haunches if we don't get there pronto, and Josh here ain't in no condition to walk."

Seeing that Willy was about to protest further, Gil gritted his teeth. He hadn't time to waste on anger and flipped Beau's reins over to Willy and commanded, "Stay here!"

Straining to see, Gil cautiously made his way down the other side of the hill toward the dark patch of trees. Willy was right, a man couldn't know what he might find.

Once on the edge of the dark growth, he stopped and listened. Over the breeze, he heard the heavy breathing of the nearby horses. And a whinny of pain. Following the sound, he spotted them. One was down.

Both horses seemed glad to see him. Their reins had been caught in the underbrush, holding them fast.

He spoke softly to soothe them, "Here, steady now. Steady." Swiftly, he knelt and discovered the badly broken leg of the small roan mare. She raised her head and whinnied pitifully.

"Thunderation, Queenie, I'm real sorry." Sorry didn't cover it, though. No matter how much he despised it, the horse would have to be shot.

He untangled the reins and unhitched Queenie from the halter. Beside him, Jogalong neighed and pawed the snowy earth as if he, too, knew what must be done. Gil led the gelding off a ways and tied him to a sapling.

Gil then took care of the unpleasant chore of putting Queenie out of her misery.

*   *   *

Jennifer peeked at the molasses cookies in the oven and decided they were brown enough. Pulling the pan out, she set it on top of the range to cool.

The boys deserved a treat; they'd worked extra hard to keep up with the chores while Gil was gone. They'd kept the paths from the house, barn, chicken coop, and bunkhouse cleared after the last snow, and even spread ashes on them to make them safer for her to walk.

Now they were in the throes of a February thaw, and outside, everything dripped as the snow melted. It left the roads patchy with mud and slush, and she'd dreaded going to town with them in that condition.

With only a little trepidation, and after more than a bit of cajoling, she had finally given consent for Zachary and Homer to go alone to town—the boys had taken it upon themselves to do her marketing for her—but not without many promises and admonitions to stick to their agreed-on route.

"Homer, you're not to be gone longer than three hours. Anything that can't be done by noon can wait until another day."

"Yes'm. But I gotta have time to exchange Piker, Oats, an' Bones fer Red an' Stockings behind Lindermans'. An' Pa wanted Oats brought 'round to the boardin'house. He's gonna keep 'im in a shed out back."

"You'll have plenty of time for your horses, Homer. Only, please don't dawdle. Go straight to town and back. Now, Zach, do you have my note to Mrs. Linderman?"

"Uh-huh. It's in my pocket, see?" He pulled it out to show her.

"All right," she said and sighed. "Keep your scarf tied about your neck, now. You've had the sniffles lately."

She let them go, waving and watching until they were out of sight. Biting her lip all the while. Maybe she shouldn't have let Zach go—he was only four.

And a half, he'd reminded her the other day.

Homer was a responsible young man of fifteen, Jennifer sternly reminded herself as she reluctantly closed the door, and they'd made the same trip a hundred times over. Gil would be proud of her for letting Zach go. He thought she'd kept their son in babyhood too long, she knew, though he never voiced his feelings in those exact terms.

She rested a while, caught up with her mending, then busied herself with baking cookies.

Outside, she heard the sloshing sounds of a buggy drive up to her front door. Surprised, she hurriedly wiped her hands on her loose, overall apron. It couldn't be Bessie—she always went to the back door. And Mary Sue and Frank had visited only two days before, to see how she and the boys were faring.

Swinging the door wide, a smile of welcome hovering, Jennifer suddenly wished she had hidden and bolted the door instead. Because her caller was Robert Quiller.

18

"*Good day to you,* my lovely Patricia," Robert said as soon as he brought the buggy to a stop. He looked at her fondly, letting his gaze travel her face with glowing appreciation. As one would a possession. It made her shiver.

She had totally mistaken that look nine years ago; she'd been entirely too naive to understand it. But Jennifer wondered that he still found anything in her face and form to desire. After all, she was nearing thirty, and her form . . .

Suddenly she was hugely grateful she'd decided to bake this morning. The overall apron she wore hung unfettered almost to her hem. Underneath, her worn dress was unfastened at the waistline to allow for her growing girth.

"How pleasant to find you at home, my darling girl. I have long looked forward to seeing you again, without the encumbrances of your husband or his son. Now we can have our long-delayed chat."

His smooth, cultured voice invited her to share his joy at their reunion. It did not match the cunning edges of what Jennifer saw behind his smile and eyes.

Again, she shivered. How had he managed it? How had he caught her alone?

But perhaps this was best after all, Jennifer decided. She could talk plainly and freely, and hopefully, put an end to this cat-and-mouse game he had started.

"Good day, Robert."

"May I come into your abode, my dear?"

"Yes, I think that would be best." She held the door wide, striving to keep her distaste for him from showing.

He removed his black beaver hat as he entered, giving her simple furnishings only a flicker of interest. The slightest twist of his lips, gone as quickly as it appeared, gave away his disdainful opinion of her home.

Wanting something to give her an excuse to be busy, she said, "I am baking this morning. You'll have to come into the kitchen."

"Wherever you say, Patricia."

"My name is Jennifer."

He gave an acquiescent nod. "Since you insist. Jennifer. But you know the line that comes to mind. A rose by any name still smells as sweet. "

Annoyance was only part of her emotions as Jennifer deliberately turned to the stove. Shame at the way his compliments had once turned her head flooded her mind. "Be seated there at the table, Robert, if you wish."

"Thank you."

The whisper of cloth against cloth told her that he removed his black fur-lined cape with the beaver collar, and then a slight scrape of a kitchen chair indicated he was seated.

"Perhaps, my dear, you would be good enough to offer me coffee?"

Without a word, she poured a mug of the dark brew that was left over from breakfast and placed it on the table in front of him. No doubt it would be bitterly strong. Years of training caused her automatically to set the cream pitcher beside it.

He watched her in silence for several moments. She did her best to ignore his intent observation as she removed the baked cookies onto a plate and then dropped cookie dough onto a clean sheet. She took time to add a stick of wood to the stove before putting the dough into the oven to bake.

"Admirable, my dear . . . Jennifer. You have become quite the staunch pioneer woman. Domestic to the hilt. But I must ask you to sit now."

It was a quiet order from a man who expected to be obeyed.

"Very well." Her few moments of activity had given her time to gather herself. She felt calmer. She seated herself in the opposite chair, folded her hands on the table surface, then looked squarely into his light brown eyes. "What is it you want, Robert?"

"Do you really have to ask that question?" Amusement flared in his eyes.

"Yes. Yes, I do."

"I want you. I always did."

"But that was nine years ago!"

"Ahh, but my dear! My desires concerning you remain the same. Surely you know that?"

"Why?"

He paid no attention to her question and asked his

own. "Why did you run away from me? After Willard died there was no need for you to be merely my mistress. You could have become my wife."

"No, I couldn't have, Robert. Never, no matter what situation you offered me. My life was in ruins."

"But I would have taken care of you. I looked for you everywhere. I followed you to Europe."

"I know."

"I lost track of you when you returned to the United States," he said, his voice complaining mildly. "And then the war hampered my search."

"I didn't want you to find me."

"But you're mine, Patricia," he said in a completely reasonable tone. "You must realize I would find you eventually and reclaim you."

His very reasonableness frightened her. How could he continue to think, in the face of all that had transpired, that she had any remaining interest in him at all? Their association had ended in tragedy!

With an effort to keep her voice steady, Jennifer's fingers tightened until her knuckles turned white. "You can't reclaim something you've never had, Robert. You must see the sense in that. I married your cousin Willard. I was never yours."

"Were you not? Remember that velvety night with a million stars when you met me under the willow tree where we kissed? Your mouth was as fresh as a newly opened rosebud, my dear, and as innocent. That was *after* you married the cold-blooded Willard. God, how I wanted you that night. I knew your passions belonged to me."

Robert licked his lips, remembering, and then continued. "Willard never suspected us, then. And how desperate I was to see you, to touch you. I attended every tea, soiree, and ball the whole season only to do that. You never objected. Then you came to me at my country estate, remember?"

Indeed, she hadn't objected at first. That was her disgrace! His practiced charm had fooled her into thinking him a friend, a family member to whom she could turn in moments of minor distress. While her husband frequently ignored her, Robert was an attentive swain who flattered and cajoled her until a polite dance embrace in public became maneuvered meetings in dark hallways and dark empty rooms where he petted and kissed her, not always gently.

She had been young and hadn't known what to do.

"You lured me there under false pretense, Robert. I never would have responded to your invitation had I known no other guests were invited."

He had dismissed all his servants after they dined, and like a lamb to the slaughter, led her to a darkened bedroom. A single candle that he held high had shown her that it was his. She had balked at the doorway.

Only God knew how she'd escaped his rape.

He laughed now in triumph. "You were a wee bit gullible, darling." His smile faded. "But so was I. I thought you only teased me when you flirted with other men and that you would eventually be all mine. Then you told me you would remain faithful to Willard. I didn't like that, you know," he ended with a frown.

"Flirted . . . yes, I suppose I foolishly did that," she answered absently. Guiltily. "It seemed all of the younger set did so then."

That was no excuse, she now reflected. It was one of her more shameful actions of youth.

The lines in Robert's face deepened. "And Willard never appreciated a warm-blooded little bitch like you. He married you only to get himself an heir."

Slightly shocked at his harsh speech, she said, "Many marriages are based on that need, Robert. I knew that when I married Willard. Aunt Agnes—"

Robert cut in disparagingly. "Aunt Agnes! Yes, and your ambitious Aunt Agnes had much to answer for. When I laid my proposal at your feet I would have given you the whole world. But that hatchet-faced old woman accepted Willard's offer for you over mine. His wealth was twice mine."

"I didn't know about that, Robert, but—"

"I supposed you didn't, my dear. However . . ." He leaned forward and took her hands. "Now I have found you again, I forgive you. You are mine now!" Then dropping his gaze, he added, "And I see we must do something to restore your lovely hands. You have quite abused them."

Jennifer drew back, tugging at his grip. Robert held fast. She then pulled hard. Robert half rose and leaned even closer, a mixture of adoration and determination on his face.

"Come away with me now, Patricia darling. Today, this very minute. I'll adorn these slender fingers with jewels and your lovely body with gowns from the finest designers in the world. I'll take you to Paris and Italy. You'll have everything."

"Robert, I'm married—"

"Never mind that. You don't have to stay in this pitiful alliance a moment longer. I'll buy you a divorce."

"Like you did in Philadelphia, Robert?" Jennifer yanked her hands free at last and blurted out the suspicion she'd lived with for nine years.

Robert leaned back in his chair. "Do you know about that, then? But it was only to help Willard along. He wouldn't give you up unless I had pushed the issue. And you wanted me, too. Didn't you? You were a hot little bitch in heat that night under the stars."

Jennifer tried hard to keep her emotions under control, but old outrage, shame, and fear caused her to shoot up from her chair. She stood glaring at her accuser and tormentor.

"So it *was* your doing? You created even more scandal than there already was, didn't you, Robert? You led everyone to believe I was your mistress."

"I had to, Patricia, don't you see? I had to get you free of Willard and you had too much conscience. Now you're mine again and we needn't worry about him any longer. Or anyone else. Now darling, why don't you just get your cloak and we can be on our way. You needn't take anything else."

Jennifer blinked rapidly. The man did not recognize her repeated refusals. Was he deaf to them? He pretended she saw the situation as he wished. Why? Why, after all this time and thousands of miles later would any sensible man continue . . . any *sensible* man?

Then it dawned on her. Robert wasn't rational! At least where it concerned her. She searched his face for clues as to what would make his thinking so unbalanced, but what she saw was a smiling, gracious man with adoration written there. He was in a world of his own.

All at once, she realized the source of her past problems. Robert's involvement had been even deeper than she knew, and what he had done wasn't from mere malicious intent—*he believed in his own fantasy.* Why hadn't she seen it before?

Now she had the precarious task of convincing this man that she was not going with him without upsetting his balance any more than it already was.

Jennifer swallowed hard as her arms went around her middle in an unconscious gesture of self-protection. And now for the protection of her unborn child as well.

She took a deep breath and spoke softly. "No, Robert, I am not yours. I belong to myself, I am my own woman. You must understand me—I'm a different person now. I am Jennifer Prescott. I haven't been that flighty young girl named Patricia for a long, long time."

Robert stood to face her, reaching to stroke her cheek. "You are still so beautiful. Didn't you hear what I said, my darling girl? I forgive you for all this"—he waved a hand about, as though her home was a sin for which she would be magnanimously pardoned—"we won't speak of it again. Let me take you away to Paris."

"Robert, please." Jennifer moved away into the parlor. She had some idea of leaving the house entirely if she needed to, and wanted to be nearer the front door.

The door abruptly flew open and Zachary raced into the room. Just as abruptly, he skidded to a stop. His wide dark eyes stared at the eastern man. "Who's here, Mama? Me 'n' Homer saw the carriage outside."

Homer ambled through the door, spoke shyly to the visitor, then threw a puzzled glance at Jennifer before going through to the kitchen to deposit his wooden box of groceries.

Jennifer stood tall, holding herself together with thankfulness at seeing the boys and a need to get Robert out without upsetting him further.

"You remember Mr. Quiller, don't you, Zach?"

"Yes, ma'am. How do, Mr. Quiller."

Robert nodded. Harsh disappointment robbed him of speech. If those brats hadn't come in, if he had had a few more minutes, he could have convinced her to come with him. She would have been his by nightfall.

Homer sidled into the parlor and leaned against the wall. He stared at Robert, then glanced away. "Somethin's burnin', Miz Jennifer."

Indeed, the odor of burning cookies filled the air, but Jennifer refused to move until her enemy was out of the house. She spoke, her chin held high. "Thank you for calling, Mr. Quiller. But as you can see, I am quite occupied with my duties here. I don't need anything," she said as she drew a deep breath, leaving out the words *from you* that screamed through her mind. She hoped he grasped her meaning anyway, and finished her sentence with a dismissing "even though it was kind of you to offer."

For one instant, Robert let his control slip. Pure hatred and spite shot from the glance that swept the boys and her home. Seeing it made Jennifer decidedly nervous and sweat ran down her brow. Determinedly, she held herself straighter. She would not cower in fear.

But how far had he gone nine years before to ruin her? How far would he go now?

Unconsciously, Jennifer swept the bottom of her apron up, blotting the dampness from her temple. Hopefully, she moved toward the front door and pulled it wide. *Why wouldn't he go?*

Robert remained where he stood, and it was a moment before Jennifer realized where his gaze rested. At her belly. His face looked frozen; his skin paled as she watched. He raised his eyes slowly, his gaze boring directly into hers with bitter accusation. "How could you betray me thus?"

"Robert, I think our business is concluded. I suggest your interests will be better served back east. But you won't find what you want here in Kansas."

His mouth tight, he left without looking at her again. However, as he passed her, he hissed, "We shall see."

Gil used a torch, roughly put together from a gun-cleaning rag and a piece of wood, to lead them back to the overturned wagon.

Yelps and growls reached them before they saw the dark shapes. Gil shoved the torch into Josh's hand and yanked out his handgun, popping off three shots in rapid fire. The wolves ran, but not very far.

"Get a fire going, Willy," he grimly commanded. "I'll look after the horses."

Josh slid to the ground from behind him. "I c'n help." Unsteadily, he kicked snow aside for a campfire.

Gil slowly rode around the wagon. The hides seemed intact, but the meat lay scattered. Only daylight would tell them if they could salvage any of it.

He widened his circle, alert to the glittering eyes of half a dozen slinking animals that watched his every move.

"Fire's goin'," said Willy.

"See if you can find the coffee," Gil said.

"Gil." Josh spoke uneasily. "Them wolves're bolder'n a two-bit whore. They're stealing our meat." He nodded toward the outer reaches of the meager firelight.

"Yeah. Going to be a problem. Willy, build another fire on the other side of the wagon. And another, yonder," he said as he pointed in a third direction.

"'At might eat up our firewood supply," Willy warned.

"Can't be helped. Josh, if you're feeling better, drag

that meat into a pile by the wagon while I ride line. We'll look at it in the morning. If you find some that's already no good, throw it to the wolves. Maybe they'll have enough and leave the rest alone."

They kept it up for hours. Eventually, Willy slept while Josh tended the fires. Gil rode in circles, often shooting into the darkness. After he hit two of the predators, the noise of ravaging sent his horse into nervous snorts.

He patted Beau's neck to calm him down. Hell, his own nerves were taut as a fiddle bow, Gil thought. He'd never had a run-in with more than two wolves at a time before.

After that, Gil surmised their threat was less, but he couldn't take any chances. He didn't know how many wolves still stalked beyond sight.

About midnight, he shook Willy. "Get up, Willy. Guard duty."

Willy rolled out of his blankets, but not without a few curses. "Damn them mangy wolves. Robbin' a man of sleep is worse 'n anything."

Gil ignored him. "Okay, Josh, your turn. Get some sleep."

"What about you, Gil?"

"My turn'll come." Gil hastily swallowed some coffee, then unsaddled and watered Beau. His mount needed rest.

He checked his gun and replaced his ammunition, then started to walk the flattened circle. Toward dawn, it seemed to him that there were fewer eyes and furry shapes on the edges. He roused Josh before rolling into his own blankets.

A hail woke him. He rose swiftly, his gun in hand.

"Whoa 'ere, Gil. It's only Miles an' Merritt acomin'," Willy said.

Gil went forth to meet the oncoming wagon. Miles drove the mule team while Merritt sat in the back, leaning on a pile of hides.

"I sure am glad to see you two ain't lost," Gil half joked. Only now did he admit to his real concern over the brothers. "What happened, Merritt? Saw your mount hightailing it over the hill, but you were nowhere in sight."

"Fool horse stepped in a prairie dog hole," Merritt said, then stopped talking as he glanced around at the scene.

"Wolves?" asked Miles, his eyes searching the ground.

"Much damage?" Merritt asked.

"Yep. Enough. Haven't had time to assess all of it. Lost one of the horses, too. How'd you boys find us so quick?"

"Saw smoke. Smelled cookin'." Merritt swung over the back of the wagon carefully and limped to the fire.

"How badly were you thrown?" Gil asked, watching him closely. Losing some of their meat and two horses would put a decided crimp in their efforts, but two men injured might put an end to their hunt altogether.

Merritt shrugged. "Got coffee?"

Gil raised his hat and ran a hand through his hair. His mouth tasted like leftover rotten eggs—he'd had to eat some during the war—and his head felt fuzzy from lack of sleep.

Besides all that, the low sky promised more snow.

"Willy, make some coffee and rustle up breakfast. Reckon a powwow is in order."

In the end, all five men voted to stay out one more week before starting back home. They decided to backtrack for a day and pick up whatever hides had been left in their hunt, then go on north to Topeka, Lawrence, and Ft. Leavenworth for the better markets.

However, it would be slower going, with two horses lost. They would be later getting home. Gil hoped Jennifer wouldn't be too upset with worry.

"Gil ain't home yet?" became the worrisome question Jennifer faced from a number of people with every trip she made into town. She hated answering it but was determined not to show her real concern about her husband's overdue return. Especially after noticing Zachary's searching gaze during one such conversation with Mr. Tige outside of the mercantile store.

"He will be home very soon, now," she replied in a positive tone. "There are things he wants to get done around our place before spring."

"Yeah. Yeah. Reckon so." Mr. Tige nodded in acknowledgment of the work that awaited a country man.

Robert approached and bowed, sweeping his hat from his head. His greeting was entirely too elaborate for a casual acquaintance. "Good day, my dear Jennifer. How lovely to see you in town this morning." He tipped his head and gave her a knowing smile. "I do hope you are feeling better than the other morning when I called."

"Yes, thank you, Mr. Quiller. I am very well. Now if you'll excuse me."

Without giving politeness another jot of attention, she pivoted and walked away, holding Zach's hand so tightly the boy fairly ran to keep pace with her. But not before she heard Robert remark, "What a beautiful woman."

Open admiration for another man's wife didn't set well with western men, Jennifer knew. It implied a connection, whether unsavory or innocent. Robert knew exactly what he did with such a greeting.

It was enough to cause her to stay home. Except that now, everyone would know that Robert had called on her while her husband was away. The townspeople would speculate about where he was going every time Robert rented Sam's buggy.

Toward noon of that same day, Gil drove his wagon into Osage Springs with Beau hitched alongside Jogalong. Merritt and Miles had chosen to go directly home.

Gil was reasonably satisfied with the results of their enterprise, though by the time he paid off Willy and Josh, subtracted his losses, and paid a few bills, his profits would cover only about half of the calves he'd hoped to purchase in the spring. However, he would be free of debt and those few calves would give him a new start in ranching, he reasoned, and besides, he still had other endeavors that brought in cash.

All in all, Gil was happy. And he could hardly wait to get home to see his wife and son—he was ragingly hungry for even the sight of Jennifer—and renewed his vow never to leave his home again.

He pulled the wagon up to John Perry's store and swung down to unload a canvas-wrapped bundle of frozen meat. Josh hopped down and shouldered it while Willy sat in the back of the wagon.

"Papa!"

Gil pivoted at his son's call. The boy raced up the muddy road toward him, already yards in front of a smiling Jennifer.

"Howdy, sprout," he greeted, catching Zachary up as the child hurtled himself three feet into the air at him. He hugged him close, then looked beyond. "Jennifer."

Only the consciousness of the fact that they stood in the middle of town prevented Gil from crushing her in his arms. Her blue eyes smiled into his, tumbling his heart like a butter churn. "Did you miss me, Teacher?"

"Oh, Gil, I'm so glad you're home at last. We've been very worried. The army said . . . oh, never mind, I can tell you later."

Feeling badly for giving her cause to be anxious, he murmured, "Well, I'm home, now. And this time I mean it. I'll not leave you again."

"Did you shoot a hundred buffalo, Papa?"

"Uh-huh. Near 'bout."

He took a quick gander at the busy street. Awareness that he was back was starting to take hold along the road. People were heading their way.

"'At 'n wolves," said Willy.

"Wolves, Papa?" Zach asked, his eyes rounded.

Gil's gaze returned to Jennifer, his free hand rubbing the rough beard he'd allowed to grow. He wanted to kiss her something fierce, and if he didn't move he'd end up embarrassing her in front of all the townsfolk who were coming around, eager to hear how the hunting party'd made out.

"Yeah. Three or four."

Mr. Perry came out of his store, then, and Mr. Tige hailed him from his mercantile. Gil turned, his arm around Jennifer.

Robert Quiller stood with his back to the mercantile's front glass, his hands resting on the knob of his cane as he observed them. Gil's immediate reaction was acute dislike for the man. He looked at Jennifer too boldly, and somehow, lasciviously. Not for the first time, Gil felt a roaring jealousy.

Quiller smiled slowly while a knowing cunning entered his gaze. Very slightly, he nodded.

Gil was left with the impression that the man held a secret and wanted him to know it.

19

The boys were eager to tell Gil about coming home to find Robert Quiller in their parlor. Something about the visit made them uneasy and neither of them liked the scene they'd walked in on, Gil knew. Zach said the man had a mean mouth and looked at his mother funny, while Homer, with a shy, dawning understanding of a man's needs and feelings, said Quiller made Teacher plumb nervous.

On the other hand, Jennifer had said nothing about it at all after she mentioned the bare fact of the visit. That made *him* nervous. And furious. And scared. The damned weasel was after his wife.

Quiller, by all accounts, had a great deal of wealth and fine living to offer her. It galled him that he didn't.

Gil was slow to anger, but once roused, he became a tornado of wrath, and right now he felt the storm building. By thunder, the man's growing attention to his wife was intolerable. He had to put a stop to it or he might explode.

Gil sought Quiller out about a week after his return. He found the eastern dude in the hotel dining room, ensconced at "his table," directed there by the impressed clerk.

"Ah, Mr. Prescott." Robert greeted him as though he had been expecting him, and indicated a chair. "Please join me."

"No, I'll stand. This won't take but a minute."

"I see. Well, then, what is your business with me?"

"I haven't any. But I have one strong suggestion, Mr. Quiller," he said, his voice low but hard. "One that I'd advise you to take. Stay away from my wife!"

"Well, now. Well, well, well." Quiller leaned back in his chair and puffed on his thin cigar, contemplating him with arrogant humor. Gil's nostrils quivered as he took in the fragrance of the fine tobacco.

Robert let his gaze drop to the long reed in his hand. Then he raised contemptuous eyes. "Would you care for one, Mr. Prescott?"

"No." Gil stood with his feet apart, feeling mulish with dislike. This highfalutin gent sure did put his back up. Did he think to bribe him with the offer of a cigar? "Did you hear what I said?"

"Yes, yes, Mr. Prescott. I heard you."

Quiller spoke as though he was king of all he surveyed and talked to a rather slow-minded minion; Gil's hands balled at his sides.

"I do think you ought to reconsider and seat yourself," Quiller continued. "We might have business to discuss after all."

"What do you mean?"

Robert paused a long moment, his face a triumphant smirk. "I have known the woman who is now your wife for a very long time, Mr. Prescott."

March came in like the proverbial lion. It snowed and blew heavily the first week, then dripped and thawed through the day and froze again at night. Gil suggested that Jennifer stay at home when he went to town. She gladly gave in and let Gil do her shopping. She was content with the company of the boys while he was gone. On Gil's orders, they stayed close by, she noticed, which made her chuckle. Her husband had grown even more protective since his return.

Jennifer didn't mind. Her movements were rather clumsy these days, and mindful of her previous loss, she didn't fuss at the bit of pampering on which the men seemed bent. Homer and Zachary had even taken on the additional chore of seeing to the chickens lately, and if Zach forgot to feed his dog, Homer or Gil reminded him.

Then one night, Gil sent the boys to bed early. Noting that he seemed to have something on his mind, Jennifer watched as he picked up a dish towel and silently proceeded to gallop his way through drying the dishes.

"Slow down there, Gil. They're not likely to wiggle out of your rope," she teased after he nearly dropped one in his haste. "What is it that has you in a lather, anyway?"

"Sorry, Teacher. Just been thinking, that's all."

His gray eyes flashed at her, then away. She hadn't seen that look of uncertainty on his face for months. "Thinking, hmm? Want to share it?"

He laid the last plate on the table and draped the drying towel over a chair. He took a few steps toward the parlor, then turned back and circled the table. He rubbed the broken ridge of his nose. "Jennifer, what would you say about moving into Osage Springs again?"

"What do you mean? For my confinement?"

"Uh, yeah . . . but, no. Permanently. You must be tired of being stuck in the country all this time, a big-city woman like you. Going days, sometimes weeks without seeing other people. Other ladies."

"Have I complained?"

"No, but then, you wouldn't. Well?"

"How would you like it, Gil?"

"Um, I reckon I'd like town living well enough."

"But what would you do to make a living?"

Gil shifted his feet. "I'd keep this place. Ranch it with a manager, maybe. Already running back and forth anyway. And Homer might come to stay for good, even though his pa says he wants him back in town soon to help run the livery. Sam's never said a word to me about selling it, like his wife says. Maybe I'd hire on with Sam. Army's moving out. Spring's round the corner."

Jennifer wondered what was really behind Gil's rambling thoughts, but she chose to answer his one remark about their proximity to town.

"Yes, we're close enough to town. I've never felt truly isolated here even though we're rather off the main thoroughfare into Osage Springs."

Putting that thought aside, she went to another. "But part-time ranching won't fulfill your dream, Gil. You've been talking of little else but ways in which to get this place together again and how to expand it ever since you arrived home from the war. Everywhere you can, you've saved your pennies toward that goal. Why have you changed your mind now?"

"I haven't, Teacher." He stared down at his boots suddenly as if he wished he hadn't said that.

"Gil, what is all this about?"

"I just . . . I want you to be happy, Jennifer."

"But I am, Gil. Why—" Why would he think she wasn't? Perhaps because rumor gave him cause to think it? What poison had Robert blown into the wind? What seeds had taken root in Gil's mind and heart?

She was afraid to ask, afraid to probe. Licking her dry lips, she murmured, "This has become our home, Gil. This is where I belong."

Gil gave her a long, thoughtful stare before turning away. Restlessly, he reached for his coat, murmuring something about checking the animals.

Behind him Jennifer felt the full blast of cold air before he closed the door behind himself.

After the weather cleared, Jennifer set out for town again. She longed for some female company and planned to visit with Maude; she admitted to herself that she sometimes did miss womanly discussions, but she wasn't about to tell Gil that. And letting Gil choose threads and buttons didn't always work for her. She liked doing that for herself and thought to stop in at the yard goods store as well.

But her happiness in these simple tasks was cut short when Robert very obviously put himself in her way again.

Feeling annoyed as well as half-frightened, she wondered how he knew when she was in town and where she would be.

But her patterns of life were easy enough to discover. She lived a country wife's schedule.

Robert always greeted her politely enough. No, Jennifer couldn't complain about anything Robert said, at least in front of other people. It was the sly, intimate way he spoke to her, subtly implying there was more than mere acquaintance between them. It angered her deeply. But she kept thinking that if she just avoided him as often as she could and ignored him the rest of the time, he would finally grow tired of his game.

But it wasn't to be this time. When she approached Lindermans' grocery store, he was there. Courteously, he held the door wide for her to enter.

"My dearest Jennifer. You look blooming this morning."

"Thank you, Mr. Quiller," she said and made to move toward the back of the store.

Mrs. Tige gave her a long glance and pinched her mouth as she nodded her how-do-you-do's. Mrs. Dillon spared her a sympathetic "Good morning," but then hurried away on the excuse of being very busy.

And the disappointment of it was that Maude seemed swamped with customers this particular Saturday and couldn't get away from her counter long enough for a cup of tea.

Well, if that was the worst of it, Jennifer decided, she'd hold her head high and live through it. Gossip wouldn't kill her. She simply wouldn't let it take the toll on her that she'd suffered before.

Jennifer managed to leave the store without any more marked encounters thirty minutes later after she was sure Robert was gone. But when she stepped outside, he bowed to her from across the road, effectively letting her know that he observed her comings and goings with a close eye. She hurried away to meet Gil and Zachary at the livery barn.

No, gossip wasn't the worst of it, Jennifer sadly observed on the drive home. Because Gil was too quiet, unlike himself, when usually he talked of the things going on in town or a new idea for making money. He seemed to look at her with new questions in his eyes, too. Had she grown another head? He apparently didn't know where to focus his gaze.

Jennifer didn't know what to do about it.

She ought to try telling Gil all the details of her past and the part Robert had played in it, she told herself more than once over the next weeks. But it seemed she'd run out of courage. She couldn't bear it if he didn't believe her, or in her love for him and Zach. And it seemed that he shied away from discussing anything except the necessities of the daily chores as well.

Yet at night he still held her tenderly. It kept her going through her devastating periods of doubt.

Gil cleaned up the old rusted plow, putting it to good use around the end of March when he turned the garden earth, expanding its perimeters as well. Jennifer loved her vegetable patch and had asked him to make the old space about twice the size. He'd make it larger three times over, if that was what she wanted; anything, he'd do anything to please her. Anything to keep her.

Zach brought him a cup of water from a half-filled bucket and he paused in the plowing to drink it. "Thanks, son. This is thirsty work," he remarked, wiping a trickle of sweat from his brow.

Down by the barn, the low bawl of one of his new calves drifted into the spring morning. Last week, he'd worked till past dark for days in rough fencing a section of pasture land that would keep the small herd close to home. He wanted to oversee their progress without it putting him too far from the house and Jennifer.

"Uh-huh. Mama says so too," Zach said, swinging the bucket around, watching the way the water splashed out. "Mama says she's glad we have a well that works right outside the house."

"Yep. That new well is a dandy, isn't it?" Gil was proud he'd remembered to say "isn't." His language was something else he'd been paying particular attention to. He wanted Jennifer to notice his attempts to improve his education. "I won't mind a'tall either, not having to haul water all the way from the spring."

Gil took another swallow of water and continued to make idle conversation with his son as he gazed down the gentle slope toward the house. Lord A'mighty, he hated to think on how hard Jennifer had slaved in the garden last year. Rough work had ruined her hands, Quiller had pointed out. Rough work—the likes of carrying those buckets of water all that way, of heavy wash loads, of cleaning the henhouse, of all the other demanding work that came from being a country wife—was making her into a drudge, Quiller'd said.

Well, he'd sure as hell agreed with the man there! That's why he'd made sure Jennifer didn't have to haul water this season. Besides that, Gil didn't want her to even think about the planting in her condition. He'd do it.

Yep, he took pride in his improvements of the past few months, yet there was still so much to be done.

Lately, he'd been scheming to find the money to buy a pump and pipe so he could bring water directly into the house. He'd do that, too, by thunder. He'd go back to hauling stone into town and mending firearms. He didn't mind.

"Papa, there's a buggy coming."

Gil turned to look. One of Sam's rentals, his best vehicle pulled by his showiest team—the one that Robert Quiller had used ever since he came to Kansas—rolled at a spanking pace down their road.

Gil's hands clenched on the wooden plow handles before he dropped them and strode toward the house. He'd be strung up by his thumbs before he let that slick sidewinder into his house again.

That day they'd talked, the dirty-minded little man'd had the go-to-hell gall to imply he and Jennifer had once been lovers and wanted to be again. Moreover, Quiller had boldly proposed to give him a very large lump settlement to dissolve his marriage and let Jennifer go. Gil had never heard the like. As though Jennifer could be bought!

Outraged to speechlessness, Gil'd been torn between throttling the man right there in the hotel dining room and totally ignoring him as a man gone completely mad. The thought even crossed his mind to report the incident to Osage Springs's new sheriff, Jack Logan, but he didn't cotton to making himself a joke of the town. In the end, he chose simply to turn his back and leave.

But Quiller's voice trailed him with promises to offer Jennifer his whole fortune to leave Kansas. He'd accused Gil of tricking her into marriage, of abusing her and robbing her of her youth and beauty.

The hell of it was, Gil fumed, he already felt guilty

enough over all Jennifer had done and sacrificed for him. He agreed that some of Quiller's accusations were true. But damn it! She was his now, and she was pregnant with his child, so guilty or not, he damn well wasn't about to let another man steal his wife. He'd fight any odds to keep her.

However, the doubt that had him in an all-fired cold sweat was, *What if she wanted to go?* It tumbled round and round in his mind. Could he stop her from leaving if she did?

Now the brazen bastard had come to call on Jennifer again.

Gil wiped the dust from his hands along the seat of his pants, glancing at Zach. He couldn't stand the thought of his son witnessing the confrontation with Quiller. Or his father's possible defeat. "Son, I want you to go, uh, check Flossy. She's down at the bottom of the pasture."

Zach started to protest, but he recognized that Gil's low "git!" wasn't to be argued with; he turned and trudged away.

Gil found the house empty, the front wide open to the spring sunshine. The yeasty smell of rising bread wafted his way. Jennifer, he thought, must be checking her hens. Just as well. He could send Quiller on his way without her presence.

Gil took his rifle from its wall hook beside the door, then he stepped outside, cradling it. Impatiently, he waited for the buggy to roll to a stop.

When it did, Quiller put one shiny, unscuffed half boot onto the carriage fender, preparing to descend without waiting to be invited. "Mr. Prescott—"

Gil had no desire for cordial greetings. "Don't bother to get down, Quiller. You ain't welcome here."

A bit of shock flooded the older man's face. "My good man, I—"

"I ain't your good man. You heard me. Don't bother to get down. You ain't staying."

Quiller's lips pressed together tightly. He looked down a haughty nose, his affront at Gil's harsh commands showing. "I am calling on Patricia, not you."

Thrown off guard, Gil asked, "Who's Patricia?"

Startled in turn, a quicksilver look of panic shone from the depths of Quiller's eyes before his expression suddenly turned blank, as though he pulled drapes over his thoughts.

"I do beg your pardon." He paused a moment before saying, "I merely came to bid Mrs. Prescott adieu. I am leaving Osage Springs."

For the first time in weeks, Gil felt something like a bowstring on his nerves relax. "You going back east?"

"Yes. My business interests there need my attention."

"In that case, I'll pass along your message. But don't ever come back here, Quiller. My wife wants nothing more to do with you."

Quiller's eyes darkened with wrath. He looked as though he were bursting to say something scathing.

Gil inched his rifle toward the front, its barrel coming closer in alignment with the offensive intruder. "Never again."

It was enough. Quiller picked up the reins and tooled the horse team in a tight circle and left. Gil watched the buggy out of sight. Toward the top of the rise in the road, he saw the cruel way in which a whip was laid onto the horses.

God A'mighty, he was glad to see the back of that skunk.

*   *   *

Spring. Jennifer's heart sang with it along with the birds. On her way to the garden to check for the earliest lettuce sprouts, she sniffed the air. She loved these fresh mornings when the sun rose earlier each day.

The planting was too new to expect much, but she loved looking for tiny green shoots each day anyway. Gil had planted vegetable seeds of everything for which she'd asked. Lettuce, early peas. Green beans and limas. Cabbage, turnips, radishes, carrots, potatoes, beets, corn, and cucumbers for her pickles. He'd put the squash and muskmelons and pumpkins over by the side where they'd have more room to run.

She even laughed at herself as her ungainly movements slowed her usual pace, and shook her head for the near impossible tasks she'd set herself. She might be doing the weeding crawling on her hands and knees. But she had only a few weeks left before the baby was born, and by the time the garden's fruits were ripe, she would be feeling herself again. And my, wouldn't Maude be pleased with what she brought in to sell.

Thinking of pickles made her mouth water. Were there any still left in her cellar? No, she'd served the last of them weeks ago. She chuckled at herself. She should've passed the stage of craving odd things to eat, but pickles . . . she suddenly wanted a whole jar of them. Or kraut. Now, kraut might do and she knew three jars of the vinegary cabbage were still on a back shelf.

She glanced at the sun. It was a long time until dinner. A little snack wouldn't hurt anything.

Deciding to indulge herself, Jennifer went around

the side of the house to the cellar. Gil had replaced its rusty hinges and added a pulley to help her open the heavy door. It now worked more quietly. Gratefully, she had no trouble at all, and descended into the small room. She didn't need to light the candle that she kept ready in a niche by the door, however, because daylight flooded through the opening.

She had to stretch to her toes to reach the desired kraut. Actually, the jars were just beyond her fingertips. Pivoting, she looked for the crate she used to climb on—but she turned too fast and lost her balance. Grabbing for the shelf, she fell against it heavily, bumping her head before landing on her knees. Jars rattled, and one fell, bouncing against the dirt floor.

As her fingers came away from the shelf, she was left with a tiny scrap of cloth in her hand. She stared at it fuzzily. A fragment of fine cotton. Blue and gold plaid. Where had it come from?

She'd had a dress of similar plaid once, hadn't she? When she was eighteen or nineteen? But the dress hadn't been in her possession in years.

Robert? Had Robert left this?

Her heart began to pound as the blood drained from her head. Jennifer wasn't sure, later, if she lost consciousness for a moment or not. But she suddenly was aware that she sat crumpled against the rough stone wall, a sharp edge digging into her back. Slowly, she became aware that her head hurt.

Well, she had been totally foolish this time, and she'd most likely sport the bruises to prove it. But she didn't think she'd seriously injured herself. Until she tried to rise.

Struggling to get her feet under her, she found that her legs didn't want to hold her up. Awkwardly, she tried again, clutching the edge of a wooden shelf and pushing against the wall. She gained her feet only to lean on the wall to help her from sliding back down. Her baby turned inside her and pressed low in her belly.

Her heart raced. Her head hurt, her knees stung, and a hundred other scrapes and aches came to her attention. But it was the sudden fear of losing the baby that roared through her mind. Please, God, no.

"Gil!" Her call was futile if he was still in the barn with Zach and Homer. They'd never hear her down here. She called again anyway, louder this time. "Gil! Zach!"

Although she expected no answer, Jennifer listened. Silence.

If they had gone out into the pastures, she'd never reach them, she thought. The bell that Gil had rigged on the outside wall beside the back door was meant to send a call for meals or any other need, but it sure wouldn't help her now. She had to get to it.

Inching along the wall, she found the steps. She felt a little stronger but sat to catch her breath. One step at a time, she climbed up, ignoring the harsh rock against her palms. Five. Four. Three to go. She rested.

A sudden bark sounded above her head, and Jennifer sat up. "General! Oh, here, boy, here!"

Excitedly, General bounded down to find her, happily licking her face. "Hello, boy," she said, petting him. "Yes I'm very glad to see you, too! General, go find Zach. Where's Zach, General? And Gil! Go find them," she ordered and pointed.

General tried to get his wiggly body by her. He wanted to investigate unknown territory. "Yes, yes, I know, you aren't usually allowed to come into the cellar. But now isn't the time. Go!"

General raced upward and out of her sight. She

heard him bark again and wondered if he had found a rabbit. But General usually wasn't very far from Zach. Maybe . . . "Zach! Zach, are you there? Gil!"

"Mama?"

Jennifer heard the faint call and she responded immediately. Only a moment, and Zachary's head popped into view. She was so glad to see him that she was teary with it.

"What's the matter, Mama?"

"Honey, go find Papa." She sniffed. "I fell."

Jennifer didn't have to finish her explanation because Gil was there. His eyes alarmed, he didn't wait for any either before he was beside her, running his hands along her legs and back while she tried to tell him she was only bruised. Finally, he simply scooped her into his arms. "Hush, Jennifer honey. We'll see better after we get you into bed."

Jennifer felt more confident. "Gil, I think I'm only bruised. I feel stronger, now. Really," she insisted a little too desperately.

He spared her a frowning glance. "That's good, honey, but we aren't taking any chances. Zach," he said and pointed with his chin. "You run ahead and pull the spread down for Mama."

Low in her back, a tightening ache began. Jennifer bit her lip and waited for it to pass. She hated to worry Gil this way. But more than that, real fear began to draw her. It was too soon for the baby to come. Too soon.

But what if she'd caused something to break loose?

No, this couldn't be happening again!

Gil carried her through the house and laid her on the bed. "Gil," she whispered. Her head felt a little swimmy and she couldn't keep the tears from rolling down her cheeks. "Don't leave me."

"I'm right here, sweetheart." With sure movements, Gil stripped her of shoes and stockings and began to unbutton her dress, all the while searching for any injury more serious than broken skin.

He turned away, intent on gathering a pan of water and washcloth.

Panic swept her and she grabbed a piece of his sleeve. "Gil, don't leave me."

20

Gil frowned while he fought to keep his thoughts to himself. Something had scared Jennifer, something more than her fall.

He knelt by the bed, letting her clutch his hand while he stroked her cheek. Her eyes glittered with pain. "I'm here, Jennifer. Is it the baby coming?"

In spite of all her efforts to remain calm, Jennifer was frightened. Her foolishness in wanting the kraut had led her to this, and now she might have to pay the penalty with early labor. And what had happened to that tiny scrap of plaid fabric? "I—I don't know. But please stay with me, Gil. It's too early, but it may be . . ."

Zach came through the doorway. "Is Mama hurt?" His bottom lip quivered. Beside him, General wagged his tail and jumped up onto Gil.

Jennifer rose to her elbow to reassure the child. "Only a little, Zach. I'll be all right."

"Zach, get your dog out of here. Pronto!"

The boy's eyes pooled. His father had never spoken to him so sharply before.

"Oh, honey, don't cry," Jennifer said, giving Gil an admonishing glance. "General's been a hero today. He found me and led you to me when I needed your help the most. Why—" She felt strange and let herself fall back against the pillow, then worked to keep her tone even for Zach. "Why don't you find a bone in the kitchen for him and take him outside to eat it."

"Yeah, Zach, that's a good idea," Gil said by way of an apology. "I'll be out in a bit, but let me see to Mama right now, okay?"

His hand on his dog's head, Zach backed away, his gaze never leaving Jennifer's white face until he was out of sight.

Gil returned his attention to Jennifer. A spreading discoloration lay against her forehead. Smoothing her hair back, Gil felt the knot where she'd hit her head. He pondered that perhaps she'd been hurt worse than he thought.

He wondered if she had passed out because of it or if the bump happened when she fell. She'd fainted once before, he remembered, the night he discovered her condition. It scared him spitless then, and scared him more now. But Jennifer's health had seemed all right these last months.

A baby coming early was always a worry. They might lose the child. Many families lost children. . . .

Some women died in childbirth.

All his insides clutched at his heart. Not for the first time, Gil wondered how exacting the ordeal would be. What price would Jennifer pay? Pain and suffering, to be sure. He cringed at the thought of it, fought the very idea of her in pain.

How would he face it? What toll would he have to pay?

Nothing in his war experiences, even watching men die right beside him, had wiped away his anguished memories of sitting outside the tepee and listening to the muffled moans of Morning Rain as she struggled to give Zachary life. And he'd never seen her alive again. For years he'd lived with the guilt of her death.

Now Jennifer faced the same experience and she looked to him for comfort. "Gil . . ." Jennifer needed the doctor. She needed Maude, or someone.

He bit down his fear and fought for a soothing tone. "How is it, Jennifer? Are you in labor?"

"No, it's odd, but I don't think so, now. But I may need you."

"All right, Teacher," he said gently. "I won't leave the house. But I must get some water to bathe these scrapes. Don't want infections, you know."

He rose and went to the kitchen. Zach stared at him, his eyes wide and questioning, his little body stiff, daring his father to refuse to give him a straight answer. It struck Gil that his son seemed very much older of a sudden.

"Is my mama all right? Did she hurt herself bad?"

"Zach—" Gil ran his hand through his hair. "Zach, son." He went on his haunches to search the boy's face. Dare he ask a child so young to make the three-mile ride to town alone? "I don't know how badly Mama is hurt. She needs the doctor. I can't go—"

"I'll go, Papa. On Major!" Major was the fastest horse they had in their string, now, outside of Beau.

Even in his concern, Gil noted Zachary's declarative tone. He wasn't crying now, only bent on doing what he needed to do.

"Do you think you can?"

"Yes, Papa, I can do it. We've been to town a hundred thousand times, I won't get lost."

Zach seemed so sure. He had to take the chance.

"All right. But don't wait to saddle up, ride bareback. Go straight to Lindermans' and tell Maude or Peder to get the doctor out here, then go and stay with Homer at the livery barn. If you have to, stay the night with him, okay?"

"All right, Papa." Zach was gone in a flash.

Gil hurriedly dipped water into the wash pan and yanked a clean towel from the stack Jennifer kept in the corner of the dry sink. He stepped to the front door in time to see the boy thunder by, clinging like a leech to the sleek brown horse.

"Hurry, son," he murmured before turning toward the bedroom. "For God's sake and your mother's, please hurry."

Gil kept up a running stream of commentary on how his calves were thriving and the string of horses that he could count as his in exchange for his work with Sam Burns. He tenderly helped Jennifer off with her dress and then bathed her hands, knees, and other scrapes. He put any thought of where Zachary might be on the road out of his mind, mentally praying his boy would be safe.

Pretty soon, Jennifer relaxed and her distress seemed to ease, and his heart did too. Perhaps nothing else untoward would happen to cause the baby to start just yet.

By the time he heard a buggy outside, Jennifer was dozing lightly.

"How is she?" Maude asked before she was through the door.

"Better. Doc with you?"

"He's getting his bag."

"Thank God. Zach?"

"You've got some little boy, there, Gil. The child was as cool and precise as any grown man. I'll never forget how he looked comin' into the store."

Dr. Rosenberg took a long time to examine Jennifer.

Gil almost chewed through his lip, standing against the wall just outside the bedroom door, then pacing the parlor. Maude made tea.

The tall slender physician finally called him into the bedroom. "Well, Doc?"

"Hmm, it doesn't look as though you'll have a baby just yet, Mr. Prescott. You've been lucky this time. But Mrs. Prescott did get shaken up a mite and I think it would be best if she stayed in bed for a while."

Gil felt almost drunk with relief. "By thunder, Doc, that's good news. I'll see to it, Jennifer will stay in bed. For how long?"

"Really, Dr. Rosenberg, must I?" Jennifer asked.

Dr. Rosenberg didn't believe in pussyfooting around. He nodded to Jennifer but he spoke to Gil, for it had been his past experience that he had to make the husbands responsible in cases like this one. "For the next few weeks until she has the baby, I want Mrs. Prescott to lie flat on her back for the most part. Only sit up once or twice a day, half an hour."

Gil didn't mistake the seriousness of what the doctor meant. "You can bet your bottom dollar, Doc, that I'll follow your orders to the letter. We'll take care of her."

"Good. Now I'll leave an ointment for those scrapes and something that'll help her sleep."

Maude brought Jennifer a cup of tea, then suggested the men take theirs in the kitchen. Gil offered the doctor a shot of whiskey, instead.

"Don't drink, as a rule," Gil said. His hands were still shaky and he laughed at himself as he held them up for the doc to see, before pouring a couple of fingers of the amber liquor into each of two glasses.

"Don't give it a thought, Mr. Prescott. Most men would rather walk through hot coals barefoot than have anything to do with childbirth. Too many mysteries about it, I suppose, and too much pain. But I think your wife will do fine. Just follow my orders."

"Doc," Gil said, shaking his head, "I wouldn't cross those orders for all the tea in China," he said, using an old saying of his mother's.

Maude expressed her reluctance to return to town. "I'll stay the night if you need me," she told Jennifer.

"No, Maude, you know Peder can't get by without you."

Maude smiled like a young girl. "That's true. But Jennifer, we have the Schiller children with us now. You were right. That dog-eared good-for-nothin' Schiller was happy as a lark when Peder offered him an 'apprentice fee' for Lavinia and George. He didn't even question that we wanted all three children, little Molly included. Signed over their custody like he would a bill of sale for horses or cattle."

"Did he leave town?"

"The next day, I heard. Didn't come by to say a last good-bye or nothin'." Maude shook her head in disgust.

The doctor had given Jennifer something to soothe her nerves, and she yawned. Hearing about the happy solution that served both the Lindermans and the Schiller children, however, was just the thing she

needed to take her mind off herself, she decided. "Are
the children all right?"

"Right as rain, now. Outfitted them first thing.
Lavinia . . . well, she hugged me closer'n a mama bear
would her cub when she realized they would be livin'
with us. She's taken to helpin' with the store like a
duck to water. Molly's been braggin' to everyone
who'll listen 'bout her new clothes. George might
take some time, but we ain't worried. He'll come
around. He came straight from school yesterday to
help Peder stack cans. We're sure crowded, though.
Looks like we'll haveta add on to the back of the store
soon."

"Oh, Maude, you must be so happy. Tell me, how
have the children adjusted in other ways? You know,
with the fact that their father's gone for good?"

"Well, Lavinia doesn't say much. But George!
George told Peder he was good riddance. Little Molly
sometimes cries, but I think as long as Lavinia is
there she'll be okay."

"That's settled then. You and Peder will do a wonderful job with those children, Maude, but you must
get back to them. They'll need you."

"Well, I hate to leave you like this."

Gil stepped to the door. "Uh, Jennifer, we have
another visitor. It's Bessie Terrell. Looks like Zach
brought her."

"What do you mean, Zach brought her?" Jennifer,
despite her sleepiness, raised to an elbow. "How
could Zach bring her? Where is he?"

"Um, don't know, exactly." Gil didn't know how
Zachary had found Bessie and didn't dare contemplate where, either. But she had arrived riding Major
behind Zachary.

He berated himself for upsetting Jennifer, but he'd been caught off guard, himself. "Calm down, Jennifer honey. The boy's home, now, and is just fine."

Bessie followed Zachary through the front door. The boy raced to the bedroom. "Mama, Bessie's here."

"That's nice, Zach. Where have you been?"

"Been to town. Papa sent me to fetch the doctor, so I fetched Bessie, too."

"You did what?" Jennifer sat up completely.

Bessie, just inside the front door, waited for a challenge from either Gil or Maude. When none came, she said, "I came to help Miz Jennifer," then followed Zach.

Her voice drifted in to Gil and Maude. "Now Miz Jennifer, you ain't got no worries 'bout little Zach, here. Looks like he done taken grown-up lessons behind your back."

"I suppose so."

"Uh-huh. I'm almost five!"

In the parlor, Maude smiled at Gil. "Well, it looks like you have the help you need, Gil. I reckon I'll get on back, myself. But you let me and Peder know if you need us, hear?"

"Sure thing, Maude. Much obliged for coming out." Gil opened the door and ushered Maude and the doctor to the buggy.

By the time supper was over that night, Gil and Bessie had come to an understanding. Bessie would stay for as long as she was needed and she would have the upstairs bedroom. He and Zach would move to the bunkhouse.

Gil swirled the last of his coffee in his mug. "Can't pay much, Bessie."

Bessie looked at him over her own. "Did I ask for any pay? Did I? I owe Miz Jennifer more than you know, Mr. Prescott, 'sides which, she's my friend. So don't go insultin' me. You wait 'til I ask."

He sighed. He was tired tonight. Tired, dispirited, and disgruntled at having to leave Jennifer, however much it was necessary. However, Zachary was too young to be out in the bunkhouse alone, and Jennifer would rest better if she had the bed to herself. "Much obliged, Bessie. Reckon I'll go get my stuff."

Jennifer's supper tray sat on the table beside the bed. She leaned against the pillows, staring at nothing.

"You didn't eat much," he remarked. "The doc won't like it if you don't eat."

"I don't want any more."

"Okay. Then it's time to lie down again."

"I suppose." Jennifer scooted down, then let Gil tuck a quilt around her. She watched in silence as he gathered his bits and pieces of clothing. "Gil, I want to talk to you."

"All right." Gil eased down on the side of the bed. His wife had most of her color back, he was pleased to note. He took her hand, rubbing his thumb over her slender fingers, then over the scar on the pad of her thumb, which she'd gotten learning to peel potatoes. He needed her touch, needed to make the connection.

"It's nice of Bessie to come stay," he said softly.

"Yes, it is. But I'm sorry you and Zach have to sleep in the bunkhouse."

"It's for the best, Jennifer." He didn't want to go. He really didn't. He heartily wished Homer was still here so that he could be the one to stay in the bunkhouse with Zach. Then he would sleep on the floor beside the bed, beside Jennifer, where he could hear her if she called. But Homer was busy with the livery barn at his father's bidding.

"It won't be so bad and you'll sleep better. This way you'll build up your strength for when the baby's born," Gil said, hoping his common sense words reassured her better than they did him.

"Hmmm."

"And the days will fly, now that spring is blooming. You can open your window soon." She would hate staying in bed for weeks, he mused.

"Mmm." Jennifer acknowledged Gil's attempt to cheer her, but something else tickled her thoughts. "Gil, where were you this afternoon?"

"Down by the far pasture checking the calves. Why?"

"Oh, I . . . nothing. Gil, have you noticed anything different happening?"

"Different? Like what?"

"Well, lately, have you noticed anything odd around our place?" Her hand on his tightened. "Like, um, signs that someone has been around when we're not home. Like . . . like perhaps the night riders have been around."

"No. Why would you think the night riders would bother us, Jennifer? Most of the border raiders have melted away, and besides, we've done nothing to draw anybody's ire."

"Oh, I—" She bit her lip and decided to drop the vague suspicion. It was too nebulous, anyway. "Oh, phoo. I'm just imagining things, I guess. Gil, I . . . there is something else. About Robert . . ."

He patted her hand. "Don't distress yourself, Jennifer. He ain't a fit subject."

"But there are things I need to explain—"

"Not now, Jennifer honey, there'll be plenty of time

to tell me about him another time." He got up from beside her and rolled his clothes into a bundle. "Besides, you've got yourself and the baby to put your thoughts to right now. You gotta conserve your strength."

"Gil, please."

"Jennifer, I don't want to hear about the little weasel! He ain't worth the breath talking about. Now I want you to try to sleep, okay?"

She answered slowly. "All right." Did her husband refuse to talk of Robert Quiller because he truly didn't think the man worth the time or because of what he might hear? Was Gil afraid he'd hear things about *her* that he couldn't face? Or maybe he had already heard them.

Perhaps she no longer sat on a pedestal.

On Sunday afternoon, Dora Burns and Mrs. Dillon came to call.

"Heard you were laid up, Mrs. Prescott, and thought we would bring you some Christian cheer," Dora Burns said.

"That is very thoughtful of you, ladies. Won't you sit down?" Jennifer indicated the two kitchen chairs that Bessie had brought into the bedroom for her guests.

Mrs. Burns gave the young woman a scandalized look from beneath her lashes and nodded stiffly. Amused, Jennifer wondered what it would take for Dora to actually speak to Bessie.

"I brought one of my special three-egg cakes, Mrs. Prescott," Mrs. Dillon said quietly. "I gave it to Bessie as we came in."

"Why, that is very kind of you, Mrs. Dillon. We will enjoy it, I'm sure. Have you decided on a new teacher yet?"

"Oh, yes, we have, Mrs. Prescott," Mrs. Dillon said, her brown eyes lighting, "and the questions you suggested we ask during our interview were of great help to us. I think we've found a perfect candidate. A young man by the name of Nathan Saunders. He comes from Lawrence."

"Excellent, Mrs. Dillon. I'm almost tempted to send Zachary in next year. He'll be only five, but he's quite bright and already knows his ABCs and numbers."

"Yes, I must say, little Zachary is much smarter than . . . um . . . well, you know, the usual Indian child," Dora Burns said, lowering her voice as though she had something unusual to impart. "I told Sam, I said, that child is an exception to be proud of. I'm sure it's due to your fine efforts, Mrs. Prescott."

"Well, of course I have taught him here at home, Mrs. Burns, and it would be a joy to continue to do so. But Zachary has no need for special tutoring, you know, and neither, I suspect, would the other children of Indian heritage. Most of them are very intelligent, from all I hear and read."

"Oh, do you really think so? Well, I—I didn't mean to imply . . . well, it is only that some of them . . . well . . ." Dora Burns sat straighter, not willing to concede the point all the way. "Not all children are gifted with an educable mind, don't you know. Like Homer, poor boy."

She'd been abed too long by half after only a week, Jennifer decided, for a sudden desire to set the cat amidst the cream surfaced in her mind. "Actually, Mrs. Burns, Homer is a joy to teach as well. Has he recited one of his poems for you and his father yet?"

"Poems?"

Jennifer quite enjoyed Dora's startled face.

"Yes, poems. As in speech that has meter and rhyme."

Dora Burns not only looked shocked, she appeared stunned, and as though she couldn't quite grasp what language Jennifer was speaking. "Homer? Poems?"

"Yes. Homer, it turns out, has a genius for poetry. He understands a great deal of it and is trying his hand at it himself."

Thereafter, Jennifer and Mrs. Dillon conducted a delightful conversation of wide range concerning Osage Springs's educational needs and ambitions with very little input from Homer's stepmother.

Jennifer wakened slowly. She lay still a moment before opening her eyes wide to the dark bedroom, not knowing what had wakened her. Listening to the quiet around her, she heard only the faint breeze. It wafted spring fragrances of new grasses growing and wildflowers through her partially opened window. Drowsily, she breathed deeply. She loved spring and the promise it brought.

Before she remembered, she slid her hand across the sheet looking for Gil, for his warmth and comfort. Her hand found only cool nothingness. Restlessly, she eased to her side, feeling heavier than ever.

Ten days of sleeping alone hadn't reconciled Jennifer's feelings of abandonment, no matter how often she recounted all the very good reasons why Gil and Zachary were now in the bunkhouse. Something about it felt completely different than when Gil was away altogether. As though she'd been through this before . . .

Sighing, she shifted once again. And tried to reclaim sleep. Beyond the garden, she heard General give a low yelp. He must've found a rabbit.

Down at the bunkhouse, Gil heard General's bark, too. He rose silently and went to the door, opening it to stand for a while looking out at the dark, idly wondering what creature General was after.

He hadn't been asleep anyway. Too much on his mind, too many demands. He'd put in eighteen hours today—not unusual for a rancher—and he should be tired enough to sleep.

Instead, he only wanted Jennifer.

He listened to the night sounds. Nothing unusual. General came trotting back, his forays satisfied. "Had enough roamin', huh?" he murmured, watching the dog curl up at Zach's feet. "Me too," he added on a whisper.

He let a gusty sigh out and went back to bed. To try to sleep. But oh, God, he hated this separation.

21

"*Bessie, this one is beautiful,*" Jennifer exclaimed, holding up the paper that held the dress design she liked best of the dozen Bessie had shown her. They had talked for weeks of Bessie's plan to open a dressmaking business, with Jennifer as a silent partner. "The detail is very stylish. And this one, and yes, that one, although it may be a little too daring for the, um, um . . ."

"Respectable lady," Bessie finished for her. "It's okay to speak plain, Miz Jennifer. I done heard it all, so you aren't gonna hurt my feelin's none."

"Oh, Bessie."

"An' if we're gonna be partners in settin' up our dressmakin' establishment, you gotta speak plain."

"Very well. This *is* a very good design and will be flattering to the . . . um . . . abundantly blessed figure."

"You think everything looks invitin' these days, Miz Jennifer. You been in that night rail too long. What else? What's your *but?*"

Jennifer chuckled, then gave Bessie a grimace. She was tired to her backbone at being abed and her friend knew it.

"Well, I think we must decide what trade we want to draw. We can't possibly hope for success if wives and daughters, when they shop, are likely to come face-to-face with women who . . . who make money with their womanhood and sometimes rob them of their men. Respectable women will refuse to patronize the shop."

Jennifer shuffled through the other designs, glancing at each again. "But perhaps if you were to offer a couple of evenings each week, open only to a certain trade . . ."

"Miz Jennifer, you got the delicate notions of a lady all rolled up with a real nose for business," Bessie said and grinned, her teeth flashing very white against her dark complexion. She took the stack of designs that Jennifer held out to her. "But evenin's prime time with sportin' ladies. They can't give up their best workin' hours. Howsomever, I'll cogitate on it some."

"What're you cogitating on?" Gil asked as he came through the parlor.

Gil wore his spurs today and Jennifer listened to his musical jingle as he came. He had gone into Osage Springs early this morning to bring out a new string of horses that Sam had bought last week. Gil thought them half wild and said they'd take some training.

"Oh, nothing much, Gil. Bessie is merely keeping me entertained with her dress designs."

Jennifer had told Gil of Bessie's plans but had omitted telling of her part in helping to finance and make decisions for the shop. He refused to use her money for the ranch, she reasoned, so she saw no reason not to invest it in Bessie's shop, but she thought Gil might object. She'd decided to wait to tell him until the shop was really established and counted on his own attention to be well and truly focused on the ranch enough not to notice.

"It helps pass the time," she added. "Where's Zachary?"

Gil nodded absentmindedly as he rummaged in the corner trunk for something. "That's good. Anything to keep your mind peaceful for right now will do it."

Jennifer hid a smile. If Gil only knew how exciting she found the fun of planning the shop, he might not be so complacent about it. However, once the shop was running smoothly, her part in it would be over. It was, after all, Bessie's endeavor.

Besides, she mused, there was more than enough to do as a rancher's wife and with children of her own to care for. Automatically, she placed a hand against her abdomen. The expected one frequently moved so vigorously, Jennifer wondered if the babe already knew how to turn somersaults and if she could keep up with it after it was born. She was counting on Zachary's enthusiasm to help. Lately, though, its movements had quieted.

"And what about your son?" she reminded Gil.

"Stayed down at the barn to help Homer. I told the boys to keep the new string in the near pasture 'til we see . . ."

Gil had a dozen items stacked up on the floor by the trunk. A quick breeze from the opened window blew at the pages of his mother's Bible. The wind smelled fresh, like rain in the air.

"What are you looking for, anyway?"

"Some of Pa's papers. The original deed shows our

western line going . . ." Gil pulled out a packet wrapped in oiled cloth. "This is it. Got to talking in town this morning with Mr. Withers, the land agent. He thinks Pa bought more land the year before he took sick. I said I'd check."

He stood, shuffling through the papers before singling one out, then remained very still for a long moment as he read it. He raised his gaze and stared at her, his expression excited, hopeful, while his mouth went soft. "Jennifer."

"What is it, Gil?" She pushed herself up on the pillows.

"These papers verify it. Pa bought more land in sixty-three. I can hardly believe it. Why, it gives us another third of what we already have now, and . . . and that rocky area I've been working, that's ours. I thought it was open land and I'd plumb lose it sometime this year because somebody would take it up."

"Oh, Gil!"

"Think of it, Teacher," he said, his grin lighting up his face. "We're better off than I thought, even though we're still land rich an' cash poor."

He bent swiftly, kissing her once with fervor, then strode purposefully out.

"Gil, where are you off to now?"

"Town. Have to double check everything with Mr. Withers. Don't want no mistakes about this. Don't wait dinner."

"But Gil, Bessie's—" It was no use. He was out of hearing range.

Bessie came into the bedroom. "Don't fret now, Miz Jennifer. I c'n go in tomorra, just the same."

They heard the faint gallop of Gil's leaving on Beau.

Jennifer laughed. "No, no, Bessie, you must go

today, and you should leave right away. It looks like rain coming by this afternoon, if it holds off until even then. Besides, you've had your heart set on it all week and Mr. Tige expects you today and is ready to sell. A location next to his mercantile is a prime one and with all the new people settling round about, we can't risk losing it."

"But Miz Jennifer, you shouldn't be left here alone."

"Nonsense, I'm fine and the boys are someplace around. They'll be coming in looking for something to eat in a couple of hours. Besides, I haven't had a twinge of discomfort"—she laughed again and amended her statement—"that is, of labor pains for weeks, now. I think this baby has settled down to wait it out just like I have."

"Are ya sure?"

"Yes. And Bessie, you need to get those letters off to those mills requesting the fabric swatches. Can't set up a shop without goods to sell, can we?"

"Uh-huh, sure 'nuff do and uh-uh, sure 'nuff can't. All right, I'll go," Bessie consented after a long moment. She fluffed Jennifer's pillow and rearranged the one under her knees. "I'll lay out some bread an' cheese to keep those growin' young'un's from starvin' before I get back. Now you promise to stay in bed, hear?"

Jennifer dutifully promised and Bessie set off in the buggy. She opened a book but found she couldn't get comfortable and soon laid it aside. She dreamily watched the way the breeze played with the curtain awhile, and contentedly sniffed at the spring grasses and listened to the low thunder rumbling distantly.

When it died away, she tried to hear something of

the boys above the breeze and the occasional moo, but she could not. Even the dogs were silent or too far from the house to be heard. Only a faint creaking sound came to her and a sudden squawk from one of her hens.

Raising her head, she intensified her concentration. Bessie said there was a varmint getting some of them—they'd lost three.

A scrape of something against the side of the house caused her to turn her head, then she heard the faint creak of the wide opened front door. She felt no immediate alarm.

"Zach?"

There was no answer. Zachary usually called to her as soon as he came into the house.

"Homer, is that you?"

But Homer, although often still shy, would also have let her know it was he. All she heard was a floor squeak.

Had one of Bessie's varmints gotten into the house? But if it had been of a four-legged variety, she would hear more—more awkward movement, more noise.

She started to call again, then halted. Slowly, she pushed herself up against the headboard. Anyone she knew would have announced themselves.

Apprehension left her with chill bumps along her arms. Lone men frequently roamed the countryside, honest drifters looking for work or handouts, many working their way west. Gil had invited two or three to a meal over the past year, and she certainly didn't mind feeding someone who was hungry.

But an honest man would've answered her call. Would have identified himself.

Her mind darted to where her old gun had gotten to—the one she'd kept close by during the years without Gil. The last time she'd seen it, it was in the desk beside the front door. Jennifer doubted, in her ungainly state, that she could reach it before encountering whoever was there.

Swinging her feet over, she sat on the bedside and paused to get her balance. She had been so long abed, it took her a moment to find it.

As soft as a whisper, she heard a footstep from the parlor. Her heart began to thump painfully. Latching onto the headboard, she put her feet to the floor. If she couldn't reach the gun, what weapon was at hand?

But there was no more time to think about it. A shadow was cast over her lap. Her gaze flew to the doorway.

"There you are, Patricia."

Her breath caught in her throat. "Robert."

Frightened, she was yet more puzzled. The man standing before her bore little resemblance to the impeccably groomed person she'd always known. He looked dreadful. His eyes were bloodshot; his rumpled suit appeared as though he had lived in it for days. Unshaven, unkempt, his hair too long. And dirty!

"What has happened to you?" she asked on a near whisper. "Has there been an accident?"

"Accident?" His brown-eyed gaze was cloudy. "Oh, no, my dear. This is no accident. I am here by design."

Jennifer let that go by even while knowing he had misinterpreted her question. "Have you been ill, then?"

"No, of course not. You know I am never ill!" He sounded a bit testy, and impatient with her questions.

"Well, then, why have you come?"

"Now, Patricia, don't be dull, my dear. I came to see you!"

Her fright growing, Jennifer gathered her schoolteacher's voice. "Robert, I wish you wouldn't call while my husband is absent. Gil—"

"Your husband," he said, spitting the words out. "*Your husband* wouldn't allow me to see you when last I called."

When had that been? Jennifer fleetingly wondered. Gil mentioned only that he'd heard Robert had decided to return to the East.

She stared at his growing fury in dismay, then rose, gripping the bedstead tightly. She had to face him down, despite her own anxiety. Maybe then he would go.

A tightening waved across her lower back. She waited for it to pass. "I am here, now, Robert. You may say what you meant to say then."

Her even tone seemed to soothe him, for his anger slowly abated. "You must dress, Patricia." His gaze traveled down her nightgowned body with no acknowledgment of her extended belly. "Quickly. I have come for you at last."

It was as though he hadn't understood her at all the last time they had had this discussion. Did he really think she wanted to go with him?

"Robert, you must see that I cannot go with you," she said, trying to reason with him. She made to move past him, reaching for her robe on a hook beside the doorway. A lamp would be on the fireplace mantel.

Robert overrode her words. "My darling girl, I wanted to come sooner, but they kept guarding you." His face was spiteful. "Even that whore."

Jennifer searched his face for a spark of lucidity. He had simply ignored her refusal. How had he known Bessie was here, unless he'd been watching the ranch? But how? Surely he hadn't been sleeping out in the open all this time. Not Robert Quiller.

But his appearance told a story of its own, and part of her mind darted with relief to the tiny scrap of cotton plaid found in her cellar. She hadn't imagined it after all.

She tried a new direction. "Where have you been, Robert? I understood you were going home, back east."

He seemed puzzled by her assumption. "I couldn't leave without you. Though I am sorry for my tardiness. It took longer than I anticipated. But we can go now, Patricia."

Once again, she tried reason. "No, Robert, I cannot go with you. You really must understand. My place is here with my family."

"Family?" He looked at her more directly. "You have no family left but me. I saw to that. You are mine now."

"How can that be, Robert." Jennifer spoke firmly. "I have a husband. I am Gil Prescott's wife! I bear his child even now!"

For the first time since he came in, Jennifer thought his mind had finally focused on what she actually said. Awareness crept back into his gaze. "Child . . . yes, you are great with child." His gaze dropped to her abdomen. "*His* child! Willard's. It should have been mine!"

Lightning fast, he grabbed her arm. With the bed at her back and Robert filling the doorway, Jennifer had nowhere to go. A mild tightening began again.

Breathing deeply, she held her expression to blandness while it eased.

"Not Willard's child, Robert. I lost that one. You do remember that, don't you?"

His eyes glittered with unholy fury. Jennifer twisted in his grip, while panic clutched at her as never before. It dawned on her at last. This man's confusion and obsession went much deeper than she'd thought. Robert was truly mad!

"I wanted you to have *my* child. Even as *you* should have been mine! But Willard, damn him, offered your aunt more than I could ever hope to. He did it to spite me, you know. Took the woman I wanted above all others. He rubbed my nose in it, too, letting me escort you to all the highest social functions in his place while gloating behind our backs with the taboos in place. You, my cousin's wife, never to be mine!"

Jennifer winced at his pounding words while another pain rippled along her lower back. Placing a hand against his chest, she gently pushed so that she could straighten. She had to reach him, she just had to. The poor man was so deluded.

The discomfort in her back eased once more. She drew a deep breath. "Robert, listen to me. Please, Robert. I'm very sorry you did not get what you wanted from me, but you must know I was never yours even in the beginning, and I am not yours now."

His face took on new bewilderment. "But Patricia, I fixed it so you would be free. I made sure Willard couldn't bother you again. Is that why you ran away?"

What did he mean, he had fixed it so that she could be free? And Willard? She had indeed counted Robert an enemy. He had ruined her socially, and her marriage, causing her all kinds of hell. Was that all there was to it?

"You shouldn't have left, Patricia. You owe me." He yanked her arm, causing her to fall against him, then grabbed a fistful of her hair. "Now, come, my darling girl, no more of this protest. We are leaving now."

He dragged her into the parlor. "Robert, wait." The pain across her back repeated, this time with pressure. Despite his grasp on her hair, she bent low, and she knew! Her baby was coming.

Hearing a low whistle from outside, she realized the boys were back. Zachary's running footsteps preceded him by mere seconds. "Mama, you know what?"

Racing through the front door, he skidded to a stop. His face and hair gleamed lightly with raindrops. His delighted, expectant look faded.

"Zach! Don't—" she said, struggling inch by inch to straighten.

"What're you doing with my mama!"

Robert was diverted. Looking down his nose at the boy, he said, "This lady is not your mother, you stinking little bastard. She doesn't love you at all. I found out all about you. You're nothing better than a worthless coyote pup, whelped from an Indian slut. Patricia only took you in because your father paid her to do so."

Thunder rumbled directly overhead.

Zachary didn't exactly understand the intent in everything the man said, but he remembered his papa telling him to ignore that ugly word. He didn't like this man, hadn't liked him before. His face looked mean, and something told him his mama didn't like him either. Tears ran down her face.

"You let her go!"

Robert laughed nastily. "Look at the child. A pure savage throwback. You can almost see the feathers in his hair. Is this what your husband gets on his women?" He sneered at Zachary. "Your pa won't want you anymore after he gets another son. A white one!"

"Zach, don't listen. Run. Run, Zach."

Uncertainty filled the boy's eyes. "No, Mama. He wants to hurt you."

Robert twisted Jennifer's arm, bending it up between her shoulders. She couldn't hold back a cry.

"I'll hurt her worse than that, brat, if you don't get out of my way. We are leaving now."

"Robert, I can't . . . leave," Jennifer said, panting. Even in her distress, she fought for reasonableness. If she could reach his sense of social correctness, something that was such an innate part of his training, she might be able to stall him. "I'm not dressed and—and besides, you didn't bring your carriage . . . with you. How do you expect me . . . to leave without a carriage? Bessie has mine."

Robert's eyes flashed with a mixture of admiration and humor. Mad humor, Jennifer recognized in the sudden lightning that streaked the room.

"Very good, my dear," he spoke sarcastically. "But you do know we can solve that problem." He pushed her arm higher. Unwillingly, she stumbled forward out of the front door and into the rain.

"Down at your barn, slut." He shoved her again.

Zach launched himself at Robert's back, his fists flailing. Robert let go of Jennifer, and the momentum sent her to her knees on the rough ground, her outflung hands preventing a worse fall. Twisting, Robert backhanded Zachary smartly. The boy tumbled like a small stone and lay still.

"Zach," she screamed, terrorized.

Instantly, Robert pulled a snub-nosed derringer from his coat pocket. "You owe me, Patricia. You owe me yourself, you owe me a child. I can put an end to this one, if you choose, or you may come with me without any more fuss, and spare him. What is it to be, my dear?"

In desperation, Jennifer stared at him as the rain began in earnest. From the corner of her eye, she saw Zachary move, thank God!

Her whirling thoughts focused on Robert's face even as she felt another labor pain begin. She had to get this madman away from the ranch. "I will go with you."

22

Jennifer pushed stiffly to her feet, her mind whirling. She had never known him to use a weapon other than his duplicity before, but she didn't underestimate the deadliness of the small derringer or the extent of his rage.

"I'll go with you, Robert," she repeated.

Robert's aim at Zachary remained unwavering.

Stall. Stall! Stall for time.

Her heart beat erratically as the word repeated itself in her mind. Homer needed time to notice something wrong. Gil needed time to get home from town. But she couldn't put Robert off, not with that gun pointed directly at her little boy.

Please God, please. Help me. I need help.

Jennifer slowly straightened, gritting her teeth against discomfort, fear, and desperation. She wanted to cry out, to reason with Robert to just leave, but that hadn't worked inside the house, and now his craziness might cause him to pull that trigger.

Zachary stirred and pushed himself to his elbow. Jennifer held her breath.

"Robert!" Her cry was too shrill, too agitated. She had to calm down!

Reaching for composure, she prayed for control. "We can go on horseback."

Only the slightest of easing appeared in Robert's stance. "Do we have a bargain then?"

"Yes. A bargain. Come, Robert, give me your arm."

Homer was at the barn. He'd come find Zach. Together, they'd be smart enough to go after Gil or find help from somewhere. But right now she had to get Robert away from her son.

Slowly, Robert lowered his arm. "Yes. Yes, we must be going."

He hurried her down the well-worn path. Damp earth flew up onto the hem of her white nightdress. Jennifer scarcely felt the stones digging into her feet or her hair streaming wetly down her back. Another tightening cramp circled her abdomen. Without thought, she clutched at the barn door, gasping for breath.

The barn was dark inside except for the lamp glow from the tack room. She didn't want to enter. Old, frightful memories of a dark place invaded her mind. Her baby, that first tiny little mite, had been lost after a dreadful fall in a dark room. And Willard. She'd bumped into Willard in the dark, swinging from a rafter with a rope around his neck.

Gil, come home. I need you, your son needs you, this unborn child isn't going to wait.

Drawing a deep breath, she wondered if she had the strength to get past the next hurdle. But again, she felt a softness flow through her body, as though she drew peace from beyond herself.

"Come, come, what is it now?"

"Nothing. I—I only needed to rest . . . a moment."

They stepped through the door. Homer appeared, squinting at them in the gloom. "Miz Jennifer, what're you doin' outa bed?"

Beside her, she felt the hard nose of the derringer easing forward in Robert's hand. She didn't think Homer could see it.

"Homer, Zach needs you. Up by the house."

The youth thrust out his chin as he suddenly recognized her companion. "What's this here gent—?"

"I am merely showing Mr. Quiller a horse, Homer. Please go up to the house."

"Miz Jennifer, yer in yer night rail. I don't think—"

Robert cut him off, shoving the derringer into plain sight. "Do you wish to cause your own destruction, boy?"

Homer paused, his gaze growing more resolved.

"Please, Homer," Jennifer commanded in her teacher's voice. "Follow instructions. Go find Zach, *please!*"

Reluctance in every step, Homer backed away through the door. The last Jennifer saw of him, he had turned and trotted toward the house. She prayed that he would find Zachary was all right.

In the barn's dim interior, Jennifer smelled the pungent odor of fresh horse dung and knew that Homer was preparing to take some of his charges to the livery in town.

Robert dragged her behind him as he inspected the contents of several stalls.

"Ah, yes, I know this mount. And this one. Two of Sam's finest. These will do nicely. Where are your saddles?"

Jennifer clamped a hand over the top of a stall rail. Everything inside her insisted she bear down. She resisted the instinct with all her might, but not without effort.

"I . . . there aren't any, Robert. We . . . we own only two, and Zachary's is too small for either of us, and Gil has the other one." Jennifer wondered if she could sidetrack his attention once more, and asked, "Where is your transportation?"

Her contraction eased, thank goodness, but her diversion lasted only a moment.

"I lost it," he spoke tersely. "Damned horse spooked one night out there—" He stopped and looked at her suspiciously.

"Never mind," he snapped. "Get your saddle."

"I told you, Robert!" she snapped right back. "We have none."

He gripped her shoulder, his fingers digging past her flesh to the bone. "Quit lying! You must own a sidesaddle."

Her head twisted as she tried to smother her gasp. His assumption that she wouldn't deign to live without every possible luxury didn't surprise her, but it did remind her to speak calmly.

"Not at all. I have no need of one and I usually have the buggy. But Bessie took that today, to attend to business, you see."

"That damned strumpet has it, eh? Well, what about that brat of Sam's? Where is his saddle?"

"He frequently rides bareback, especially when his father can't spare a saddle from the livery."

"Barbaric. But if that is what we must do, my dear, then we'll do it."

Jennifer recognized his implacable demand. He

would expect her to mount a horse regardless of her condition.

"There is the buckboard." Since she had little choice in the matter, she thought the wagon her best bet. Soon, her baby would make greater demands to be born, and the buckboard afforded a little protection.

Robert tightened his hold on her arm and shoved her toward it.

"There! There's the harness. Now get those horses and hitch them," he ordered and let her go. "We need to be gone from here."

Moving more awkwardly than ever, Jennifer reached for the leathers hanging from a nail over her head. A clash of thunder made her jump. She dropped the harness, part of it still dangling from its nail, and grabbed for the post to steady herself. At the same time, the horse in the stall snorted and kicked against the boards.

"Patricia?" Robert shrieked.

The delayed lightning flashed, and it showed her that Robert had his back partially to her. Somehow in the near darkness and the clap of thunder, he had lost his focus.

Jennifer didn't even think about it. Snatching at the harness, she grabbed as many of the leather strips as she could and flung the multiple pieces forward over the slight figure. He cried out a curse and went down, his pistol discharging a shot. Quickly, she used the noise to cover her own movements into an empty stall.

Huddling against the wall lended only a temporary hiding place. If she could remain undiscovered for only a few minutes . . .

Another crash of thunder came. The horses snorted

and kicked at their barriers. A sudden barking chorus from the two Generals added to the din. Above them all, Robert screamed his curses.

Then even that was drowned as a roaring louder than a freight train filled her ears. A pressure seemed to flatten her against the outside wall. Throwing her arm in front of her face, she then tried to curl around herself, thinking to protect her unborn child. She whimpered with another birth pain, cried Gil's name and Zach's in fear. The wind blew it away. Something crashed around her.

Long moments later, she could think again. Almost abruptly the roaring diminished. She could only hope that some of the storm had lifted. She listened for sounds of Robert but heard only her own breathing and the churning stampede of two horses racing past her stall.

Tornado. For years she'd heard of them. Was this it? Had this been a twister? All the stories she had heard seemed to have just proved true.

Zach! Homer! Were her boys safe? The house. She had to get to the house. Would it be there?

And Gil! Was he still in town?

Bending almost double, she waited for another wave of cramping to ease. She no longer cared where Robert was. She thought only to make sure the boys were all right.

Now, she reasoned, while everything was in chaos, was the moment she could escape. She had to try.

She struggled to her feet, clutching posts and the sides of the stall for support, then made her way out into the main part of the barn. The sky was lighter, giving her more illumination. Everything seemed out of kilter as though the barn leaned. She glanced toward the huge front doors only to discover they were gone from their hinges.

She cautiously stepped outside. All around her was a tumbled yet oddly swept-clean appearance. The rain had gone. No one was in sight, not even her enemy. But, thank God, the house stood. She started up the path.

Behind her an ominous squeaking began. She looked over her shoulder as the sound became a sudden, horrific crash. Before her eyes the barn fell, boards and beams piling up on top of each other in wild abandon. From the nearby attached corral, a lone horse squealed and took quick advantage of the sudden opening to run free.

Oddly, she smelled the lilac bushes that Gil's mother had planted along the path. They weren't quite in bloom, yet.

Twister! While still a mile off Gil studied the dark cloudy vee as it dipped to touch ground. And it appeared to head right for his place. He hoped to God his family were in the cellar!

Raking his spurs across Beau's flanks, he raced toward home. Closing the distance, his horse began to fight the bit. The wind became a fierce enemy.

But then the storm vee widened and seemed to turn. East by northeast. Away from the house. Gil questioned what he saw but as the seconds passed and the sky began to lighten, his acute anxiety lifted a degree. He harbored a hope that the center of the deadly storm had bypassed them.

Racing into the house yard, his eyes darted everywhere. His mind barely acknowledged the flattened garden or the pile of debris or the rooster that angrily stretched its neck as it strutted across his path.

He vaulted himself out of the saddle and leaped for the front door. "Jennifer! Boys!"

He didn't stop to listen, racing straight through and out of the back door to the cellar. He grabbed the handle and heaved. Greeting him was the silver nose of a pistol.

With one stroke, Gil tweaked the gun from the hand that held it as instantaneously he recognized Homer and Zach staring at him from below, their eyes wide with terror.

"Is your mother with you?" he rapped out.

"Papa! Papa! That bad man came!"

"Who? What man?"

"Quiller," Homer said, coming up the cellar stairs. "He forced her to go with 'im, Gil. I'd a done somethin' but he had a derringer an' Miz Jennifer begged me to see to Zach."

"I wouldn't let him, Papa. I tried to stop him. But he hit me—"

"Where'd they go?" Gil demanded. "Which way?"

"Don't rightly know as they even got started, Gil. They was in the barn when the storm come—"

"Homer and me were going down to the barn to get her away, Papa. Then Homer said we had to get in the cellar."

"Saw the twister," Homer explained.

Gil only grunted. Pivoting, he saw emptiness where the barn should've been. He took only a step before he heard a sharp cry. Almost a scream. Jennifer.

A hundred yards down the barn path, Jennifer had tried to answer Gil's muffled shout for her. Instead, her knees gave out and she caught the ground with her hands, pushing against the earth even as her baby pushed inside of her.

Seconds later Gil found her on the rocky path. Pure shock gave him pause. She lay curled around the ball of her belly, the once white nightgown plastered to her body, her bare white feet and ankles covered in mud. Her hair lay wetly dark against her skin, almost hiding her face.

Dropping to his knees, he gathered her to him, rocking her against his chest. He thought his heart would burst out of it with anguish. "Oh, God, Jennifer, I've done this to you! I've brought you to this."

"Gil, Gil."

"I'll get you to the house, sweetheart. Just hold on, Jennifer, please, hold on."

"No time. Don't leave." The pressure demanded all her effort and she could speak no more.

"No. No, I won't." Seeing her in so much pain tore at him until his own despair and helplessness seemed overwhelming.

"Mama." Zachary was sobbing, kneeling at her head. Homer unabashedly let tears stream down his cheeks.

Something about his son's tears jerked Gil up.

No! By God, no! None of his war years had prepared him for this, but they had given him a great knowledge and training for imminent action, instant judgment calls, immediate performance of a kind. Damn it! He'd watched calves being born, and horses, hadn't he? He'd even helped his pa while attending births. Surely, a woman couldn't be that different.

Gathering every bit of command he possessed, his eyes bore into Homer's. "Get blankets off the bed, all you can find, and lamps and a knife—my skinning knife. And bring water! Zach, go with Homer and hush those tears! Mama needs you to be strong."

Jennifer needed *him* to be strong, Gil admonished himself. She had given and given to him, unselfishly filling all his needs and demands while complaining of nothing. She was a woman of powerful character, tenacious of mind and fortitude, the strongest woman he had ever known. He could be no less of a man.

With his decrees in place, he eased her down.

Then the boys were there once more and as gently as they could, the three of them lifted her onto a pad of blankets beside the lilac bushes. It felt soft and smooth under her after the rocky path. Gil tucked a sheet over her. She heard him direct Zach to remain at her head and talk to her while he helped the baby come.

"It's a boy!"

A boy. Another son. Then she heard the miracle of a resounding wail. She gazed up at the sky. It was blue and the sun dappled her face between the lilac buds. And she couldn't stop sobbing.

Gil tenderly placed the baby in her arms and she snuggled him close. She used the corner of the towel he was wrapped in to wipe his little forehead, noting the shape of his head and eyes. "Look, Zach. He looks like your papa, too."

Beside her, Zach remained uncharacteristically silent.

Bessie came, seemingly from nowhere. Jennifer heard her exclaim in a flurry.

Gil fed Jennifer whiskey while Homer went after the doctor and Zach was sent back to the house to prepare his mama's bed and to be out of the way.

They put her to bed, and Gil urged her to take more of the potent brew, but she waved it away. She was so tired.

The baby whimpered. He would need nourishment soon, Jennifer thought hazily. Oh, she did want so to hold him again, to smell him, to put her lips to his little cheek. To reassure herself that he breathed.

However Gil was there, and Bessie, and they seemed more concerned with her. She tried to tell them she was fine, only sleepy, tried to warn Gil to beware of Robert, and to tell him to find out what had happened to the scoundrel and where he'd gone, but Gil only shushed her. When she asked for Zach, Bessie insisted he was in the kitchen and she mustn't worry.

But it was unusual for Zachary not to be right there, wanting to be in the middle of whatever was happening.

Her mind went over the jumbled events of the day. It all had piled up on her, like the barn piling boards and beams and hay in a wild stack. Well, they could build a new barn and replant the garden, she supposed. Gil could round up the scattered stock and repair the corrals. But what about Zachary?

Out of it all, her thoughts kept revolving around Robert's cruel words to the boy. Jennifer knew how badly mere words could hurt. They could plant a seed of doubt and distrust which, if not nipped immediately, could grow into real damage. How much had Zachary taken in of Robert's ugliness? Would Zach doubt her and his father's love for him after hearing the degrading things Robert had said?

Years of habit told her she should talk to Zach right away about what had happened. To undo whatever she could. Yes, right away.

Instead, exhaustion claimed her.

The doctor came and went. Jennifer nursed the baby, but slept again immediately afterward.

Long hours later, she woke to the demanding cry of hunger. "Hate to wake you, Miz Jennifer," Bessie said by her bed, "but this young'un needs his milk. Ain't gonna be good if he has to wait any longer."

"Oh, you should've wakened me sooner," she answered, and eagerly accepted the tiny bundle of wailing humanity. Late afternoon sun streamed into the bedroom, giving no indication of the earlier storm. It was as though a topsy-turvy world had righted itself while she slept.

She put the baby to her breast. It didn't take him long to discover what it would give him. Jennifer laughed in pure delight.

"That child ain't gonna have no trouble in this world in making a place for himself, I'm thinkin'," Bessie commented, chuckling along with her. "Born in a whirlwind storm out in the yard an' under a lilac bush! Don't that beat all? Don't never want to tell 'bout that lilac bush, though. People'll think he's soft."

Gil added his opinion as he watched from the doorway. "Nobody's gonna think he's soft, Bessie. They'll only remember the twister bringin' him and how brave his mama was." His voice soft with tenderness, he added, "They'll only talk about how handsome he is, having sunny yellow hair like his mother."

Zach sidled in and stood by Jennifer's head, staring at the baby.

"Oh, Zach, where have you been, honey? Sit down, here, right by me."

She waited while Gil lifted the child to sit beside her.

"I'm sure glad you're here, Zachary. Look at your brother. What do you think of him?"

"He's too little. When will he walk?"

"Oh, he'll need time to grow. And then he'll crawl first, remember? Like little Frankie?"

"But he's all scrunched up."

Jennifer chuckled. "That will change very soon. Here, Zach, you can touch him if you like. One finger, now. Gently. See? See how soft he is?"

Zachary stroked the tiny cheek in wonder, then said, "I'm browner than he is."

Jennifer glanced at Bessie, whose brown eyes were painfully wise, and then sought her husband's blue-gray gaze. They hadn't yet heard the extent of what Robert had done.

She thought it a perfect time to set the record straight. "That's right, honey, you are. But you know, the sun has kissed you and you'll always be a little darker than your brother."

She reached out and laid a hand against his cheek. To her, the difference in their skin tones had never mattered. "But Zach, you are always going to be our firstborn son. Always and forever. I am so grateful to your birth mama for giving you to me. Before you came along I didn't have a little boy of my own."

Zach grinned. "That's why you liked me, isn't it, Mama?"

Jennifer felt her heart ease. It appeared she could put the one worry aside. "Yes, indeed. You filled my heart up with so much love that it made it grow and grow and now I have room for more love than ever."

"That's right, son," Gil added. "You're our first son. And like your mama pointed out, you and the new baby have eyes just like me. Everybody will know you're brothers the first time they look at you."

"Uh-huh," Zach said, his eyes lighting up. "And he'll have the same last name as me. Zachary Prescott. Gabriel Prescott."

"Uh, Zach," Gil began. They had never truly discussed a name for the new child and Zachary hadn't mentioned it again since Christmas.

"Well, I hadn't considered . . ." Jennifer had been too afraid, before, to choose a name. "I . . . I . . . Gil?"

Gil gazed at his wife. He adored this woman. She'd been through events of mountainous proportions today and she still thought of him. Did she remember choosing a name almost five years gone?

Placing a hand on Zach's shoulder, he pronounced, "Gabriel is a right upstanding name. If Teacher—if Jennifer agrees."

Jennifer, too, thought of the night she and Gil named Zachary. She'd barely made his acquaintance, then. "Yes. Yes, I think Gabriel a fine name for our newest son."

"Gil!" Homer called from the kitchen. There was something quiet about it, an urgency.

Gil stepped out of the bedroom. Jennifer heard their low voices conversing in the parlor. Everything within her tightened, waiting for the announcement of another disaster. Then Gil appeared once more.

Over the baby's head, Jennifer searched his face. His expression almost suspended, she read a dawning relief there, a hope, a waiting.

"Jennifer, you needn't worry about Quiller any longer. He'll never threaten any of us again."

"Why? What has happened?"

"He's dead. Homer found him under the barn rubble."

23

Gil listened very closely to Jennifer's account of what had happened when the sheriff came to collect Robert Quiller's body the following morning. He was particularly quiet during her statements concerning the attempt to kidnap her. He asked no questions of his own. Jennifer wondered at it.

The sheriff shook his head, dumbfounded. "Quiller was a queer duck, I reckon. But the folks in town seemed to think he was right generous in his dealings, and harmless enough, though he liked to charm the ladies. He—"

"'Scuse me, Sheriff, but I got somepthin' to add to this here discussion," Bessie said from the doorway.

"Why, certainly, Miz Bessie," the sheriff said, giving the young woman an indulgent smile. "What is it?"

"Well, that Quiller fella wasn't exactly harmless. No way no how, not when he had one of his headaches.

He was outa his head, some, I think." Bessie shook her head. "Anyhow, he done worked me over that one time real good."

"Ya never said nothing to me, Bessie," the sheriff said, giving her a steady look.

"No, sir. Reckon I didn't. But you know nobody pays much attention when a whore gets what fer."

The sheriff twitched a shoulder as though he felt the guilt of Bessie's mild accusation, but made no comment. He turned back to Gil. "And you, Mr. Prescott. What do you make of it? What was Quiller's purpose in harassing Mrs. Prescott that way, d'you think?"

Gil's expression was hard. "Can't say, exactly, Sheriff. But the man had a fixation on my wife."

"Yes, so I've heard from a number of people. Homer Burns told me Quiller cozied up with his stepma. Asked her a lot of questions about Miz Prescott here. Told me he thought the man even came out here an' threatened her once."

The sheriff's dark-eyed gaze was bland, but beneath it, Jennifer sensed a keen search. He seemed almighty suspicious of Robert's death. But why? Then she no longer wondered as Gil told of his confrontation with her former suitor in town.

"Yep, that's true, Sheriff. Quiller was an arrogant son of a bitch!" Gil spared her a glance of apology. "Sorry, Jennifer."

Her husband drew a gut-level breath and continued, "Anyway, when I faced him down, he told me all about how he had a prior claim to Jennifer, left over from back east. Named off all the things he could give her— a mansion to live in, jewels, an' the like. Hell, it was enough to make a princess proud. And he rambled on and on about setting her free. Said he'd done it once before and he'd do it again if he had to. Said a lot of other things."

Gil stood abruptly, shoving his kitchen chair back roughly. "Yeah, I had reason to kill 'im, Sheriff, if that's what you're lookin' to find out. The man was threatenin' my home. And I reckon I might've if it had come to that, but I didn't. The simple fact is that a beam fell on 'im when the barn collapsed."

The sheriff pursed his lips, then nodded. "All right, Mr. Prescott, take it easy. Reckon I'll take your word on it. Besides, all the evidence points to just what you're telling me." He got up to leave. "By the way, Mrs. Prescott. Quiller left a trunk behind full of clothes and papers and a few other knick-knacks. Reckon I'll have to go through 'em. Do you know if he has kin or someone else back east I should send the things to?"

"Ahhh, no, I . . . Wait! Yes. Send it to this lawyer," she said as she pulled a paper from the small desk in the parlor and wrote an address on it. "He will know."

The sheriff thanked them both and left, taking the body of Robert Quiller with him.

As the days and weeks trickled by, Jennifer learned just how deep the gossip in Osage Springs had gone. Bessie, as counted on, had told her the truth as she heard it. Robert had done his dirty work, all right. He had set the tongues to wagging and most of them believed him to have once been her lover.

Jennifer feared for how much of it Gil believed.

Some weeks later, she was determined to find out. She carefully wrapped the fresh cherries Bessie had brought from town only that morning in a clean white

napkin, then placed them on top of the thick sandwiches, pickles, lemonade, and butter cookies she
already had in the basket. "There. That should do it."

Bessie gave her a decidedly lascivious grin and
winked. "Yes, ma'am, it should. Now you be on your
way, Miz Jennifer. Time's awastin'."

"Mmm," was all Jennifer answered, but she glanced
doubtfully at two-month-old Gabriel sleeping peace-
fully in his cradle, nonetheless. He should last at least
three more hours before demanding another feeding,
but sometimes he seemed bent on rearranging all her
plans for free time.

She needed every moment of that time, too.
Jennifer had schemed with Bessie for days, now, for
the freedom to have a much-needed talk with Gil.
Alone and uninterrupted. Now was the time, and
waylaying him with a picnic dinner on his way home
from the quarry site was the how.

Gil had traded stone for the lumber to finish the
new barn; he had hired men to put in the stone foun-
dation—again, bargaining goods for labor. Tomorrow, a number of friends and neighbors would be
there to raise it. A huge supper party would follow.
She wanted things settled between her and Gil before
then.

Yes, now was the time. Zach was gone, helping
Homer herd the livery horses back to town for the
second time that week. And since Sam had expanded
his horse string—Jennifer reckoned poor Dora had
lost her battle to coax Sam into selling his business,
and instead, to help her with hers—they transported
more horses than ever.

It appeared their place was coming to rights at last.
Gil's calves thrived, Sam was beginning to pay cash

for Gil's care of his mounts, and when he had time, Gil occasionally repaired a gun or two. He'd put in his one field of wheat, replanted her garden, and put some money aside toward a house pump. Every endeavor that Gil put his hand to seemed to be blossoming.

Jennifer's heart turned over. Everything except their marriage. Gil hadn't once come close to her in the last three weeks since the doctor had told her it was all right to resume her wifely duties. She had expected Gil to move back into her bed with all the speed and eagerness of an attacking mountain lion, and with as ravenous an appetite as well. After all, their first months of marriage had been like that, both of them starving for the blaze of passion between them, and equally so for the tenderness and teasing that grew deeper each day.

She had cherished it, held it close to her heart and soul. She had felt cherished in return.

Only the restoration of trust between them could bring it about again. She feared she had lost Gil's, lost it to the half truths that Robert had spread around town.

Now she almost cried at Gil's mannered good-nights. He was polite during supper, solicitous throughout the remainder of the evening, playful with Zachary. He cuddled Gabriel for a time after supper each evening, then bid her a distant good-night and went to his cot in the bunkhouse. Not only had he kept to himself, he barely looked at her directly anymore.

He'd urged Bessie to stay on as well, and when Bessie had insisted that her store was ready to open and she needed to move back to town, he'd made noises about hiring a girl to help in the house, instead.

Gil had little extra money to pay for a hired girl.

Unless he thought he *must* have one. But why would
he unless he thought his wife would no longer be
around to take care of things? To take care of him
and Zachary? That was the rub. If he had lost faith in
her, no longer trusted her, he might think . . .

Oh, blazes! Jennifer could no longer guess what to
make of it all, but the rejection and abandonment she
felt by Gil's ignoring her hurt worse than she wanted
anyone to know. It was so horribly familiar.

She carried the basket and a blanket as far as the
lone tree just beyond the spring. It was the way he
would come home. There, she spread both the blanket and the picnic.

It had been a long time since she had been down
this way; wagon ruts now marred the grassy plain
where Gil often traveled. Leaning her back against
the tree, she wrapped her arms around her drawn-up
knees and stared out at the land.

Hearing the wagon, she stood. Gil drove around
the curve of the low hill and spotted her. A joyous
surprise lit his eyes before he swiftly shuttered his
thoughts.

Her own heart leaped at the sight of him. He wore
his shirt unbuttoned against the hot July sun and his
sleeves were rolled high above his elbows. His skin
had bronzed these last months, playing up the ripple
of his taut muscles as he hauled on the reins. Dark
ashy-brown hair hung a bit over his forehead under
his pushed-back hat and more of the same shade of
hair feathered down his torso.

She remembered exactly how it felt beneath her
fingers.

He pulled the team to a halt, taking in the blanket,
the basket, and her. Jennifer had prepared well; she'd

washed her hair that morning and then brushed it to
a shiny mass of curls that she wore loose, tied only by
a blue ribbon. The dress she'd chosen was also blue,
an old print that Gil liked. Bessie had taken the lib-
erty of lowering the neckline to a shameless level and
adding a bit of lace to show off her creamy bosom.
Jennifer had complained she would never again be
able to wear it in company, but she hadn't hesitated
to wear it for her husband.

Gil stood up in the wagon. A frown brought his
brows low and his underlip thrust out. If Jennifer
hadn't known him to be as gentle as a spring lamb,
she would think him fierce. His gaze seemed to
devour her, yet she saw the war within his emotions.

"What are you doing out here, Jennifer?"

"I came to wait for you," she answered softly, gesturing to the basket. She lifted the jar of lemonade,
something she knew he was unlikely to refuse.
"Would you like some lemonade?"

Without answering, he slowly dropped over the
side of the wagon and came forward. He held her
gaze a moment, then accepted the tin cup and drank
thirstily.

"I . . . um . . . I brought dinner. Sandwiches and
deviled eggs and . . ." Jennifer let her hand drop while
she tried to gauge his reaction. He seemed to be
weighing all the facts of her being there, where she
had never been before, and the allure she offered.

"Reckon I ought to water the team first," he finally
said.

He strode from her and took the horses down to
the spring. When he returned, he had scrubbed the
dust and sweat from his face, neck, and arms. Water
droplets ran down his chest.

Jennifer had to turn away lest he see the desire in her eyes. She wanted so badly to touch him, but she had much to say before she allowed passion to rule.

If she could bring it about again. The passion and tenderness.

She knelt and spread a napkin. From beneath her lashes, she watched him fold down opposite her. His back remained straight as a bean pole. She laid a chicken salad sandwich in front of him, and one of thickly sliced beef. Without saying much, he began to eat.

Gil kept his eyes on his boot heel and chewed staunchly. Almost painfully, he swallowed. He might taste the food better, he reckoned, if he wasn't so damned scared she might be here to tell him she had had enough of him. Enough of his coldness, enough of his rude ignorance, enough of his poverty.

He knew the strain between them; he'd fostered it.

"All right, Jennifer. Say it."

Jennifer put down her own half-eaten sandwich. Her hope had been steadily draining away as the minutes ticked by and she realized he held himself with such rigid control. All her carefully thought out openings seemed flat against it. "And what am I to say?"

"Whatever you have to, I reckon."

"Well, you've guessed rightly. I did come here to . . . to talk to you. I . . . please, Gil. Look at me!"

Startled, his gaze flew up, full of pain, a gray ragged shimmering that she didn't understand.

"Gil." She let her own pain lace her words. "I tried to tell you, once. You shouldn't have put me on a pedestal. I knew I could only fall off. But it's my own fault, I suppose. I should have told you everything."

Gil saw the hurt on Jennifer's face and realized she

was speaking of the rumors that had made the rounds in Osage Springs. That damned lunatic would likely haunt them all for the rest of their lives, he thought.

"If it's about Quiller, I don't want to know." He threw down the bread crust from his hand.

"I can't tell you without including him," she pleaded.

Gil rose, and turned his back, thinking only to save her a humiliation. "You don't have to say it!"

"Yes! Yes! This time I do."

"Teacher, it don't matter."

"But it does. Don't you see?" He said nothing, his heart tearing apart. She wanted to tell him the truth? That she'd loved that rich arrogant bastard who treated her like a piece of property. But he couldn't stand the thought of the little weasel having any part of his lovely Jennifer.

Behind him, she touched his hand. "Please."

And he could refuse her nothing. As hurtful as it would be, he resigned himself and turned back.

At her urging, he sat down once more, his hands locked around a raised knee. Jennifer clasped her arms around her waist and began.

"Did . . . did you or your family ever . . . ever follow the social news from the East?"

"No." Surprised at the question, he wondered to what she referred. "Nothing much interested us from the East except the war news and politics, of course."

"That's what I surmised. Anyway, a mere social scandal would never have made the papers here in the border states. That is why I chose to come and settle here. But a wrongful death might have."

Gil held her gaze at last. The shutters were gone.

Jennifer took a deep breath to steady her nerves,

then continued. "It's a long story, Gil, and I need you to be patient while I tell it."

She waited for his nod, then began. "Back in Philadelphia, I was the center of a terrible scandal. It was truly awful. I didn't know how to stem it and no one believed the truth."

"Start from the beginning, Jennifer."

Gratefully, she accepted his encouragement. "Remember when I told you that I married my first husband when I was eighteen? That was true. His name was Willard Mitchell. He and Robert Quiller were cousins, and both from Philadelphia's finest families. They courted me at the same time, and I thought . . . oh, I know how foolishly vain it sounds, but I thought it was all fun having two handsome, wealthy gentlemen vying for my hand in marriage."

Jennifer talked and talked, trying not to diminish her own blame in the series of events that had ended in her social ruin and ostracism. She wanted Gil to know it all. Finally, she ended with "That's when Willard began divorce proceedings, accusing me of adultery and Robert as a correspondent. Nothing I could say would convince him of my innocence or dissuade him. After all, Robert told him and others that he and I were, indeed, lovers. The scandal made all the front pages."

"Aw, the damned mongrels! Is that when you left?"

"Not quite. I was planning to. I wanted nothing more than to leave it all behind me. But the worst . . . the worst came after . . . Gil, a few days later, Willard hanged himself."

"My God, Jennifer! Hanged himself?"

"Yes. It was the worst night of my life, I guess. Most of the servants had the night off. I . . . something . . . it was dark, but something caused me to go into that room. I called out, then bumped into Willard's swinging body. I hadn't been out of bed but a day or two from losing the baby and I—I fainted. When I came to, Aunt Agnes was there, screaming at the top of her lungs. A maid ran in from the back of the house and another went for the doctor. The authorities . . . they all suspected foul play and asked me questions and questions, hatefully so and with no respect.

"But in the end, they let me go. I had done nothing wrong, you see, nothing against the law. The papers, as one might suppose, however, raked up every tittle and jot of the stories about me and reprinted them. When they didn't know it all, they made allusions. It took weeks to die out. It killed Aunt Agnes. One day her heart simply gave out. She died in deep shame, believing all the worst of me."

Jennifer paused, wiping the tears from her cheeks with the heel of her hand. She could no longer look at Gil. He had thought her an ideal woman, a pure and unsullied soul. She couldn't stand to gaze upon any doubt or bitter loss in his eyes.

"Now you know it all, Gil. In Philadelphia, I am known as an adulterer and worse."

Long moments of silence stretched between them. Finally, Jennifer could stand it no longer and turned her gaze on him. His expression was a mixture of compassion and sadness. She wondered about the sadness. But the burning question she had been asking herself for weeks had to be spoken.

"Do you wish to dissolve our marriage now, Gil? Do you want me to leave?"

Gil couldn't have been more shocked if she had poked him with a hot iron.

"Whyever would I want you to leave, Jennifer? Don't you know I love you with every fiber of my being?"

"I thought you did," she said, barely above a whisper, her heart building a hope with his confession of love. "It's how I love you. But those ugly rumors—"

"Hell and damnation, Jennifer! I never believed any of 'em. How could you think I would? What's more, most of the town folks never did either."

"Are you sure, Gil?"

"Sure as the sun sets of an evenin'. Everyone knows you, honey. They know you to be the fine woman that you are. They saw all that talk of Quiller's for what it was, the wishful thinkin' of a rejected man. I only wish I hadn't misjudged the danger he was capable of."

"Oh, Gil. Oh, I hope so. I want my friends to think the best of me. But Gil, what do you think? Do you think less of me now that you know all about . . . Philadelphia?"

"Think *less* of you? *Less?*" Incredulous, he raised to his knees in front of her and, throwing his hat down, ran a hand through his hair. "Jennifer . . ."

He braced his hands on her knees and leaned toward her. Jennifer longed for him to put his arms around her; she so needed his reassurance. She took hope in his earnest blue-gray eyes—they reflected the richness of his love. Jennifer basked in it, soaked it into her very pores.

"How could I ever think less of the woman who was faithful to me for years through real bitterness and poverty, who gave up every comfort to take on a motherless boy, and then a husband who nearly killed her with too much lovin'? You're so precious to me

I'd pure die if you left me. I never loved anybody like I love you, Jennifer, gut wide and marrow deep. I love you so much that it hurts. I look at you an' I see . . ." He hauled in a breath, wanting to express his feelings but so overwhelmed with them he wasn't sure he could ever say it all in a hundred years. "I see life itself. The wonder of it is what you see in me."

Jennifer shook her head, then laughed shakily. "Oh, my darling Gil. Don't you know? You gave me your most precious gift that night you brought me Zachary. You gave me your trust. Ever afterwards, I could trust myself."

Gil took her hand and toyed with her long fingers. As before, he ran his thumb over the scar on hers as though to read something there or gain some knowledge he needed. Slowly, he began to speak. "I left more of myself than Zachary, that night, Teacher. But I didn't understand it for a long time."

He lifted her palm to his mouth and pressed his lips there, then glancing at her briefly, lowered it to his knee. But he held it tightly. "You see, I got somethin' shameful of my own to confess."

He drew a deep breath. "For three long years, every time I was in town I'd walk by the schoolhouse, or hang close by your house on a Saturday night, hoping for only a glimpse of you. I watched you every time I got a chance. But I never even spoke to you because I . . . Well, folks said you were still grievin' for your dead husband and didn't welcome any courtin'. I didn't think there was a chance for the likes of me.

"But I was hot blooded and a fool, to boot. I got lured down to the Indian camp looking for a quick . . . well, you know. I wasn't never a saint. Anyway I met Zach's mother. She was sweet an' giving. To my shame, I went back for more. Often. Pa and I fought; he hated Indians an' forbade me to have more to do with her, but by that time Zachary was on the way. To my everlasting sorrow, Jennifer, I married Morning Rain simply to defy my father!"

Gil's voice rose and fell as he related his own past hurts and wrong motives and Jennifer knew his empathy with her had been based on his own wild youth.

"But I came to love her an' I would of stuck by the marriage if she'd lived. When she died, I grieved. But I grieved more for all the wrong I'd done her. Can you understand that?"

"Yes, I think I do." Reaching up, she stroked his hair. All the tenderness that had grown between them was in her touch.

"She *died,* Jennifer, to give me a son! And I hadn't loved her when we conceived him."

"Oh, Gil. She forgave you, I'm sure of it. She wanted you enough to give herself to you. By your description of her I don't think she would want you to carry the guilt of her death with you for the rest of your life. And you have Zachary with which to remember her."

"But don't you see? That's why—" He looked at her beseechingly, begging her to understand his fear.

And Jennifer did. Her own past history fed it. "That's why you've stayed away from me these last weeks and months?"

"Oh, Lord, yes! D'you think I've wanted to? It's been hell, Jennifer, pure hell not even touching you. But I can't risk it. If I touch you, you know what happens. Hell, I go up in cinders just looking at you. But I'd rather live the rest of my life out in that dad-blasted lonely-as-a-glacier bunkhouse than risk getting you pregnant again. I—"

All the heaviness Jennifer had carried these last months lifted like a heavenly cloud. This was a problem she knew how to solve. Her husband still wanted her. Joyously, she put a hand against his mouth.

"Now, Gil Prescott, you just listen to me a minute," she said decisively. "I know Gabriel's birth was a bit traumatic."

Gil snorted at her understatement, but Jennifer gave him a shushing stare. She continued, "But all that was due to circumstances that had nothing to do with my health. I'm fine. Dr. Rosenberg says there is absolutely no reason I shouldn't have another child. And another, even."

Jennifer dropped her hand from his mouth and took his, placing it on her breast. His fingers, hot and needy, stretched to the bare skin above her neckline, and his palm flattened out against her fullness. Her breath caught, her nipple hardened. All of her cried out for more.

His voice was gruff as he said, "Aw, hell, Teacher."

"Mmm, no, it feels like heaven," she insisted in a low murmur, leaning into him. "We have two fine sons, Gil. Don't you want a daughter?"

"Oh, Jennifer, you make it so . . ." He slid his other hand against her round bottom and brought her up against his hard arousal. "Oh, God, I have no willpower against your coaxing at all," he said on a moan.

"Then kiss me, Gil. Make love to me, right this minute. I want you something fierce."

"Never could resist a bossy woman."

Gil kissed her almost frantically, long and drugging kisses as though he couldn't bear to break the contact long enough to progress any further. Then Jennifer ran her hands over his chest while he worked at her buttons. They slipped easily from their holes, and he released her full breasts with an excited cry of triumph. He lowered her down to lie fully on the quilt while she arched against him. The last conscious thought he had was that he had to slow down.

A long thirty minutes later, they lay entwined, covered only by the skirt of her dress against the hot July sun. "Did I get it right this time, Teacher?" he teased, a lazy grin spreading.

It hadn't been he who had led the rush this time.

Jennifer blushed, but she grinned back and answered, "Oh, you most certainly did, Mr. Prescott. You deserve an unqualified A. But if you wish to maintain your grade, I do think more practice is needed. Every night, perhaps."

"Every night, mornings, noons like this, every chance I get, wife!"

Jennifer's long-held slender thread of hope turned into the most certain thing of her life. She took Gil's face between her hands, stroking tenderly where his nose had once been broken. She didn't think he would ever understand the depth of her love or the gift he had given her.

Gil, on his part, knew he'd remember the exquisite beauty he saw in Jennifer's face at that moment, and the shining light from the blueness of her eyes, until the very second he died. He had to swallow against its brightness as she murmured in answer, "Loving you will take a lifetime, husband!"

LORD OF THE NIGHT
by Susan Wiggs
A Venetian lord dedicated to justice suspects a
lucious beauty of being involved in a scandalous plot.

ORCHIDS IN MOONLIGHT
by Patricia Hagan
Caught in a web of intrigue in the dangerous West,
a man and a woman fight to regain their
overpowering dream of love.

A SEASON OF ANGELS
by Debbie Macomber
Three willing but wacky angels must teach their
charges a lesson before granting a Christmas wish.

National Bestseller

Winner Take All by Terri Herrington

Logan Brisco is the smoothest, slickest, handsomest man ever to grace the small town of Serenity, Texas. Carny Sullivan is the only one who sees the con man behind that winning smile, and she vows to save the town from his clutches. But saving herself from the man who steals her heart is going to be the greatest challenge of all.

The Honeymoon by Elizabeth Bevarly

Newlyweds Nick and Natalie Brannon are wildly in love, starry-eyed about the future...and in for a rude awakening. Suddenly relocated from their midwestern hometown to San Juan, Puerto Rico, where Nick is posted with the U.S. Coast Guard, Natalie hopes for the best. But can true love survive the trials and tribulations of a not-so-perfect paradise?

Ride the Night Wind by Jo Ann Ferguson

As the only surviving member of a powerful family, Lady Audra fought to hold on to her vast manor lands against ruthless warlords. But from the moonlit moment when she encountered the mysterious masked outlaw known as Lynx, she was plunged into an even more desperate battle for the fate of her heart.

To Dream Again by Laura Lee Guhrke

Beautiful widow Mara Elliot had little time for shining promises or impractical dreams. But when dashing inventor Nathaniel Chase became her unwanted business partner, Mara found his optimism and reckless determination igniting a passion in her that suddenly put everything she treasured at risk.

Reckless Angel by Susan Kay Law

Angelina Winchester's dream led her to a new city, a new life, and a reckless bargain with Jeremiah Johnston, owner of the most notorious saloon in San Francisco. Falling in love was never part of their deal. But soon they would discover that the last thing they ever wanted was exactly what they needed most.

A Slender Thread by Lee Scofield

Once the center of Philadelphia's worst scandal, Jennifer Hastings was determined to rebuild her life as a schoolteacher in Kansas. She was touched when handsome and aloof Gil Prescott entrusted her with the care of his newborn son while he went to fight in the Civil War. When Gil's return unleashed a passion she had ignored for too long, they thought they had found happiness—until a man from Jennifer's past threatened to destroy it.